DARK ANGEL

BOOKS BY D.K. HOOD

Her Bleeding Heart

Chase Her Shadow

Now You See Me

Their Wicked Games

D.K. HOOD
DARK ANGEL

bookouture

Published by Bookouture in 2023

An imprint of Storyfire Ltd.
Carmelite House
50 Victoria Embankment
London EC4Y 0DZ

www.bookouture.com

ISBN: 978-1-83790-384-9
eBook ISBN: 978-1-83790-383-2

For those who strive for a better world and never give up

INTRODUCTION

My father was a serial killer, and by the time they placed me into foster care—so was I.

I watched my father murder my mom but that's a secret I must keep locked away forever. No one will ever know that during those terrifying few seconds, he triggered my dark side and gave me a reason to kill monsters like him.

Life experience has taught me that most people have lost their primal instincts, and yet mothers are willing to die to shield their child or a man will risk his life to save a stranger. This is the remaining primal character of a warrior—a protector. Could you stand by and allow someone to abuse a child or slaughter an innocent person if you had the power within you to prevent it happening? Let's be honest here. Well, could you?

I can't. That's for darn sure.

Psychopathic serial killers come in many flavors—the careless, the smart, and the invisible—and then there's me. I figure the others are sick freaks, and you might ask what makes me different? You see, in my world they're the prey and I'm the predator.

PROLOGUE

Where am I? Disoriented, Missy Angelo shook her head to dislodge the burlap bag covering her face, and panic gripped her when the cord tightened around her neck. Trying to be brave, she ran her fingers over the lumpy ground beneath her and reached up her tied hands to find a metal box surrounding her. The sounds of an engine and country music drifted toward her. The air around her smelled like gas and the only fresh air came from wind whistling through a rusty patch on the floor. Through the loose weave of the bag, she could make out the blacktop flashing by, and the light flickering through the hole was a comfort. Why was she in the trunk of a vehicle? How long had she been trapped in the dark?

Terrified, confused, and with her face wet with tears, Missy curled into a ball with her mom's words echoing through her mind. She should never have gone with the janitor. *Don't talk to strangers. Don't accept candy from dirty old men.*

She'd made a terrible mistake and Mommy would be cross with her. Heart pounding, she kicked at the trunk and pounded with her fists. "Let me out. Let me out."

The music cranked up louder and the vehicle swerved, tossing her from one side of the trunk to the other. Now she'd made him angry. Why was he doing this to her? She tried to think straight. He hadn't been a stranger or a dirty old man. The janitor worked at the school. The teachers called him Jared and he was nice to everyone. He'd often sweep close to her and smile. Sometimes he'd whisper funny things to her about the teachers, as if it were their little secret. He had a friendly smile and wasn't dirty. When she'd seen him outside the girls' bathroom, she'd believed him when he'd said her mom had wrecked the car and her dad had asked him to take her to the hospital. She'd cried and he'd led her to the janitor's storeroom and given her a can of soda. He'd told her to be brave and not to worry. If her parents died, he promised to take care of her.

Sobbing, she'd drank the small can of soda and didn't move from the chair when he'd left to get his vehicle. By the time he returned, her legs had gone all wonky and he'd wrapped her in a blanket so tight she couldn't move her arms. He told her if she made a noise, the cops would take her away and she'd never see her parents again. Suddenly very afraid, she'd believed him. Her head swam and her mouth wouldn't form words. So tired, she couldn't keep her eyes open and must have fallen asleep.

She screamed again and again until her voice came out in a croak, and her hands hurt from striking the top of the trunk. The music stopped and the vehicle slowed and turned. As it bumped along, Missy peered through the hood at the hole and could see a dirt track. Dead grass and vegetation clawed at the sides of the sedan like nails on a chalkboard. Bounced around, her head banged on a toolbox and she cried out in pain. She traced a small lump on her scalp with trembling fingers. Her throat was dry from screaming. Why couldn't anyone hear her? "Let me out!"

The sedan stopped. A car door creaked open and sometime later the trunk lid opened. Jared peered down at her. She could just make him out through the hood. He looked different wearing coveralls and yellow plastic gloves. He gave her a silly smile. His eyes moved over her and he wet his lips. Afraid, Missy shuffled away from him. "I want my mommy."

"She's dead and so is your pa." Jared grabbed her hair. "Be a good girl and do as I say or I'll drag you along by your hair."

Missy screamed long and loud, gasping in big breaths and kicking out at him with her feet. "Get away from me. I hate you."

"Scream all you want, no one will hear you. This is my special place. I bring all my girls here and they really enjoy it. None of them have left me. They're all here and you'll meet them real soon." Jared grabbed her legs and, swinging her out of the trunk, tossed her into the dense dry vegetation.

Winded, Missy scrabbled to her hands and knees and tried to get away. Her tied hands made it difficult to run as she moved through the long grass, tripping over weeds tangling around her legs. Behind her, she could hear him coming. He was laughing. The next second, the weight of Jared's body crushed her to the ground. Prickles dug into her cheeks as she gasped for breath. "Help me. Somebody help me."

Pain slammed into the back of her head and she bit her tongue as hands tore at her clothes. A metallic taste spilled into her mouth and she wet herself. She blinked as a shadow fell over them. Someone had come to save her and the sun shone around the shadow like an angel's halo. A whisper came over the heavy breathing behind her.

"It's judgment time."

A rush of hot fluid splashed over her as Jared's weight crushed her. She turned her head as a playing card landed on the ground just in front of her eyes and floated in a sea of crimson. The soft voice came again and drifted to her as if on the breeze.

"Don't move, little one. Help is coming. Don't look behind

you. He can't hurt you now. I'm close by, watching over you. Be strong."

Calmed by the soft voice, Missy closed her eyes. A miracle had saved her. "Thank you."

ONE

Special Agent Beth Katz backtracked to her vehicle. She had spatter from the kill and needed an excuse to cover the stains. Blood from slicing a throat gushes in all forward directions, so grabbing the hair and cutting from behind usually avoids splash back, but she had drops on her sleeve. She tossed her examination gloves and the bloody razor in a container of Lab Clean and swirled it around. The solution would remove all traces of blood and DNA in seconds. After pulling on clean examination gloves, she dried the razor and dropped it back into her pocket. She had seconds to create an alibi. Moving fast, she closed the trunk and ran to open the door to her Crown Victoria. She reached for the radio and called her boss. "I still have eyes on the suspect. His vehicle has left the highway and is heading along a dirt road toward the Clawsfoot Mine. I'll park some ways in and head in on foot. I don't want to spook him into killing the girl."

"*I'm coming in hot.*" The engine of Mac's SUV roared. "*ETA five minutes. Don't do anything stupid. I want this guy alive.*"

Feeling an overwhelming glow of satisfaction, Beth smiled. "Copy."

After tossing the radio back inside the vehicle, she took off at a run. The roar of Mac's engine echoed in the distance. She bounded through the long grass toward the slaughtered man and stared at him in disgust. She fell to her knees beside him. Trapped under him in a pool of blood, lay a young girl face down. Right now, Beth needed her charming, charismatic psychopath's persona to calm the child. It was, after all, her true nature but one she needed to keep hidden to avoid the scrutiny of FBI profilers, should they ever discover her in the wrong place at the right time. Being nice was easy, natural, and having to act the abrasive co-worker was tough but it kept her safe. Her acting skills had worked so far but every day as a hardheaded FBI agent was a challenge.

With gentle care, she untied the hood and pulled it away from her face. Wide-eyed and past crying now, the girl was almost catatonic. Beth stroked the child's hair and kept her body between the girl and the dead man, blocking her view. "Hang on, sweetheart. We'll have you out of here real soon. Keep looking over there at those wildflowers. They're so pretty, sitting there all on their lonesome. Don't look back here, okay?"

The girl's head moved in a slight nod and her lips moved but no words came out. Jared Small's head rested above the waist on the girl's back, his thick torso pinning her under him. Footsteps came thumping along the dirt road, and Beth pressed the gaping hole in Small's throat, in what she hoped appeared to be a futile attempt to stem the bleeding. She turned and sat on the ground as Mac came into view, weapon drawn. Shaking her head, she looked at him. "He's gone. I'll need help to get the girl from under him."

"Dead?" Mac holstered his weapon and stared down at the inert body. "Did you shoot him? Dammit, I wanted him alive." He pulled on gloves and snorted in disgust.

Meeting his gaze, with her best shocked expression, Beth shook her head. "No, I didn't shoot him. I found him like this, Mac. His throat's been cut."

"What?" Mac pulled his weapon again and peered around. "Did you see anyone?"

Trying to look confused, Beth stared at her blood-soaked gloves and sleeves. "No. I saw this animal on the girl, that's all."

"Okay." Mac holstered his weapon. "I'll turn him over, and you pull out the kid."

Concerned, why Mac hadn't shown one ounce of compassion for the little girl, Beth crawled on her knees toward her and as Mac turned Small onto his back, she lifted the little girl free and carried her some distance away. Making soothing sounds, she examined the little girl and, finding nothing life-threatening, then turned her away from the carnage. From the way Missy stared blankly into space, she was going into shock. Beth wished she had something to cover her, but if she used her jacket, she'd contaminate the evidence on the child. Instead, she gently pulled her clothing around her and sat her on a boulder. "Just sit there, sweetheart. I'll be right here. Look at those pretty flowers while I speak to Mac."

As she returned to the body, a waft of blood and excrement slammed her in the face. She coughed. "I'll never get used to that stink."

The dead man's eyes had fixed into a blank stare and his mouth hung open. Under his chin, a wide red smile stretched from ear to ear. She looked at Mac. "I tried to put pressure on the wound, but he didn't stand a chance. I couldn't see how bad it was. I figure he bled out before I arrived on scene." She glanced at Missy. "We need to get her out of here."

"Not until I've spoken to her." Mac pulled up the dead man's T-shirt to cover his death stare and went to the girl and crouched down in front of her. "It's Missy, isn't it? You're safe now. Agent Katz will sit with you."

He beckoned Beth to follow him some ways away and lowered his voice. "I'll call forensics and the paramedics. Tread carefully, she doesn't look so good." He indicated with his chin to the man on the ground. "You were right about Jared Small. We interviewed him for the Cindy Walker case. It must be six months ago. Remember?"

How could I forget? Beth nodded. "Yeah, I had a hunch it was him all along. I wonder if he has any bodies stashed around here?"

"We'll leave that to the forensic team." Mac removed his gloves and tossed them near the body. "Go talk to the kid."

Beth removed her blood-soaked gloves and dropped them beside Mac's. CSI would collect them later. She folded up her sleeves and then, pulling on a fresh pair of gloves, she went to the girl and gently ran a hand down the girl's head. When the girl's eyes moved over her, she sighed with relief. At last, she was becoming more responsive. "I'm Beth and this is Mac. We're FBI agents. Are you hurt?"

"I banged my head." Missy picked at the drying blood on her hands. "He was a bad man. Is my mom, okay?"

Beth cut a glance to Mac, who shrugged. She had no idea if the kid's mom was okay but guessed it was a ploy Small used to get her into his vehicle. "Yeah, she's fine and so is your dad. They'll be at the hospital when you get there. Why?"

"He said mom had been in a wreck and Dad had asked him to take me to the hospital." Missy wiped at her tear-stained face and shuddered. "That's why I went with him."

"Keep her talking." Mac moved away, pulling out his phone.

Allowing her psychopath's charm to surface, she looked at the girl. Being the sweet colleague or the perfect neighbor was a mistake many of her kind made. She had it in spades and could turn it on and off like a tap when needs be. With her FBI counterparts now studying psychopaths' behavioral traits, acting hardnosed at work avoided any trace of suspicion. With kids,

Beth made an exception. It was normal, even for her, to offer comfort. Speaking nonsense, she disregarded the contamination protocol for the good of the child. She drew the blood-splattered child into her arms and rocked her like a baby. An overwhelming sense of despair for the child gripped her and she cuddled her closer. "He was a bad man, Missy. You can't trust everyone. Some people tell lies."

"Are you a cop?" Missy looked her straight in the eyes. "You don't look like a cop."

Beth nodded. "I'm an FBI agent. Do you know what FBI agents do?"

"Sort of. You catch the bad guys like the cops." The little girl's eyes swiveled to her and examined her face. Missy took a breath and then blew it out. She stared at her unblinking as if reliving a memory. "I know who killed him."

Heart thumping, Beth kept her facial expression neutral. No one had ever discovered her secret. *Don't let it happen—not now, not in front of Mac.* She admired him but if he discovered her calling, he'd never understand her, not in a million years. What happened next would shape her entire life going forward. Taking monsters like Jared Small out of existence depended on her continued survival. Most times, the cops found the bottom dwellers on the food chain of murderers, but so many smart and ingenious psychopathic serial killers slipped through the system, escaped or convinced a parole board they were rehabilitated. The problem was they killed again the moment they stepped free.

Out of the six-hundred thousand cases of missing persons in the US per year, more than ninety thousand people are never found. No bodies, no murder scene—zip. She'd been working for five years taking out the unstoppable psychopaths and had barely scratched the surface. As a special agent in the FBI, she'd use the law to hunt down the also-rans and they'd do their time. Most were never released from jail, but it was the others who gained her attention. She hated the child killers, the murdering pedophiles, the sex slavers, and the perverted sadomasochist serial killers with a passion. All of them needed to meet her dark side to bring them to justice. It had taken her adolescence to understand her psychopathy was different. Beth had never been like other psychopathic serial killers, who became slaves to their fantasies and addicted to killing. Her dark side only sought vengeance for others.

Psychopathic serial killers hid behind masks of decency and lived in plain sight. They were the best friend, the sociable neighbor. In fact, they came in every flavor and were the most vicious of killers, but she recognized them as if they wore a flashing red light on their heads. *It takes one to know one.*

"Well, I'll be..." Mac pulled clean gloves from his pocket and bent to examine something on the ground. "It's a tarot card. The Grim Reaper... the death card." He pulled out his phone and took pictures. "Are you sure you didn't see anyone, when you arrived?"

Beth huffed out a sigh and faked a long shudder. "No and I'd have mentioned it if I had but I wasn't looking for another perp because I was kinda busy trying to save this clown's life."

"I'm ordering you to take a psych review after this take-down. You don't look so good." Mac looked at Missy. "She'll be in counseling for the rest of her life, poor kid."

Acting distressed came easy for Beth, she shook her head. "I don't need to see anyone. This was no more traumatic than a car wreck and we've seen plenty of those."

"You'll do as I say. It's different when kids are involved." Mac gave her a long hard stare. "You've been out too long on your own. I figure you're close to breaking point. Take the test and prove me wrong."

Beth blew out a long sigh. "Okay, I'll take the darn test."

"That's settled then. Leave everything in situ but as soon as the ME arrives, we'll get Missy out of here. The paramedics are on their way." Mac bent down and looked at the trembling child. "Missy, did you see anyone else here?"

With her heart pounding, Beth closed her eyes, held her breath, and waited to be cuffed.

"Yes, it was an angel." Missy smiled. She had one tooth missing and blood caked her hair but her eyes had filled with wonder. "An angel saved me."

TWO

Sirens and cruisers surrounded the area. Beth moved away from Missy and endured questioning by detectives and then again by FBI agents. She answered all their questions and satisfied them with her answers. When the forensics team complete with Dr. Shane Wolfe, a respected medical examiner from Black Rock Falls, arrived in a chopper, she swallowed hard. The Texan's work bringing down serial killers was legendary, and he traveled all over Montana processing crime scenes. "Wow! I get to meet Dr. Wolfe."

"Yeah, the boss called him in as the Tarot Killer is involved." Mac raised one bushy eyebrow. "If there's evidence here, he'll find it."

I hope there isn't any. Beth looked down at her blood-soaked clothes and shuddered. The smell was getting unbearable and she needed to shower. She looked up as footsteps came close by and found a tall broad man with white-blond hair and piercing gray eyes staring at her. It was as if he was taking in the scene and analyzing it with one sweeping gaze.

"Agent Katz, I'm Shane Wolfe, the medical examiner. Why don't you tell me what happened here?"

Keeping her story precise, Beth gave him a rundown of her story. "I heard screaming and ran from my vehicle. It was hard to miss him beside the track. He was bleeding real bad, but the girl was my first priority. She had a hood over her head and I pulled it up to check on her first. She was breathing and staring into space, catatonic. I spoke to her, but she didn't respond. I pulled on gloves, checked for a pulse on the bleeding man and found none. As he was still bleeding, I assumed he must still be alive and tried to put pressure on the wound. He was facedown over the girl and I couldn't see the extent of his injury at the time. Then Mac arrived. He turned over the victim and I pulled out the girl. Mac covered the victim's face with his T-shirt to hide it from her. That's about it."

"Was the blood gushing or dribbling out when you arrived?" Wolfe turned to look at the area around the body. "Did you move the victim?"

Beth pressed the back of her hand to her head. "Dribbling and, yeah, we moved the body. We rolled him onto his back. He was crushing the kid beneath him. What else could we do?" She glared at him. "Like I said, my duty of care the moment I arrived on scene was the girl's welfare. It was obvious he was attacking her."

"Missy said she saw an angel?" Wolfe narrowed his gaze on her. "Was she referring to you?"

Shaking her head, Beth blew out a breath. "I don't think so. She mentioned seeing a halo and would have mentioned me when Mac asked her. I really don't look like an angel wearing this black woolen cap." She pointed to the tarot card. "Maybe it was the person who left that card?"

"It seems that way." Wolfe glanced over at the girl and then back to her. "Y'all know what the tarot card means? The Tarot Killer is a vigilante who takes the law into his own hands. Some say he's a myth, but I've seen what he can do to psychopathic serial killers. Trust me, he's no myth. You're lucky to get out alive."

Beth snorted. "He was long gone by the time I arrived, but if he is a vigilante like you say, why would he attack me? He'd already killed the predator. I wouldn't be a threat to him."

"Now don't y'all go taking the Tarot Killer lightly. Don't you have a shoot-to-kill order for him?" Wolfe lifted his chin. "He'd be aware of that by now, so yeah, all law enforcement is a threat and you'll need to watch your back in the future." He nodded as if to himself. "I'll need your clothes. If you left trace evidence on Missy or the corpse, I'll need to eliminate your DNA from my investigation. One of my team will give you a suit to cover them." He handed her a large evidence bag. "We'll meet up at the office later. I'm afraid you'll be stuck behind a desk until the results of the psych test come in. Look, I know seeing a shrink is a pain but it's for your own good."

Agitated, Beth blew out a sigh. "Okay, but I don't really have a choice, do I?"

"You were involved in a highly stressful situation." Wolfe examined her face. "It's protocol, Agent Katz. People suffer PTSD after incidents like this one and we don't want FBI agents freezing on the job. It's not a big deal, just a psych test."

Letting her shoulders slump in a show of resignation, Beth nodded. "Yeah, I understand. I just hate being stuck behind a desk. I'm sorry to be difficult. I'm kinda jumpy."

"It's a normal reaction." Wolfe looked sympathetic. "I'm sure everything will be fine. Mac mentioned you've been working a ton of homicides lately. I'm sure all you need is a break for a time."

The last thing Beth needed was a break. She wanted to be up close and personal with killers, so she had a choice: take them in or take them down. That couldn't be achieved sitting behind a desk but for now she'd be the perfect agent and go with the flow. She needed to keep her job. Being out of the loop on crime would make her lose control and then the hunter became the hunted. She looked at Wolfe. He was well named: his alert gray eyes wouldn't miss a thing. "Can I get out of here now? I stink on ice."

"Yeah, suit up and you're good to go." Wolfe turned back to speak to one of his team.

After pulling blue coveralls over her blood-soaked clothes, she found Mac. "I'm heading back to the office. The forensics want my clothes and I need a shower."

"Hang on, I'll get someone to drive you." Mac looked around.

Beth removed her gloves and tossed them into the evidence bag. "I can drive myself, Mac. I'm fine."

"Technically, you're under evaluation." Mac shook his head. "I'll get one of the cops to drive you."

Annoyed, Beth shook her head in disbelief. "Give me a break. How will that look to the uniforms? I'm not a head case and right now I look like a blood-splattered blue snowman. I'll need my vehicle to drive home."

"Okay." Mac's gaze moved over her and he frowned. "You still look way too calm to me. That's not a good sign after experiencing a traumatic event."

"It's been two hours. The shock has come and gone." Beth walked away, giving him a wave. "I'll see you back at the office. Now we know the perp's name, I'll see if he's left a trail on the net."

Beth climbed into her sedan and headed back to the highway. Making sure no one followed her, she slipped into a busy parking lot. She pulled open the coveralls to remove the razor from her pocket, and slid it into a concealed sheath attached under the seat. She didn't need anyone finding that on her when they took her clothes. Minutes later she was inside the office, grabbing clean clothes from her locker and heading for the shower. Her skin tingled as her mind replayed the kill. She'd planned it right down to the last second and hadn't left any evidence behind. Finding Jared Small and being there just at the right time hadn't been a fluke. Already a suspect due to the rusty old vehicle he drove, Small was interviewed by them at the school months ago on a different missing child case, but Beth recognized the signs. He was oh so nice—the charmer hiding behind the mask of a monster and he'd fooled everyone, except her. She'd gone deeper and discovered he was a member of a group of predators using the dark web to share their experiences and disgusting image files in a chat room. They believed the group was safe from prying eyes and no doubt law enforcement, but nothing buried deep on the dark web or anywhere else in cyberspace was safe from her. She existed in data streams and had been able to manipulate code from the moment her young fingers touched a computer.

It amused her that some of the men like him found it necessary to boast about their crimes and plans. She'd traced his whereabouts easily enough and read his posts about his "dates." He liked to visit his killing field once a week and gaze on the victims he'd tossed down an old well. Patience being a virtue she had in spades, she'd watched and waited until he'd led her to the Clawsfoot Mine.

Beth smiled as she dried her hair. *He hadn't counted on me spying on him.* Persistence always paid off, and after reading his last post, she'd hit the streets, telling Mac she had a hunch about Small and would be cruising the neighborhood around the school. When Small left the schoolgrounds, she'd followed him to the mine. The next minute the call came in about the missing girl. One thing for sure, Jared Small would never harm another child. He was gone and her dark side was appeased for a time.

She headed back to her desk and turned on the computer. After bringing up Small's dark web files, she heard voices behind her. Mac was giving her a concerned stare and Wolfe was speaking in hushed tones beside him. Were they discussing her?

"The forensic team has discovered six bodies down a well at the mine." Mac moved closer to her desk and shook his head in disbelief. "This Tarot Killer, whoever he is, saved number seven. There's no evidence at the scene, not as much as a footprint. Are you sure you didn't see or hear anything, Beth?"

Beth pushed both hands through her long damp hair and stared at him. "I'm sure."

"I know, y'all figure this Tarot Killer is some type of cult hero, but committing murder even when it's a killer is still homicide." Wolfe looked at her closely. "We can't have people taking justice into their own hands—even if we figure they deserve it."

Cult hero, well that's a first. Beth smothered a smile. "I'm an FBI agent, Dr. Wolfe, not a silly schoolgirl who reads romance novels." She raised one eyebrow. This was a seriously handsome man and the way his trained eye moved over her it was as if he could see through her own perfectly fitted mask of deception. "I didn't see anyone apart from Small and Missy."

"Okay." Mac leaned one hip against the desk. "Did you pull up anything on Small?" He looked at Wolfe. "Beth came to us from cybercrime. She's also worked undercover on a number of cases and has serious talent."

"Thank you." Beth smiled. "Small's been a busy boy on the dark web. I found his website and his dedicated followers. I've been reading his posts and discovered a series of instructions dedicated to the abduction, rape, and murder of children. Details of where to cruise the streets and the best places to grab a kid at random. He advised them to follow kids walking home alone from school or going to the store and the best way to lure them into their vehicles."

"Did he mention anything about Missy?" Mac let out a long breath. "Now he's dead, we don't have a clue to his motive."

"I figure his motive was clear enough, but psychopaths don't need a motive." Wolfe folded his arms across his broad chest. "It's more like a craving. Sooner or later, it gets the better of them." His gaze settled on Beth as if he could see her dark side dwelling just under the surface. "They can't control the beast and have to feed it to keep their sanity. It's been there for as long as they can remember, so they adapt and blend into society. The ones we catch are those who lose control."

Giving him her best concerned expression, Beth nodded. He understood psychopaths but lumped them all together and that was a mistake. She could control her dark side and killed only unstoppable murderers. She looked at Wolfe and wondered, if she confided in him, would he stick to his Hippo-cratic oath or have her arrested? She wished she could discuss how the need to take out Small before he destroyed more young lives had burned through her veins like liquid gold. She under-stood a predator's thought processes and recognized the monster behind Small's smiling face. "You can say that again. I've just been reading his posts over the last week or so. He mentioned he'd been watching Missy and how each day before lunchbreak she'd go to the bathroom. The school was quiet at that time with all the kids inside the classrooms. He figured he'd have time to drug her, get her into the trunk of his vehicle, and then leave on his break. The teacher would be too busy to notice Missy hadn't returned, the lunch bell would ring, and she'd be forgotten. He'd have one long hour with the girl and then return to work at the usual time."

"It was a stroke of luck you happened to be watching when he drove out of the schoolgrounds." Mac shook his head and stared at her. "How the heck did you figure he'd planned to take the girl today?"

Shaking her head in frustration, Beth let out an exaggerated sigh. "I didn't know for sure, Mac. I had a hunch, is all. I guess it comes from working undercover. I'm used to listening to my gut feeling and he's been on my radar since we interviewed him for the other missing girl. After reading his posts on the dark web, I'd bet a dollar to a dime she's one of the bodies taken from the well." Acting casual, Beth pulled back her hair and fastened it with a band from around her wrist.

"Did someone give you the tipoff he was going to strike today?" Mac leaned closer, spilling cigarette-tainted breath over her. "Come on, Beth, nobody has a hunch that good. If you have a CI or someone else was involved in these murders, I need to know."

Lifting her hands and dropping them to her sides in a frustrated move, Beth met his gaze. "If I had a confidential informer, I'd tell you and be putting in a request to finance them." She stood hands on hips and lifted her chin to add attitude to her expression. Being nice didn't work, so she'd try another angle and go on the defensive. "Don't I get points for initiative, Mac?" She glared at him. "Okay, let me spell it out for you. Remember the call the local cops received about a rusty old Dodge cruising the streets last Tuesday? When we interviewed Small and I got a look at his vehicle, it fit the description, so I followed up. I had a gut feeling he was involved when we spoke to him. I discovered he finishes up early on Tuesdays, and figured I'd head to the school and trail him to see where he goes. I was heading toward town when the call came in about the girl and then he drove right past me. It took me time to turn around in the traffic and catch up with him. I called you the moment I set eyes on him. I was in the right place at the right time, is all. It was a lucky break."

"If Beth suspected him as the killer, then the Tarot Killer had him in his sights as well." Wolfe cleared his throat. "He has ways of tracking down serial killers and there was obviously a pattern to the homicides you missed, Mac. I guess he sees what you don't. He sure has investigators scratching their heads. He never leaves evidence behind and witnesses give a different description— male, female, fat, thin, tall, short. This is why no one can pin him down. I've been to a few of the crime scenes and he always leaves the same tarot card behind. It's not a card we can match anywhere. He evaporates after the crime without a trace. It's like he doesn't exist."

Taking the advantage to plant a seed of doubt, Beth shrugged. "Have you considered he might be more than one person? There could be a whole team of them out there taking down serial killers that slip through the net."

"That sure would make more sense." Wolfe rubbed his chin. "The way he moves all over it would suggest a team effort." He smiled at her. "I'll run that past my people. Thanks for the input." He looked at Mac. "Seems to me, Beth used sound judgment and investigative skills to prevent another murder. She's been through emotional hell and back today. Maybe you should cut her a break?"

"Okay." Mac straightened. He examined her face again and nodded. "I've scheduled psych tests for you for next week. I'll send someone to take down your statement. When you're done, make sure your case files are up to date. You'll be at your desk until the results come in. Don't look at me like that, Beth. It's for your own good."

Annoyed, Beth watched them walk away and sighed. *What if I don't pass the psych test?*

THREE

TWO WEEKS LATER

Dumbfounded, Beth stood in front of the assistant director's desk. "You want me to go where?"

"The Rattlesnake Creek field office." The AD looked up at her over his spectacles. "You'll be assisting Senior Special Agent Dax Styles. Rattlesnake Creek is a small town in central Montana. It backs onto the Rocky Mountains, so pack a ton of warm clothes." He handed her an information sheet.

Beth blinked a few times, trying to wake from the nightmare. "What can someone with my skills do in a backwoods town out west? Do they even have the internet?" She sighed. "I was informed I'd be remaining in DC."

"After the psych reports, I've decided to give you a break from homicide and retest you in a year or so and see if your stress levels are lower." The AD smiled benevolently. "You're too young and valuable to lose, Agent Katz. Agent Styles is a loner and getting the reputation of a maverick and we feel having a partner would benefit him as well."

Trying to process everything, Beth swallowed hard. Her dark side would run riot unless she channeled it into taking out society's lowest forms of life. She lifted her chin. "A maverick?

Do I assume by that he takes the law into his own hands at times?" She shook her head. "An out-of-control megalomaniac, that's all I need."

"It's deep in the Central Montana Rockies. I hear you can see Crazy Peak from the top of town. That's the highest peak in that area. Everyone carries a weapon. Girls marry at sixteen. There are a ton of ranches but it's a mining town. Gold and silver, as far as I'm aware. Styles assists the local sheriff at times and uses what force is necessary when required to keep the peace. Out there, law enforcement is a little different. Let's say, more flexible. You'll be using your own judgment a good deal of the time. The field office covers Central Montana, so you'll be traveling all over. You like working alone, so that is an option, as you'll find Agent Styles is often away on a case. Should you need backup, the Snakeskin Gully field office is about half an hour away by chopper." He linked his fingers on the desk and smiled at her. "It will be like a vacation. The scenery is second to none." He cleared his throat. "Go home and pack. You'll be reviewed in two or three years, so I suggest you rent out or sell your apartment. You have ten days. Styles will be waiting for you at the Helena airport at ten o'clock on Monday morning the week after next. Your flight there gets in at nine. Head for the helipads. Lucky for you, he's a chopper pilot."

Bewildered, Beth returned to her desk and sat for a time thinking. In those few seconds, everything had changed. Without freedom to move around, and trapped in a small town, she wouldn't be able to take down the monsters without becoming the prime suspect. Now, she'd need all her expertise going forward. Once she'd gotten the lay of the land, she could devise a scheme that enabled her to slip away unnoticed. Her dark side would always be there but now controlling it would take skill. She'd faced many obstacles during her life, and Rattlesnake Creek and Dax Styles were just another rock in the road. *I can do this. I must.*

Using her skill, she accessed Dax Styles' file The thirty-two-year-old man with light brown hair in a buzz cut had a chiseled, interesting face. The intense cornflower-blue eyes and scar on his chin reflected his tough-guy maverick image. The picture screamed, *Don't mess with me*. His record was impressive but confusing. A West Point graduate, he'd served as a commissioned officer in the military police. He'd risen fast to the rank of captain and received two Silver Stars and a Purple Heart but then decided not to re-enlist and was honorably discharged after eight years. He'd joined the FBI five years ago and all was well until he was removed from DC after using excessive force on two occasions during takedowns. He'd been in Rattlesnake Creek for two years with no complaints against him but hadn't requested a transfer. Why she'd been sent to Rattlesnake Creek became abundantly clear. As a commissioned officer, part of Styles' responsibility during his time in the Army would have been to watch over subordinate officers, devise special training, and assess if they were fit for duty. She stared at his image and the darkness rose up inside her. "I figure you've bitten off more than you can chew with me, Dax Styles."

FOUR

Tired from lack of sleep, Beth pushed her luggage cart onto the glass-enclosed section set on the tarmac and spoke to the person at the desk. "Agent Beth Katz. I think that's my ride." She pointed to the FBI chopper being refueled. "How will the pilot know I'm here?"

"He'll come and get you." The man behind the counter stared at his computer screen. "Agent Styles is heading back to Rattlesnake Creek at eleven."

Relieved, Beth nodded. "That's him, but I thought we were leaving at ten?"

"Nope. He arrived at nine-thirty and has to refuel and do his preflight check. His flight plan is already logged. You can leave your luggage here, Agent Katz. I'll make sure it's loaded. If you walk through that door, you can get coffee and there's a restroom." He smiled and pointed to a door on his right. "The pilot will take a break before he leaves."

Beth pushed her luggage into a bay next to him and waited as he placed tags on all her bags. "Thank you."

"You're welcome." The man smiled at her.

After buying a cup of coffee and a packet of cookies,

Beth waited for twenty minutes before a tall man in a Stetson, faded jeans, a thick black jacket, and cowboy boots walked straight past her to the counter and purchased a coffee and a ham on rye. She stared at him with interest. The image in his file was only a couple of years old but this man's hair curled over his collar. He appeared taller than the six-two in his file and had an impressive muscular physique, but when he turned and walked toward her, the scar along his chin and the intense stare matched the picture. Her first impression had been correct. He radiated danger. *So, this is Dax Styles.*

He came over to her and placed his to-go cup of coffee and takeout bag on the table. His gaze flicked over her two-piece black suit. She'd wanted to impress him by wearing a typical FBI outfit, but she'd worn slightly higher heels than normal to make her appear taller. At five-six, she was average but he would tower over her. She stood and offered her hand. "I'm Beth Katz. It's nice to meet you, Agent Styles."

"You're gonna freeze your butt off dressed like that, and the sidewalks, where there are any, aren't suitable for heels." Styles kicked a chair out from the table and sat down staring at her. "I make it my business to blend in with the townsfolk. Being an outsider makes them suspicious, and when they're suspicious, people get shot."

Beth had never taken a backward step in her life. "I didn't come here to be liked Agent—"

"Styles." His intent gaze seemed to penetrate right through her, as if he were reading her mind. "Drop the *agent*. We're not in DC. I know you figure coming to this remote part of Montana is a demotion, but I've read your file. Your expertise in cybercrime and the contribution you gave as an undercover agent in apprehending serial killers is impressive. That's why I agreed to your position." He waved absently as if dismissing something. "That nonsense they put you through over the Small case was demeaning. From what I can see, you handle messy murders in your stride."

Soothed by his support, she nodded. "Yeah, I do. Losing my position in DC was a setback I didn't need. I'm not likely to get a promotion stuck in Rattlesnake Creek."

"You should consider the move as a promotion. You're head of cybercrime here and the only undercover agent." He sipped his coffee and then leaned back in his chair and observed her for a beat. "If you're willing to come down from your high horse for a time, we might be able to solve crimes together."

High horse? What was he talking about? She ignored him and dipped a cookie into her coffee and ate the melting delight. Gathering her thoughts, she looked at him. "That will be difficult. They've labeled you as a maverick. Is that why you're here?"

"I play by my own rules at times, yeah." Styles shrugged nonchalantly. "Rattlesnake Creek is old school. It puts the *wild* back into Wild West, twenty-first-century style. There's one sheriff, no deputies, and finding deputies in this neck of the woods is difficult. Fights break out, people steal from each other in the mining camps. When I arrived here, there was a fentanyl distribution racket hidden underground in a local ranch. They purchased the pure drug, cut it, and sold it on the streets making millions. So, I had to break a few heads to get my point across, but it worked." He gave her a long look. "Why did you try to save Small? He was trying to rape a kid. Makes no sense to me at all."

The way he was looking at her made her fully aware of this man's profiling skills. As a military cop, he'd have the ability to read people. It would be his downfall if he messed with her, but she could play the part of a distressed victim better than most. She swallowed hard and looked at her hands. "Instinct, duty of care, call it what you will, it seemed the right thing to do at the time."

"I'd have let him bleed out and worried about the girl. He was cut through to the backbone and didn't stand a chance. You should have seen that." Styles shook his head slowly. "The girl was your priority, not the perp. That's why they sent you here." He met her gaze. "You didn't know that, did you?"

Astonished, Beth lifted her coffee cup and drank to avoid his gaze. "No."

"They figured you didn't act fast enough to help the girl and they believe the homicide cases are getting to you." Styles pushed the last bite of sandwich into his mouth, chewed slowly, and washed it down with coffee.

Beth gaped at him. "Me? That's a downright lie. I was the one looking after her. Mac didn't give her a second look. I wasn't traumatized from the crime scene. Blood doesn't worry me and I've seen my fair share of dead bodies. Mac's the one who needed a psych test, not me."

"How does that make you feel?" Styles waved his cup at her.

Anger rising, Beth glared at him. "What are you, my shrink now?"

"I just want you to be honest with me." Styles turned his to-go cup around with the tips of his fingers. "Can you do that, Beth?"

The use of her first name startled her. Was it a ploy to get under her guard? She pushed down the need to allow her charismatic nature to deal with him. He expected her to be prickly and any change would make him suspicious. In truth, the sight of a bloody crime scene didn't affect her, but her dark side rose up like an avenging angel when she witnessed young lives destroyed by murder or other despicable means. When kept under control, her dark side was like a virus grown in a lab, only lethal when it escaped.

She lifted her chin. "You want honesty? Can you handle the truth?"

"Yeah, I can. Shoot." Styles' mouth twitched up at the corners and his eyes flashed with amusement.

Holding back the rush of anger, Beth took a deep breath. She'd become a convincing liar. After all, she'd had years of practice. "I distance myself from the victims because I have nightmares about what happened to them." She lowered her voice. "Yeah, I tried to save Small, but not because I gave a darn, because I wanted to know what he'd done with the other girls. They asked me why I didn't shoot him when I saw him on the girl. The chance of a through and through and hitting the girl wasn't worth the risk." She stared at him and swallowed. "The truth is, if I'd had a darn knife with me, and seeing him on that girl, I'd have cut his throat myself."

"That's a normal response." Styles chuckled. "I'd take him down in that situation too and save the taxpayers the cost of a trial and a life sentence. I follow my own rules when there's no doubt of their guilt."

Interested, Beth leaned forward in her seat. "And what are your rules?"

"If they draw down on me, I shoot to kill. They don't get a second chance. It's within the procedural guidelines. Nowhere does it say we should allow an armed perp to shoot first. When someone draws down on me, it's every man for himself." He checked his watch. "You done here? I suggest you use the restroom. It's two hours to Rattlesnake Creek and I don't stop at gas stations along the way. I'll go and load your bags into the chopper. Don't be long. We leave at eleven sharp." He stood and strolled out of the door and then stopped to look at her over one shoulder. "I'll show you where you're staying. A vehicle is supplied. It's old but it will get you around. We'll be eating at Tommy Joe's Bar and Grill tonight and in the morning. I'll show you around town." He cleared his throat. "Have you packed boots and jeans? If not, the general store has everything you need."

With her bags stuffed with everything she could possibly need, Beth nodded. "I googled the climate and what to expect, but I'll likely need more winter gear."

"Okay, I'll give you a rundown of the best stores in town in the morning." He headed for the door. "Don't take too long. Wheels up in ten."

Beth stared after him. Her life had been turned upside down and it was only a matter of time before her dark side reared its ugly head again demanding to be fed. With a man like Styles as her partner, she'd need to be watching her back every step of the way.

FIVE

The scenery was spectacular as they flew over the mountains. In her ear, Styles gave Beth a running commentary of the local places of interest. They flew over an alpine region with sparkling waterfalls, lakes, and a forest that went on forever. She turned to Styles. "I've heard of Black Rock Falls. I figure anyone in law enforcement would be interested in their homicide cases." She had visited the area during her last vacation, but no one needed to know, least of all Dax Styles.

"Their local FBI field office is Snakeskin Gully. Agents Carter and Wells are our backup if we ever need them. They are farther west, about thirty minutes from us by chopper. Black Rock Falls is where Dr. Wolfe, the ME, is located. Our local doctor, Nate Mace, handles the uncomplicated deaths in town. Anything remotely suspicious, we call in Shane Wolfe."

The chopper rounded a high snow-covered peak, and as they passed over the forest, Beth noticed the raw patches on the landscape. Bare areas stood out littered with brightly colored industrial machinery against the open spaces. Scars from where they'd mined dotted the landscape. She adjusted the mic on her headset to speak. "Is that mining damage?"

"Yeah, well that's private land. The miners take the soil from where the old gold miners used to dig and pass it through a machine to remove gold particles from the soil. When they're through, they're required to return the ground to its previous condition." He sighed. "It's never the same again, but if we're lucky, some of the miners plant trees and shrubs before they move on. The grass grows back quickly enough. It's not just gold. There are minerals too."

The chopper swung in the wind as they rounded a rocky outcrop, and Beth caught her breath as they descended into a magnificent valley surrounded by majestic peaks, forests, and waterfalls. The colors of late fall made the scenery resemble an old master. It was spectacular, and after seeing the mining operations, she hadn't expected to see acres of unspoiled land surrounded by creeks and mountain ranges. She could make out the sprawling town, sitting on one side of a wide fast-flowing river fed by three separate waterfalls. She turned to look at Styles. "Is that Rattlesnake Creek?"

"Yeah. Nice, huh?" He gave her a satisfied smirk. "I figure the creek was a might smaller during the gold rush back in 1865."

As they descended, more details came into view. The main road was wide, lined by redbrick buildings with brightly colored façades. Vehicles lined the street, all parked nose in. It was a prosperous, alive town. Astonished, Beth stared at him. "It's beautiful."

"It's our little secret but don't let its looks fool you." Styles landed the chopper on the top of a redbrick building. "Women are in the minority around here and the men are as tough as nails. Weekdays, it's not so bad, but when the miners come into town to blow off steam, it's chaotic."

Beth unclipped her seatbelt when Styles cut the engine and removed her headset. "That's not our problem; that's the local sheriff's concern."

"Oh, I lend a hand when necessary." Styles flipped switches and then opened his door. "Most of our work is from out of town, although we have had a few murders. The people who come here are looking for a fast buck. You can look through the case files. The crime rate here is high for such a small town and the sheriff really needs a few good deputies but it's difficult getting people to stay."

Beth waited for him to pull her bags from the chopper and grasped the one on wheels and one other. "I'll come back for the others."

"I've got them." Styles gathered them up and headed for the stairs. "Watch your step."

She followed him down a flight of stairs that led to a long passageway. "What is this place?"

"This is the FBI field office building." Styles walked up to a door, placed one of her bags on the floor and pulled out a set of keys, opened the door and waved her inside. "This is your apartment." He followed her into the passageway. "We take up the top floor and I live down the other end of the building—the last door. There are two other apartments, but the end ones have all the views. The elevator goes to our office or down to street level. You'll need to scan in your palm print to use the elevator and access our office." He dumped her bags on a leather sofa in the family room.

Staring around the spacious apartment, Beth frowned. "So, you're saying the FBI figures we don't need personal security? Just the building? That makes no sense at all."

"Any threat would need to come via the roof and in truth anyone wanting to get inside our apartments would only need to kick in the door." He shrugged. "No one has tried to get in here yet."

Beth moved along the passageway; three bedrooms, one converted into an office; a spacious and surprisingly modern kitchen with appliances. She turned and looked at him. "I'll need transport and food."

"Well unless you're into tofu, I've stocked the refrigerator and freezer. Eggs, milk, bread, bacon, vegetables, cereal, butter, and anything else I figured you'd need. There's a pharmacy and general store if you need anything personal. There's a truck out front if you need it, FBI issue, so not the latest model, but most times we'll be on cases together." He rubbed his chin thoughtfully. "I'll show you around when we've eaten. You'll need to change into something more practical. Jeans and boots would work." He gave her a long look. "Freshen up and I'll meet you at the elevator in, what, twenty minutes?" He handed her the keys to the apartment. "Will you be able to start work first thing in the morning?"

"Sure." Nodding, Beth followed him back down the passageway and shut the door. She leaned against it, his words running around her head like an earwig. *We'll be on cases together.* She ground her teeth at the idea. *Not if I can help it.*

She inspected the apartment. Surprisingly everything had been supplied: linen, towels, a new coffeemaker, and a good supply of quality coffee. After dumping her bags on the bed, she dragged out jeans, a sweater, and a long jacket she'd purchased the moment she'd known her fate. She'd need more clothes and fast. Winter would be here before too long and nothing she had would be warm enough. She glanced at her watch and took a hot shower. The trip had taken most of the day and her back ached from sitting in economy. She tied up her long hair and made the elevator with seconds to spare. After Styles took her through the process of scanning her palm print into the machine, they headed down to a red truck. "You have a red truck? That's not very FBI, is it?"

"That's the point." Styles grinned at her. "Blending in with the community." He pointed to a few stores. "Pharmacy, general store, deli, bank, all close by." He slowed and parked in a space. "This here is Tommy Joe's Bar and Grill. Good food and more of a meeting place for the townsfolk. You don't get moved along here if you've finished your meal."

Beth climbed from the truck. "Is this the only bar in town? It must be crowded at the weekends."

"Nope, we have three saloons, two here in town, one on the highway. Two have gentlemen's clubs in the back. We have three motels too and I suspect one of them runs an escort service. I've been there and watched for a time. I never witnessed any soliciting, but the same women seem to be having drinks with a variety of men before they leave with them."

Beth blew out a long breath. "Again, that's the sheriff's problem. I'm here to work on crimes the local sheriff can't solve."

She walked into the bar and scanned the room: two pool tables, a jukebox out of the 1950s, and a bar with the usual assortment of bottles displayed along the wall. On one section was a printed menu and on a chalkboard a list of specials. She took her credit card from her purse and waited for someone to come to the counter. The swinging doors to the kitchen opened and a tall, handsome man in his thirties walked through. His smile at seeing her lit up the room. Beth hadn't expected a welcome. Most people treated her with suspicion.

"Ah, you must be Styles' new partner." The man wiped his hand on the apron around his waist and held it out to her. "Tommy Joe Barker, but my friends call me TJ."

Beth shook his hand. "Agent Katz. Is this your bar?"

"Yeah." He flicked a glance at Styles and then back at Beth. "What can I get you?"

Beth actually liked the man. She had an instinct about most people and no alarm bells were ringing. "Steak, medium, with all the trimmings."

"I'll have the same." Styles rubbed at a scar along his chin as TJ vanished back into the kitchen. "Like I said before, you need to drop the *agent* when you're in town. It makes people nervous.

Nervous people shoot first and ask questions later, if you get my meaning."

Drawing in a deep breath and letting it come out through her nose, she waited for TJ to return from the kitchen and ordered a cup of coffee. "It's nice to meet you TJ. You can call me Beth." She handed him her credit card. "Put our meals on here."

"Sure." TJ looked at Styles and raised both eyebrows. "Why don't you take a seat, Beth, and I'll bring the coffee right over."

"I like my back to the wall." Styles led the way to a booth in the corner. "Thanks for the meal, but I prefer to pay when I'm with a woman." He shrugged. "I have a reputation to uphold."

Beth gave him a broad smile and snorted with laughter. "Oh, do you now? We might be dining in an Old West town, but this is the twenty-first century and, like it or not, I'm your equal. You can pay next time if your ego needs a boost."

"Mac mentioned that you say it like it is." Styles turned the salt cellar around in his fingertips. "I like people who are straight down the line. It makes life uncomplicated. I figure we're gonna get along just fine." He winked at her.

He actually winked at me. Beth bit back a reply and looked away as her dark side rose up and shimmered just under the surface. At that moment, she wanted to strangle him real slow.

SIX

"Mom, I'm going over to see Skylar." Brooklyn Daniels stuffed the cookies into her mouth and washed them down with milk. "I'll be back before dinner."

"What about your homework?" Her mom walked into the kitchen, opened the freezer, and pulled out a frozen lasagna.

Brooklyn grinned. "We haven't any, apart from studying for a quiz tomorrow. I can do that after dinner." She looked up at her mother. "We're going to pick wildflowers. There's a bunch of them right behind Skylar's house."

"Okay." Her mom looked at her watch. "Don't make me come looking for you."

Backing out of the door, Brooklyn snatched up two more cookies from the plate and headed for freedom. It was a cold, windy, sunny afternoon but the fresh air was wonderful after spending the afternoon sitting beside Tommy Higgins. He smelled and he kept kicking off his shoes and waving his stinky feet under the desk. He thought it was funny and so did the other boys. She ran along the sidewalk and met Skylar at her gate. She handed her a cookie. "I told my mom we were picking wildflowers behind your house."

"We can't tell anyone about the secret garden." Skylar fell into step beside her. "If we tell, the Warlock won't come back."

Lifting her shoulders to her ears, Brooklyn shivered against the blast of cold wind whistling down from the Rocky Mountains. "He'll be happy we brought him cookies, but I don't have any beer."

They made their way along the railroad track, stepping from one wooden crosstie to the other. Leaving the track where it disappeared through the tunnel in the mountain, they headed for the forest. They'd discovered the fairy grotto, a small clearing in the forest where the sun shone down on a patch of wildflowers during the summer, but the Warlock had only met them the previous day. They'd both spoken to him for ages online in the game chat room but didn't really believe he existed for real. Seeing a man with a flowing cloak and long fair hair appear without a sound had scared them at first. He'd told them to leave his grotto because the Queen of the Fae would be arriving soon. He'd sat on a boulder, head in his hands, saying he was in trouble. Curious, Brooklyn had asked him why and he'd replied that he had nothing to give her because an elf had stolen his magic. She'd asked him what they could do and he'd asked for food and beer. He'd made them promise not to tell anyone they'd seen him or he'd be banished for speaking to humans. After giving their solemn promise, he'd bowed and disappeared into the trees.

Excited, Brooklyn led the way into the grotto and looked around but saw no one. She turned to Skylar. "He's not here, we're too late. He's been banished."

"The poor Warlock." Skylar's face dropped. "It's our fault, we should have helped him yesterday."

"You still can." The Warlock emerged from the trees and smiled at them.

"We have cookies but no beer." Skylar held up her cookie.

"That's wonderful." The Warlock bowed and looked her in

the eye. "The fairy queen will see one of you. The other will be given a special magical power if she does exactly what I say."

"I want to see the fairy queen." Skylar held out her hand. "Give me your cookie. I'll give both of them to her."

Nodding, excitement shivered through Brooklyn. She would be given a special power. "Okay."

"I must blindfold you first and tie your hands." The Warlock stared at Skylar. "The fairies are frightened of humans."

Hoping to catch a glimpse of the fairies, Brooklyn stared into the trees. As the Warlock blindfolded her friend, she looked at him. "What do you want me to do?"

"Drink this magic potion." He pulled a small bottle from his pocket. "Drink it all and stand on this blanket." He spread out a red blanket on the grass. "Don't move. I'll be back very soon." He led Skylar away. "I have potion for you too. You can drink it when we get there."

Lightheaded and sleepy, Brooklyn sat on the blanket. It seemed to be a long time before she heard the Warlock walking back through the trees. She looked at him and smiled. "Where's Skylar?"

"The fairy queen is very pleased with her." He moved onto the blanket and sat beside her. "Don't worry... I've saved the best for you."

SEVEN

After spending what was left of Monday afternoon visiting stores with suitable clothing and boots, Beth had returned to her apartment and made use of the washer and dryer. Wearing stiff unwashed jeans and shirts wasn't going to happen. When her phone buzzed, she stared at it for a few moments before picking it up and reading the caller ID. "Yeah, I just got in, Styles. What's the problem?"

"No problem. As it's your first night here, I figured you'd like some company. Do you want to have dinner with me at Tommy Joe's Bar and Grill?"

Starting any type of relationship with a colleague wasn't in her future, but was he just being nice? Co-workers in her last office often dined together. Perhaps this was what Styles expected and her concern wasn't necessary. She thought for a beat and then nodded. "I'll need to get back into having a partner. I'm used to working alone. I find having someone constantly interrupting my thoughts is counterproductive."

"Counterproductive, huh?" Styles cleared his throat in what sounded like a bad attempt to cover up a snort. *"Well, I've been managing here alone for some time now and, apart from the sher-*

iff, I haven't needed anyone to brainstorm ideas with to catch killers. It was just me and it worked out just fine, so having you come by and cramp my style wasn't the kind of news I welcomed either."

Well, he was being brutally honest with her. She was starting to like this guy. Lately men seemed to tiptoe around her, as if too scared to say the wrong thing. At the airport a man had held the door open for her and then apologized. With her hands full of luggage, she'd smiled and thanked him and noted the relieved expression on his face. "In that, the feeling is mutual. Nothing personal. I've worked alone since joining the FBI, mainly because I was working cybercrime and had my nose stuck to a screen for long hours. After, I moved around most of the time and worked undercover some of the time, so having a partner never happened. I worked under Mac and gave him a report of my progress, is all. Being here is a new experience for both of us."

"Not for me. I was a captain in the Army, in military police. This is why you're here with me. Mac sent you here to assess your functionality in the field."

Swallowing the taste of deception, Beth screwed her hand into a fist. "You know darn well the reason I'm here. I found a dying perp. He was planning on raping a kid, but the Tarot Killer got there before me and cut his throat, which I hear is tame for him." She sighed. "I did a psych test and the consensus was I needed time away from the city. They figured if I had PTSD, I might freeze up if confronted by a killer."

"Would you?" Styles sounded interested.

Beth barked a laugh. "Well, as I haven't met one since, your guess is as good as mine. What you said earlier about my lack of caring is wrong. I did care for the little girl and I prevented her from seeing the perp's body. I've thought about her often and had nightmares about the guy gushing blood, but before you ask, no, I don't suffer from PTSD."

"Okay, okay." She could hear Styles scratch the stubble on his chin. *"No more talk about that old case. It's closed. Are you meeting me for dinner or what?"*

Smiling to herself, Beth blew out a breath. What harm could it possibly do? "Yeah sure, I'll be there. What time?"

"I have a table booked for eight-thirty. I'll be there early, playing pool and having a few beers as it's walking distance away." He let out a long sigh. *"Catch you later... and I'm paying this time."* He disconnected.

Beth dropped her phone on the counter and went to the bathroom to take a shower. As the hot water spilled over her it gave her time to think. Working with Styles was going to be a problem, but she'd overcome many difficulties in her lifetime and he was just a small bump in the road. The one constant in her life was the stream of psychopathic killers and the victims who needed justice. Her mind went to Dr. Shane Wolfe. The man intrigued her, especially now that she'd met him in person. Not that he was like her, but they shared the same ethic in a twisted way. She'd once read a paper he'd published on why he became a medical examiner. He wanted to be the voice of the dead and tell their story to bring their killer to justice. So, in truth they had the same goal. The only difference was she played on the same team as the killer. She understood a psychopath's need to kill but her focus was different. Her dark side only sought vengeance and she murdered people because they deserved to die. Removing a predator from society was her priority. She made logical decisions and targeted seemingly uncatchable psychopathic killers committing horrendous crimes. Now with Styles as her wingman, she'd need to re-strategize her endgame.

An hour later, Beth stared at her reflection in the closet mirror and shook her head in disbelief. Agent Beth Katz had been transformed. She'd replaced the black suit, white shirt, and heels with blue jeans, sweater, and jacket. She pulled on flat leather ankle boots and straightened to slide the black Stetson on her head. The fact that everyone including the kids she'd noticed around town wore cowboy hats had forced her hand. She'd walked into the Mountain Range clothing store and explained what she required and left with a trunk filled with packages. The Stetson she'd purchased from a store situated down a small alleyway. The hat had been fitted and steamed into shape to suit her, the store owner insisting the hat was made to last a lifetime.

It was just after eight when she left the building. A cold wind brushed her cheeks, bringing with it the fresh smell of snowcapped mountains. Most of the stores had closed signs hanging in the doors, but lights blazed from the saloons, pizzeria, the gas station, and Tommy Joe's Bar and Grill. As she made her way along the sidewalk, a delivery guy came out of the pizzeria in the distance, carrying a pile of boxes and headed toward a pickup. She raised her eyebrows, surprised such a small town delivered pizza, but then the town's size was deceptive and miners would likely be their best customers.

Out of the shadowed storefronts a group of men emerged. Some carried beer cans, and from the remarks, she figured these were the local bullies. Before the delivery guy had made it to the truck, they'd surrounded him, stealing boxes from his stack and pushing him around. Beth quickened her pace to intervene when Styles came barreling out of Tommy Joe's carrying a pool cue. Words were exchanged and the delivery guy collected his pizzas and escaped to his truck. Beth moved closer, keeping to the shadows. The men had Styles surrounded, but as no loud insults carried to her on the wind, she assumed he had the problem in hand.

Before she'd taken her next breath it got nasty. Beth picked up her pace, as one of the men swung a punch at Styles and all hell broke loose. She stared open-mouthed as Styles broke the pool cue over one guy's head in a shower of splintered timber, twirled the broken end in one hand, and swung it low to take out the legs of another. Men rushed him but Styles ducked and twisted, missing blows. The thumps and gasps meant Styles' attackers weren't so lucky. Cries of pain rang out as the men ran straight into fists or the heel of Styles' boot and fell gasping to the blacktop rolling around in agony.

One man grabbed the broken pool cue from the ground and ran at Styles, screaming a war cry. Beth's hand went to her weapon but froze as her partner grabbed the man's wrist and spun him around, wrenching his arm so high up his back she could almost hear the tendons snapping. Running to assist, Beth reached the sidewalk beside Tommy Joe's Bar and Grill in seconds and pulled her weapon from its shoulder holster. As cool as a cucumber, Styles curled his mouth into a smile and he held up a hand for her to stop.

"I said, go home before I send you to the hospital." Styles tossed the man away and stood relaxed with his hands loose at his sides. There wasn't a mark on him. "You know the deal in this town: no gangs, no bullies. Draw down on me and you'll die."

The two men left standing looked at each other and came to a silent decision. One lurched forward, dancing like a prize-fighter, ducking and weaving before aiming a punch, but Styles just smiled. He struck out like a rattlesnake, and as fist met bone in a sickening crunch, blood ran down the man's face and he howled with pain. "Should I be using words of one syllable so you understand?" Styles dropped his hands again and stared at the remaining man. "Pick up your buddies and go back to camp. Playtime is over."

Beth stood to one side and waited for the burly men, all between twenty-five and thirty, to disperse. They limped away, holding tissues to bloody noses and cursing. She'd just witnessed Styles dealing with six men, who could have been armed, although she had read in the documentation on

Rattlesnake Creek that the miners camps prohibited the carrying of firearms. Styles must be crazy or enjoyed fighting to take such a risk without backup. Shaking her head, she stared at him as he turned back to walk into the bar. "Are you hurt?"

"Oh, you *do* care." He grinned at her. "There's Mac's lack-of-empathy case shot to bits."

EIGHT

After returning to her apartment from her dinner with Styles, Beth dropped into one of the comfy leather chairs and considered the primal being that was Dax Styles. He'd surprised her. The quiet, seemingly introspective man was akin to a bottle of nitroglycerine—one jolt and he exploded into a completely different person. Not a psychopath—she understood the difference—this man was in control every second of the time. He gave a warning, and if not heeded, then a whole world of hurt came tumbling down on whoever had stepped out of line—and oh boy, those who called his bluff ended up in the hospital. She had no doubt that Styles kept himself on the right side of the law, but she could tell just by looking at his eyes, he'd kill without a second thought. She stared at her reflection in the black screen of the wide TV. "If I cross that imaginary line, he'll take me down without hesitation." She smiled and leaned back in the chair. The idea of eluding a strong adversary excited her. "Life just got interesting and I sure do love a challenge."

She stood and went to the kitchen to pour a glass of the wine she'd brought with her from DC. She'd ordered comfort food to make her time in Rattlesnake Creek as pleasant as possible. Her extravagant lifestyle, fed from various income streams via the dark web, meant that she lived comfortably, ate the best food, and drank the best wines. It enabled her to use and discard disguises when she needed to disappear. Working as a special agent was the perfect cover. In her profession, she was up close and personal with crime investigation. Having a first-hand look at the crime scenes made her choices easier and ultimately gave her exposure to the deadliest criminals.

At first, it had surprised her just how many serial killers used the dark web. Many had followers hidden in the data streams, and it was these particular dominant psychopaths who caught her interest. These notorious killers thrilled their devotees with each increasingly brutal murder. The fact they had so many followers concerned her. The others held no thrill value for her and she'd willingly participate in a team or alone to capture the grab-and-slash killers. The opportunistic killers rarely had the brains to plan a murder. The fast-kill, no-thrill, out-of-control frenzied killers usually died in a hail of bullets. No, the psychopaths in her sights had a high intelligence, murdered frequently, and planned ahead. They hid their secrets well and took dangerous to a new level. They were a worthy challenge.

Many had killed ten or twenty victims before she discovered their MO. All of them eventually convinced themselves of their infallibility and escalated into an out-of-control state. These people needed to be stopped, permanently. If allowed to live, they would be dissected by the FBI behavioral analysts who would discover secrets they didn't need to know about the other reality that existed on the dark web—her sanctuary. The place where the monsters waited to strike, deals were made and secrets shared. In cases like these, it took the brain of a psychopath to take them down and once she set her sights on one of these killers it was game on.

NINE

TUESDAY

After a peaceful night's sleep, Beth changed into running gear and headed for the local park. She ran, feeling the cold numbing her cheeks and the mountain air burning her lungs. Maybe from now on she'd find a better way of keeping fit. After breakfast, she took the elevator to the office and used her palm print to access the entry. She stepped inside a bright modern office with large windows overlooking spectacular scenery of the river, forest, and mountains. The mountains seemed close enough to touch and surrounded one side of the town and then went on forever in the distance to meet up with the snow-covered Crazy Mountain Range. Dax Styles hadn't arrived and she glanced at her watch. It was five after eight. Perhaps he was a nine-to-five operative.

The room was clean but had a distinct male locker-room aroma overlaid with aftershave. She wrinkled her nose and walked over to the window and pushed it open to allow the fresh mountain breeze inside. The cool wind lifted papers pinned to a whiteboard and she turned to examine what must be Styles' current case.

The images of young girls smiling pinned beside graphic

crime scene photographs caught her by surprise. Styles hadn't spoken of any cases. His chatter over lunch and dinner had been about himself or the virtues of Rattlesnake Creek. She walked along the whiteboard, but half of the images didn't correspond to the victims. Pushing her hair behind her ears, she looked closer, taking in the details. As she stared at each of the fifteen images, the door to the office slid open and Styles walked in surrounded by a cloud of cologne. She turned to look at him. "Morning."

"You're early." Styles grinned at her. "I'm usually here by eight-thirty. First person in makes the coffee." He held out a takeout box from the bakery. "I'll supply the food." He dropped the box on the counter and slid a carton of cream into the small refrigerator set into the kitchenette.

Beth walked over and peered into the overflowing box. "I'll walk to the deli for lunch. I get hyper on too much sugar." She chuckled, imagining running through the streets with a carving knife after indulging in a box of donuts. "It's not a good look."

"In the bag there are sandwiches, bagels, and muffins." Styles shrugged. "I'll eat whatever you won't. Maybe you should work out?"

Beth nodded. "I usually do but I'll need to find a gym that opens around six. I went for a run this morning, but the cold is murder on the lungs."

"No need." He placed the sandwiches in the refrigerator. "The gym is the door before my apartment. When they renovated this building for the FBI, as we are expected to live here, it was included. It has everything you need to keep fit. I even have a baseball pitching machine in a batting cage I can use to let off steam. If nothing works for you, there's the option of sparring with me." He chuckled as if it were a remote possibility. "And there's a hot tub. Great for warming up on cold winter nights."

Rolling her eyes at the wall, Beth filled the coffee machine with water. "I use weights and a punching bag most times." She flicked him a glance over one shoulder. "Sparring would be good but I don't want to hurt you." She chuckled. "Although after the show you gave me last night, you'd be a worthy opponent."

"You're on." Styles took down the tin of coffee beans and lifted down a grinder. "I've read your file You excel in all schools of hand-to-hand combat but you won't hurt me."

Laughing, Beth raised both eyebrows. "Don't be too sure. I might be average in size, but I've taken down my fair share of perps."

"Yeah, but in this town you need to be street smart. The miners gangs are just louts, most carry hunting knives but rarely firearms. The rest of the population, men and women, if you draw down on them, it will be a gunfight, so try to avoid that at all costs." Styles shrugged. "As you witnessed last night, there are no rules. When they come at you—and they will—they'll use every dirty trick in the book." His eyes rested on her face as if waiting for her to contradict him. "This office covers many remote towns, mountain areas with unknown threats. You'll need to be ready for anything. Are you ready to face the unknown, Beth?"

"Oh yeah, I am but that's why I carry a weapon. I'm not planning on being beaten down by a group of thugs. Did they tell you I'm a marksman too? Or should that be marksperson?" Not wanting to divulge the extent of her skills, which included being an herbalist of the deadliest kind and a knowledge of drugs and their effects that would rival a specialist, Beth met his gaze. "The problem is, by taking the law into your own hands, you risk prosecution. Have you had many complaints made against you?"

"The miners work in camps, so they're always in gangs." Styles scratched his chin and dropped his gaze. "Do you figure they'd like everyone in town knowing I beat them in a fight? The local townsfolks are grateful I'm here to assist the sheriff."

He sighed and lifted his gaze. "This is the way I roll, Beth. I hope you're not gonna be a problem?"

A problem? Not at all, Beth admired the maverick trait in him. She shook her head. "Me? Now you're making me sound like a spoiled brat." She snorted and, hiding a smile, pressed her fists into her hips. "What I saw was five or six bullies beating down on a pizza delivery guy. You called them out and they attacked you." She raised one eyebrow. "You handled it. End of story."

"That's good to know." Styles smiled at her. "I'll sleep easier knowing you're not here to keep tabs on me."

That goes both ways, I hope. Beth turned away and indicated to the whiteboard to change the subject. "Is that our case?"

"Yeah, well it's out there for everyone. The first two murders are in the cold case files now. The others are live but now we know he's still out there. There was a break of two years and then we found another, same MO, less than a month ago. She died and her best friend is missing. He hasn't stopped killing. This one happened just last week. There's no autopsy report, just a local MD's report. The body is on ice until someone figures who to call." His gaze narrowed. "Seven murders and seven missing girls. He's taking them in twos, killing one and, we assume, taking the other to places unknown."

Beth walked up and down the whiteboard and examined each photograph with care. "These are familiar. There was a psychopathic killer with a similar MO working out of Idaho." She moved from image to image, pointing at a pile of neatly folded clothes set beside each body. "What does this behavior say to you?"

"The guy was a neat freak." Styles looked at her and raised an eyebrow. "Most animals that rape and murder girls are in kind of a hurry."

He was missing a crucial point. Beth blew out a breath in frustration and then poked a finger at the images one by one. "I'm seeing an organized psychopath living out a fantasy. Everything he does is part of the vision in his mind. He's reliving his first kill over and over. It's not unusual. Serial killers often do this. Can't you see the bodies were laid out post-mortem? He wasn't in a hurry. He took his time and enjoyed himself. The clothes folded neatly beside the victims is a signature. It's his calling card." She turned to look at him. "Did they find any evidence at the crime scene relating to any of the other missing girls?"

"As far as I recall, they found one shoe alongside the highway." Styles shrugged. "Apart from that, nothing." He poured coffee into two tall cups and looked at her. "I'd like to know how he does it." His Adam's apple moved up and down as he swallowed. "How he separates the girls and keeps them quiet long enough to murder one of them." He sipped his coffee. "Both girls should be screaming or trying to escape, but no one ever hears a sound."

Allowing the old case to filter through her mind, Beth added cream to her coffee and took a sip. She regarded Styles over the rim. "The Idaho killer had a similar MO. They called him the Pied Piper, like the old story about the kids from a village disappearing never to be seen again. The Idaho killer only took one girl at a time and the murders stopped some time ago. Did the bodies of the girls this new guy abducted ever show?"

"Nope." Styles rubbed the back of his neck. "We never found a trace of them. No bodies. Nothing."

Everything was so familiar. Everything she understood about serial killers told her the Pied Piper had found a new comfort zone. He was out of control and would make a mistake soon enough. The hairs on the back of Beth's neck prickled and she looked away. She'd once seen her reflection when her dark side was out for vengeance, and seeing the brutal fate of so many innocent lives had set off a chain reaction. Fighting to gain control, she stared at the whiteboard. Her throat tightened as she scanned close-up images of the victims. "Do we have the autopsy reports? Anything more on the crime scene?"

"Yeah, we do." Styles pulled a cookie from a jar on the counter. "It's harrowing reading."

Gathering her wits, Beth snorted. "Harrowing is an understatement. What kind of guy does that much damage to a child and then hangs around to fold up their clothes? We need to take down this guy. This isn't someone who can be rehabilitated. This is an animal." She stared at him. "Don't you agree?"

"It just happens that I do. I figure we have as good a chance as anyone to catch him." He gave her a searching look. "From what I hear, you never give up." He sighed. "As much as I'd like ten minutes alone with this animal, when we catch him we'll let the courts decide his fate."

Beth smiled. "That's why we're carrying the badges."

"Yeah, that's right." He stared at the whiteboard and shook his head slowly in dismay. "All we can do is hunt down leads and hope we find a trail that leads to him."

Beth smiled. "Oh, there's always a trail. We'll just have to look harder."

"Talking about animals." He gave Beth a long look. "Do you like dogs?"

Animals? Beth blinked, wondering what animals had to do with the current case. Had she missed something? "I like dogs fine, as long as they don't jump all over me. Why? Is it pertinent to the case?"

"Nope, I guess not." Styles stared at his cowboy boots for a beat before shrugging. "It's just that I usually have Bear with me here in the office. He's a Belgian Malinois and used to being by my side. He's not keen on being left alone all day."

Containing a smile, Beth nodded. Actually, she preferred animals to humans. Animals were predictable. They were placid or batshit crazy, and it only took a few seconds to determine which way they leaned. She understood her empathy for pets was unusual in a psychopath, but she considered it to be one of her more redeemable traits and it deflected any scrutiny. Most behavioral analysts wouldn't consider someone like her capable of loving anything, least of all a pet. "Is he part of the team? What's his background?"

"He is primarily an attack canine, but I've trained him in search and rescue." Styles leaned against the counter as his expression became animated. "He won't jump on you."

Interested Beth smiled. "I knew you were a military cop, but your file doesn't mention being a handler. How did a K-9 end up with you?"

"Bear was injured the same day as his handler was killed in action." Styles gaze narrowed. "I'd worked with his handler many a time and knew Bear well. K-9s often won't work with a different handler, but as Bear knew me, and needed time to recover, I offered to give him a home. We left the service on the same day. Now he works with me. The bureau pays for all his expenses and supplies his FBI coats." He shrugged. "So yeah, that makes him part of the team."

Wanting to meet this remarkable dog, Beth smiled. "Well, go get him."

"I will." Styles headed for the door. "Thanks."

Moving back to stand in front of the gruesome images, Beth nodded slowly as her dark calculating side crept back beneath her skin. This killer was very particular about the age and type of girls he murdered. The bodies were all of very young blonde-haired girls, but the friends were of varying appearances. Her mind went back to cases she'd investigated, and faces of similar girls raced into her mind. A copycat, or had the Pied Piper been a busy boy? She turned and stared out of the window. He was out there somewhere and she would find him. He'd crossed her line of acceptable behavior and, yes, she had standards and killing little girls was at the top of her no-go list. She wanted to go to the window and scream out that she was coming for him but instead lowered her voice to just above a whisper. "When this blonde hunts you down, you rabid kid-killing monster, she's going to make you suffer."

TEN

WEDNESDAY

Styles' phone buzzed and he stared at the caller ID. It was the local sheriff, Cash Ryder. "Morning, Cash. What can I do for you?"

"*Two girls have gone missing from Rainbow—Brooklyn Daniels and Skylar Peters. The locals have been out searching since Monday night. They found a body an hour or so ago and believe it's Brooklyn. I went by, as Rainbow is in my jurisdiction. I took Nate with me. We'll need you here to cast your eye over the crime scene.*" Ryder cleared his throat. "*That case on your whiteboard. This is the same MO. I figure we've got ourselves a serial killer.*"

Scrubbing a hand down his face, Styles stared at Beth. "Okay, find me somewhere close by to set down the chopper and send me the coordinates. We'll be there ASAP." He disconnected and explained the situation to Beth.

"If the body has been there since Monday, why hasn't anyone smelled it? Two little girls couldn't have walked far." Beth pulled her dark blonde hair into a ponytail and secured it with a band from around her wrist. She stood and collected her things. "Didn't they search for them when they went missing—and who is Nate? So many new names, I've lost track."

Styles attached a holster to his thigh, checked the load in his revolver, and grabbed a Kevlar vest from a hook on the wall. "Not a problem. Dr. Nate Mace is our local doctor. He's young and up to date. I've never had a problem with him taking care of the victims, dead or alive." He collected a forensics kit. "Grab some of the food to take with us. We could be gone for hours." He spun the chamber in the revolver and checked the load.

"You carry a .357 Magnum?" Beth looked at him and blinked. "Really?" She tossed food and energy bars into a carrier and added bottled water.

Pulling on gloves and setting his Stetson on his head, he gave her a lazy smile. "I'll have to take the city girl out of you. We're in the Montana Rocky Mountains, and it's home to an endangered species of bear. Grizzlies like it here and this time of year they're hunting for food to stay them over winter. If one of them decides we're his next meal and the usual distractions don't work, we'll need a backup plan." He touched the hilt of his gun. "This will stop one intent on killing us, or the noise will frighten a black bear away, but trust me, it will only make a grizzly mad." He tossed her a Kevlar vest with *FBI* in tall yellow letters front and back. "Put that on. There's a killer out there or maybe two. The Tarot Killer is in Montana. There're two positive cases he was involved in over the last couple of months. This perp is perfect for him, so we'll need to watch our backs."

"I didn't read anything about him killing cops." Beth hoisted the bag over one shoulder. "Have you?"

After whistling Bear to his side, he shrugged. "There's always a first time." He bent and rubbed the dog's ears. "Stay here, boy. We'll be back soon." He glanced at Beth. "He likes to come with me, but he's not been to too many murder scenes. I figure we should leave him behind this time."

"He's your dog." Beth glanced around. "What if he needs to pee?"

Styles bit back a grin. She actually cared about his dog. "He just had a walk. He'll be okay. Worse case, I mop it up. It's not a big deal. He has food and water and a warm place to sleep. He'll be just fine." He headed for the door. "Okay. See you later, Bear."

Taking a new agent as a partner was difficult. Deep in thought as he took the chopper alongside the mountain range toward Rainbow, Styles pondered what it would be like to trust someone to watch his back again. He'd always been a loner. Fresh out of Quantico, he'd found DC restrictive and, used to doing things his way, had gotten him into trouble. After spending six months behind a desk, he volunteered for the most remote posting. Due to his military career, the FBI had no qualms about sending him out alone to a remote mining town in Montana. He enjoyed the solitude and had his own demons to fight. The current case had unearthed memories he'd rather forget, but what had happened so long ago was the reason he'd become an MP.

At eight, he'd walked with his sister to the local park. She'd always wanted to be in charge and he'd been a jerk. He'd run away from her, dashing into the forest and hiding. He'd heard her calling him and hunkered down and ignored her. When he'd come out, she'd vanished. He'd walked home alone and told his mom, but in fear of getting a beating from his pa, he'd lied and told her Ginny had left him alone in the park. He remembered the panic, the neighbors running back and forth, people coming from everywhere all calling her name. They never found her. Someone had taken her but he'd never known the details until he'd joined the FBI. The cops had found evidence of a struggle, hair, and her shoes but nothing else. What had happened caused a domino effect in his life. Soon after, his parents split up and then his father took his own life.

His mother had never told him the truth about his sister's disappearance, even after he'd confessed about lying. No one had been brought to justice for taking his sister and the case had gone cold. He glanced at Beth and wondered if he should tell her. It was obvious since she arrived that Beth had an analytical mind. It had been a long time ago, but whoever had taken, killed, and buried his sister could still be out there. He'd never discussed the case with anyone and one day he'd get to the truth of what really happened, but for now he'd keep it to himself until he'd gotten to know her better.

"You always this quiet?" Beth looked at him and raised her eyebrows. "I feel like an intruder."

Styles laughed. "Sorry, I'm used to being alone. It's usually just me and Bear and he isn't good at holding a conversation. What's on your mind?"

"Apart from the case, absolutely nothing." Beth took a sip of water from a bottle and shrugged. "I know nothing about you apart from what's in your file. If we're going to have each other's backs, we should at least try and be sociable." She grinned. "I'm guessing the people who put us together are having a good laugh at our expense right now."

Nodding, Styles swung the chopper toward the coordinates. In the distance the flashing lights of the sheriff's truck lit up the field like a beacon. "Yeah, but I figure we can keep out of each other's way if necessary. I'm sure, like me, you enjoy time alone to think. We can discuss cases, and as soon as you get to know the area, you can investigate alone, if that's what you want."

"I don't need your permission to do that." Beth narrowed her gaze. "I've found being a woman is an advantage. People are more likely to talk to me. I'm not perceived as a threat... and I don't have the reputation of taking apart the locals."

Styles grinned at her. "Ouch!" He flew over the landing area, a rough patch of soil running alongside the forest left from gold excavation. "When we get some downtime, I'd like to pick your brains about a cold case that's been bugging me for years. Two heads might be able to solve it."

"Sure, I like puzzles." Beth stared around the area. "How far to the crime scene?"

He shook his head. "I don't know. Cash... ah, the sheriff... is here to give us a ride. Grab what you need. We might be gone for a time."

They climbed out of the chopper and Styles handed bags to Beth. He did a mental check of everything they might need. He grabbed a Thermos of coffee and stuffed a few energy bars in his pocket. Going into the forest without supplies could be fatal. He followed Beth to the sheriff's department truck, and Cash Ryder climbed out to greet them with Dr. Nate Mace close behind. "Cash, Nate. Good to see you." He turned to Beth. "This is Special Agent Beth Katz from DC. She'll be working out of my office for a time."

"You picked the short straw, huh?" Cash held out his hand. "Sheriff Cash Ryder and this is Doctor Nate Mace."

"Nice to meet you." She shook their offered hands and looked at Ryder. "What have you got for us?" She pulled open the back seat of the truck and climbed inside.

"Not much." Ryder slid in behind the wheel. "This murder goes way above my pay grade, so I'll follow your lead. Around these parts, it's brawls, stealing, and cheating that get my attention. Nate here does an examination of the deceased and that's the extent of our knowledge. Murder crime scenes, I figure we leave to the experts, but I'm willing to learn."

"That's good to know." Beth leaned back in her seat. "There's no doubt it's murder?"

"Nope. The poor little girl is real messed up." Ryder indicated to Nate. "Nate wasn't sure he should touch anything."

"I'm a GP." Nate shrugged. "I'm not trained in forensics. I checked for life signs, made sure I wore gloves and booties, and we taped off the area."

"I asked a forest warden to stand guard." Ryder sighed. "And we have search parties out looking for the other girl."

Styles flicked Beth a glance and raised one eyebrow. "Who was first on scene? Who found her? Have you detained them and taken statements?"

"Yeah, I followed protocol." Ryder blew out a breath. "It's my first homicide but I knew what to do. I took photographs of the scene and everyone involved. After we secured the area, I called you."

The truck bumped along a fire road and they headed deep into the forest. Styles scanned the area, searching for trails or cabins close by, and found nothing. "How far from her house did they find the girl?"

"Half a mile." Ryder pointed to the right. "There's a track into Wandering Bear Forest not far from the residence but it's closed, with a boom gate across it. No one goes into this part of the forest because of the old mine shafts. The kids all know it's dangerous. It's signposted and the school gives out warnings all the time. It's dark and overgrown. I can't imagine young girls going in there alone. It would be way too frightening and there's nothing to see in there. It's just dense forest, apart from the clearing where we found Brooklyn Daniels."

"Yet they did go in there. The question is why." Beth folded her arms across her chest. "Someone lured them into the forest. You'll need to speak to their friends. It could be a secret. That's how predators work, they take their time to groom the kids before they pounce. This has been going on for a time, and dollars to dimes, this guy is working the area. There'll be others dangling on his hook and he is just waiting to reel them in one by one." She looked at Styles. "I figure we need a forensic team out here. You mentioned our to-go-to contact is Dr. Shane Wolfe, the ME out at Black Rock Falls. I've worked with him before, and his team is what we need here. He handles serial killer crime scenes all the time and is the most qualified."

If this was the same killer the FBI had been tracking across the country, they'd need all the help they could get. Styles looked at her. "Yeah, call him. It would be better to have his involvement from the get-go. If he's in Black Rock Falls, he'll be an hour or so away. He moves around the state, so if he's not available, we might need to call in a team from Helena."

"Either will do, as long as we get a forensic team here." Beth lifted her chin. "I'll make the call and then we'll preserve the crime scene. Don't move anything until he gets here." She looked at Nate's aghast expression. "I know it's going to be hard on the parents, but if possible, can you go with Ryder when he informs them? You're someone they trust and you'll need to explain the situation in your best bedside manner."

"They'll want to come on down." Nate examined her face. "You know that, right?"

As a doctor, Nate should be familiar with dealing with people in shock after hearing bad news. Styles nodded his approval. "Yeah, go with him but be on your guard. We have more than wildlife in the forest to worry about right now."

ELEVEN

Wheatgrass moved with a sigh as they trekked toward the forest. Seeds from the long flowing tops swirled around in the air along with particles of dust whipped up by the chopper blades. Beth followed the men, who chatted about everything other than the crime scene. She slowed her pace, searching along each side of the narrow trail running deep into the forest. She touched Ryder's back to get his attention. "Are there any trails leading from the crime scene to a secluded road? If he's taken the other girl, he must have left transport close by. Has anyone checked out the trail he might have used?"

"Yeah, I walked the trail and kept everyone away from the immediate area. It is not a direct route from the main road to where the body was discovered." Ryder pushed up his hat and slowed his pace. "There are other trails but most of them lead to old mine shafts. The area is riddled with them, and the locals keep well away. It must have been something special to lure the girls into the clearing. The only way they could have walked is dark and overgrown with weeds."

Beth nodded. "Which way did the search party come from town?"

"They came in from the west and searched the tracks that lead from the fire road." Ryder rubbed a thumb over the end of his nose. "I found a shoe, same as in the last murder." He shrugged. "I have the same evidence on my whiteboard as you do. This is how I know this is the same person who murdered Scarlett Chester and abducted Aisha Santiago out in Deep Springs. What we need is a medical examiner to give us more detail about the murders. It's gruesome but there's not blood all over like you'd expect."

Allowing information on the cases to drift through her mind, Beth scanned the area as they approached the clearing. "I'm glad that you were able to keep the scene uncontaminated. Who was first on scene and did you get every detail of what they did when they arrived here?"

"Yeah, it happened to be two of the forest wardens, so we were very lucky." Ryder dodged a low branch and held it back for her. "They have been trained in the correct procedure for discovering a body or any type of crime scene in Wandering Bear Forest. It's much the same as if they find a poacher. They take photographs and preserve the scene. We have one of them here now and the other one is just on a break. They've been taking turns along with other volunteers to prevent sightseers."

The smell hit Beth way before they reached the clearing. The rancid stench robbing the clean forest air of its unique freshness. Ahead Ryder called out to warn the forest warden they were on the trail. When they arrived on scene, Beth noticed how pale the poor man appeared as he stood solemn-faced with his back to the body. She'd walked the narrow trail beside the doctor, who insisted she call him Nate. He kept the subject away from the murder and Beth wondered if it was for his own peace of mind after seeing a horrific murder scene.

She took in the man beside her. Strong, dependable, and kind was written all over him. He was like all the mountain men she'd met, tall and muscular, but was clean-shaven and had a decent sense of humor. She stared at him and swallowed hard, suddenly tongue-tied. Her life had never been normal, and she'd never found anyone remotely desirable. She ran both hands down her face. Was the feeling as if she'd just been dropped down an elevator shaft attraction?

"Are you sick?" Nate's hand closed around her arm. "Perhaps you should sit down. There's a fallen log a few yards away."

His hand seemed to burn through her clothes and, confused, she quickly stepped away. "Sorry. I'm fine, just deep in thought." She avoided his gaze and turned to Ryder. The sheriff wasn't such a threat to her sanity. "Ryder, Nate is right. You'll need to keep everyone away. We don't want sightseers trampling evidence, and if the parents see her like that, they'll remember her like that for the rest of their lives. Close the trail both ways with tape. Make it clear no one is to pass."

"Copy that." Ryder gave her a mock salute.

"You figure this will happen again?" Nate's face drained of color as he looked at Beth. "Here in Rainbow?"

Mind reeling over her unusual response to Nate, Beth tried to avoid staring at him. *Why him? What makes him different from everyone else?* "It depends how wide his comfort zone is right now." She pulled out a notebook and made a few senseless notes. "If this is the Pied Piper, he could be living right next door or working right beside you and you'd never know."

Stopping at the edge of the clearing to take in the entire scene, Beth swept her gaze from one side to the other checking the perimeter of the forest for any disturbance. She noted the four separate pathways. Most all of them were simple animal trails. The body of the girl appeared so very small, laid out under one of the surrounding trees. She turned to Ryder. "Has anyone disturbed this area at all?"

"Not that I'm aware." Ryder tipped back his Stetson and let out a long sigh. "It doesn't feel right, leaving that young girl exposed. She should be covered. Seeing the ants crawling all over her makes me sick to my stomach."

Seeing his face drain of color, Beth pulled her face into an expression of concern. "I'm afraid we must leave her in situ until the medical examiner arrives. He will bring a team with him with the latest forensic equipment. If we are planning to catch this guy, we need all the help we can get, and trust me, Wolfe is the best. I'll call him." She pulled out her phone as Ryder's buzzed.

"No need to call him. Dr. Shane Wolfe is in the air." Ryder closed his phone and moved to her side. "Due to the similarity of the Deep Springs case, and the spate of murdered and missing girls, he was notified by the Snakeskin Gully FBI field office. He requested coordinates. He wants to take a look at the body and the scene."

Incredulous, Beth stared at Styles. "Isn't this our patch?"

"It's a big state. We can work together if needs be." He smiled at her. "It's called cooperation. A little goes a long way."

Agitated, Beth pushed both hands through her hair and turned to look at Styles. "I've worked on serial killer cases. In fact, you could say it was my specialty. What I don't like is having people looking over my shoulder all the time. I know about the team in Snakeskin Gully. They have an incredible reputation, especially since they've been working in Black Rock Falls, but I don't think we should call for assistance until we have analyzed the crime scene ourselves. As nobody has discovered zip about this murderer, I can't see a reason for calling them in on this case."

"Jo Wells is one of the top behavioral analysts in the country or maybe even the world." Styles pushed his hands in his back pockets and stared at her. "Surely, if she is available, you would welcome her input?"

That's all I need. I can just imagine having a meaningful conversation with the psychopath whisperer. Beth blew out a long sigh. "First up, we analyze the scene ourselves." She scanned the clearing. "The body was moved. From the way the grass is lying flat in the center of the clearing, and from the shape, I would say a blanket was spread out there. That area needs to be preserved for the forensic team. The killer could have left trace evidence all over that patch." She walked slowly toward the body and stared down at the forlorn figure. "See the pressure marks on the side of her cheeks? There's your reason for not hearing the girls' screaming. That is a large handprint, and by those lines, he was wearing leather gloves. That is a typical mark a glove makes on the skin using extreme pressure."

"Do you figure he removed her clothes after or during the attack?" Styles crouched down to examine the body. "I've seen rape victims before and there are usually burn marks on the skin from where the clothes were ripped from the body. I don't see that here."

Knowing how predators groomed children, Beth shook her head. "It may be hard for you to comprehend the way a psychopath's mind works, but I figure somehow he convinced her to remove her clothes herself." She shrugged. "What people don't understand is that these people can appear to be special. They have a charisma that can lure people to their deaths."

"I have read a bit about them myself." Styles rubbed his chin and stared at the girl as if trying to see her in a different light. "So, you're saying that these kids don't see this man as a threat—they see him as a friend?"

It was almost like watching the cogs fall into place and the wheels in Styles' brain start to turn. "So, we should be looking for someone who works with children? A teacher, a preacher, the guy in the ice cream van, people like that? The kids know them but maybe their parents don't?"

Surprised by his fast acceptance of her theory, Beth nodded. "Yeah, that's exactly who I mean."

Keeping her distance from the corpse, she walked around

examining what she could see without touching or contaminating the scene. "There's no blood. Not here or on the flattened grass. The injuries to the body were inflicted postmortem."

"Why is she posed like that?" Ryder stared at her with a tragic expression. "We should cover her." He cleared his throat. "Why does someone do this to a kid?"

Having lived her life juggling both sides of the coin, Beth understood the thought process that led to the murders. The one thing that eluded her was what he'd done with the second victim. She turned to Ryder, surprised a sheriff would find the crime scene so distressing. She stepped a little to one side to block his view of the victim. "The killer needs to make excuses for what he's done. It's never their fault; it's always the victim's fault. A psychopath never believes he is to blame. I would say the flowers in her hair were placed there before the attack." She sighed. "He probably took photographs of her to show her innocence and then posed her after the attack as his excuse. In his twisted mind, he believes that she lured him to do this, so he posed her like that to show everyone what she's really like."

"So why does he keep on killing?" Nate Mace came to her side. "Hasn't he proved his point?"

Trying to drive her dark side back into the recesses of her mind, Beth stared at the ground. This monster needed to be taken down and fast. He'd left clues, subtle but enough, and she'd hunt him down, but it would take time, especially as her team seemed to be growing by the minute. "He keeps killing because he can. No one has caught him and his list of kills is undetermined. He believes he is invincible and has convinced himself that every little girl who befriends him is a temptress. This is his proof." She waved a hand toward the body. "He figures, he's right about them because they all come to him, don't they? They must all follow his instructions. He's not abducting them from the streets. He's luring them with a promise or a treat."

"They go like lambs to the slaughter." Styles rubbed the back of his neck, his eyes fixed on the corpse. "We gotta stop this guy."

TWELVE

When Sheriff Ryder went to meet the medical examiner, Styles left the doctor and the forest warden to guard the body. He turned to Beth. "We need to search the trails. I want to know where he parked his ride."

"What direction is the fire road?" Beth stared into the forest. "That would be the most logical place."

Styles led the way along the narrow trail leading to the fire road that ran parallel to the crime scene. It was difficult to determine if the crushed vegetation and the layer of disturbed pine needles had been caused by man or beast. They took their time, moving slowly and scanning left and right, but found nothing apart from another small clearing fifty yards or so from the crime scene. The second small clearing had an abundance of wildflowers, and the variety matched the garland found on the victim's head. Styles stopped walking and turned in a slow circle. "I figure this is where he picked the flowers." He indicated to a slight indentation on the edge of the clearing. "What do you make of the flattened grass here?"

"It's small. Perhaps an animal slept here overnight?" Beth stared at the ground for a minute and then dropped to her knees. "Take a look at this." She handed him a pair of examination gloves. "You'll need these."

Pulling on the gloves, Styles crouched and peered into the grass. A line of ants, carrying what appeared to be cookie crumbs above the heads, marched in a procession into the undergrowth. With care he brushed the grass back and forth. On the level of the soil, he discovered a few cookie crumbs and gathered them up with care before dropping them into a small evidence bag. "Now we know what he did with the other kid. Somehow, he convinced her to come with him to this clearing. He gave her some cookies as a treat and no doubt told her to wait for him. What happened next is anyone's guess."

"Let me think on it." Beth paced up and down the small clearing, hands on hips and staring into the distance.

In the short time that Styles had known Beth, she'd impressed him with her analytical mind. From the first moment she set eyes on the whiteboard in the office, he could almost see the wheels turning in her head. He'd always considered himself to be a good detective and he had solved his share of cases, but she seemed to come to the table from different angles. As she'd specialized in cybercrime, he found her insight interesting and a surprise. Her undercover experience, which meant she could turn her hand to just about anything, was another bonus. During his time in law enforcement he'd spoken to many behavioral analysts, and they all had their own ideas of how a psychopath thought, but Beth's untrained conclusions were perceptive. Perhaps her time delving into the dark web and seeing the dregs of society in the raw had given her an edge a behavioral analyst could only wish for. He took in her almost blank expression and sighed. As she obviously needed time to think, he moved around the clearing looking for other small trails that headed in the direction of the fire road. After following a few narrow animal tracks, he turned back.

"Did you find anything?" A flash of annoyance moved

across Beth's face. "I believe those tracks are way too narrow for him to lead a child through, and if he carried her, you would notice damage to the vegetation and maybe some strands of hair caught on the pine trees. There's none evident."

One thing's for darn sure, Beth Katz didn't hold back on her opinion. If he didn't know better, he'd assume she didn't have a filter, but Quantico trained agents in people skills. He wondered if her experience in Helena had caused her unsocial attitude problem. "This isn't my first case, Beth, and you're not speaking to a rookie." He straightened and stared at her. "I was doing my job by checking any possible trails the killer could have taken. We both know that psychopaths figure they can outsmart us, so why would he take the most obvious route out of the forest?"

"If you want my opinion, he went that way." Beth indicated toward a narrow pathway on her right. "He has a little girl, who thinks he is all that, so he needs to keep her happy to get her out of the forest and into his vehicle without making a noise. That trail follows a path of wildflowers. It's nonthreatening unlike the others that go into darkness. That one in particular has less of a canopy than the others and rays of sunlight stream through in long beams. It's almost magical."

Surprised she hadn't bitten back at his comment, he nodded. "Okay, that makes sense. Have you come up with any ideas about why he's killing one and taking one?"

"Only the obvious." Beth gave him a long considering look. "You have to remember that people like him would probably regard the two kids differently. He's chosen one to murder. The types of girls on your whiteboard are similar in appearance. The ones we don't find are all different. What does that say to you?"

Styles held up both hands. "You lost me back at the one he chooses to murder. Why do you think they are always blonde?" He rubbed the scar on his chin, annoyed at the way it tingled when he became agitated. "Why has he suddenly changed his

MO to two girls and why is he only murdering one of them?
What is he doing with the other one and why can't we find a
body?"

"That's what I've been thinking about while you've been
wasting time." Beth's lips curled up at the corners in an almost
mocking smile. "The blonde represents the trigger that started
the killing in the first instance. Why he is taking two kids now
has me stumped. I can only give you an example of what I think
it might be." She met his gaze. "In simple terms, people are like
objects to psychopathic killers. They are only useful to them
while they are serving a purpose. He has been grooming these
kids for a time, so they will come to him when he asks them.
The reason he kills the blonde one we've already discussed. She
is the excuse to behave the way he does." She blew out a long
breath and eyed him with apprehension in her gaze. "Have you
ever gone into a bakery and purchased something you want to
eat now and something you want to save for later?"

Absorbing all the information as fast as his brain would
allow him, Styles pushed his hands deep into the front pockets
of his jeans. "Yeah, hasn't everyone?"

"Okay, so now you understand." Beth slowly removed her
gloves and rolled them into a ball before pushing them into her
pocket. "So, you enjoy the first cake, dump the wrapping in the
garbage, and never think about it again."

Styles swallowed the rising bile. "Sure, but what about the
second cake?"

"The first one would be your favorite, because everyone eats
their favorite cake first, right?" Beth's eyes bored into him. "The
second might just be used to satisfy a lingering hunger... or what
else would make you purchase a second cake?"

Not wanting to consider another option, Styles looked
away. The implications of his next words could change the
entire outcome of the investigation. Incredulous be stared back

at her. "You don't think he's taking her to share her with a friend, do you?"

"You asked for my opinion, and that's my thoughts." Beth stared toward the last track leading from the clearing. "None of the second girls who are missing have ever been found. There could be a number of reasons why this has happened. For instance, he's killed and buried them, or they're being kept as sex slaves but not by the killer. He's too smart to keep them around, so he likely passes them on to a pedophile ring."

Shaking his head, Styles straightened and looked at her. "He can't have killed them. We've never found the bodies of the missing second girl. Why could you even consider he's murdering both of them?"

"You know as well as I do that there are many different ways to dispose of a body." Beth removed the tie from her hair and refastened it. "The second girl is never blonde and so she doesn't offer an excuse for his behavior. He has no reason to exhibit her. For all we know, he could have them all buried in the crawl space under his house." She stared at the pathway. "I bet you dinner we'll find a shoe along this trail. It's his way of telling us he's taken the other girl with him. It's him leaving us a little clue. It's all part of the 'catch me if you can' game."

THIRTEEN

Beth led the way through the forest, although it was difficult to examine the ground due to the beams of sunlight casting zebra stripes along the trail. The forest had a damp smell to it of leaf mold intermingled with the fragrance of wildflowers. Even with the shafts of sunlight brushing her face as she walked, the cold breeze from the mountains was ever present. Through the trees, she caught glimpses of the snowcapped mountain ranges. If it hadn't been for the breeze, she would never have noticed the pink ribbon caught on the branch of a pine tree. She dragged an evidence bag from her pocket and used it to snag the ribbon. Holding the ribbon up in triumph as Styles walked toward her, she smiled at him. "I told you they came this way."

"Good find. For a computer geek, you sure know a ton about psychopathic behavior." Styles examined the ribbon. "That sure fits the description we have of the missing girl." He barked a laugh. "Now if we find a shoe, I'm gonna think your psychic."

As the trail opened up into the fire road, Beth hadn't taken two steps when she spotted the shoe. "There it is. He's not only left it behind for us to find but he's placed it on this tree stump so we can't miss it." She stared into the distance picturing a truck driving away. *Game on.*

"Well, I'll be. I'll take a couple of shots of the shoe and then we can bag it." Styles pulled out his phone. "I can't see any footprints or even a sign that there's been a vehicle in this area. Why don't you check over there, along the edge of the road? The soil on that side looks a little softer."

Beth searched up and down walking some ways up the track toward the highway but found no signs of a vehicle. She headed back to see Styles coming back from the opposite direction. "There's nothing at this end of the road. Did you have any luck?"

"Nope." He stared into the sky and then back at her. "I hear a chopper. We'd better be heading back. I checked out the ME when he was first recommended to me. Did you know he flew a medevac chopper in Afghanistan? Instead of resuming his practice as a GP, when he left the service he studied forensic science, obtained all the qualifications necessary to become a medical examiner. All the while caring for his wife and three young children."

Beth looked at him. "Yeah, I heard something about his wife dying of cancer. The people I worked with in Helena mentioned he wanted to get away from the memories in Texas and moved to Black Rock Falls. He has certainly made his name there. Now he is in high demand all over."

"Yeah, apparently the Helena office isn't too happy with him for headhunting Dr. Norrell Larson, their top forensic anthropologist, for his team. He converted an entire wing of his building for her to use."

Following him back along the path, Beth continually scanned the forest for more clues. "Yeah, well I guess he wants the best team around him he can get. She is one of the best. It seems to me the sheriff of Black Rock Falls is lucky to have his team and the Snakeskin Gully field office as backup."

"I'd never have expected to be working a serial killer case from Rattlesnake Creek. This case in particular is mind-blowing. I mean, who the heck is this guy? No clues, zip, and now he brings his nasty games right to our doorstep." Styles walked backward looking at her and cocked one eyebrow. "I always say a ray of sunshine appears when you least expect it. I've gained a partner, who seems to know her way around a murder scene, and now we have access to Wolfe's team."

Amused, Beth snorted. "Trust me, I'm no ray of sunshine."

"It's just as well." Styles turned back and his shoulders hunched a little, but he kept walking. "You figured it was tough in the big city. Trust me, that was a cakewalk to what you'll encounter here."

The smell of death increased as they headed closer to the crime scene. As they entered the clearing, Beth's attention moved over the three people surrounding the body. She recognized Wolfe by his white-blond hair. The small young woman beside him was a mirror image in hair color and had the same slate-gray eyes. This had to be his daughter and medical examiner in training, Emily Wolfe. She'd met his assistant, Colt Webber, a badge-holding deputy from Black Rock Falls, at the last murder scene she attended in Helena, prior to her coming to Rattlesnake Creek. She walked over to him and introduced him to Styles. "My second kid murder in a row. I'm surprised we were called to deal with this case. Usually, they use the Child Abduction Rapid Deployment Team."

"The sheriff didn't suspect an abduction." Wolfe glanced over at Ryder and then back at her. "He mentioned things like that didn't happen here. I guess mainly because few women live in a mining town out in the mountains. So, there's not many kids."

"Maybe a few years back but not so much now." Styles pulled a piece of wheatgrass from the pathway and chewed on the long stalk. "The mine owners have made Rattlesnake Creek their home and have families. The people who run the stores and saloons all have kids. Well, most do."

"Okay, what have you got for me?" Wolfe stared at the evidence bags in Beth's hand.

Holding them up for inspection, Beth indicated to the trail behind them. "We found a pink ribbon along the trail and a shoe we figure belongs to the other missing girl, Skylar Peters. They match the list of clothing the sheriff obtained from the parents. We assume from the hair color that the deceased victim is Brooklyn Daniels."

"I always find it a problem to assume anything in a murder case. This young lady will be referred to as Jane Doe until I get a positive ID from the parents." Wolfe's gaze narrowed over the top of his face mask. "If this is Brooklyn Daniels and she was last seen on Monday afternoon, then I would say from the state of the body, insect infestation, the livor mortis, and the fact that rigor has come and gone, she likely was murdered a short time after she left home." He shook his head. "I'll need to take a closer look once I get her back to Rattlesnake Creek. The ER there has offered me their facilities to conduct an autopsy. I'll be taking any trace evidence I find back to Black Rock Falls for analysis." He turned to look at Sheriff Ryder. "I'll call you once I'm done and you can make arrangements for the parents to view the body for ID."

"What else can you tell us?" Styles removed his Stetson and ran a hand through his hair before pushing the hat back on his head. "Do you figure the damage to the corpse is by animals or mutilation?"

"I'll need to check saliva and other factors, including trace evidence left by either animals or her killer." Wolfe gave instructions to his team to remove the body and then turned back to Styles. "From my preliminary examination, the burst blood vessels in the eyes and the marks on the face would indicate suffocation. The bruising on the thighs and vaginal area would indicate a sexual assault. From what I can ascertain, all the other injuries occurred post-mortem." He waved a hand to encompass everyone in the clearing. "I want the names, hair samples, and fingerprints from everyone who came close to the body for elimination purposes. Emily will start with the forest warden as he was the first on scene."

Beth held up the evidence bags. "Do you want these as well? Or do you want us to log them into evidence?"

"I'll take them." Wolfe held out a hand. "He might have been careful with this one." He indicated with his chin toward the body bag on the gurney. "Sometimes, with a second victim they make mistakes." He gave Beth a long look. "How come you're working in these parts now?"

Beth shrugged. "I'm here so that Styles can assess my capability in the field." She shook her head. "Apparently, the psych test they gave me showed that I didn't show enough care for the victim—the child, not the rapist." She lifted her chin and stared at him, hoping her dark side wasn't showing through. "The truth is I was concerned for the child and she was my first consideration. I kept her calm and removed the hood covering her face. I told her to look at a patch of wildflowers and not look behind her. I figured seeing a guy bleeding to death all over her would be more traumatic. The monster trying to rape her had his throat cut, and to be perfectly honest, I didn't consider him to be a victim, so when the psychiatrist asked me if I was concerned that he'd died in front of me, I told her the truth."

"Which was?" Wolfe raised one eyebrow.

Trying to stop her lips quivering into a smile, she shrugged. "I told her I hoped he'd rot in hell."

FOURTEEN

Styles stared at Beth in disbelief. He'd been trying to make people believe she was an asset. If a report that she was unstable went in from someone like Dr. Shane Wolfe, she'd be fired. He opened his mouth to jump to her defense when Wolfe gave a hearty laugh. He cleared his throat. "I'm sure she doesn't mean that. You don't do you, Beth?"

"I can see why a comment like that would ruffle a few feathers." Wolfe smiled at her. "Trust me, many victims of unspeakable crimes come across my table. I look at mutilated bodies and wonder what kind of animal can do that to another human being. This is why I work in this field of medicine." He indicated to the body bag. "A young girl is dead and most people would say she has no way of telling us what happened, but she does. Once I've examined her, I'll be able to place a timeline of what occurred, starting from her last meal, what it was and how long before she died she consumed it." He removed his mask and smiled at Beth. "Like me, we're all like Lady Justice. We must look at both sides and not favor either. If you stick to the evidence, the victims will get justice."

"Maybe in a perfect world." Beth's mouth turned down at

the corners. "You've worked on many serial killer crimes. Just how many do they murder before they're caught?" She gave an exasperated sigh. "How many escape and kill again? This young girl should never have been killed if people were doing their jobs. He's been on a killing spree." She stared at Wolfe. "You want honesty? The only thing that stopped me shooting him was the chance of killing the girl. I would have killed him without hesitation. Using my weapon to club him over the head would have been my next move if I hadn't seen the blood."

Horrified, Styles touched her arm. "I'm sure Dr. Wolfe doesn't need to hear all this stuff, Beth."

"It's okay." Wolfe squeezed Beth's shoulder. "You felt responsible for the girl by not getting there in time to stop him assaulting her, but you did save her. Trying to protect her by the only means possible is perfectly normal. You couldn't have lifted a man that size to free her. You had no choice. The fact you actually tried to save the rapist's life was commendable and I told Mac the same thing. He asked me for my professional opinion and my personal thoughts don't apply. I can only give him the facts. My team went all over the crime scene and searched for a murder weapon and found nothing more than a few drops of blood heading toward the road. This evidence and the tarot card points to him taking revenge on an unstoppable child killer. You arrived shortly after and found the carnage. The psych test is normal procedure. Don't concern yourself about it. The work you're doing here is solid and I figure Styles needs a partner." He looked at Styles. "I heard about the gang bullying the pizza guy. I figure y'all need to calm down some and try and work together if you're planning on catching the Pied Piper."

Ears heating from the reprimand, Styles nodded. "So, you figure it's the same killer?"

"Unofficially, yeah, I do." Wolfe indicated to the pile of neatly folded clothes. "This fact isn't something that's been released to the media, neither is the shoe. It can't be a copycat. Y'all need to be hunting down suspects who move around. He establishes comfort zones—places where he can travel to kill and then return to base. He must work close by the towns where he kills. That alone is enough to pin him down. You get at it and I'll do my job and find you the evidence you need for a conviction."

Styles nodded. "Yeah, I understand the concept, and Beth has tracked pedophiles and sex offenders on the dark web. She understands how a psychopath's mind works."

"You've studied psychopaths?" Wolfe raised one eyebrow.

"Yeah, I've read everything Dr. Jo Wells, the behavioral analyst, has written." Beth shrugged. "Her prison interviews are very enlightening. Now I know she's here in Montana and working out of the Snakeskin Gully field office, I can call her if we need advice."

"That's good." Wolfe smiled. "We're done here. I don't need to revisit the scene. I'll be in touch with the report ASAP."

Removing his gloves and rolling them into a ball, Styles walked over to Ryder and Nate. "The ME has released the crime scene. We'll have to assume its Brooklyn Daniels, so when you find her next of kin, explain they'll need to identify the body. Send me their details and inform them that Wolfe will contact them when the body is ready to be identified. Maybe mention their daughter is in the Rattlesnake Creek Hospital morgue."

"Copy that." Ryder pushed his hat firmly on his head. "You both heading back now?"

"Yeah." Beth removed her mask. "We need all the time we can get to hunt down this killer and find Skylar Peters before he murders her as well."

"No one has found a trace of her." Ryder stared blankly into the forest. "They never find the second girl, do they? I wonder what he does with them?"

"It's past the forty-eight-hours comfort zone." Nate stared at

Beth. "You know more about these maniacs than I do. Don't most of them kill them within the first few hours after the abduction?"

"Unfortunately, no." Beth's eyes flashed with anger. "Sometimes when these monsters abduct a kid, they keep them for years or pass them around. So many go missing and are never found."

Shaking his head, Styles stared at Nate. "We found a shoe that the search party missed and a ribbon. Seems to me no one has the resources in these small towns to find a missing dog let alone a kid." He looked at Beth. "Let's go. I'm not giving up on finding her alive just yet."

It was late in the afternoon when they arrived back at Rattlesnake Creek and after dropping by the office to check on Bear, it didn't take too much convincing for Styles to persuade Beth to join him for supper at Tommy Joe's Bar and Grill. They hadn't eaten anything since breakfast and the coffee in the Thermos was only just warm by the time they got back to the chopper. He sure needed a strong cup of coffee. They took a booth toward the back of the room and Styles moved the salt cellar around the table trying to wrap his mind around the case. "It seems obvious to me that this Pied Piper guy has a place close by where he's keeping the second kid. Even in this weather, a body soon stinks. If he was in town, someone would have reported him by now. This makes me believe he has a cabin somewhere in the forest or alongside the creek."

"Yeah, it would be isolated, but with a decent road in and out for fast access." Beth refilled her coffee cup from a pot on the table and added the fixings, stirring slowly. "If Wolfe is correct and he is moving from one place to another for work, we're probably looking at a miner. When we get back to the office, I'll plot all the other murders on a map and we can see at a glance if they all occur within the vicinity of mining towns."

Sipping his coffee, Styles nodded. "Which also means that this is his first in this area, and looking at his previous episodes, we can expect another murder soon. The problem is we are surrounded by mining towns and we don't have resources to watch every kid in the neighborhood."

"Maybe not, but we do have access to the media and we can use them to our advantage." Beth leaned back in her seat as TJ arrived with the food. She looked up and smiled at him. "Thanks, the steak here is spectacular."

"Yeah, I think the food is pretty good too." TJ grinned. "I convinced our chef, Wez Michaels, to move here when I was taking a vacation in Texas. There is one thing a Texan knows about and that's steak. He cooks a mean barbecue too. His ribs are about the best around these parts. You should try them sometime. The fish is always good. Everything comes fresh from the creek daily."

"I'll look forward to it." Beth looked at her plate and sighed. "My compliments to Wez Michaels." She picked up the silverware and sliced into the steak. "Mmm, I've been looking forward to this."

Downing his coffee to wash the smell and taste of death from his head, Styles found her reactions to walking from a gruesome and heart-twisting crime scene unusual, but then he'd known people to put on a brave face in front of colleagues and fall apart later. Yet her enthusiasm for food surprised him. He'd lost his appetite the moment he'd walked into the clearing.

FIFTEEN

THURSDAY

When he'd arrived in the Montana Rockies, the Warlock believed he'd have trouble finding the right girls. The small towns didn't have the large family communities he'd seen throughout the West. This made it difficult for him to find the places young kids played after school, on weekends, or during their vacations. It also meant working around his job to be there at the right time. He'd been lucky in Rainbow. The small mining town was owned by a company that preferred to employ married men with families, and housing went with the job. It was an expanding community, with a high school and a number of churches. The college in Rattlesnake Creek covered the needs of the older children, with a school bus service supplied between towns. He'd discovered during his time in Rainbow that most of the children preferred to play in small areas of the forest and along the narrow riverbed running through a woodland area. Like Rattlesnake Creek, Rainbow had a number of rivers fed from mountain ranges, so it wasn't unusual for visitors to be seen hiking or fishing in the area.

He exploited this fact to the max, using his disguise as a fisherman to follow kids through the forest. It was very rare to see a young girl alone in the forest as the area was deemed unsafe by parents, but they often allowed them to go in two or threes to play in the nearby parks on the edge. If he found a girl he wanted, he would make himself visible to her in short bursts. Wearing long flowing purple robes adorned with yellow stars and the pointed warlock's hat usually caught their interest. Kids were so gullible, even in this time of the internet and TV news stories about kids being kidnapped and murdered. They all looked at him as if he was something special. Swearing them to secrecy was easy, and if one of them ran screaming to their mommy, he'd pack up his things and be on his way before anyone discovered who he was and where he'd come from. In truth, he didn't come from anywhere. He moved about so often there was no such thing as home base. He figured the last place he'd lived was the place he called home—if anybody asked him.

He'd become an expert in abducting children and had three sets of young girls vying for his attention, but then he excelled at everything he put his mind too. Excited, he moved along a small path in the forest that led to a clearing. The sound of young voices drifted on the breeze as two girls, maybe seven or eight years old, sat around a stump of wood, playing with their dolls. The dolls were both fairies, which made life for him much easier. He loved the country kids. They still played with dolls and had a special innocence about them. The city ones were contaminated by progress and were street smart by six. He went back down the narrow trail, inhaling the scent of the forest. Winter would be here soon, and kids didn't play in the forest when it was snowing. He rested his backpack on a tree stump and pulled out his costume. A long white wig and Santa Claus beard covered his face. He pulled on the costume and shoved on the hat. He filled his pockets with candy and, holding a leather-bound faux ancient book of spells in one hand, walked slowly toward the girls, chanting softly under his breath.

Their first reaction was usually a startled stare, and his reaction mirrored their own. He'd turn, looking behind him and then both ways as if confused. Most times the girls would laugh, as if finding their reaction to seeing him funny. He would close his book and tuck it under one arm, and then give them a low bow. "It seems that you have me at a disadvantage, my ladies. Did you summon me here?"

There were usually more giggles, and then they would speak to each other in hushed tones. He would ask them their names and what they desired. Most times they asked for candy, which he had in his pockets. He would spend a short time with them, asking them about their day and how many times they came into the forest and had they met any fairies before. After extracting all the information he required, he'd tell them that the fairy queen was waiting for him just over yonder. He swore them to secrecy, saying he was in fear of being banished from the magical world forever if one word got out of them seeing him. As a reward for their loyalty, he promised to visit again when they called, and then he'd walk away, searching for a place to hide the second girl. Nothing ever happened the first time they met.

He'd usually head back to work, consumed by the fantasy of meeting the girls again. He couldn't wait but prided himself for being in control, it was one of his assets. Often, he would go back and meet the girls two or three times to gain their trust. They were all the same, the blonde would sit on his lap if he gave her everything in his pocket. Most times the other girl would stand back but not always. As time went by the fantasy became unbearable and he'd meet the girls for the last time. He hoisted the backpack onto his shoulders, picked up his fishing rod, and slipped into the trees. His stomach flip-flopped with excitement as he heard girlish giggles coming from their secret meeting place. The last time was now.

SIXTEEN

After spending the entire morning searching through databases and eating egg salad sandwiches at her desk for lunch, Beth had spent most of the afternoon hunting down local sex offenders in the area and men working in the mines who had been recently released from jail. She ran both hands through her hair in frustration. It seemed that the mines were a perfect place for parolees. A vast number of local miners were people from all over, with many of them recently released from jail for a variety of offenses. Maybe they were prepared to work in the rugged conditions. It couldn't be worse than jail. Although after scanning the employment pages online, she saw that qualified people were in high demand. She stood and went to the whiteboard to add the most probable suspects and then turned to Styles. "I have a list of potential suspects. After going through the databases to discover anyone who had recently been released from jail and the usual suspects, including stalkers, pedophiles, and other sex offenders, I've narrowed it down to these four guys. Roderick Soto, Howell Marshman, Christopher Wheatly, and Francis Baldwin. Two of them work at a gold-mining outfit at the bottom of Longhorn Peak. The other two are out at a place called Lost Gem Valley, and wouldn't you know, they're mining for gemstones."

"I've been hunting down other types of employment, where people move around our local area." Styles rubbed the scar on his chin and looked up at her with a weary expression. "Lawrence Dawson is a courier driver who moves between three of the towns in our area. He doesn't have any priors, but he seems to work his own hours. When someone needs a courier or something delivered urgently, like fresh food or documents, they call him. He arrived in town three months ago and apparently does this for a living all over. I guess he just likes to move around and is someone we should interview."

Beth put her hands on her hips and stared at him. "Is that all you've come up with? One guy?"

"Nope, I have another two potential suspects." Styles grinned at her. "My, you are feisty today and what have you done with my dog? He's had his head on your lap the best part of the day. You planning on stealing him away from me or something?" He cleared his throat at her glare. "Not many people move around constantly between the towns. If people want anything from the outside, they usually use the railroad and go pick it up themselves. We don't have that many freight drivers coming up the mountain, so I couldn't include the few who actually made it here and back without either breaking down or driving over the side of the mountain."

Exasperated, Beth shook her head. "So, what's the names of the potential suspects you've come up with who actually move around the towns?"

"Ainsley Rice and Emerson Green." Styles leaned back in his chair, making it creak alarmingly, and placed his snakeskin boots on the desk and crossed them at the ankles. "I don't have any reason to place them on our potential suspects list, other than they arrived in town recently and they move around all over the state. They both live in Rattlesnake Creek and currently work at the hospital as male travel nurses." He held up one finger. "But they can be called out to any of the towns if asked at any time or during an emergency by the local doctors. So, they both move around inconspicuously and in plain sight, just the same as the other guy I mentioned."

Rubbing her temples, Beth wrote the names on the whiteboard and stood back and looked at them. "Okay, who do we go and see first?"

"It's brewing up a storm out there." Styles indicated to the window with his thumb. "I've been watching it rolling in over the mountains for the last half an hour. I'm not taking the chopper up in an electrical storm, and it will take us time to hunt down a suitable place to land close to the mines. That's if there is a safe place to land. I'm thinking we'll probably have to drive there." He dropped his boots, picked up his hat from the desk, and stood. "It looks like we go see the nurses."

Beth gathered her things. "Okay, and by the way, I've no intention of stealing Bear's affection from you. He likes me, is all, and when you're not looking I bribe him with doggy treats." She grinned at him.

The telephone on Styles' desk rang. He rolled his eyes at her and reached for it. Beth waited as he listened to a one-sided conversation from Wolfe. She expected him to put the phone on speaker, but he ignored her frantic waves.

"Yeah, thanks for letting us know." Styles glanced at her and then looked away. "The morning will be fine. We're heading out to interview a few potential suspects. No, we haven't found anything positive yet. Okay, bye."

Beth leaned on the desk and stared at him waiting for him to explain. "I wish you'd put the phone on speaker so we could have both spoken to Wolfe."

"It wasn't necessary." He shrugged into his coat. "Wolfe just called to tell us that the victim has been identified as Brooklyn Daniels. He's sending the autopsy report over first thing in the morning, although it's a preliminary report as he's taking all the swabs he collected back to Black Rock Falls for identification. He has everything he needs there to run DNA and trace-evidence testing. He said it wouldn't take long as he has the best equipment available in his lab." He gave her a long look. "You might think I take a long time to work a case, but this way I don't make mistakes. One thing for darn sure, we'll work together much better if you take it down a notch or two."

Picturing the rabbit and the tortoise inside her head for one crazy moment, she laughed. "So, you can't handle a feisty woman, huh? I'm used to working at breakneck speed. In case it slipped your mind, we still have a kid missing out there."

"Yeah, I know, and we also have every person available out searching for her. We all have jobs to do, Beth. The search teams have been running all daylight hours since she went missing. Trust me, Ryder has it covered. Searches are something he's good at and the townsfolk all get behind him. We've lost people in snowdrifts and he's found them." Styles pulled on a pair of gloves. "If we'd joined the search, we wouldn't have hunted down this list of suspects, would we? We need to allow the local law enforcement to do their job." He indicated to a list on the whiteboard. "Did you check to see if any of those people on your list own cabins in the forest? We know this killer is taking the second girl somewhere isolated. If we can discover where he's taking them, it would be a start."

Fortunately, Beth could see his point and she nodded. "Yeah, I've checked, but none of them own any properties in the immediate area. Discovering where the killer is taking the girls will be near impossible."

"The problem is there are hundreds of hunting cabins throughout the forest. Many have been there since the first mines, way back. Some are occupied but most of them are deserted or only used during hunting season. Just about anyone can build one and live off the grid out there and no one would know." Styles went to the coffeemaker and filled a Thermos. "How long before you're ready to leave?"

Dragging on her coat, Beth went to his side and filled her pockets with energy bars. She looked at him and smiled. "Just in case we're held up. I want to be eating supper before midnight."

Beth's phone buzzed in her pocket and she stared at the caller ID. She glanced at Styles. "It's Ryder." She swiped her phone to answer. "Beth Katz."

"We have a problem." Ryder sounded agitated. *"There's a van heading out of town with a bound and gagged girl in the back."*

Excitement shivered through Beth. "Stay on the line." She stared at Styles. "This could be the Pied Piper. Let's go."

SEVENTEEN

Running for the door, Beth pressed the phone to her ear. "Okay, we're on our way. Give me the rundown."

"The woman who called it in said she followed the van and called me. She had to stop as it was heading up the mountain in the direction of Silver Fish Creek. I'm out at Rainbow coordinating the search for Skylar Peters." Ryder let out a long sigh. *"It would be an hour or more before I get there, especially in this weather, so I can't act as backup."*

Beth glanced at Styles as they climbed into the elevator. "Do you have the coordinates?"

"Styles knows the area, but I know a shortcut. The road to Silver Fish Creek is steep and narrow and it will be slow going for a van. If you head out through Rock Valley and go through the town of Rosewood, you'll come out halfway along the mountain road. The trail up the mountain is little more than an old animal track. The mines laid some gravel over it at one time but it's steep and narrow, but Styles' truck should handle the going without a problem."

They dashed from the elevator and Beth pressed her phone

to her ear. "We're leaving now. I will update you as soon as I know anything."

"Copy that." Ryder disconnected.

Outside was like walking into a hurricane. The wind howled like a freight train, bending the trees and stripping leaves. Lightning flashed and thunder rolled on for long seconds. The rain came down in freezing sheets, and as Beth ran for the truck, hail pinged off of the hood. She threw herself inside and strapped in as Styles backed out of the parking lot and, lights and sirens blaring, drove away at high speed. They made their way along Main. The road met up with Clear Spring, a highway that wound its way through the local forest. "What do they call the forest?"

"Eagle's Nest." Styles accelerated but the noise of the rain pelting the roof of the truck drowned out the sound of the engine. "It covers all of Rattlesnake Creek, from the highway right through to the mountain range and then some. It's broken by the highway over the bridge that leads into Rainbow. The forest there is known as Wandering Bear."

Gripping tightly to the edge of the seat, Beth nodded. "Yeah, I heard Ryder mention that name when we were there."

They raced out of the forest and headed alongside the railroad track for about three miles before turning back toward the forest. Beth noticed a signpost ahead. "Rock Valley is coming up on your left."

"Yeah, I know my way around town, and if we happen to get lost, we can always use the GPS. There's a satellite sleeve in the glovebox for my phone if you can't get any bars." Styles slid the truck around the corner, the back wheels fishtailing in the deluge of water rushing down the mountain.

Fear gripped Beth as the truck bounced over debris spilling from the torrents of rainwater, coming toward them in wide muddy rivulets. She could hardly make out the road ahead between the *swish, swish, swish* of the wipers. It seemed that Styles didn't have a problem driving at top speed in dangerous conditions. They flashed past a signpost that pointed the way toward Rosewood and hurtled along a narrow winding road. Ahead, a flash of lightning illuminated a herd of deer careering down the mountainside toward the road. The brakes on the truck screamed as they bumped over fallen rocks and skidded. It seemed to take forever to stop, and Styles had the truck sliding sideways toward the terrified herd.

Nails digging into the upholstery, Beth hung on for dear life. With her heart in her mouth, she stared at the soaked deer scrambling to get away. Finally, the truck came to a jolting stop, and beside her Styles huffed out a long sigh. She relaxed her fingers and looked at him. "That was a little too close for comfort."

"It's not gonna get too much better either." Styles righted the truck and kept going. "The road the van has taken around the mountain is very narrow. There's often mudslides, especially in this type of weather. It's obvious to me he took this route to avoid being seen. It used to be a cattle track before a team mining the area widened it ten years ago. There were so many accidents, vehicles plunging down the side of the mountain and into Silver Fish Creek, the mine was abandoned."

Horrified Beth stared at him. "Where does it lead to now?"

"A fire road. About two years ago the Forestry put through a fire road with a lookout. The fire road runs through the forest and eventually ends up at the main highway. If I wanted to live off the grid, that's where I'd head. Apart from the forest warden living in the lookout over the wildfire season, there wouldn't be anyone around that part of the forest, except those people who don't want to be found."

Scratching her head, Beth looked at him, she didn't understand the reference to Silver Fish Creek. "So, we're heading up the mountain, right? Shouldn't we be going down toward the creek if that's where we assume the van is going?"

"Nope." Styles turned onto a narrow trail. "The creek is way down at the bottom of the mountain. This road got its name from the mine. Hang on, it's going to get rough."

Thunder crashed and lightning flashed all around them as they wound their way at breakneck speed up the steep incline. They seemed to be traveling through intermittent patches of clouds. Swirling mist and sheets of rain surrounded them. The truck hugged the side of the mountain as they maneuvered the narrow road higher and higher. It was as if they were traveling upstream. The swirling water brought with it leaves, pine cones, twigs, and chunks of dirt. As they turned a tight bend, the back of the truck slid out over the deep ravine, the back wheels barely getting purchase on the wet rocks before Styles regained control.

Heart thundering in her chest, Beth stared ahead at certain death. Under the rock formation that formed a bridge, the swollen creek had fast become boiling rapids and rushed down the mountain in a raging torrent of water. Swallowing her fear, she searched the winding road. "There, look, that has to be the van. It looks as if it's having trouble driving up the side of the mountain. Do you think we can catch it?"

"I'm going as fast as I can without killing us." Styles shot her a glance. "At the speed he's going, we'll catch up with him soon enough. I doubt he's stupid enough to try and cross the bridge." He cut his lights and sirens. "Maybe it's better he doesn't know who we are right now. I don't want him to do anything stupid."

The young woman in the back of the van would be terrified and Beth held her breath as the vehicle attempted the narrow bridge. Water cascaded down the mountain, flooding the bridge, and it was obvious what was going to happen. The back wheels of the van seemed to float out over the edge of the ravine and the next moment the van lifted up on the swell of water. The back spun almost gracefully before it surfed backward down a torrent of water at high speed. In seconds it joined the raging river and slammed into the rocks. The massive boulders pinned it in place, but the bubbling torrent had no mercy and spun it around and around, like water down a drain. The front windshield exploded in a rainbow of broken glass and the river claimed its prize. She stared in horror as the van vanished beneath the water, the back wheels barely visible in the rapids. Speechless she gaped at Styles. "How do we get down there in time to get them out before they drown?"

"We wait, or we'll be washed off the side of the mountain along with them. The water is already subsiding, and by the time we get to the bridge, we'll get through if the rain holds off. That's not the problem. See how the road kinda disappears from view?" Styles stopped the truck and stared at the mountainside. He rubbed the scar on his chin and gave her a determined stare. "The road there is banked by rock on both sides. It's great for not being washed over the edge but right now it could be a river. This truck has been through water before but it's not invincible. Our only option is to wait. Turning back is impossible as there's no turnaround areas for at least half a mile. We'd have to go back down in reverse."

Not wanting to miss the opportunity of catching the Pied Piper, she shook her head. "We can't go back. We must at least try and get them out of there." She stared at the sky. "It's not raining so hard now. Go when you figure it's safe."

"I know you're concerned about the girl's welfare, but it's too late to save her." He shook his head. "There's not one chance in hell they would have survived the fall and it only takes four minutes to drown and we've gone way past that. You should call it in. Contact Ryder, and he'll arrange for a search-and-rescue team to meet us at the end of the fire road." He stared down at the swirling creek. "From there is access to the riverbank. It's become a popular fishing hole since the fire road went through. It shouldn't be too difficult to get a tow truck in there and drag it out. The main problem will be getting someone willing to risk their life to hook it up." He put the truck into drive and they crept up the winding road.

Gravel and mud slicked the blacktop and the back wheels of the truck spun each time they hit a patch of flowing water. Beth's fingertips dug into the seat, terrified that the next moment they would slide over the edge and tumble into the ravine. Even though Styles had proved to be a very competent driver, she was used to being in control of her own destiny. Driving herself had always been a priority because the simple truth was that she didn't trust anybody. Now thrust into a life-or-death situation, she stared at the road ahead. The dim light of a stormy day intensified as they entered a tunnel like part of the road. It was awash with water moving at a rapid rate. She turned as Styles caught his breath. "It's worse than you thought, isn't it?"

"Yeah, but it's not too deep." Styles white-knuckled the steering wheel, his attention fixed on the road ahead. "We're committed now. There's no turning back."

The truck slid sideways as a torrent of water came down behind them, lifting them up and carrying them like a piece of flotsam on the rush downward. Heart in her throat, Beth bit back a scream as the side of the truck fishtailed back and forth between the ragged rocks, bouncing from one side to the other as they rushed along. It was like being in a waterfall, there was no way to steer the vehicle, fate had them by the neck and was squeezing hard.

Metal screamed as a pine tree ripped from its roots rode the waves with them and slammed the truck against one wall. They had become an out-of-control missile careering down the side of a mountain. Breathless with fear, Beth dragged her eyes away from the horror before her and chanced a glance at Styles. "What's at the bottom of this tunnel?"

"A line of small boulders above an upward rise and then it turns onto a road beside the river. I'm hoping the wheels will touch bottom on the rise, so I can gain some control." He stared ahead and winced as the truck scraped along the rock wall. "It's insured but I think it's about time I put in a requisition for a new one. This one is going to be toast by the time we get out of here."

Gipping so tight that her fingers hurt, Beth glanced down at the trickle of water seeping through the door seals. "The water is up to the window on my side, if it smashes, we're in big trouble."

"You don't figure we're in trouble now?" Styles turned the wheel, but it didn't seem to make any difference. "It will get worse if I can't get the truck out of the water. At least the engine is still running. That has to be a plus."

Unnerved, Beth dragged her eyes off the swirling mass of dirty water and debris rushing them down the mountain at high speed to look at him. "How much worse can it get?"

"We could be washed into the river and then all bets are off." He blew out a breath. "It's gonna take split-second timing. The end of this tunnel widens out to a flat trail, so with luck the water will spread out some and the tires will grip enough for me to get us out of trouble. Hang on, it's not far now."

Overhanging branches whipped the side of the truck, threatening to pierce the windows. Beth flinched as the out-of-control truck headed for an overhanging boulder. Sure they would hit it, she leaned toward Styles, but the water seemed to lift them up. The back of the truck spun out to one side and sent them sideways, headlong down the last part of the tunnel. As the tunnel widened ahead, the truck struck the rocks, and swung around again to face in the right direction. The water level dropped, and ahead Beth could see the boulders on the rise and the flatter area that Styles had mentioned. She held on tight, pushed her feet hard into the seat well, and for once in her life, put her trust in somebody else.

Beside her, Styles wrestled with the steering wheel, turning it this way and that. Beth held her breath as they hit bottom and the tires gripped on the water-soaked gravel alongside the trail. The truck bumped and skidded, fishtailing as Styles pushed it onto higher ground. They came to rest wedged between two saplings, and beside her Styles laughed. He actually laughed. Trembling from shock, she turned slowly to stare at him.

"Wow! What a rush." He looked her over. "Are you okay?"

Incredulous, Beth gaped at his amused expression. "Yeah, I'm fine, but I figure this ride scared a few years off my life." She turned in her seat. "Can you see the van?"

"Nope but the river is behind that boulder." Styles indicated with his chin. "Just follow the flow of the water and you'll find it." He touched her arm. "Wait up, we can't stop here. We need to get out of the mud and check the damage on the truck."

Realizing how close they'd come to dying, Beth squeezed his arm and smiled. "Sure. Great job by the way. I thought we were a goner halfway down that slope."

"Well thank you kindly, ma'am." Styles touched the tip of his Stetson. "We'll make a note of these coordinates for search and rescue and then head to the fire road. You can call them from there."

Beth nodded. She had seen something in Styles she hadn't expected. His military training obviously kept him cool and under control in perilous situations. She had been shaken to the core, and he'd enjoyed the ride. His behavior reflected his maverick attitude but was it something she could exploit, or would she be needing to constantly watch her back?

The storm had passed by the time they'd gotten to the fire road, and while Styles climbed out to check the damage to the truck, Beth contacted Ryder. "We have eyes on the van. It was washed off the road and is currently upside down in the creek."

"Dang. What else is going to happen?" Ryder whistled. *"Did you bring this bad luck with you from DC?"*

Speechless for a moment, Beth stared at her phone. "Wow. I

know it's been a tough few days for you, Cash, but don't take it out on the people who are trying to help. Can you get someone out here to haul this van out of the water? Styles said it is close to the popular fishing hole out at Silver Fish Creek. We'll wait at the fire road for you."

"Okay. They've called off the search for Skylar due to the weather, so I'm heading back to town. I'll gather the troops and meet you there, but it might take some time." He disconnected.

"Don't let him get you down. I figure this is his first murder." Styles leaned in the window. I guess it's a little over-whelming for someone used to a quiet life."

Beth snorted at the irony of it all. "I don't know why he'd say that. As if I have anything to do with serial killers..."

EIGHTEEN

It took hours for the search-and-rescue team to drag the van out of the creek. At least it had stopped raining. It had taken six men tied with harnesses to the trees to bravely go into the swirling water and hitch up the van. The grinding noise as they winched it free was like the screams of the tortured as metal ripped across rocks. It was a pitiful sight inside, both people had suffered numerous injuries and shocked men had laid the bloodless limp bodies of the driver and the young girl on the riverbank. It was obvious both were past resuscitation, but the search and rescue tried without success. After searching the van and collecting evidence, Beth turned to see Nate arriving with Ryder. Nate's professionalism calmed everyone. He examined the bodies and pronounced them both dead at the scene.

As Nate walked away, she stared at the young girl's face and turned to Styles. "That's not our missing girl, but I recognize her, don't you?"

"Yeah, she is familiar." He pulled out his phone and scrolled through his files. "This has to be her." He held out his phone so she could see the image. "If this is Aisha Santiago, she went missing from Colorado about six months ago." He handed her a wallet. "The driver had this in his pocket."

After examining the wallet, Beth pulled out her phone. "I'll call Wolfe." She made the call and brought him up to speed. "We just hauled the van out of the creek, the driver was deceased and from his license, he is Ricky Tallis out of Butte. In the back of the van, we found a young girl restrained with zip ties and gagged. We couldn't resuscitate her. The thing is, we recognized her from our list of missing persons. I'm on scene now but I figure she's from a recent case where two girls went missing in Colorado some months back. We checked the files and think her name is Aisha Santiago. We might have found the Pied Piper."

"If it is the Pied Piper and he's dead, it means we will never find the rest of the girls. His secret will have died with him." Wolfe cleared his throat. "He could have them holed up anywhere in the forest. Unless they have a way of escaping, they'll all die of starvation."

As Beth stared at the lifeless figure lying on the side of the creek, Wolfe's words hit home. She looked away from Styles as her dark side pushed its way to the surface. The part of her that wanted vengeance wouldn't be satisfied if the Pied Piper had drowned. The death was too easy for the suffering he'd caused. She lifted her chin and stared at the raging rapids. "What do you want us to do with the bodies? We have an ambulance on standby and Nate has recorded the time of death."

"Have Nate take them to the hospital. They have a morgue there. Make sure nobody touches them. Leave them in the body bags and get them on ice. I'll fly out first thing in the morning and collect them." Wolfe sighed. "Any sign of Skylar Peters?"

Beth shook her head, desperately trying to calm her dark side and dropping her gaze to the sandy soil at her feet. "No, nothing. I don't figure they'll find her in Rainbow. This guy has her some other place. How can we possibly find her in this wilderness?"

"There's always a way. Keep looking. I'll call you when I've completed the autopsies." Wolfe disconnected.

Beth waited patiently for Nate to finish examining the bodies and make notes, and then went to his side. "Wolfe will be here in the morning. He said to leave the zip ties on the girl and don't allow anyone to touch them without wearing gloves. He wants them on ice at the hospital morgue. Can you handle that for me?"

"Yeah, not a problem." Nate glanced at the weary search-and-rescue crew. "I'll take swabs from the men who touched the bodies, but I doubt there'll be any trace evidence on the girl. The running water would have destroyed it."

Beth nodded. "Thanks. I'll get their prints before they leave as well. I have a scanner with me."

"Okay, as soon as Styles has finished recording the scene, I'll get them into the back of Ryder's pickup." Nate gave her a slow smile. "He'll be thrilled."

"I'll be thrilled about what?" Ryder walked up from behind them.

Exchanging an amused look with Nate, Beth turned to him. "We can't leave the bodies here. They'll be taking the ride to the morgue in your truck."

"My day just gets better by the second." Ryder rolled his eyes, turned, and his shoulders slumped as he walked away.

Slightly amused, Beth stared after him. "Is he always so much fun?"

"Yeah." Nate narrowed his gaze. "He's a good cop and is well respected in town... well, all over. I just figure he believes his towns have suddenly lost their innocence. It was okay for brawls and roughhousing, the odd bit of cattle rustling, thieving, but murdering kids takes it to a whole new level. I guess it takes some getting used to." He let out a long sigh. "I'd better get to work." He walked away, leaving her staring at the damaged van.

The storm had passed and sunshine cast rainbows over the still raging river. If the driver of the van had only waited another hour or so before attempting to drive up the mountain road, he'd have been on his way to his hideout by now. She turned at the sound of footsteps on gravel. Styles was heading her way. "Did you get everything you need?"

"Yeah. I've recorded the scene and thanked the search-and-rescue team." Styles came to her side and stood beside her scanning the area. "Everything we found inside the van is in evidence bags in my truck." He smiled. "The damage to my truck is cosmetic—scrapes, dents, and a nice coating of mud, but it started okay. The bodies are ready for transport. I figure once Nate has removed them, we're good to go."

Beth nodded. "That's good to know. We'll write it up and then decide what to do next. Finding a girl from a different crime makes the case complicated. To be honest, I assumed he'd killed them all by now. Six months is a long time to keep a kid hidden. I'm wondering how many more he has holed up somewhere." She turned to stare at the bodies. "If that's the Pied Piper, it's over. I seriously doubt we'll ever find the missing girls. The idea they'll be facing starvation, after what he's already put them through, makes me sick to my stomach."

"I'm not planning on giving up anytime soon. Now we have a name, we'll hunt down his friends. Someone might know if he has a cabin somewhere." Styles shrugged. "We'll get his name out to the other agencies. We don't have to shoulder this alone. Someone, somewhere knows this guy. He'd have a job and pay taxes. We'll dig deep and find out what he eats for breakfast." He gave her a long look. "I thought you knew your way around computers? Chasing down his ID would be a start. Is he really Ricky Tallis out of Butte?"

After years in cybercrime and her intimate knowledge of

the dark web, Styles' comment amused her. On the web, she could find a particular strand of hay in a haystack. It was a place she moved through like a shadow, without leaving a trace of herself behind and collecting information she could store for later use. So many dark souls roamed the data stream, so many out for personal gain or for pure hatred. It was a minefield and negotiating through it was dangerous. Many people believe knowledge is a good thing, but some knowledge could get a person killed. She met Styles' grin with a blank stare. He knew he'd rattled her cage and was enjoying the moment. She blew out a sigh. "Yeah, I guess I can manage to run a search when we get back to the office." She turned away and headed for their truck. "Nate and Ryder are heading out now. Let's get out of here."

NINETEEN

Tommy Joe's Bar and Grill was packed to capacity when they arrived in town, and as they walked to a table in the back, Beth couldn't help noticing the way people avoided her gaze. Overhearing mumblings from people close by, it was obvious that the accident on the mountain was common knowledge in town. When Josie, one of the servers, came to their table to take their order, Beth smiled at her. "I'll have a burger with fries and a lemon soda." She placed the menu in its holder on the table. "It's very busy in here today and everyone is talking up a storm. Has something happened we should know about?"

"The crowd in here today are all gold miners. The storm washed them out, so they're waiting for the rain to clear before they get back to work. I doubt they'll go back today." Josie glanced over at Styles and flashed him a white grin. "The usual for you, Dax?"

"Yeah, thanks, Josie." Styles leaned back in his chair and tipped up his Stetson. "They all went kinda quiet when we walked in. What's happening?"

"Some say you were chasing a van up the mountain and caused it to go over the edge." Josie cleared her throat and looked around furtively. "They say a man and his daughter died when they hit the river."

Wondering how anybody could have seen them driving up the side of the mountain, Beth flashed a look at Styles and raised one eyebrow. "Isn't it strange how rumors start? We had a report of a girl gagged and bound in the back of a van and we pursued them up the mountain. They had at least a fifteen-minute start on us, so we were a long way behind them when they were washed off the mountain by a torrent of water. It's doubtful that the driver knew we were following him. We didn't have the lights and sirens on, so whoever is spreading that rumor needs to get their facts straight." She lifted her chin and allowed her gaze to move purposely around the room. "It's obviously common knowledge the girl was bound and gagged. Whoever called it in, is spreading gossip. The truth is the driver was transporting somebody he'd kidnapped. The girl in question was a missing person and definitely not his daughter."

"Oh, I see." Josie's cheeks pinked. "I'll make sure everyone knows the truth."

"See that you do." Styles removed his Stetson and placed it on the chair beside him. He looked at Beth as Josie walked away. "You were kinda tough on her. It's not her fault that people are talking about us."

Surprised at his reaction, Beth sipped from a glass of water and eyed him over the rim. "I don't think I was harsh. I was just giving her the facts. Sometimes the truth is the best policy in a small town like this. I figure if we keep too many secrets, the townsfolk will stop trusting us." She thought for a beat, noticing his discomfort. "Ah, is she someone special to you?"

"We've dated a few times." Styles drummed his fingers on the table. "I don't have anyone special in my life. I figured getting close to someone in a small town can only cause trouble, but I'm only human and, living on my lonesome in that old building for years, sometimes I do need companionship. I've dated a few of the women in town." He gave her a long look. "Is that going to be a problem or do you figure FBI agents should distance themselves from the locals?"

Not quite sure where this conversation was going, Beth thought for a beat and stared at the lemon wedge bobbing about in her glass. She needed to get along with Styles but didn't intend on being joined to him at the hip or forming any type of romantic attachment. She had to admit he was a good-looking man who could take care of himself and that was something she admired, but having someone in law enforcement in her life would cause a problem. Sooner or later, someone with Styles' investigative ability would discover her secret. She'd had casual dates with people outside of the FBI. It gave her something to talk about with the others when they asked about her personal life. Unfortunately, it didn't matter where she worked or who she pretended to be at any time, people always wanted to know personal details. Accepting the odd dinner invitation, however much she disliked socializing, made her appear perfectly normal to the inquisitive mind of a colleague. Dating was one of the many parts she played in her life.

She raised her gaze to Styles to find him staring at her intently. Not wanting to be abrupt or rude to him, she cleared her throat feigning confusion. "I've only been here a few days, Dax. I'm finding my feet just now. I've never lived in a small town before, so I guess the rules are different here. My problem is, if I look like I'm competition to the locals you're involved with, it might cause friction, but I don't expect you to change your habits just because I'm here. Perhaps if you make it clear that I'm your partner at work, it might prevent a misunderstanding." She smiled at him. "I'm basically a loner. I do date but not frequently. You'll find I often take off on my own for days between cases to clear my head. This is a beautiful area and I plan to explore it in my downtime. Not in that wreck you call a truck they supplied for me. I've already ordered something more suitable and hope it will be delivered soon."

"That's good." His smile lit up the room. "I was planning on asking you to come along with the boys and me when we go on our next fishing trip. There's just one thing I want you to remember when you go on your explorations. The wildlife in this area is exceptionally dangerous. I suggest you go from motel to motel if you want to see the sights. I don't want to find you torn up by a grizzly way up there in the mountains."

After waiting for Josie to put their meals on the table and leave, Beth picked up a fry and nibbled on it as if contemplating his words. "No, I wouldn't go hiking alone, but I do plan to visit some of the towns in this area. When I researched Rattlesnake Creek, I discovered many of the outlying areas have craft shops, pottery, leatherwear, and handmade jewelry from the gems found in the mines. I need to make my apartment a home, so gathering a few personal items is on my list."

As they finished their meal, Styles' phone buzzed. Beth stared at him as he frowned at the caller ID and then looked up at her.

"It's the San Francisco office." He handed her one of his earbuds. "Use this. I can't put the phone on speaker in a public place. "Agent Styles."

"This is Agent Dominic Lowe from the San Francisco office. We believe that one of your current investigations includes the Pied Piper cases?"

"Yeah, that's us. Do you have any information?" Styles took out his notebook and pen and, using one hand, opened it to a clean page.

"Four days ago we fished a young woman out of the bay We figured she was a sex worker, and after subsequent investigation discovered she worked for a pimp along with another six girls in his stable." Lowe sounded disinterested and bored with the conversation. "No one claimed her body, so we ran a DNA test

*on her and discovered that she is one of the missing girls from the
list we assume was abducted by the Pied Piper. The case went
cold, but I believe you have all the case files on the cold cases that
we've attributed to the Pied Piper over the years. This girl is a
Montanan, Scarlett Chester. From the autopsy reports, she was
high when she drowned."* He sighed. *"We haven't notified next
of kin or taken the investigation any further. We figured you'd
wanna take the lead in this case from the get-go."*

Beth nodded emphatically and stared at Styles. Two girls
from past crimes suddenly popping up in different parts of the
country was too intriguing to let go. There had to be a link
between the Pied Piper and whoever was holding this girl. She
had no doubt in her mind Scarlett Chester had been sold into
slavery.

"Yeah, we would." Styles checked his watch. "We'll leave
first thing in the morning. It's around a six-hour flight. Can you
possibly arrange to have a vehicle waiting for us at the airport
from about two in the afternoon?"

*"Yeah, not a problem, and there is a hotel just across the road
if you're planning on staying for a couple of days."* Lowe had
brightened considerably. *"We'll see you tomorrow."* He
disconnected.

Beth pulled out the earbud and handed it back to Styles.
"This case is starting to get crazy. How can the Pied Piper's
victims suddenly start showing up at the same time? San Francisco, how did Scarlett Chester end up there and working on
the streets? It's not something she would have done on her own.
This is pointing to the Pied Piper, raping and murdering one
girl and selling the other. It's a lucrative market and would
account for the fact the girls are appearing all over the country."

"We've considered comfort zones." Styles folded his notebook and pushed it into his pocket. "It seems to me the whole
darn country is his comfort zone." He pushed his feet. "We'll
need to make plans. I figure that Wolfe will want Scarlett

Chester's body in his morgue at Black Rock Falls. We'll need paperwork to take the body." He picked up his Stetson and pushed it onto his head.

Beth stood and pulled on her jacket. "You chase down the paperwork and I'll contact Wolfe. I'll get onto Ryder about doing a background check on the guy in the van, Ricky Tallis. I won't have time."

"Let's go." Styles led the way out of the door.

Hurrying after him, Beth tugged on his arm to slow him down. "What about Bear? You can't leave him alone while we're gone. Is there anyone who can take care of him for you?"

"He'll be coming with us." Styles glanced at her over one shoulder. "He likes to ride in the chopper. He has K-9 status, so can go everywhere we do." He gave her a long look. "Unless you have a problem with that?"

Shaking her head, Beth pulled open the truck door. "Not at all. I like having him around."

TWENTY

San Francisco

After landing to refuel and grab something to eat, Beth sat opposite Styles in a typical airport diner. The chair was made of aluminum, as was the round table that wobbled when she placed her coffee on the top. Without saying a word, Styles took a coaster, folded it in half, and wedged it under the short leg. She took a packet of wipes out of her pocket and cleaned her hands, before tossing them to him. She indicated a cleaner, wiping down the tables with the same dirty rag. "I wouldn't put anything on the table if I was you."

"Thanks, the coffee looks like weak tea, but what can they do to ruin an egg salad sandwich?" He poured bottled water into a dish he'd brought with him for Bear and the dog lapped, splashing water all over the floor, and then lifted his head and looked longingly at Beth as if willing her to feed him.

Beth lifted her sandwich to her lips. "I guess I'm gonna find out." She chewed and nodded. "It's fresh at least." She wanted to feed Bear. He looked so cute in his FBI coat and she tossed him the crusts of her sandwich.

"Please, don't feed him at the table." Styles looked at her. "He shouldn't be accepting food from you at all." He picked up the sandwich and sighed. "My wife used to make curried egg sandwiches and we'd eat them with tomato soup in winter. She made everything from scratch apart from the bread. My job was to keep the vegetable patch producing everything she needed." Styles let out a long sigh. "Before you ask me, it lasted six months after I joined the FBI. She wanted me to take a desk job. In fact, she wanted to rule my life. If I came home five minutes late, she'd want to know where I'd been and what I'd been doing, how much money I'd spent. You know it's impossible to work nine to five on the job. Most times I was given cases that took me out of town, and never being home caused a problem."

Interested, Beth leaned forward. She'd read about this type of behavior and wondered if he'd been a victim in his marriage. "What kind of problems?"

"Demands mostly." He sipped his coffee and grimaced and then put the cup down on the saucer. "One time she cut up my credit cards. Another time she cut all the legs off my pants to prevent me from going to work. I figured she was insecure and took some personal time to try and sort things through, but then it got to a point where she didn't want me to leave the house. I explained I needed to work to earn a salary." He stared into space for a beat and sighed. "When I finally persuaded her to allow me to go back to the office, she called me every half hour. She'd tell me she was watching me, and if I as much as spoke to another woman, she'd kill herself."

Aghast, Beth washed her sandwich down with a mouthful of the disgusting coffee. "So, what did you do, divorce her?"

"Nope. I loved her and we went to counseling and tried to work through her insecurities. I figured we had everything under control, but then one day I was out on a job when she showed." He opened a bottle of water and sipped. "I'd been interviewing the same woman about her husband over a few days. It was a murder case and part of a serial killer investigation we were doing at the time. I was speaking to her on her front porch, when out of nowhere Sharon came running toward me. Before I could react, she pulled a gun and shot the woman. She didn't kill her and, long story short, she's doing time and won't be out anytime soon. So, I filed for divorce." He met her gaze. "It kept me awake for a time wondering what I did wrong. This is the reason I accepted the position in Rattlesnake Creek, to get right away from all the memories. I don't visit her or have any contact with her whatsoever and it's been years. She said things to me after the incident that I'll never forget or forgive."

Surprised that Styles had confided such a personal part of his life to her, she nodded. "Coercive control is what they call that type of behavior. It happens due to a number of different problems. The controller can be a narcissist or have borderline personality issues. It can start off small and escalate into physical abuse." She cleared her throat. Could she actually be feeling empathy for Styles? A strong man like him, to have suffered at the hands of someone he obviously loved must have been very difficult. "I honestly think when things like this happen in our lives it only makes us stronger."

"Ha!" Styles leaned back in his chair and grinned at her. "I don't know about making me stronger, but I am more careful about the women I choose to befriend, that's for darn sure." He gave her a scrutinizing stare. "Okay, fess up. I showed you mine, now you show me yours. What dark secret are you hiding? What happened to you to make you so hungry to bring down serial killers?"

Fortunately, being gullible wasn't one of her traits and his opening up and laying bare details of his disastrous marriage told her more about his true character than he'd ever realize. He might have a tough, uncaring exterior, but in truth, to tolerate spousal mental abuse to such a degree was a true indication of a deeply caring man. She ate her sandwich, chewing slowly to mull over his question. Her past life wasn't a secret. What happened to her as a child, the time in foster care, and the adoption were all on record. When she joined the FBI, her troubled past was taken into consideration. At the time, she'd passed all the psych tests and everything else they put her through with flying colors. In fact, she outscored many of the men in her class. She wondered if this was a test, for surely if Styles had been asked to supply the director with an assessment of her work in the field, he would have been advised of her past. She shrugged and met his gaze full on, hoping that her dark side wouldn't creep to the surface and reveal itself. "I don't have any secrets. My life is an open book. I don't have any stories to tell you about past lovers because I haven't met Mr. Right yet." She could almost see him regroup and try another tactic. "Is that what you mean, because not having a steady doesn't really relate to the job does it?"

"I was thinking more in the lines of why you decided the FBI was for you." Styles shrugged. "We all have a reason to want to take down criminals. It's not everyone's first choice of employment."

Beth nodded. "Ah, I see where you're coming from. My father is a serial killer and I'm trying to make things right."

"You can't be held responsible for what he did." Styles bit into his sandwich and chewed slowly. "Did you ever witness anything?"

Shaking her head, Beth lifted her sandwich to her mouth and hoped he couldn't read a lie in her expression, as the memory of seeing her father murder a young woman flashed into her mind. Her father's actions had changed her forever and triggered the dark side lying dormant in her genes. After witnessing her mother's death by his hand and years of suffering in foster care, she hated her father for creating the monster inside her. Bringing the burning need to kill under control had taken all her willpower, and from that day on she'd vowed to make serial killers pay for destroying families.

"No, thank goodness. The psychiatrist tried hypnotism, but if anything happened in front of me, I've blocked it out. I could have retrograde amnesia. If so, it will likely never surface. I don't remember anything before my mom died, and first thing I recall is being told my mom had died. The next thing, I was in foster care without a clue of where I came from or any memories of a family. I didn't know my father was a serial killer until I turned eighteen—or that he'd killed my mom and fifteen other women. My adopted parents decided I should know the truth. It played on my mind for a long time, still does. The moment I left college, I applied to join the FBI. After researching ways of finding serial killers, I decided to put my skills in computer science to work in cybercrime, but I needed to be on the job and asked to work some cases in the field. The director figured I was perfect for undercover gigs because I'd been hidden in cyber-crime and I can take care of myself. I went through the training and went to work. It was interesting being inside the lion's den." She leaned back in her chair. "After the last undercover gig, I went back into cybercrime and then they put me out on the streets. It was good being out of the office."

"So, what happened to your dad?" Styles rubbed the scar on his chin.

The thought of him made her stomach churn. "I know my father is still alive in jail somewhere but I've never wanted to discover where he is or even what he looks like now. As far as I'm concerned, he can rot there."

"They say it can be hereditary." Styles finished his sand-wich. "Does that worry you?"

Beth laughed. "Aw, come on, Styles, be honest with me. What you really want to know is, do I have a hankering to murder someone?"

"Well, do you?" Styles sipped his water and stared at her, his expression solemn.

"Yeah, when I see a kid raped and murdered, I want to tear the perp apart with my bare hands." Beth raised both eyebrows. "I'm told that's a normal reaction. The abnormal reaction is doing it."

TWENTY-ONE

After arriving in San Francisco, they were met by Agent Dominic Lowe and driven straight to a hotel in a dark blue Taurus. Beth dropped her bags and coat into her room and walked next door to Styles' room to speak to Lowe. They were speaking in hushed tones when she arrived, but the door was open and she walked straight on in. "I think it will save time if you give us both the information on the Scarlett Chester case at the same time."

"Oh, we were just discussing sports." Lowe was dressed in a dark suit and tie, the usual agent attire. "Now you're settled here, I'll take you to the office. It's just across the road. I can walk you through the case, but in truth it's been put on the back burner by this department, mainly because streetwalkers die here just about daily."

Disgusted, Beth shook her head slowly. "So, I guess if a dog got hit by a car, you'd be out in force?" She glared at him. "Where's your duty of care? Did you miss the bit about everyone being equal under the law?"

"Look." The tips of Lowe's ears turned pink. "It's not like that at all. All murders are usually covered by the local PD, but as this woman is a missing person connected to the Pied Piper case, it falls into FBI hands. No one on our team is covering the Pied Piper case, and as the most recent murder attributed to him happened in your area, naturally we called you in."

"Okay, we've been traveling all day, so let's get on with it." Styles removed his thick jacket and hung it on the back of the chair. "It sure is warmer here than in Rattlesnake Creek." He exchanged a meaningful glare with Beth and, beckoning Bear to his side, followed Lowe out the door.

Lowe looked at Bear with interest. "You brought a K-9." He chuckled. "I don't think you'll need him on this case."

"You never know." Styles waited for the walk sign to flash and headed across the road. "Anyway where I go, he goes."

Inside the FBI office they went to Lowe's cubicle and he handed them a hardcopy of the file. "This is what we've got on the case so far. It's mainly information from the local PD. I became involved when she was taken to the morgue and formally identified."

Beth leaned over the table, staring at the file as Styles turned the pages. "Identified how? This girl has been missing for three years. She is barely a teenager."

"We used Snapshot DNA profiling." Lowe leaned over to flick through the file to a photograph. "Are you familiar with the process?"

Beth nodded. "Yeah, it's relatively new. They take a DNA sample and the machine produces a likeness from their DNA profile. It's very accurate." She lifted her gaze to him. "Problem is, it doesn't give a name."

"Yeah, well we ran the image through the missing person's database using facial recognition software and got a hit for Scarlett Chester. We hadn't realized she was so young." Lowe turned to the autopsy images. "As you can see, she'd been in the water for a time. At first glance, you wouldn't consider her to be a young girl. She was fully clothed and dressed like a street-walker. How she got into the river is a mystery. The case is open, but she was high on heroin, so she probably fell into the river."

"Is this all the interviews that you have from people who knew her?" Styles waved two pieces of paper. "I find it difficult to believe the names on here are real. Where can we find these people?"

"They come out at night." Lowe gave Styles a long considering stare. "Maybe you can cruise up and down the street and pick one of them up. They'll spill their guts for twenty bucks."

The instant dislike that Beth had formed for Lowe was growing by the second. "Do you honestly believe that women choose this profession? Most choose this rather than being homeless and raped on the streets. The problem is that to enable them to cope they turn to drugs and then what had started as a fast-moneymaking idea turns into a vicious circle. They become hooked and have no other way of paying to feed their addiction."

"They could go to a shelter." Lowe shrugged. "It comes down to choice in the end, doesn't it?"

Beth caught Styles' warning glance but couldn't let it go. "The chances of gaining a place in a shelter would be minimal in any city. Don't you think that people would rather be in a shelter than living in a cardboard box under a bridge?" She lifted both hands in the air in exasperation, blew out a long breath, and stared at Styles. "First up, I suggest we go to see the medical examiner who performed the autopsy. Can you give us his name and where to find him, please?"

"It will be on the documents." Lowe waved his hand toward the file dismissively. "I'll leave you to it."

"We'll need a ride." Styles straightened to his full height and looked down at him. "Which way to the parking lot, and where do you keep the keys?"

"Keys are on the board over by the door." Lowe indicated

with his chin. "Head straight through the door and you'll run into the parking lot." He lowered his voice to a whisper and said something to Styles that she missed.

When Styles turned to stone and just stared at Lowe, Beth could almost feel the air crackling between them. Lowe's face turned beat red, and he backed away and then headed out of the office with Styles' stare boring into his back.

"We'll need a copy of that file." Styles turned to her. "I guess in this office it's every man for himself."

Nodding in agreement, Beth collected the documents, and shoved them back into the file. She went to the copying machine and slid each page through and then stapled them together. She dropped the original back onto Lowe's desk and looked at Styles. "Let's go."

Outside in the parking lot, Beth waited as Styles used the remote to find a vehicle. She turned to look at him. "What did Lowe say to you just before?"

"He was just being a jerk." Styles led the way to a sedan, opened the back door, and waved Bear inside. "We'll need to stop on the way and grab a couple of bottles of water. It's warmer here than I thought."

Annoyed, Beth walked up behind him. "Being a jerk is a given. What did he say?" When he gave a shake of his head, she touched his arm. "I need to know where I stand here."

"He suggested I keep my mutt on a leash." Styles pulled open the door and raised one dark eyebrow. "Forget about it. He's just a jerk and I figure he got the message, that I didn't consider a comment like that appropriate." He slid behind the wheel and turned to look at her. "I just happened to agree with everything you said and I'm not saying that just to keep on your good side."

Amused, Beth chuckled. "I haven't got a good side." She glanced at him. "Surely, you've figured that out by now?"

TWENTY-TWO

The medical examiner was a man in his sixties, with graying hair and a handlebar mustache. Styles smothered a grin. The man looked as if he'd just walked out of a historical movie. His long white lab coat hung way past his knees covering brown trousers and matching loafers. He'd given Bear a look of disdain, but on Styles' command the dog sat down to wait outside in the passageway. The usual stink of a morgue surrounded them as they stepped inside the examination room. The cool air a stark difference from the humidity outside. Styles dipped one finger into the mentholated salve and wiped it under his nose and then handed it to Beth. This was part of the job he didn't enjoy, especially when young people were involved. It seemed such a waste to see a young person murdered usually just because they happen to be in the wrong place at the wrong time. He fastened a mask over his nose and mouth and waited in the large room for the ME to slide the body from the refrigerated drawers in the wall. He moved closer alongside Beth and peered at the bloated, discolored face of Scarlett Chester. "Can we get her out of here so I can take a look at her under the light, please?"

Patiently standing to one side as the ME moved the body on the gurney under the light, he allowed his gaze to travel over the victim, searching for any signs of damage. Needle track marks were evident on both forearms and between the toes. He looked up at the ME. "Did you find any signs of a struggle?"

"She has bruises all over." The ME indicated to a few discolored patches on the surface of the skin. "They're in different stages of healing, so indicate a recurring factor over a period of time. I would say she was beaten regularly or engaged in rough sex. There are marks across her back, which suggests the use of a leather strap."

"What exactly is the cause of death?" Beth circled the body slowly, examining every inch.

"She drowned under the influence of heroin." The ME shrugged. "It happens more than you realize."

"Did you collect samples of water from the lungs and cross-match them with the river water?" Beth lifted her gaze to stare at him.

"Yeah, I did, and it was a match." The ME sighed. "I didn't order a full toxicology screen and just tested for heroin due to the needle track marks on both arms."

Unconvinced, Styles shook his head. "It would be very unusual for someone to just walk into the river and drown. Are there any injuries consistent to her being thrown off the bridge?"

"Not that I'm aware." The ME shrugged. "The local PD and the FBI didn't request any X-rays or MRI scans to determine if she fell or was pushed from the bridge."

Styles looked at Beth and raised both eyebrows. "Okay, I'll need her suitably refrigerated and packed for transport. I will also need a copy of your files. We'll be leaving first thing in the morning. You'll need to have her at the airport chopper terminal by nine."

"I haven't received any requests to release the body." The ME looked taken aback and covered the body with a sheet. "I can't do anything without the completed paperwork."

"I'll complete any paperwork you require. This girl went missing from Montana. We are taking over the case, and she is going to the Black Rock Falls medical examiner, Dr. Shane Wolfe." Beth stared him down. "Is that going to be a problem?"

"No, I'll have her ready." The ME went to a computer, slipped in a thumb drive and a few minutes later handed it to Styles. "These are the files. You will need to give a copy to Dr. Wolfe." He went to a drawer and pulled out a document pad. He thrust it toward Beth. "This is the required documentation. You'll need to complete that before you leave."

Styles glanced at her. "I'll go and wash up. I'll meet you out at the car. I want to sift through those files again."

"Sure." Beth leaned against the counter and took the pen the ME offered her. "This won't take long."

The visit to the ME had been a complete waste of time. He hoped that Beth's faith in Dr. Shane Wolfe was justified because something about this girl's death didn't sit right with him. It was very unusual for an ME to go to the trouble and expense of completing a Snapshot DNA analysis to discover her identity but not fully investigate the cause of death. It didn't take a doctor to notice the new bruising on the back of the girl's arms or the blushing across her shoulders. It could be consistent with hitting the water from the bridge. One thing for darn sure, it wasn't the result of livor mortis. He walked to the sedan and settled Bear in the back seat. He slid behind the wheel, went over the case file, and made a few notes as he waited for Beth.

He looked up as Beth came out the door of the medical examiner's office and then glanced at his watch. As she slipped into the passenger seat, he turned to her. "If you're not feeling sick after being in the morgue, we should find a quiet restaurant and work out what we're going to do next. We are going to hunt down the pimp, right? I have his name from a statement by one of the streetwalkers. So there's a lead we can follow, if we can find this woman by the name of Billie Jean. The pimp is known as Spike."

"Well, there's no way a hooker is going to climb into the car if I'm there, and chances are they'll recognize this ride as law enforcement." Beth shrugged, reached for a bottle of water, and screwed off the top. "I figure we split up. I'll go grab some clothes from Target and hit the streets. I'll attract attention from the girls. They don't appreciate others taking their spots. I'll see if I can locate Spike. He wouldn't be suspicious of me, and I know I'm older than most of his girls, but with enough makeup I can probably convince him to take me into his stable. So, we hit the stores first and then work out our plan."

Convinced Beth had lost her mind, Styles stared at her. "I'm not sending you out there without a wire and the chances of organizing that this late in the day are impossible. How the heck am I going to know if you're okay?"

"You won't, but if this guy is running a stable of underage girls, I'll need to get them out of there, so having you waiting in position with this big old sedan will be good enough." Beth smiled at him. "You don't have to worry about me, Styles. I'm a big girl."

He looked at the diminutive Beth Katz and shook his head. "So, you get them out of there and then what? All that will happen is he'll recruit another group. You know darn well there's a network of pedophiles out there who move kids around. Working the streets is the end of the road and where kids end up when their owners need a new toy. They don't care if the girls die, take their own lives, or overdose. They're just a commodity. Removing the girls from him won't solve the problem. You know that, right?" He started the engine and headed toward a shopping mall.

"I know this is just the tip of the iceberg, Styles." Beth

sipped her water and sighed. "It would take me maybe weeks, months, or years to surf the dark web to discover where and who these people are, but they're out there." She leaned back in her seat. "Right now, we save the ones we can and continue our work on the Pied Piper case. Once we have this guy, we can concentrate on hunting down the major players in this sex slave ring and bringing them to justice."

Styles nodded. "One case at a time. I know you want to save the kids, but right now taking down the Pied Piper is a priority. We know he'll strike again soon."

"Oh, we'll find him." Beth huffed out a long breath. "He's already made two mistakes, the two girls he abducted showing up alive. Well, for a time after he abducted them at least. This indicates he is holding the girls somewhere, and then moving them on." She shot a glance at him. "You know he'll never give up a name. He'll keep his secrets to the grave, but we'll stop him." She drank more water. "Then we'll go chase down everyone he associated with, and if he thinks they can hide on the dark web, he's mistaken."

Allowing her words to sink in, Styles stared at her. The dark web was a mystery to him. "So you see this pedophile or slaver ring as a large web of people with one fat spider sitting in the middle directing traffic?"

"I guess you could look at it that way." Beth smiled. "Unless you understand how to negotiate code streams and discover the dark web universe, that would be a good analogy. The dark web does spread out in countless strands of data. The problem is most of them go nowhere. This is where my expertise comes into play. I know my way around and I never give up."

Suddenly seeing Beth in a different light, he eyed her with curiosity. He'd heard she was like a dog with a bone. He nodded. "Finding the pimp might give us a clue we can use. If we take him in, we might be able to persuade him to give up his contact's information in a deal. I'm confident that together we can cut off at least one leg of the spider."

"Oh, trust me, when we do this, the moment I find the first leg I'll be squashing the whole spider." Beth grinned at him. "That spider is mine."

TWENTY-THREE

After gathering everything she needed, Beth dumped the shopping bags in the back of the sedan alongside Bear. She enjoyed this part of her work. The thrill of a dangerous mission made her feel alive. Although, joining the undercover unit had been a ploy to avoid attracting suspicion. She needed an excuse to explain her disguises and now they'd become a necessary part of her job, but being careful to never be perfect, like her alter ego, was the key. As the Tarot Killer, she became the person, but as the FBI undercover agent, her disguise was a simple facsimile.

She smiled at Styles. "I have everything I need."

"Good, I'll find a restaurant." He turned the vehicle around and headed downtown.

During the meal they scanned the case files, hunting down names they could use. As Billie Jean had mentioned the pimp by name, Beth would use her as a contact to get an introduction to Spike. She checked her watch and looked at Styles across the table. He looked weary and she hoped he wouldn't fall asleep when she needed him watching her back. "This could take hours, you know. These people all know each other, and I need a darn good cover story to get inside."

"Going undercover takes weeks of planning, listening devices, and a complete team of people watching your back." Styles turned his glass around in his long fingers and shook his head. "I'm going to be completely useless sitting down the block in a vehicle they'll make as soon as I stop at the curb." He blew out a long sigh. "Having me close by will only draw more attention to you, not me."

Shrugging, Beth pulled out her phone and scrolled through advertisements for rentals. "Look at this." She held up the screen. "Casual rentals—open twenty-four hours a day." She checked the location. "Drop me at the hotel and then go and pick up a van or something inconspicuous." She shrugged. "They have them available." At his pinched expression, she pulled out her credit card and handed it to him. "Put it on my card."

"That's not necessary. We have an expense account. I'll use mine." Styles pushed it back toward her. "Although, I'm not too sure we'll get the cost of everything you purchased at Target reimbursed."

Beth smiled at him. "Don't worry, I'll pay for them. Now go. I'll get dressed."

Later in the hotel room, Beth stared at her reflection in the mirror. She'd tucked her dark blonde hair under a platinum-blonde wig that hung down to her waist and had full bangs. Contacts had changed her blue eyes to bright green and she'd squeezed into a tight white elasticized top and a leather miniskirt. A pair of red stiletto heels completed her outfit. She'd added a few other accessories from the stash she'd hidden in her luggage. The dangly gold earrings were in fact lock picks and her belt, once unclasped, transformed into a garrote. She arranged the wig and pushed a pair of eight-inch long hatpins into each side. The decorated tops made them resemble a normal hair clip. She'd had these pins made especially from steel and kept the points deadly sharp. The brooch she attached to her top held a detachable shuriken. The Japanese throwing star was held in place with a magnet. She'd used this method of killing before and was an expert at throwing them. Going undercover to her was just like moving from one place to another, she'd done this so many times before as she stalked her victims. Over the years, she'd discovered that being prepared for anything and paying attention to details gave her the edge over anyone that she preyed upon.

The FBI agent side of her wanted to get the young girls in Spike's stable away without any bloodshed, but then there was Spike. They needed information from him to hunt down the ringleader of the operation supplying these kids, but the serial killer side of her needed to appease her dark side and remove the piece of trash from existence. She considered the problem and sighed. Spike was likely the end of the supply chain. Her dark side seeped into her consciousness in a whisper. It certainly had a convincing argument and she smiled in the mirror, seeing her other side reflected in her eyes. After all, what was the value of one piece of trash in a ton of garbage?

She picked up a small purse, carrying some of the same items she'd found in the purses of prostitutes she'd searched during raids. She'd aged the shoes and bag by rubbing them with a steel wool scrubber. Adding a spray of very cheap perfume, she slipped out of the door and knocked on Styles' room. As he opened the door, she smiled at him and gave him her little girl voice. "Ready to party?"

"Ah... I think you have the wrong room." Styles shut the door in her face.

Laughing, Beth hammered on the door. "Open up, Styles." When the door opened, Beth did a twirl. "I can't believe I fooled you."

"Beth?" Styles stared at her, his expression incredulous. "I would never have recognized you. You look like a kid and even your face shape is different." He looked closer. "Your eyes are emerald-green. How did you do this in such a short time?"

In her time in the FBI, Beth had used a number of half-truths to get by. She had, in fact, completed a special-effects makeup course, and many other useful courses to enable her to transform into different identities when the need arose. She'd passed as both male and female many a time and with her skill could change into a different person like a chameleon in a very short time. She considered her reply for a beat. "Oh, I was very involved in the drama society in my hometown. If I hadn't been so driven to join the FBI, I would have turned my sights toward being an actor."

"Well, you'll need all your skills to deceive Spike." Styles looked her up and down and then turned to grab his jacket. "I just hope he doesn't ask you for a demonstration." He told Bear to stay and shut the door before leading the way to the elevator. "Here, put my jacket around you before anyone sees you with me." He scowled at her grin. "You know darn well if it gets back to Lowe that I've had a hooker in my hotel room, it will get back to the director. What we're doing here tonight isn't something I want to explain. It goes against procedure putting you at risk like this."

Beth moved to the back of the elevator and handed him his jacket. "You go first and I'll meet you down the block. Where did you park the van?"

"Opposite the diner. I'll meet you there. I'll go inside and grab some coffee. It's going to be a long night." He gave her a searching look and shook his head. "I must be crazy agreeing to this plan."

Beth stuck one foot in the elevator door and counted to one hundred before following Styles out of the hotel. She found the van, a gray Ford Transit, suitable and nonthreatening, opened the passenger door, and slipped inside. When Styles joined her, she turned to him. "I have a burner phone. Give me yours and I'll put in the number. My name is Silver, so if you call, make like you're making a date with me in case anyone is listening. If I say I'm busy tonight, I'm fine. If I tell you to call back later, I need help. If I call you, come running." She took his phone and added the number to his contacts list. "I've checked out the area and there are alleyways all through. I figure if we take one of the side streets and you drop me at the opposite end of one of the alleyways, I'll be able to walk through and mingle with the other girls."

"I still think you're crazy." Styles headed toward the sleazy end of town. "How about here?" He indicated to a twenty-four-hour fast-food restaurant. "If I park here and make like I'm eating takeout, I won't look so conspicuous." He pointed to an alleyway. "That one there will come out in the right area. I checked on my phone and they all go right through on this block."

Beth slid out of the seat. "That works for me." She gave him a smile, tossed back her long hair, and falling into character, strutted across the road.

TWENTY-FOUR

The negative reception Beth received when she walked down the trash-laden sidewalk didn't surprise her. To the other women trying to turn a trick, she was invading their territory. After negotiating through the miasma of cheap perfume and rancid sweat, she tried without success to speak to a few of them. Ignoring the derogative threat-laced comments, she made her way across the road to a greasy spoon obviously used by the streetwalkers. She went to the counter and ordered coffee and then sat on one of the high stools, beside a young African American woman with needle track marks up each arm. She'd added these telltale signs to her own arms and the dark circles under each eye. She turned to the young woman and nodded but said nothing.

"Are you the new girl?" The woman gave her a lazy smile. "You know this is the end of the road, don't you?"

Beth shrugged. "Are you with Spike?"

"Me?" She laughed. "I'm way too old for his stable. No girl, I'm with Brutus."

Beth nodded slowly. "Is he here? Billie Jean called me and said he had an opening."

"You sure you want to be involved with Spike?" The woman blinked slowly as if trying to focus on her. "You do know his girls have got a best-by date and then they end up in the bay or in one of the dumpsters? I could speak to Brutus. You'd do better with him and he doesn't keep his girls locked up."

Thinking on her feet, Beth shook her head. "I have the feds after me. I need to be hidden for a while, maybe I could make a deal with him?"

"Spike?" The woman waved a hand dismissively. "Honey, he ain't gonna make any deals with you. He'll keep you working and high until you die." She indicated to the door. "There he is now. "Hey, Spike. Look here, some prime real estate just walked in looking for you."

Spike stood at least five-ten, a handsome solid brick wall of African American manhood. She turned to look at him under her lashes and waited for him to speak to her.

"You looking for me?" Spike moved his gaze slowly over her. "You look like a cop to me."

Beth lifted her gaze. "Do I? Well, I'd consider that a compliment. It would be good to be on the right side of the law for a change."

"Stand up." Spike moved closer. "If you're not a cop you'd allow me to search you, before we have any dialogue."

Sliding off the chair, Beth handed him her purse and waited while he checked her phone.

"You don't mind if I turn this off now do you?" He lifted out the tarot card and flipped it over in his fingers and then searched her face. "The Grim Reaper. I have a tattoo of him on my back. Now why do you carry that?"

Beth shrugged. "Some preacher gave it to me, to remind me that drugs kill or some shit." She wanted to grin. She'd never touched that card and now his fingerprints were all over it. "Keep it."

"I will." He slid it inside his jacket pocket and then turned back to her. "Lift up your arms." Spike did a very thorough body search and then stood back and nodded slowly. "Why do you want to speak to me?"

Beth took the phone from him and slid it back inside her purse. "I need to hide for a time. I mentioned it to Billie Jean and she said you had just lost one of your girls. I figured I would ask you if I could join your team for a couple of days, maybe fill in until you find another girl?"

"My team?" Spike flashed a white smile and scratched his cheek with one finger. "I noticed you have a bottle of liquid heroin in your purse, so why do you need me? I pay my girls in H."

Beth shrugged. "That won't last long and I'm desperate. I'll do anything to be off the streets right now." She shrugged and made to turn away. "Don't worry, I'll go and ask Brutus if he can help me."

"How old are you?" Spike grasped hold of her chin and turn her face from side to side. "You still look fresh but you're too old for my clients. They like them young, but I am a girl short, and they might just take you if I offer them a discount. Maybe if I turn down the lights in your room, you might fool them." He shook his head. "I have a reputation to uphold but you are kinda cute."

Avoiding the question, Beth smiled at him and wet her lips. "I'll make them happy. I always leave them wanting more. Trust me, no one leaves me disappointed."

"Okay, I'll give you one night's trial and that's only because I have a full house tonight. If they like you, we'll see what happens next." Spike grasped her by the arm and pushed her out the back door of the greasy spoon.

She stumbled down the alleyway tripping over garbage. Her heart raced as he pressed her against the wall and pulled a bunch of keys from his pocket to open a metal door. Pushed into a hallway with open doors leading to rooms each side, she tried to slow down to take in the group of men inside. She didn't have a chance to see more than a glimpse before he opened another door and thrust her down a flight of steps and into the cellar. A blast of cheap perfume and sweat hit her in a wave. She blinked at the brightly lit room divided into sections and each with its own door. At the top of each door was a window, and as she passed by, she could see young girls and their clients.

"This is your room. Sessions are timed at fifteen minutes max and then I give you ten minutes between clients to clean up. Make sure you look good. I have a reputation for clean merchandise." Spike grabbed her purse and rifled through it. "I'll keep the phone." He slipped it inside his pocket, opened a door, and waved her inside. "Welcome to Spike World."

The door clicked shut behind her and a key turned in the lock. There was no handle. She hadn't figured on being trapped. The lights inside dimmed and she could hear Spike walking away. The sound of sobbing came through the thin walls and Spike's footsteps stopped. A door opened and a shuffling sound came from the passage outside. Beth pressed her face to the window and stared at the young girl being dragged along by her hair. She flinched as Spike backhanded the girl across the face and then landed a punch to her belly. The girl doubled up and fell to her knees sobbing in pain.

"What's worse, him or me?" Spike dragged her up and held her nose to nose with him and then pointed to a man standing in the doorway. "You'll stop crying and tell him how much you love him. Hear?" His large hand went around her neck and he squeezed, lifting her to her toes. "Or we're gonna have a problem."

The girl's eyes bulged and her lips went blue. Her eyes swiveled toward him and she nodded. Mascara ran down her cheeks to mix with the tears. Spike dropped her and she fell to the floor gasping. He smiled at the man and then dragged her roughly to her feet and shoved her back inside the room. He turned to the man. "You wanted a fresh one. Some of them just need a little convincing, is all. I'll give you extra time with her tonight." He shrugged. "Next time she'll call you Daddy. If not, you'll get Delores for free."

"I'll take Delores now." The man wiped his mouth with the back of his hand. "I'll wait upstairs." He walked away pulling on his jacket.

"Okay, time is up, gentlemen." Spike peered through the windows and then opened the doors and glared in at the girls. "Clean yourselves up. We have a full house tonight." He followed the clients up the steps.

In a flash, Beth's dark side reared up, and the need to rid the world of men like Spike tore into her. Just how long had he been torturing young girls? What did he do with them when they became too old to please his clients? Did he sell them on or toss them into the bay? Rage tore into her and she bit the inside of her mouth so hard blood spilled over her tongue. Desperate to stop him, she took deep breaths. Losing control now would cost her and the girls their lives. Calming, she looked around the tiny room. Inside was a sink, a chest of drawers, paper towels, and a bed. On one side of the door was a red button, which she assumed was used when the clients wanted to leave. She sat on the edge of the bed to consider her situation. She could get out of the room easily enough using her lock picks but getting the girls out past the men and Spike would be difficult. She needed to come up with a plan. With ten minutes between clients, she at least had a chance to think. A buzzer sounded, which she assumed was the end of a session. What a strange way to run a brothel, but then it seemed a pedophile would do anything to gain access to children. Beth removed her earring and went to work on the lock. It opened in seconds and she replaced her earring and moved into the hallway. After checking each room, she opened the doors and beckoned the five girls into the hallway. Speaking to them in a group was a risk. If desperate enough, one of them could go straight to Spike and spill the beans. She looked at the desolate faces and took the risk. "Do you want to leave this place?"

To her surprise they all nodded in agreement, although they all wore the same vacant lost stare. It was as if they'd lost hope. She smiled at them. "If you do as I say, we can get out of here together."

"Spike will never let us go." One of the girls shook her head. "If he catches us trying to escape, he'll beat us and then with-hold the drugs until we're screaming."

Beth moved her gaze from one to the other. "He won't catch us. What we need to do is to clear the clients from upstairs. I figure he has a reputation for supplying the best girls, so he won't want to ruin that and we can use it to our advantage."

"How can we do that from down here?" The girl leaned sleepily against the wall.

Convinced she had a good idea, Beth smiled at them. "You must all get sick. You can pretend to be vomiting, can't you? He'll think he's given you something bad to eat or there's some-thing wrong with the drugs. He wouldn't risk sending down valuable clients when you're spewing." She looked at them again, trying to gauge if any of them would rebel against the idea. "Once we get rid of the clients, I'll deal with Spike."

"We're not going to get far on the streets dressed like this." The girl lifted her chin. "Someone else will grab us and we'll be in more trouble. At least we're inside here and not out on the sidewalk."

Trying to be calm and patient, Beth sighed. "You'll have to trust me, won't you? I can get you out into the alleyway. You turn right at the end of the alleyway and head for the fast-food restaurant. There's a gray van out front. The man inside is with me and will keep you safe. We'll help you get free of drugs and back with your families." She smiled at them. "I promise you'll be okay, but we all have to stick together. For this to work, everyone must get sick at the same time. The moment you hear the next clients arrive, fill your mouth with water and spew all over them. I figure that should have the right reaction and they'll hightail it out of here on the double." She waited until they all agreed, some even giggled. "Okay, get back to your rooms. Leave everything to me."

TWENTY-FIVE

When people make plans, something inevitably goes wrong, and Beth waited for something bad to happen. The girls were drug addicts and under the influence of heroin. They might panic, believing their source would be terminated if they left Spike. Stomach cramping with anticipation, and just waiting for someone to tell Spike she had a van waiting at the end of the alleyway, she sat on the bed. To her surprise, as the clients started filtering into the hallway, including the elderly man Spike had chosen for her, the sound of spewing came through the walls. She stood and looked at the man eyeing her with a lecherous grin.

"You're new, but I prefer my girls no older than twelve. You're way too old. I'll wait for one of the others." The man turned to go, one hand poised over the red button.

In a wave of disgust, Beth grabbed him by the hair, pulled him against her, and wrapped her hands around his head. He flapped at her and the stink of unwashed old man wafted into her nostrils. With one quick twist and a satisfying snap, he collapsed onto the floor without a sound. She stared down at him and smiled. "Well, I prefer my pedophiles dead."

Beth stepped over his twitching body and pressed the button. She could hear voices outside as Spike apologized to the clients and ushered them back up the stairs. She banged on the door and waited for him to return. When the door opened, she indicated with her thumb to the dead man lying in a pool of urine. "He died."

"Dammit, he's a judge and we needed him." He stared at the body. "Heart attack?"

Beth shrugged. "How should I know? He clutched his chest, peed himself, and fell down." She lifted her chin. "I know I'm drop-dead gorgeous but I didn't expect this on my first day."

"You're older than what he usually likes but attractive and sassy, but not hot enough to kill him." Spike blew out a sigh. "Dammit, with one girl down, I figured you'd be able to take up the slack, but now all the girls are sick. I can't just have you working with them all spewing close by. It's not good for business." He looked around as if trying to make up his mind. "I'll need to get him out of here without anyone seeing. He can't be found here and if you know what's best for you, you'll keep your mouth shut." Spike stared at the man, shaking his head. "I'll wait for the clients to leave and then bring my car around. I can't involve anyone else, so you need to help me get him into the trunk." He smiled at her. "I'll toss him in the bay"

Beth nodded. "Fine by me. I heard they pulled a girl's body out of the water That wasn't your missing girl, was it?"

"Scarlett?" Spike leaned over her, crowding her. "Who told you she was dead?"

Sitting on the edge of the bed and casually crossing her legs, Beth smiled at him. "Word gets around, and one of my johns mentioned you had a girl called Scarlett here. She was a favorite but then went missing a couple of days ago, so I assumed it was her. He also told me about your setup and that's when I asked Billie Jean where I could find you."

"Billy Jean needs to keep her mouth shut." Spike straight-ened. "What else did she tell you?"

Beth chuckled. "I hear lots of things, like who supplies the young ones. It's a guy they call the Pied Piper, right?"

"Nah, never heard of him." Spike shook his head. "People who know me know I don't do street deals. The only way to get clean merchandise is from an auction on the net." He stared down at the dead body. "Man, that guy's already stinking out the place. My Lincoln is in a parking garage. I'll be back in fifteen minutes." He left the room shutting the door behind him.

Being able to keep time in her head, Beth waited for the footsteps to recede and attacked the lock again. Heart racing, she crept to the top of the steps, eased open the door a crack, and peered into the hallway. She could hear Spike explaining to his clients that the girls had all come down with something, and as soon as they'd stop puking, he would let everyone know. He'd offered them a discount to smooth things over. As if sensing her looking at him, Spike suddenly turned, but Beth anticipated his move and shut the door softly. She moved silently down the steps unlocking the doors to the girls' rooms as she went along the passageway. "Turn off your lights so Spike can't see you're missing. Grab a blanket from the bed and wrap it around you. You'll be running for your lives, so wear something sensible on your feet or nothing."

She looked at the assembled group of five wide-eyed girls. "Remember to creep out, one at a time. The doors to the rooms along the passageway are all open, if you hear someone coming, get into the room and hide. There are plenty of sofas in there. Keep out of sight and wait for my command to move on."

"What happens if Spike comes back?" One of the girls stared at her with dead eyes.

So many times, Beth had seen that pathetic drug-induced state. It wouldn't be long before the girl would need medication.

"You hide in the shadows by the dumpsters. You must get to the van, so don't stop for anything. Just get the heck out of here."

A wave of panic gripped her when she heard a voice coming from one of the rooms. Beth lowered her voice to a whisper. "I hear someone."

"It's the parrot." The girl with the dead eyes blinked at her. "He's a pet. Spike walks around with him on his shoulder."

Beth shook one girl to get her attention. "When you're all safe. Tell the man in the van to wait at least one hour before he comes looking for me, okay?" She glared at the girl. "One hour, got it. No earlier or we won't catch Spike. Tell him that, okay?"

"Sure, one hour." The girl pulled a blanket around her and joined the others.

Taking a deep breath and hoping Styles was still waiting inside the van, Beth waved them up the steps one at a time, paused at the door, and then sent them running outside and along the alleyway. The clock inside her head was telling her time was running out fast before Spike returned, and the girls were moving slower than she anticipated. Her heart missed a beat each time a set of headlights flashed past the entrance to the alleyway. She had no idea which way he would be coming and if he caught sight of the girls running across the road and gave chase, Styles would arrest him. She figured, by using Spike's estimation of the time it would take him to bring the car around, she had about seven minutes remaining. Dashing back along the passageway, she checked each room. Out the back of one was a kitchen and this led to a bedroom obviously used by Spike. His cheap cologne still polluted the air. She grabbed a towel and used it to prevent leaving prints. Flinging open doors and searching drawers until she found a box of latex gloves. She pulled them on and ran through the house using the cloth to remove her fingerprints from anything she'd touched. Bolting back down the stairs, she reached the door to her room just when the metal outside door clanged shut.

Stepping inside, she avoided the body on the floor, peeled off the gloves, and tossed them into the garbage and then pushed the towel under her mattress. Nervous anticipation shivered through her as footsteps sounded on the steps. The next moment the door opened, and Spike filled the space. He swore and then covered his face with one hand. She looked up at him. "I hope you have gloves. I'm not getting his stink all over my hands."

"There's a ton of gloves in the top drawer of the dresser." He gave her a knowing smile. "I'm sure you'll find other uses for them." He pushed the door wide open and attached a clip to hold it.

Keeping a wary eye on him, Beth turned away and using her shirt opened the drawer. She gloved up and spun back, using one hip to close the drawer, and then looked at him. "Okay, I'm ready. What do you want me to do?"

"Go ahead of me and open the doors. Leave the front door open. I'll need to go back inside before we leave." He tossed her his car keys. "Use the fob to open the trunk."

As he hoisted the man easily over one shoulder and indicated for her to walk in front of him, it was obvious he didn't need her help. She caught something in his eyes that sent up a red flag. It was a flash of an expression, a decision made, but it hadn't slipped past her. She might be useful in helping him remove the body, but she'd seen that look before. The calculated sidelong look meant he'd already made plans for her. He considered her to be a witness he couldn't risk leaving behind and she'd be going into the bay alongside the judge.

TWENTY-SIX

Moving up the stairs, Beth pulled open the door and stood to one side. She needed information and she needed it fast. The girls should be with Styles now, but that didn't mean he wouldn't be keeping a close eye on the alleyway waiting for her to return. Having him so close was cramping her style. He was unpredictable and could come to the rescue at any minute—but would he risk leaving the girls alone in the van unprotected? He did have a duty of care to them and what if he called in backup? Mind reeling with different possible outcomes of her current situation, she had no choice but to play the cards as they fell.

Beth attempted to act jittery to give Spike the impression of being a drug addict close to needing a fix. "There will be people all over the streets. How do you intend to drop him into the bay without anyone seeing?" She moved ahead of him along the passageway. "I'm in enough trouble with the cops as it is. I can't be seen helping you do this."

"You won't be seen. I'm not using the bridge. I'll head alongside the bay to a boat ramp not far from here and at this time of year the mist is heavy coming from the water. I'll back down the ramp, pop the trunk, and we'll haul him into the water. He'll

float away on the tide. It will look like he fell from the shore."
He grunted and hoisted the guy more firmly over his shoulder.
"If the cops do a drive-by, we'll just act like a couple making out.
Worst-case scenario, they'll tell us to move on." His mouth
turned down in disgust. "Can't you go any faster? He's dripping
stink all over the carpet."

The heavy metal door loomed up in front of Beth and she
heaved it open, hoping not to find San Francisco's finest waiting
outside in the alleyway. She poked her head around the door
and looked both ways. Her heart missed a beat seeing the direction Spike had pointed his Lincoln. He must have driven right
past the girls. How he'd missed seeing them escape was close to
a miracle. She fumbled with the car keys, but eventually the
trunk popped open. The inside was spacious, more than big
enough for two bodies. A mingled rush of fear and thrill surged
through her as she allowed her dark side to rise. She took a step
toward Spike as he dropped the man inside the trunk and bent
low at the waist to roll him toward the back. As if between
heartbeats, Beth pulled one of the hatpins from her hair, lunged
forward, and drove it deep into Spike's ear.

He gasped in pain but didn't go down and lurched forward
deeper into the trunk. Why wasn't he dead? She glanced both
ways along the alleyway as he thrashed about like a zombie half
in and half out of the trunk. Without a second thought, Beth
detached the Japanese throwing star. In one swift movement,
she grabbed his hair, sliced his carotid artery, and pressed his
head hard against the other man's body to prevent splash back.
She ripped out the hatpin and waited precious seconds for
Spike's body to stop fighting the inevitable, and then using
adrenalin-fed strength, lifted his legs into the trunk and, grabbing up the throwing star, slammed the lid.

Time was moving so fast she could hear it counting down in
her head. It wouldn't be long before time ran out and Styles
called in the troops. Breathing heavily, she turned and ran back

inside, heading straight for the kitchen and to the bottle of bleach she recalled sitting under the counter. She tossed the hat pin and star into the sink, poured bleach all over them and then hightailed it back to her room. She collected her purse, dragged the towel from under the mattress, and escaped back upstairs. After frantically rinsing the bleach from her weapons, she put them back in place and then dashed into Spike's bedroom and grabbed his laptop. Running, she headed back to the vehicle, closing the door behind her.

Ticktock, ticktock, the clock inside her head was counting down the minutes. She laid the laptop on the seat and slid behind the wheel. Moments later, she was driving alongside the bay searching for the boat ramp in the heavy mist. The sign loomed up and she turned onto the top of the boat ramp, keeping the Lincoln facing the water. She climbed out and wiped down the seat, glad she was still wearing the latex gloves. Panic gripped her as the muffled sound of a ringtone cut through the silence of the night. In that second, the horrible realization hit her that her burner phone was still inside Spike's pocket with Styles' phone number in the contacts. Time was counting down so fast, and she had to get back to Styles. She couldn't be found with two dead bodies, especially as Spike had her tarot card in his pocket.

Wrenching the car keys from the ignition, she ran back to open the trunk. The smell of congealing blood and pee hit her in a wave of stench. Frantic, she fumbled through Spike's pockets and dragged out her phone. She slammed shut the trunk and answered the call. "I'm safe. I ran away and hid. Right now, I'm between blocks and I can't see any street signs. I'll need to keep moving. I'll call you as soon as I discover where I am and you can come get me."

"Okay. We need to get these girls somewhere safe. They're freaking out." Styles sounded agitated. *"Have you worked out a plan to explain them? We could both lose our jobs over this."*

Beth ran back to the driver's open door. "Yeah, don't worry. Everything will be fine. I'll speak to them. Gotta go." She disconnected.

She'd worry about explanations later. Leaning into the Lincoln, she started the engine, put the vehicle into drive, gabbed the laptop and her purse, and then stood back as the vehicle crawled slowly down the ramp increasing speed until it plopped into the bay. It rode the current before tipping to one side. The water flowed through the open windows and claimed its prize. Beth sighed with relief as the Lincoln sank slowly, vanishing in the mist.

She ripped off her gloves, pushed her phone inside her purse, and tucked the laptop under one arm. She took off at a run, sprinting to the entrance of the first alleyway, and tossed the gloves into a dumpster. Rounding the corner, she encountered a group of men leaving a club and smelling strongly of alcohol. All thought she was available to party and grabbed at her. To avoid them, she dashed across the road, ignoring the blasts of car horns as vehicles barely missed her. Ahead, she made out the fast-food restaurant and the gray van parked outside. Picking up her pace she ran toward it.

Breathless, she heaved open the door and fell inside. She grinned at Styles, who glared back at her. "What's up? I made it with five minutes to spare." She waved the laptop at him. "This could hold a goldmine of information."

"Dammit, Beth. You nearly got killed dodging the traffic." Styles shook his head. "I'm responsible for you."

Beth barked a laugh. "No, you're not. I'm responsible for me. Let's make that clear from the get-go. I don't need a nurse-maid and I can take care of myself." She took the burner phone from her purse, removed the SIM, and tossed the phone out of the window. "We don't need to involve the office in this case. None of these girls are from our Pied Piper missing persons files. Pull over in that parking lot so I can talk to them. I suggest you contact the local PD and speak to one of the detectives. Tell him by accident we stumbled onto a pedophile prostitution ring and they can take the credit because we're on another case. One we can't discuss with them at this time."

"You're joking, right?" Styles gave her an incredulous book. "They're never gonna buy that story and that darn laptop won't be admissible in court. You didn't have a search warrant."

Beth smiled at him. "The laptop isn't for them, it's for me. No one in the local PD will be able to trace the players involved. It might be one part of a jigsaw puzzle I need to solve a case in the future. These rings go deep and I'll be aiming for the kingpin, but right now we need to catch the Pied Piper."

"I'm sitting in a van with five kidnapped underage girls." Styles gave her a glare to strip paint. "I fed them but they're all strung out on heroin and will need a fix soon. The idea the local PD will just take them no questions asked is ludicrous."

Grabbing a bottle of water from the console, Beth drank thirstily and then looked at him. "Oh, they will. The local detectives will want to roll in the glory of breaking a case as big as this one. They'll get a promotion for getting all these missing kids back to their parents. The press will eat it up and they'll be heroes. Don't worry, I have a plan. We'll drop the girls in a safe place and get the hell out of Dodge. One thing for darn sure, I need a long hot shower. My skin is crawling just being inside that place."

"I'm not doing it." Styles shook his head. "You should know the local cops hate us being involved and surely the lack of assistance from the bureau in this area tells you they don't want us on their turf. Do you honestly believe we can trust them or the cops not to rat on us? This was an unsanctioned bust."

Leaning back in her seat and staring at the roof of the van for some minutes, Beth nodded. "Okay, drop me at a pay phone. I'll call the cops and tell them there's a group of very young girls standing on a corner wrapped in blankets and hardly anything else. They look like they're in big trouble. We'll hang around for a while to make sure they're okay. I'll set up a story with the girls and tell them that we need them to keep us out of it."

"You figure that will work? We can trust them?" Styles rubbed a hand down his face. "Man, I've crossed the line a few times myself, but this is obliterating it."

Beth climbed out of the cab and slid open the side door of the van. The girls all looked at her, wide-eyed and terrified. She moved her gaze from one to the other. "We're undercover agents. You do understand what that means, right?" She waited as they all nodded. "So, if the bad guys or anyone else, including the cops, finds out who we are, we'll end up dead. We want to keep getting girls like you out of trouble, so we never existed, okay? I need all of you to swear you'll keep our secret."

"So, what do we say to the cops?" One girl held up a hand as if she were in the classroom.

Anger hit Beth in waves. It was as if time had stopped for these children the moment they were taken. Their childhood ripped away and replaced by horrific memories. She swallowed hard, trying to regain control of the need to kill each and every one of the men who'd visited the brothel. She pointed to the girl who seemed to be speaking for them all. "You tell the cops that one of your clients left the door open. When Spike was busy, you opened the doors for the others and escaped. You ran into the street and waved down a patrol car and the cops took you to the police station."

"But that didn't happen, did it?" The girl looked at her with narrowed eyes. "There was no police cruiser. They'll punish us for telling lies."

Beth let out a long sigh. "Don't worry, they won't punish you. They'll help you and that will happen. We'll call the cops and they'll send a cruiser to get you so you can wave it down. Tell them the story. When they ask you to show them the alleyway, say it's on Beal between blocks six and seven. They'll go and arrest Spike. You can tell them everything that happened apart from our involvement, all about Spike and the men who came to visit you, and they'll put them in jail. We're going to trust you with our lives. Will you promise to keep our secret?" She looked from one girl to the other. "If you break your promise, girls like you will die in places much worse than Spike's. It's your chance to set them free. I need your word. Cross your heart and hope to die."

When they all agreed, Beth heaved a sigh of relief and headed back to Styles. She climbed into the front of the van. "Okay, it's all good. We'll need a burner phone."

TWENTY-SEVEN

Unsure why he'd agreed to this half-brained idea, Styles cruised the streets looking for a store to purchase a burner phone. Eventually they found a store and Beth purchased one and then walked to the entrance of a nearby Chinese restaurant to make the call. The sidewalk was in shadows and the stink of seven-day-old garbage spilled from the dumpsters in the alleyways. At her signal, he ushered the girls out of the van and into the entrance of the Chinese restaurant. The place was in darkness and offered the girls a modicum of security. After Beth had given them final instructions, they drove some ways away and parked out of sight. Concerned for the girls' safety, Styles drummed his fingers on the steering wheel and then looked at Beth. "This is a bad neighborhood. I figure we should get closer, just in case something happens. Those girls have been through so much. If they get caught up with a gang, it would be like jumping from the frying pan into the fire."

"Sure." Beth grinned at him. "Strut when you walk beside me, and people will think you're my pimp."

Styles shook his head slowly and slid out from behind the wheel. "This is why I prefer to work alone."

"You're no fun at all." Beth walked away with an exaggerated wiggle and then turned and blew him a kiss.

The city was busy, with the sounds of emergency vehicles filtering through the traffic noise, but in the distance the sound of a police cruiser's siren cut through the night. "Hey, we need to find a place to hide or we'll be hauled downtown to answer questions."

"We can watch from here." Beth disappeared into the shadows.

Minutes later, a cruiser arrived containing two women police officers. They spoke to the girls at some length and soon after a support vehicle arrived to take them away. Styles heaved a sigh of relief. "We need to get out of here. Over the stink of the garbage I can smell drugs. We're probably close to a flophouse and that's not a place I want to be right now."

"Ah... more like a crack house." Beth indicated behind him. "They don't look too happy."

Turning his head slowly, Styles took in the threat. Four men had filtered out from a doorway and stood in a semicircle around them. They were all dressed in the same baggy black jeans, T-shirts, and various jackets. He had little doubt that they all carried concealed weapons. He dropped his voice to just above a whisper. "I'm sure glad I left my cred pack at the hotel. I don't figure they would enjoy having the FBI on their turf."

He grabbed Beth by the arm and tugged her toward the street. If he made like he'd found one of his girls in the wrong place, they might just be able to walk out of this situation. As if on cue, Beth turned on him.

"It's not my fault. That guy just pushed me out of his vehicle. He has my phone. I couldn't call you." Beth actually appeared to be afraid of him. "He took my purse, so I can't give you what I don't have."

"Hey, little lady." One of the men, with a dragon tattoo running down his neck, came closer and his gaze moved up and down her as if he was purchasing livestock. "If you don't wanna go with him, our crib is close by."

"I'm fine." Beth smoothed her hair. "It's a misunderstanding, is all."

Styles pushed her behind him. "Do we have a problem?"

"That depends on how much bread you have on you, man." Dragon Tattoo pulled out a pistol from his jacket and aimed it in a slack hand. "Empty your pockets."

Recognizing the pocket pistol as a Ruger LCP II, accurate at small distances, Styles dropped his hands, keeping his arms relaxed and hands in sight. They hadn't noticed he was carrying, a fatal mistake if he'd planned on taking them all down, but he figured he could negotiate them out of the situation. "You don't really figure I'm stupid enough to carry cash in this town, do you?" He tipped his head toward Beth and smiled. "We're all businessmen here. I don't want any trouble with you, I just want to take my girl back to her corner, is all. She's not earning while she's standing around doing nothing."

"Well then maybe we should charge a release fee." Dragon Tattoo smiled, and his gold teeth glistened in the street light. "We'll take it in trade." He snorted. "You can wait out here in the alleyway until we're done."

During the conversation, Styles was taking small steps toward the street. In an alleyway surrounded by four men, all presumably armed, they didn't stand a chance, but out on the sidewalk both of them would have room to move. He could sense Beth behind him, she'd moved to his left-hand side and was continuing to move away, but was doing it so skillfully no one would have noticed. The way the man was waving the gun around, not aiming, just using it to gesture with, he didn't consider him too much of a threat. It was obvious they'd been sampling their own product and even if he took the trouble to aim, he'd miss. Giving what he hoped was a nonchalant shrug, he shook his head. "That's not going to happen. I have a reputation to uphold. All my girls are clean and ten minutes alone with you would shoot that to hell."

"You sayin' we're dirty?" Dragon Tattoo sneered at him.

Styles grinned. "If the shoe fits."

"Maybe someone needs to teach you who's the boss around here." Dragon Tattoo oozed menace and took a few steps closer toward him. "There's four of us. We don't need permission to take your girl. We take what we want. This is our turf."

Four guys high on crack would be unpredictable and if Dragon Tattoo fired at close range, it would be curtains for him and a long painful death for Beth. If she had any sense, she'd run as soon as he landed the first punch—he wouldn't draw down on them, not with his service pistol. Killing them would mean they'd be stuck under a mountain of paperwork for a week. He flicked her a glance. She'd removed her shoes and was assessing the situation. Relaxing, he sucked in a deep breath and blew it out slowly. His attention moved from the waving pistol to the man's eyes. The one thing that Styles had learned from a young age was that in a street fight you never allow your opponent the opportunity to strike first.

He took one step forward and, taking the weight on the ball of his left foot, brought up his right boot between the man's legs. As Dragon Tattoo buckled over, he kneed him in the face and then snatched the pistol from his hand and tossed it to Beth. She would have his back. As the other members of the group blindly searched for their weapons, he spun and landed a roundhouse punch to the second man's kidney, danced two steps to the left, and brought his boot down hard on the third man's knee. Three down—one out cold, two writhing in agony—one to go. The fourth guy was heading toward Beth, but she had him covered. Styles aimed kicks to his attackers' heads, and they stopped complaining. He turned at the sound of a body hitting the sidewalk. A grunt came from his left as Beth pulled the heel of her stiletto from the temple of the fourth man, and calmly replaced the shoe on her foot.

Styles gloved up and then bent to collect the weapons. He stripped them and tossed them into various dumpsters. He walked back to Beth and stared at the man crumpled at her feet. "You could have killed him doing that. What were you thinking?"

"I didn't need to think about it at all. He was a threat that needed to be dealt with and I used the appropriate force to take him down before he killed you." Beth stared at him intently. "If I'd shot him at close range, he'd be dead for sure. I figure, worst-case scenario, he'll just have a bad headache for a few days." She leaned against the wall exhaling a long sigh. "I didn't hit him hard enough to kill him." She folded her arms across her chest and glared at him. "And yes, before you ask, I do know the difference." Annoyance creased her face. "You know, you weren't exactly gentle with them either." She indicated to the men littering the alleyway.

Keeping his calm wasn't easy but Styles sucked in a breath and shrugged. "That was necessary. Four on two." When she ignored him and walked away, heading toward an open door, he followed. "Where the heck are you going?"

"I'm not done here." Beth held the pistol out in front of her and approached the door. "FBI, hit the ground, hands on your heads."

Drawing his weapon, Styles pressed his back to the wall and peeked around the door. "I don't see anyone." Scanning the room, he followed Beth inside the small brick storage space and gagged at the stench of unwashed bodies, urine, and drugs. "What are you doing now? We need to get out of here."

"Shutting down their operation." Beth smiled at him and ran a finger over the stacks of bills neatly lined up on a table, fresh from a counting machine and secured with rubber bands. "Looks like this is where they count the street takings and distribute the drugs. Look at the bottles over there. They supply the cooks with everything they need. They run the whole show from here."

Styles moved his attention over the ton of greasy bills of all denominations sitting in a pile in the middle of the table waiting to be counted. On another table a stash of drugs, broken into neat packages ready for sale on the streets. "We can't call this in, not without explaining why we're here."

He stared at her in disbelief as she pushed the small pistol into her belt and casually tossed him a wad of one-hundred-dollar bills, followed by another. She tucked two similar stacks under her arm and smiled at him. "Untraceable cash. Don't come over all righteous with me. I'm not asking you to keep it. We'll drop it by a church or shelter. It would be a shame to burn all of it, wouldn't it, when people are in need? I'll burn the pile on the table. They're mostly ones and fives."

Discovering Beth was slightly off center in her way of doing things was one thing, but taking money from the proceeds of crime, hit rock bottom in his book, and it was removing evidence. Styles swallowed hard. "No way. We'll make an anonymous call like before." He stared at the bundles of bills in his hands and then lifted his gaze back to her. "You can't burn it." He waved a hand toward the chemicals. "A fire will blow everything sky high."

"That's the idea." Beth shrugged. "Do you know how many lives we'll save by destroying this place?"

Before he could blink, Beth had taken a Zippo from the table and set fire to the pile of wrinkled dirty bills. He spun her to face him. "Have you lost your mind?"

"I don't want the money for myself, Styles, and I'm not gonna leave it for the drug lords when a shelter could put it to good use." The firelight glistened in her eyes as she looked up at him, seemingly oblivious to the fire now licking the walls. "One thing I'm not is dishonest. This"— she waved at the fast-igniting room—"is justice. Nipping them in the bud by destroying their distribution center is the only way to deal with these vermin." She pushed him toward the door as flames crackled behind her and thick black smoke rose up like an evil entity waiting to pounce. "I suggest you start running before the heat breaks those bottles of chemicals." She edged toward the door. "You know as well as I do that taking those guys into custody won't solve the problem." She ran down the alleyway, stepping over the still-unconscious bodies on the ground. "They'll believe this was a takedown by a rival gang or someone higher up the food chain. They'll probably believe they were lucky to get away with their lives."

The next second, an explosion rocked the night, blowing a hole in the roof of the drug den. An orange mushroom cloud whooshed into the moonless sky and a wave of sizzling heat licked their backs just before the concussive force tossed them like fall leaves in the breeze and they tumbled across the black-top. Styles landed on his back and Beth fell on top of him, forcing the air from his lungs. He lay stunned for a few seconds, but Beth staggered to her feet, collected her shoes, and the wads of bills, and then as if mesmerized, turned to look at the leaping flames. Gasping air into painful lungs, Styles stood as debris rained down on them in flaming pinwheels. "Beth, we need to get out of here." When she didn't respond, he grabbed her arm and, dragging her behind him, ran along the middle of the blacktop toward the van. "Go, go, go."

He slowed as the van came into sight and turned to find her smiling. Conflicted, he just stared at her. Part of him believed she was the bravest woman he'd ever met, and the other part was annoyed by her unconventional behavior. "Jeez, Beth, what happened tonight makes us worse than the bad guys. If someone made us running away, we're in big trouble." He glanced over his shoulder, searching the street for CCTV cameras but found none.

"As if anyone in this neighborhood would be running to the cops to rat on those lowlifes or risk retribution by a drug lord." Beth ran alongside him, with her heels click-clacking on the blacktop, seemingly oblivious to the flaming wood chips falling around her like spent fireworks. "By the way, there's nothing in our rule book about what you did back there either, or the fact that you denied them duty of care by leaving them bleeding on the sidewalk, when you knew darn well the place was going to explode. Seems to me you're the pot calling the kettle black."

Styles climbed into the van and glared at her. "I didn't kill them, did I? Although the jury is out on the guy you hit with your stiletto." He shook his head slowly. "Okay, okay, don't look at me like that. I do see your point but I don't necessarily agree with it. This is why I'm not a city cop. Sometimes, it's necessary to bend the rules to avoid complications, such as gunfights. Most of the guys in Rattlesnake Creek understand street justice. If the sheriff isn't around to deal with them, I follow my own rules." He sped off toward their hotel.

"So do I." Beth tightened her seatbelt. "And like it or not, you'll just have to get used to it."

TWENTY-EIGHT

It was the early hours of the morning by the time Beth made her way inside the hotel and went to her room, leaving Styles to return the van. In the distance she could hear sirens blaring as fire trucks rushed toward the alleyway. Unconcerned, she pushed her disguise into a garbage bag and stuffed it into her luggage. She'd burn it when she returned to Rattlesnake Creek. Leaving evidence behind wasn't in her game plan. She'd showered and pulled on PJs when a soft knock came on her door and she peered through the peephole to find Styles in the hallway. She opened the door to let him inside. "What's the plan?"

"What do you mean by 'what's the plan'?" Styles dashed a hand through his hair and then paced up and down the room. "In the space of six hours on the job with you, I have about twenty grand of illegal drug money in my room, four injured men, and an out-of-control fire is raging downtown. I'm not stupid, Beth. Bending the rules is one thing but what happened tonight is beyond reckless."

As far as Beth was concerned, everything had gone as planned and the drug bust had been a bonus. "I figure you need to calm down and take a breath. You're looking kind of intimidating right now."

"Well, I figure I'll calm down when you come clean about what really happened tonight." He stopped walking in front of her and stared her down. "I was watching that alleyway the entire time. The girls had barely climbed inside the van when a Lincoln came out of the parking garage and headed past me and down the alley. One of them told me that was Spike's sedan and he was their pimp out looking for them. They were terrified of him. Now one thing is for darn sure: that Lincoln never came back out of the alleyway."

Shaking her head, Beth lifted her chin. "Man, you are so intense." She gave him an outline of her plan to remove the clients and get Spike alone, but from Styles' expression, he wasn't buying a word of it.

"Now don't try and tell me nothing happened in there." He pointed a finger at her. "You had marks all over the front of your shirt."

Surprised by his astuteness, Beth sat on the edge of the sofa and raised one eyebrow. She'd just adjust the truth a little. "Spike took my phone and locked me inside what could only be described as a cubicle, which was opened from the outside. All the girls were kept in the same tiny rooms, where they serviced their clients. They sent me an old man and he got angry because I wasn't twelve. I mean like red in the face and raving on about him being a judge and how much Spike owed him. Next thing I know, he gripped his chest and dropped dead." She sighed. "It was no big deal."

"You think? He was a judge!" Styles reeled back and his Adam's apple bobbed as he registered what she had said. "What did you do?"

Surprised by his reaction, Beth shook her head. "I called Spike, and he took him away, which is just as well. He was stinking up the place. I helped him lift him out of my room, is all."

"Right." Styles didn't look convinced. "So, what did Spike do about that? I don't recall seeing the paramedics arriving."

Leaning back in the chair and stifling a yawn, Beth shook her head. "He wouldn't have risked anyone seeing his setup, would he? His only concern was getting rid of the body as soon as possible. He mentioned dumping the judge into the bay, so we can assume Spike disposes of bodies there. He was very distracted, trying to work out a way of getting the judge out of the house without anyone seeing him, so I pushed a little harder, and discovered he gets his girls from an auction on the net, so the dark web. He denied knowing the Pied Piper. He guessed he was a pimp on the street." She met his hard gaze with a smile. "That's why I took his laptop."

"Seems to me that you're leaving out a large hunk of this story." Styles rubbed the back of his neck. "You saying that Spike dumped the judge in the bay" He narrowed his eyes at her. "How did he get him out of the house without being noticed?"

Needing to keep the truth of her involvement to herself, Beth shrugged. "Look, I don't know for sure what he did with him. I was locked in a room, remember? There were clients there. I only caught a glimpse of one at the top of the stairs. They held open the door for Spike when he carried the judge out of the cellar. That was the last time I saw Spike. His vehicle wasn't in the alleyway when I left. There are two ends to the alleyway. If you saw him go in that way, he must have driven out toward the bay. The place was deserted when I came out." She stared at Styles. "Look, you knew at the get-go that someone was going down tonight. I figured it would be Spike, but it was lucky the judge collapsed because, when Spike left, I had the chance to get the girls out. How else do you figure I freed the girls from that hellhole?" She stared at him. "You know darn well we weren't going by the book on this one, and if you believe it will come back on us, you're mistaken. Nobody knows I went there. I was wearing a disguise and left no trace of me behind. Trust me, we won't get any blowback on this. As far as the local bureau is concerned, we came here to collect the body of a victim and take it to the ME in Black Rock Falls." She held out her hands wide. "If anyone at the hotel desk did notice our coming and going, they'd say that after dinner I came back and never left my room. No one was on the desk when I returned and there are no cameras in this hotel. Trust me, I've checked it out."

"It seems I'll be in a world of trouble if I report this incident." Styles stood in the middle of the room staring into space. "What I don't understand is how you can sit there looking so calm, after watching a judge die, attacking a guy in the alleyway, and setting fire to a crack house." He sighed. "Is this the lack of empathy Mac mentioned in your report?"

Beth gave him an incredulous stare. "Am I sorry a judge that not only protects pedophiles but indulges himself to the extreme died? No, I'm not, and before you ask about all the other stuff, yeah, I would do it again in a heartbeat." She shook her head slowly, her eyes fixed on his face. "After seeing you administer street justice in town the other night, I believed you and I were on the same wavelength when it came to what's right and wrong." She stood to face him. "It's fortunate the world is free of that monster because, as sure as heck, he'd never have been charged. Trust me, predators are in every walk of life and they protect each other. I wager if we investigated his cases involving pedophiles, we'd discover he allowed most of them to walk."

"I hate to say this, but as much as the cop in me is screaming injustice, I happen to agree with you." Styles rubbed both hands down his face. "Get some sleep. Order room service for breakfast. I'll meet you downstairs at seven-thirty and we'll grab a cab back to the airport. I want to be as far away as possible when the shit hits the fan." He turned to go and then stopped and looked back at her. "Tonight never happened and we're donating the cash to the church in Black Rock Falls. The father there runs homeless shelters." He waved a hand around the room. "We might be safe talking here, but we never know who is listening at the office." He glanced down at the bag of clothes beside the door, hair from the wig sticking out of the top of the bag. "Wrap your disguise better. We don't want anyone seeing it. There's an incinerator in our building. It's there for destroying the protective gear we wear on crime scenes. You can burn it when we get back to the office. It's too risky leaving it here."

An incinerator? This must be my lucky day. Beth nodded. "That works for me." She flopped back down on the sofa as he closed the door behind him.

It had surprised her that Styles had accepted her story about the judge without too much of an argument. Telling him the judge had died, even if she'd bent the truth some, was important because sooner or later he'd show up and questions would be asked. Beth stared at the door and shook her head. *What is your angle, Styles?* If he figured he could give her enough rope to hang herself, he was very mistaken. She'd feed her rope out very slowly, giving him tidbits and waiting for a reaction. To be honest, she didn't need to trust anyone, but working this close, it had become a necessity. Being comfortable alone worked for her, but for some reason, not one she understood yet, she kind of liked Styles.

TWENTY-NINE

SATURDAY

Black Rock Falls, Montana

The midday sun reflected on the rivers and lakes like a million diamonds as Styles pointed the chopper toward Black Rock Falls. The far-spreading forests never ceased to amaze him. The scenery in this area was breathtaking and beside him it was obvious that Beth was enjoying the view. She hadn't said more than a few words since they left the stopover for refueling and it had given him time to think over what she had told him about the night before. She was indeed an unusual woman. In fact, he'd never met anyone quite like her before. In the back of his mind, he had concerns that she'd completed a dangerous mission without batting an eyelid. Her lack of emotion must be the same problem that had worried Mac, although he regarded her lack of feeling a little differently, having seen the same in soldiers under his command during many tours of duty. It was rare for a soldier to think twice about killing the enemy when under fire. It was a fight for survival, and if Beth used the same method as a coping tool to endure the pressure of her experiences on the job, it was something he could understand.

In her opinion, she'd taken the only option available by removing the girls from a dangerous situation. He'd asked himself if he would have done in the same situation. The answer was in the affirmative, but he'd have included the incident in his report. He had to admit, many times he'd used street justice to deal with a problem and just walked away, leaving broken bodies in his wake. It had been the best solution at the time, and he guessed her reason to withhold the information was probably to protect him, as he'd allowed her to go undercover without backup. He flicked a glance toward her, seeing her calm and serene as if the last few days hadn't happened. She didn't seem to have any problems whatsoever and carried on as normal after an extremely stressful situation. He rubbed the scar on his chin. At first, he'd believed she would be a liability, but maybe she would become the asset he hadn't expected.

The outskirts of a town came into view. A small number of ranches spread out across the lowlands, and as they got closer to the center of town, habitation was spreading in all directions. Stores lined the main street from one end to the other, and prosperity was obvious by the hustle and bustle around the town center. He took the chopper in a full circle and passed over the hospital, the college, and the high school before the large redbrick building came into view with a helipad on the roof with a clearly visible large white stenciled *ME*. There were three chopper bays. He slowly dropped the nose down and landed one bay away from the ME's helicopter. Turning to Beth, he caught her staring at him. "Is there a problem?"

"Nope." Beth's lips twitched up into a smile. "Wolfe is as smart as a whip. It's very difficult to conceal anything from him whatsoever."

As the engine noise cut out, Styles removed his headphones. "Why would I want to conceal anything from him? We need him to assist us with our case. Do you have anything you need to keep from him? If so, I suggest you tell me now."

"No, not exactly." Beth hung up her headphones. "It's just that we deal with sensitive information sometimes. No one can know I have Spike's laptop. If you let that slip, everything will come out. If someone accidentally alerts the wrong person and it gets back to whoever is running this pedophile ring, everything will shut down and start up again somewhere else. This means the pathway to the dark web on Spike's laptop will be useless."

Nodding, Styles met her gaze. "What laptop?" He opened the door and lifted a hand in greeting as the man himself walked onto the helipad.

"It's so nice to see you again, Dr. Wolfe." Beth held out a hand. "Thank you so much for assisting our investigation again."

"That's what I do." Wolfe shook her hand. "Please call me Shane. It's Beth, isn't it?"

"Yeah, and thanks." Beth smiled at him.

Styles shook Wolfe's hand and nodded to a man pushing a gurney he recognized as Wolfe's assistant, Colt Webber, before turning his attention back to Wolfe. "We have the body of Scarlett Chester. The San Francisco PD found her floating in the bay"

"Okay, we'll take her down to examination room one and take a look at her. My assistant will get her ready for examination. You'll be wanting the autopsy report on Brooklyn Daniels?"

Glad Wolfe was so organized, Styles nodded. "Yeah, that would be great."

"Okay, we'll wait in my office and you can bring me up to date with the new cases." Wolfe went to the back of the chopper and slid open the door. After negotiating the black body bag onto the gurney with the help of Webber, he turned to Styles. "Did you bring the report from the first-on-scene officer and the local medical examiner?"

Styles whistled to Bear and then followed Wolfe into the elevator with the body. "Unfortunately, we didn't receive any cooperation whatsoever from the local FBI bureau or the PD. The only information I have is verbal, although the local medical examiner gave me a thumb drive with all the information he had on the case. I haven't had time to go over it yet. Our main concern was to get the victim to you without delay."

"This is a problem I often deal with, although not in this town. The Black Rock Falls Sheriff's Department has an impressive team that includes the Snakeskin Gully FBI field office." Wolfe led the way down a tiled passageway and into an office. "Unfortunately, it's a fact of life that in some places people are treated differently depending on their social background. People go missing all the time and are found murdered, but only a very select few make the press. You can be assured that anyone who enters my examination room is treated with equal respect." He waved them into seats. "Tell me what you know."

Styles noticed the dog basket, food, and water in Wolfe's office. He rubbed Bear's ears and the dog's soft brown eyes looked at him waiting for his next command. "Ah, before we start, will my dog, Bear, be a problem in here with your dog?"

"I don't have a dog." Wolfe sat behind the desk and smiled. "I leave refreshments for my visitors' dogs, which includes Deputy Kane's bloodhound, Duke, and Agent Ty Carter's Doberman, Zorro. They usually wait here in my office during the autopsies. Bear is welcome to wait in here and eat as much as he likes."

Smiling, Styles gave Bear the hand signal to stand down and the dog wagged his long tail and went straight for the bowls. "Thanks. Like us, he's been traveling for a time." He sat down and brought Wolfe up to date.

"I've used Snapshot before and it's great if a match is found to a missing person." Wolfe sighed. "The problem is that not everyone is reported missing, and many are homeless people or people hiding off the grid. There are a ton of unsolved crimes out there." He looked from one to the other. "While you've been away, I collected the bodies from the ravine wreck. Both victims have been positively identified. The driver's fingerprints were in the database, and as luck would have it, the mother of the female victim submitted her DNA when her daughter went missing. The results came through earlier and the girl in the van is Aisha Santiago out of Colorado. She went missing three years ago."

"That would be around the time that the Pied Piper changed his MO from one girl to two." Beth leaned forward in her chair. "With her discovery, and the body of Scarlett both miles away from each other, that leaves us with only one obvious solution. The Pied Piper is killing one girl and selling the other."

"Have y'all considered the possibility he might have an accomplice?" Wolfe stood and went to a coffee machine and pushed in pods. "From what I know of this case, the girls the Pied Piper kills are all blonde with blue eyes; the ones who remain missing are of various types. Over the last four years or so, I've been involved in the investigation of a ton of serial killer murders. It seems to me that most of them stick to the same type of victim."

As the fragrant aroma of coffee filled the room, masking the smell of death and chemicals, Styles shrugged. "I guess that is a possibility but we're not seeing any evidence to prove there was more than one man. If we had been able to get to Aisha Santiago before she drowned in the back of the van, we would have had answers to all the questions about the Pied Piper."

"Hmm." Wolfe placed the coffee fixings on the desk and handed around the cups. "If your theory is correct, the Pied Piper would have faith in the people he sold the girls to and there would be some type of contract between them to make sure they'd never surface alive." He sat down with a sigh and looked at Beth. "Your expertise is cybercrime first, and as an undercover agent second, is that right?"

"Yeah, and before you go any further, I don't believe that the Pied Piper is the kingpin in this organization, and unfortunately, I can't help by going undercover to catch him. I'm way too old for his tastes." Beth stirred cream and sugar into her cup. "Our priority at this time is to catch the Pied Piper. We're taking one crime at a time."

Styles sipped his coffee and regarded them both over the rim of the cup. "We have our reasons for concentrating on him. We know Scarlett was working the streets in San Francisco. It only took good detective work to discover she was working under a pimp by the name of Spike. The prostitutes we spoke to on the street made it quite clear that he only deals in underage girls, but all of them were too afraid to come forward. If this is the case, the Pied Piper is only a very small part of the supply chain. So, for now he is our target. Find him and we cut one head off the snake."

"And if the man in the van is the Pied Piper?" Wolfe raised one blond eyebrow, his gray eyes alert and missing nothing. "What's your next step?"

"I guess we take down men like Spike, one at a time, until we find the man in charge." Beth shrugged. "I know it will take time but I'm not a quitter."

"That's good to know." Wolfe nodded. "Predators seem to breed like rats."

Styles laughed. "Then I'm going to be the exterminator."

THIRTY

Attachment to people wasn't something Beth experienced. She rarely actually liked anyone. In fact, she couldn't recall what that particular emotion felt like, and yet Shane Wolfe intrigued her. He was an impressive-looking man, tall, strong, and chiseled, but it wasn't that type of attraction. From time to time, she'd experienced the animal magnetism people had toward each other and often wondered if it was a small remaining feral part of her, because she'd never loved anyone. Her research did mention a certain kind of love psychopaths experienced, a low-level friendship that rarely lasted. Perhaps it was Wolfe's knowledge that attracted her. He was so direct and gave a no-frills version of life that left her speechless. She stared at him as he delivered his autopsy report on Brooklyn Daniels.

"There's not too much more to tell you since my initial examination on scene." Wolfe indicated to the screens behind his desk. "Cause of death resulted from sharp force trauma. Three precisely placed wounds, forced under the rib cage and into the heart. Death would have been instantaneous. I found the positioning of the wounds to be particularly unusual, mainly because if a child was fighting for their life, they would be thrashing around, and yet these wounds are not hurried, each as if it was carefully placed to ensure a swift death."

Fighting to control the brimming rage, Beth swallowed hard as Wolfe displayed the autopsy images on the screen. "Could she have been unconscious? Would she have passed out during the rape?"

"This is another thing that's unusual." Wolfe displayed more images. "There are no bruises on her thighs. She didn't fight at all, and I've seen many murdered kids—they all fight back. All the bruising is in the vaginal area and the tears are consistent with rape. I found traces of condom lubrication, but he was very careful not to leave any other trace evidence." He sighed. "What I'm saying is there's every indication that Brooklyn Daniels was unconscious during her ordeal. It wasn't from asphyxiation or trauma. I've run tests for the usual drugs and came up with zip. Agreed, a date-rape drug might have left her system, but I was concerned by the purple stain inside her mouth. When I checked her stomach contents, I discovered a small amount of fluid. I'm convinced she was drugged using an herbal concoction. Right now, we're running tests for belladonna and valerian. Mixed together, they'd be powerful enough to render a child unconscious."

"That would make sense." Styles rubbed his chin. "He had two girls. If he drugged them, he could carry one back to his vehicle and then return to murder the second. They wouldn't make a sound."

Unconvinced, Beth frowned. "The problem with that theory is that a psychopathic serial killer like the Pied Piper is living out a fantasy. They get their thrills when their victims fight back. Their excitement increases if the victim struggles, begs for their life, screams. I'm not buying it."

"Have you heard of necrophiliacs?" Styles gave her a long look. "Maybe his fantasy is the kid is already dead. We can't see what's inside his head, can we? You said they're all different, so maybe his fantasy is different too."

Conceding his point, Beth nodded but then a knock came on the door.

"Yeah?" Wolfe stared at the door as Colt Webber, his assistant, poked his head inside.

"We're ready for you now." Colt smiled.

"Okay, we're on our way." Wolfe stood to one side and waved Beth through the door. "We'll suit up first."

Skin crawling in anticipation, Beth moved into the hallway. She disliked morgues with a passion. The smell of death was depressing, although this was part of the job and observing an autopsy often gave the necessary clues for her to solve a crime. The difference between her and others became more obvious inside a place like this. For her the sight and smell of warm blood was intoxicating. Being present at the crime scene of a recent horrendous murder thrilled her, but being in a morgue and witnessing a victim's autopsy was likened to sorting through the dumpster of a fine restaurant. The carefully prepared and delightful meal had been devoured and the leftovers tossed out to rot.

Glad of the mentholated salve, she waited in silence for Wolfe to complete the examination of Aisha Santiago. Her blood had been taken away for testing earlier and although a full toxicology screen would take a week or so to complete, Wolfe was able to test for specific drugs in his laboratory. On an array of screens, X-rays and other information were displayed. Once this victim's autopsy was completed, he changed his gloves and apron and went straight to work on Scarlett Chester. She took a step closer to the body of Aisha when he'd finished speaking into his microphone. Peering at a dead body didn't concern her, but the circumstances around her death, and many like her, were the reason she joined the FBI. Her keen sense of justice was the only thing that set her apart from others like her and she believed she'd become judge and jury for a reason. It didn't take a genius to know that a serial killer could literally get away with murder, but if she could be sure they wouldn't slip through the net to continue their murderous rampage, she'd allow justice to take its course. If not, she'd make a split-second decision on the fly.

Her gaze moved over to the pathetic corpses on the gurneys. It was obvious that these two young girls had suffered for years. The Pied Piper had instigated their torment. He might have died in the van. If not, he was an extremely dangerous adversary and one she must face alone to take down. She doubted that any prison would hold him, and he would never get to court because someone like him would have friends in high places. She figured this was the reason he'd been allowed to keep on killing. It was his reward for supplying the dark web with underage girls. She turned to Wolfe. "Can you break it down for us please? All those clinical terms you use fly right over my head."

"Sure." Wolfe walked over to the screen array. "The majority of the injuries Aisha Santiago sustained happened during the wreck. The water in her lungs is consistent with the sample of creek water taken at the scene. In simple terms, she drowned. The time of death is the time y'all witnessed the van going under in the creek." He frowned. "There are significant other injuries. She has ligature marks on her wrists and ankles. The X-rays indicate previous breaks to the ribs and the right forearm. There is strong indication of prolonged sexual abuse."

"The poor kid." Styles ran a gloved hand down his face. "We were so close to saving her."

Beth went to his side and squeezed his arm. "We did everything possible, Dax. If you're planning on blaming anyone, blame the storm. If that rush of water hadn't washed them off a road, she would be alive and we'd have the guy holding her prisoner in custody." She gave him a long look. "The guy in the van might still be the Pied Piper. One thing's for sure, if it isn't, he'll kill again soon. I hope Ryder has chased down information about him, searched his home, and any other places he frequented. He might have girls holed up there."

"It seems to me, from the evidence we have now, he flipped them, but maybe he kept Aisha for himself." Styles looked bleakly at Wolfe. "What about Scarlett? What happened to her?"

"I found a number of things." Wolfe looked from one to the other. "She had a skull fracture, which would have killed her without treatment and would have rendered her unconscious. She had heroin in her system but not enough to kill her. In my opinion, she was struck with a blunt object from behind. A hammer would fit the shape and size of the contusion. Blunt force trauma is indicated on the X-rays, and from the hemorrhaging, it's clear it happened hours before her death. She likely lapsed into a coma and they dumped her in the bay. The bruising to her upper back and arms is consistent with hitting water and happened in the moments previous to her death. Cause of death is asphyxiation by drowning. She again was brutally sexually assaulted over a long time." He blew out a long sigh. "Both these girls are typical examples of children sold into slavery."

They'd left Rattlesnake Creek in a hurry, leaving the information they needed on the man in the van, presumably Ricky Tallis out of Butte, with Sheriff Ryder. Beth leaned against the counter as Wolfe gave instructions to Colt Webber, to close up. "Did you get a positive ID on Ricky Tallis out of Butte, the guy in the van?"

"Yeah, I spoke to Ryder earlier." Wolfe removed his apron and tossed it down a laundry chute, balled up his gloves, and tossed them in the garbage. "Tallis' cause of death was drowning. The prints are a match and the guy has priors for underage dealing. Ryder is chasing down any properties he might own and hunting down any friends or relatives. There's nothing new on Skylar Peters, and he's calling off the search later today." He looked from one to the other. "I'll have a full report, including the toxicology screen, sent to you ASAP. Ryder will notify the next of kin."

Beth removed her gloves and shook Wolfe's hand. "Thank you for moving so fast on this case."

"It's what I do." Wolfe smiled and pulled a card from his pocket. "Agent Jo Wells, the behavioral analyst out of the Snakeskin Gully FBI field office, is always available to assist if you want to talk over a case with her. This is her cellphone number." He handed her a card. "So am I."

"Thanks." Styles moved to her side. "Do you want to grab a bite to eat before we head home?"

Beth nodded. "Yeah, I want to visit Aunt Betty's Café." She needed an excuse to get the cash to the local church.

"Sure, and then we'd better hit the sky." Styles led the way from the examination room and down the hallway to Wolfe's office. He threw open the door. "Come on, Bear. It's time to go home."

THIRTY-ONE

SUNDAY

Rattlesnake Creek

Before six on Sunday morning, Beth headed to the office, surprised to find Styles at his desk when a call came in from Ryder. In their absence, he'd sprang into action and asked the Butte PD to search Ricky Tallis' property. They'd discovered evidence that he'd kept Aisha Santiago prisoner in his home since she disappeared but had found nothing else to establish a link to the Pied Piper. After investigating, the Butte PD insisted he didn't own a cabin and none of his friends were willing to give up any information. They'd found a laptop that proved Tallis traded in child pornography and although the investigations were ongoing, Beth had to concede that Tallis wasn't the Pied Piper. To her surprise, at the news, Styles stood, walked along the whiteboard, looked at the images, and then left the office without a word.

After an hour had passed, confused by his behavior, Beth headed down to the gym. The thwack of a ball hitting a bat echoed through the large area. In the batting cage, Styles, stripped to the waist, was swinging at balls with an aggression she'd never noticed in him before now. The grunts as he swung the bat, and the speed the balls flew out of the machine, radiated anger. Intrigued, she went to watch. Slicked with sweat, Styles had obviously been here for the entire time. He swung and hit, swung and hit, like a professional player. Baseball was her passion and she'd watched the best. He moved fluidly, as if placing the ball, and missed few. The swishing sound as the bat cut through the air echoed in the silence until he'd exhausted all the balls. She bent to rub Bear's ears and smiled at him. "You look so sad. Is Styles in a bad mood?"

When Bear whined, she went to the cage and pushed her fingers through the wire and looked at Styles. "Feel better now?"

"Nope." Styles dropped the bat on the ground and went to collect the balls in a bucket and then fed them back into the machine.

This must be his way of letting off steam, but what had riled him so much to come out before six. "Couldn't you sleep?"

"I sleep just fine. It's when I wake up, I don't do so well." Styles turned his back on her and switched on the machine.

Slightly annoyed, Beth followed the cord leading out of the cage and flipped the switch on the wall. She turned and walked back to the cage, opened the door, and walked inside. Styles' thunderous expression greeted her. She folded her arms across her chest and stared at him. He was cut and muscular but scars marred his skin. In the first glance she'd spotted a gunshot wound to the shoulder, another to his upper arm, and a very cruel knife wound across his chest. When he turned away, she could see signs of shrapnel scars on his back. She dragged her eyes away, but the stories around the scars intrigued her.

"Is there something you need to say to me?" Styles lifted his chin and stared at her. "Or are you going to just stand there gawking at me? What, never seen battle scars before?"

Blinking a few times, Beth digested his words and then

raised one eyebrow. "I have a few of them myself. I look at them as badges of honor. Maybe one day we can swap the stories behind them?"

"It's never gonna happen." He barked a laugh. "We'll never be that close."

Beth folded her arms across her chest. "I understand having me here cramps your style, but I don't intend to become a problem for you. Yes, I'm stubborn and I want my own way, but how you lead your life or go about your business is your concern. To be perfectly honest, I don't give a rat's. I'm here to do a job, not to make friends."

"That's a typical narcissistic comment." Styles balled his fists on his hips and stared into the distance before slowly returning his attention to her. "I'm not down here letting off steam because of you or what you did in San Francisco. I'm mad because the Pied Piper is still out there. I want to know what happened to the other girls he abducted and we're still running in circles." He let out a long sigh, took a cloth hanging from his belt, and dried his face and chest. "The fact we found a pedophile ring flourishing with endless supplies of children opens up a can of worms, well about a million cans of worms." He took a T-shirt from a chair in the corner and pulled it over his head. "You mentioned that these predators breed like cockroaches. I know the truth of it. We might find one or two, but hiding in the dark are a million or so."

Understanding dawned on her and she nodded. "You have it right. Unfortunately, we'll never be able to find all of them because new people are joining the colony of predators all the time. It's worse than a secret society or any type of cult because they all move in different circles. They are secretive. Some alone, others trust a few people in a group, and then there's those who literally have an empire and use children as a commodity to make money." She sighed. "I could work for the rest of my life and only discover the tip of the iceberg. We might catch a few of the outsiders, like Spike and his clients, but the kingpin is always well protected. I worked on Spike's laptop most of the night and, apart from kiddy porn, I found nothing to lead me to his dark web contact page. I found a few pathways, but from what I can determine, whoever is running the auction site to move the kids sets up a new link for each auction. I figure the details are verbal, not sent in a text or email. Whoever is in charge knows how to evade hackers. It wasn't a waste of time because it tells me just how much deeper the investigation needs to go. It needs a team of supersmart hackers working on the problem. It's not something I could do alone."

"So even with your knowledge of cybercrime, this animal is smarter than you?" Styles shook his head. "How does that make you feel?"

Refusing to rise to the bait, Beth met his gaze. "It makes me more determined to track him down eventually, but right now, we have a homicide case to solve, so chasing down a pedophile ring is out of the question. I figure the director will take it out of my hands anyway. He wants me here as your partner, not working long hours on cybercrime, and they have offices filled with young hackers at their disposal." She sighed. "At least, I've made sure all of Spike's clients are arrested. I've already spoken to the local PD in San Francisco."

"How so?" Styles' mood visibly brightened.

Beth leaned casually against the wire. "I told them that I'd heard about the girls they found on the street corner. They were very forthcoming and even mentioned Spike's name. The girls gave them information about the brothel but left us out of the equation." She smiled. "I suggested they set up a sting operation in Spike's brothel and they agreed. It will be simple enough. They'll make sure they have enough men available to walk out the clients who show without causing alarm. Over a few days or even a week, they'll get just about everyone who frequents that place."

"The problem is some people in society believe these monsters can be rehabilitated." Styles leaned against the fence, swinging his bat. "In my experience, this isn't possible. The moment any of them are released from jail, they reoffend. Some of them take it to a higher level and add murder to their repertoire."

Rubbing her arms, Beth nodded. "Yeah, I figure that happens the first time because they're afraid of going back to jail and then they start to like it."

The phone in Beth's pocket buzzed and she pulled it out. "Agent Katz."

"This is Sheriff Caleb Addams out of Serenity, I'm sorry to call you so early and on a Sunday, Agent Katz, but I've just spoken to Sheriff Ryder and he figured I should contact you."

Beth moved closer to Styles and put her phone on speaker. "That's okay. What seems to be the trouble?"

"We had two girls go missing on Thursday. We've been searching all over since their parents contacted me around dinnertime. It wasn't unusual for the girls to stay out that late. Serenity is a very safe place to live and it's unusual for anything to happen unless it's an accident. We've searched the rivers, the caves alongside the mountain, and through the lowland to the best of our ability using dogs. Just about everyone around these parts volunteered. We headed out early this morning with a cadaver dog and found one of the girls, Hayley Quinn, deceased in a small clearing not half a mile from her home."

Beth exchanged a glance with Styles. "Was there any reason why the area wasn't searched earlier?"

"Yeah, Hayley told her mom they were walking to Stoney Bank, to collect wildflowers. So we headed out that way and widened the search in both directions. Where we found Hayley is in the opposite direction. It's all forest there and with the bears and all, the young folk usually keep away, especially at this time of the year. The direction that they mentioned they would be

heading is more open grasslands, slightly wooded with a river running down the center."

"This is Agent Dax Styles. Who was first on scene?"

"It was me and the guy with the cadaver dog." Sheriff Addams cleared his throat. *"It's an old dog, owned by the previous sheriff, and we were following a hunch. When I came out onto my front porch this morning, I saw a murder of crows gathering in the area. So, we decided we'd better take a look."*

"Describe the scene for me, please." Styles dropped his gaze to the phone.

"It was obvious she'd been murdered. There was a neat pile of clothes beside her and we found a shoe belonging to Ariana Brooks some ways off, but there's no sign of her anywhere in the area."

Two conflicting emotions hit Beth at once: First, the sickening horror that more children had been taken and murdered. Second, the thrill of the fact the Pied Piper was still in the area and waiting for her to exact vengeance. Keeping her gaze fixed on the floor, she fought to control the tingling excitement of the hunt yet to come. She sucked in a deep breath and let it out slowly. "This sounds like the work of the Pied Piper killer. We've been hunting him down for the last three years. Is the scene intact?"

"Yeah, I figured we'd need help on this one. I have two of my deputies out there protecting the scene. No one, not even the girl's parents, has been informed that she is there. I didn't want any sightseers until a forensic team had been over the area. Do you have anyone we can call?"

"Yeah, leave that to me. We have a medical examiner out at Black Rock Falls we can call." Beth looked up at Styles. "Agent Styles will need to speak to you about the location. We'll be heading out in the chopper." She handed Styles the phone.

"I'll need your coordinates. Can you text them to this number, please?" Styles nodded to her. "When we arrive, if you could park your cruiser with lights flashing in an area wide enough for two choppers to land, it will make life easier. It will take at least one hour to organize a forensic team and get to you. We'll contact you when we're ten minutes out. Will that give you enough time to get into position?"

"Sure. We'll see you soon." Sheriff Addams disconnected.

"Another dead girl and another one missing on our watch." Styles shook his head. "I've witnessed some atrocities in my time, but child murders really get to me, and knowing that the other girl has been sold into slavery turns my stomach."

The scene of Brooklyn Daniels' murder fixed in Beth's mind and rage filled her with a deep-seated need for justice. She had to stop the Pied Piper permanently. There could be no other course of action for a monster like him. Avoiding Styles, she turned her attention to the wall. Giving him a direct stare when her dark side was rising would expose her emotions. That could never happen. She nodded slowly. "It's the feeling of being useless and trying to stop an unstoppable force. In this case we must go back to basics and start interviewing the suspects on our list. Now that we know he frequents Serenity as well, we can narrow them down."

Beth contacted Wolfe and gave him the details. She turned to Styles. "Wolfe is on his way."

"We'll have time to grab a shower and breakfast." Styles checked his watch. "If you bring the list of possible suspects, we'll discuss them on the way to Serenity." He gave her a determined stare. "This was his first mistake. Serenity is a backwoods town, secluded and not many people go there. The suspect list is shrinking by the second."

With the thrill of the hunt rising in her blood, Beth pushed trembling fingers into her pockets. "Isn't life strange? One minute you think you've been dumped on the beach, and the next you catch the perfect wave."

THIRTY-TWO

A cruel icy wind swirled around Styles, trying to sneak into every orifice of his clothes, and raised goosebumps on his flesh as he walked to the chopper. After getting Bear inside and clicking in the dog's harness, he turned as footsteps came from behind him. He ran his gaze over Beth as she climbed into the chopper. She dressed so differently now and had chosen jeans, sturdy boots, a shirt, and thick sweater. It was good to see she'd purchased a heavy winter coat and was wearing it over her Kevlar vest. If she'd insisted on the FBI dress code of a black jacket and pants, she'd have frozen to death in an hour. He handed her a backpack, complete with a can of bear spray. "That's one of our many survival packs. Whenever I go into the forest in these more remote areas, I take one with me. You never know what you might run into out there."

"Yeah, I've read up about the wildlife, but my liquid Kevlar vest is in case we encounter the Pied Piper." Beth's lips twitched up slightly at the corners as she pushed the head-phones over her ears. "I'm not discounting the fact that he might be armed. It seems to me that every second person you see is carrying."

Styles took the chopper up and headed over the mountains. The wind buffeted them as they moved through the canyon and followed the river to Serenity. "Yeah, the townsfolk do, but most of the mine camps ban firearms, so usually the groups of men that come into town to blow off steam are usually unarmed, although some of them do carry a hunting knife." He flicked her a glance. "Look over the suspects list again and give me your thoughts."

"I checked them out over breakfast." Beth scrolled through the documents on her phone. "The four guys with priors are all miners: Roderick Soto, Howell Marshman, Christopher Wheatly, and Francis Baldwin. Two of them work out of Longhorn Peak. The other two out at Lost Gem Valley. I made a few calls this morning and spoke to the managers of both mines and received exactly the same response. All these men worked the week ending Friday. They work a twelve-hour shift finishing at six. A chopper gives the men a ride into town for the weekend and it didn't leave until around nine on Saturday morning." She shrugged. "On paper these were prime suspects as we have a pedophile and a stalker in that group." She glanced up from her phone. "Your three suspects are still in the running. Lawrence Dawson, the courier driver, mentions Serenity on his webpage as a delivery area. The travel nurses, Ainsley Rice and Emerson Green, could be anywhere at any given time as they move between the three town's ERs as required. We'll need to interview these three men as soon as possible. With all the delays, one of them is getting away with murder."

Styles nodded. "Call the Serenity sheriff and inform him that our ETA is approximately seven minutes." He glanced at his instruments and then looked ahead. "That's the town just ahead, nestled into the side of the mountain. It's at high altitude here. You'll notice the difference in the air quality and it's bitterly cold at this time of year."

A voice came over his radio and he recognized Wolfe's call

sign. He responded. "Yeah, ETA four minutes. Follow me in. Out."

"I see him." Beth turned around in her seat, looking over one shoulder. "He's behind us." She turned back. "I've checked out his background and he flew a medevac chopper in the Marines. Is that where you learned to fly?"

Styles flicked her a glance. "I wasn't in the Marines." He shrugged. "They're different to Army. I was stationed at Fort Novosel, Alabama, for my training. I flew Black Hawks most of the time. It was my first passion and I saw my share of tours, but then I decided to join the MP. I had the qualifications and made captain."

"Oh, I see." Beth's lips twitched into a smile. "I sense a little rivalry there, Dax."

Styles snorted a laugh. "Nope, I respect him as an ME. He's one hell of a doctor as well and saved so many lives without a thought of his own safety. It wouldn't have been easy, flying in and treating the wounded. It's just different worlds, is all." He tipped down the nose of the chopper. "There's the cruiser."

Styles climbed from the chopper, slipped on his backpack, lifted Bear down, and then waited for Beth. The ME's chopper landed and Wolfe, Webber, and a blonde woman came toward them. Webber pushed a gurney with a forensics kit perched on top of a pile of evidence bags. He walked to greet Wolfe. "You made good time. Thanks for coming." He held out a hand to the stunningly attractive young blonde woman. "Agent Dax Styles and this is my partner, Beth Katz."

"Emily Wolfe." Her wide smile reflected in her eyes. "It's nice to meet you. Shane is my dad."

"Emily has a degree in forensic science and is currently studying for a medical degree so she can join me in the medical examiner's office. I like to have a fresh set of eyes on the scene especially when we're dealing with someone like the Pied Piper." Wolfe gave him a typical father's back-off stare.

"She often rides along with me when we have interesting cases."

"Nice to see you again, Em, Dr. Wolfe." Beth smiled and turned to Styles. "I already met Emily in Helena. The serial rapist and the Tarot Killer case." She laughed. "Now look at me banished to the backwoods, but at least I get to work with you guys again."

Sheriff Caleb Addams, his face sheet white, walked out of the forest to greet them. Styles turned to see a man in uniform, followed by two deputies both looking green. "Is someone out there guarding the scene?"

"Yeah, we have one forest warden and the local doctor." Sheriff Addams waved a hand toward his deputies. "I was giving my boys a break, is all. I figured the animals got to her. It's not a pretty sight and sure as heck not one I've seen before."

"Lead the way." Wolfe appeared at his side. "If the wildlife already found the body, they'll be back. We need to get her out of here ASAP."

They walked in single file along a narrow trail through the forest. Underfoot, dry pine needles crunched with each step. All around, fall had changed the colors of the forest. The leaves on the once green vines and bushes had curled and turned to many shades of amber. Pine cones littered the way, and Styles recalled collecting them as a child and taking them home. The smell as they crackled and burned in the hearth brought back memories of a happy time in his life. There had always been smiles in his family before his sister vanished. He dragged his mind back to reality. The smell of death was coming on the breeze, and he reached inside his pocket for a face mask. Beside him, Bear's ears were pricked, and he noticed a slight rising of his hackles. Worried there might be a bear close by, he raised his voice. "Make some noise up there. If there's anything hanging around the forest today, we'll scare them off."

"We found bear scat about twenty yards away from the

crime scene but no prints or anything else close by." Sheriff Addams cleared his throat. "Although right now we're more concerned about hunting down the whereabouts of Ariana Brooks. Apart from the shoe I mentioned to Agent Katz, we found no trace of her, and we've searched in all directions and along the fire road."

"Hold up." Beth squeezed in beside him. "We're getting a pattern here. The last murder and two we have on our whiteboard all occurred near a fire road. The killer is using them to move the kidnapped girls. We can use this information to pinpoint his next kill." She narrowed her gaze on him. "The three towns are his comfort zone."

Shaking his head in disbelief, Styles stared at her. She obviously didn't realize just how far the forests stretched in all directions. "I figure he kills one of them after he gets them alone. Even if we had eyes on every fire road throughout the forests, we'd never get there in time. This isn't like traveling around the burbs. We're talking about thousands of square miles and a ton of fire roads. If we had a thousand men, we still wouldn't have enough people to watch the entire area."

"He won't kill in the same place twice." She gripped his arm. "It would be too obvious, so we hunt down a place in a town close by. Where is another town in easy traveling distance from Rattlesnake Creek with a forest and fire roads?"

Styles thought for a beat, drawing an imaginary circle on a map in his mind. "Spring Grove. If we are taking Rattlesnake Creek as the center, coming out as far as Serenity as the outer border, and drawing an imaginary circle, Spring Grove would be on that boundary line. It seems to me that this killer is well organized. Somehow, I figure he is grooming these kids to meet up with him. We still have the problem of how he is murdering one and managing to get the other one away without any noise."

"Most certainly." Beth moved in behind him to avoid running into the trees lining the trail. "He selects an area, chooses his targets, and then makes his move when the time is right. As he has gotten away with this so many times, we must be looking at someone who is not a threat to children. All kids are warned about talking to strangers, which makes me believe whatever profession he works in the children are accessible to him."

Running the suspects through his mind, Styles nodded. He walked backward as he talked to her. "All three of the suspects on our list could be the killer. Two travel nurses and a courier. People are laid-back in this part of the country. They would chat to a nurse and allow their kids to do the same. A courier usually brings things to the house, and so many things are purchased online now I'm sure he is in constant demand. He would be known to the homeowners, and they would probably greet him as a friend, which would make their children believe he was a safe person."

"Oh, that doesn't look good." Beth pointed to the numerous markers all around the crime scene.

Styles moved his attention to the clearing ahead, where Wolfe and his team were suiting up. Wolfe was issuing orders in a soft voice, and the deputies were moving around the area with crime scene tape. The smell of decayed human flesh, blood, and the distinct stench of bear surrounded them. In the clearing, it was obvious that what had once been a little girl was now a collection of body parts. The head and torso lay on a small patch of grass on its back with the long blonde hair spread out like a fan around an ashen face. The sight of one clenched fist gripping a wildflower tore at him. Seeing such violence inflicted on an innocent child, he almost spewed his breakfast. Beside him he heard Beth's sharp intake of breath and turned to her. "This is real bad."

"That damage is not all bear from what I can see." Beth pulled on examination gloves and moved closer to the head and torso. "There is sharp force drama to the chest." She looked at him and a frown creased her forehead. "Something angered him. Maybe he had problems with the other girl. What's her name?"

Styles looked at his phone, bringing up the file he'd made over breakfast this morning. "Ariana Brooks has black hair. This child is blonde like the others he murdered." He glanced around the clearing, scanning all the markers. "Look over there, the remains of an elk. That was the bear's target, not this child. They prefer fresh meat, and from the decomposition, I figure she has been here a few days, probably since Thursday, when she went missing. This damage is likely from a wildcat."

"The clothes are stacked up exactly the same as before. Neatly folded with the shoes on top." Beth was watching Wolfe and his team closely. "The sheriff mentioned finding a shoe we presume belongs to Ariana Brooks. If so, it follows the same pattern exactly."

Scratching his cheek, Styles looked at her. "What is it with the shoe? Why is he deliberately leaving one behind?"

"I figure it's the same as the Tarot Killer's Grim Reaper card." Beth hid her emotions behind her mask. "It's all part of the game. He's telling the world he's taken the other girl and that we'll never find her. The pile of clothes beside the body is him telling us how he took his time and that we'll never get to him in time to prevent what he's doing. He must have control over the girls to keep them quiet—but what?"

Sick to his stomach, Styles stared into the forest trying to gain some respite from the horrific scene before him. "From what Wolfe said, he's drugging them. It wouldn't take much to knock out a kid. He waits for it to take effect and then separates them and keeps one subdued somewhere in the forest. That's the one he takes with him, the one who doesn't fit his fantasy. He goes back to the first one and murders her. Like you said, he takes his time. We know this by the neatly folded clothes. After he has completed his ritual, he returns to the other girl. He'd carry her asleep to his vehicle and no one would see her when he drives away."

Styles made his way over to Wolfe to discuss his theory. "Did you find proof of the herbs?"

"I've run a toxicology screen on all the victims that we've processed, including samples taken from previous victims we assume were murdered by the same killer, and I found no pharmaceutical drugs in Brooklyn Daniel's system, but I did find belladonna and valerian in concentration." Wolfe paused for a beat, staring into space. "During a toxicology screen, we test for the most common drugs, the date-rape drugs in particular and others that are easily available on the streets. The thing is, this killer is using some type of herbal concoction, and the ones we tested for and found are extremely potent. There might be others, mushrooms perhaps." He turned his attention back to Styles. "I'll rerun the tests when I get back to the lab for other herbal drugs. It's obvious he doesn't want to harm the second girl. If what you say is true, he'd want her in good condition."

Styles nodded. "Thanks, I would appreciate it. We're going to walk to the fire road and see if we can find any evidence along the way. This is another part of our theory. We figure he comes into the forest via the fire road and leaves the same way. It's how he's luring the victims to him that is leaving us stumped at the moment."

He turned back to see Beth approaching the sheriff. He went and stood by her side. "Is everything okay?"

"Yeah, I was just asking the sheriff to forward us the statements from the first on scene." Beth nodded to the sheriff. "I think we've seen everything we need for now. Wolfe will send us the images of the scene and his reports. I figure we should head on home and start interviewing suspects."

Styles shrugged. "Yeah, I'm happy to do that but I want to follow the trail back to the fire road and look for evidence. I know the deputies walked the area, but we notice things they miss. It won't take us more than half an hour, and we'll be back in Rattlesnake Creek by lunchtime. That will give us plenty of time to hunt down the suspects this afternoon." He gave her a long considering stare. "He's not going to kill again today. He'll likely be spending most of his time relocating that girl. I figure he flips them almost immediately."

"Okay, lead the way." Beth pointed to a trail leading off to the left. "The sheriff said it was down that way."

Styles looked around. "We need that shoe. I've been training Bear to track scent, and he might be able to pick something up."

"I would say it's over there." Beth pointed to a pile of evidence bags resting on a tree stump.

After opening the bag to allow Bear to sniff the contents, Styles followed him when he ran along the trail Beth had indicated. "That's a good sign." He hurried after Bear with Beth on his heels.

Feeling as if he'd been trapped in a reoccurring nightmare, Styles followed Bear through the forest. Bear stopped and barked at the marker where the shoe had been left proudly displayed on an upturned log. The dog continued on weaving through the trees and stopped abruptly at the fire road and walked around in circles for a time before sitting down. They found no signs of a vehicle on the tightly packed dirt road. Again, they found a few strands of hair, caught in the branches of a pine tree. "This indicates he was carrying her, look how high the hair is snagged. He was carrying her over one shoulder. If I take this as an estimate, I would say the Pied Piper is approximately five-ten."

"Well, let's go and get him." Beth turned a full circle and went back to his side. "I'm convinced the Pied Piper is close by. I can feel it in my bones."

THIRTY-THREE

The scenic ride back to Rattlesnake Creek helped to remove the graphic crime scene images from Beth's head, but her mind was working overtime. She considered the problem from every angle and came to the conclusion that the Pied Piper wouldn't risk being seen, and as an organized psychopathic killer, the Pied Piper must be grooming his victims over time. First up, he would need access to the girls over a period of time to secure their trust. From Ryder's investigation, she'd discovered that no one was seen lurking around when the girls went missing, so either he went undetected because he was so familiar to the townsfolk or he was hiding somewhere in a prearranged meeting place. The only feasible way he could make this happen was that he used an inducement to encourage them to meet him somewhere in the forest. She turned to Styles and activated her headphones. "Is there a place you can land in Spring Grove?"

"Yeah, but why do you want to go there now? Won't that be showing our hand?"

Shaking her head, Beth looked at him. "Not today, maybe tomorrow. I'm convinced the Pied Piper is grooming the girls and I'm considering going straight to the source for information. If I can arrange it with the local school, we might be able to get clues from the kids. I know the legal ramifications of interviewing juveniles, but I was thinking about approaching it as a talk. As in, we speak to the principal and explain what's going on, but ask him if we can talk to the kids not in a one-on-one situation but by addressing the class. I could talk about the different ways predators can come at them. Maybe we can get some of them to speak up. What do you say?"

"You'd need to be very careful what you say. We're talking about children, and if they go home terrified of everything around them, we won't be very popular." Styles glanced at her. "I assume you have some idea of how you're going to approach the subject?"

Wrinkling her nose in thought, Beth shrugged. "I'll have something ready by the time we get there. I don't have a problem speaking in public and I know how to deal with kids. I won't say anything to upset anyone. I guess we can call the principal and tell him that it's Stranger Awareness Week, and mention that as there have been two murders in surrounding counties, we are just making the children aware of the dangers of speaking to people they don't know."

"I could do that." Styles' attention was fixed on flying the chopper. "People are used to seeing me around, so they'll assume that we're doing this as a community service."

Glad he'd come on board with her plan, Beth nodded. "Thanks."

When they landed in Rattlesnake Creek, they went straight to Tommy Joe's Bar and Grill for lunch. They ordered at the counter and went to sit in a secluded booth at the back to discuss the three suspects on the list. After stripping off her coat, Beth sat down and placed her iPad on the table. "Before, when we were looking at suspects, I hunted down various employment agencies and discovered a travel nurse agency situated in Black Rock Falls. It's a walk-in and online agency, and I figure Ainsley Rice and Emerson Green are registered there. As neither of them is working in one of the local hospitals for long periods of time, they seem to be on call to fill in when others are sick or on vacation."

"So, we give the agency a call and explain we need to contact them on a private matter, they can call us back on the FBI line if necessary to verify our identity." Styles leaned back in his chair making it groan under his weight. "Once we find out where our suspects are working, we'll pay them a visit. It will be easier that way. It will be harder for them to avoid us when they're at work."

Nodding, Beth chewed on her bottom lip. "Lawrence Dawson, the courier driver, is going to be a little more difficult to find. As he runs his own business and is out on the road most times, I'm not sure how we can hunt him down."

"I know." Styles smiled and rubbed his belly. "There is a small diner in Black Rock Falls, which sends pies out the same day, using Dawson's courier service. He just happens to be there on Sundays. I made a note when I was hunting him down. We order some cherry pies and get him to deliver them to us. When he arrives, we'll ask him a few general questions and feel him out. If he is willing to talk, we could move on to when he delivers to certain towns as we often need urgent courier services."

Beth grinned. "That sounds like a plan. As soon as we've eaten, we'll head back to the office and wait for him."

When Tommy Joe arrived at the table with their meals it was obvious he had something on his mind. Beth looked up at him, waiting for him to say something. When he just placed the meals on the table and smiled at her, she narrowed her gaze at him. "Is there a problem?"

"I was just told about the young kids going missing."

Tommy Joe frowned at her. "I'm trying to figure out how he knew the girls were in the forest."

"That's exactly what we're trying to figure out too." Styles refilled his cup from a pot on the table. "We haven't any idea whatsoever."

"I have two nieces around that age and they have always got their heads bent over their iPads." Tommy Joe shrugged. "The internet isn't safe these days. Do you think he's getting at them through a webpage or a game?"

Beth smiled at him. "We'll look into that. Thank you for the suggestion."

"Not a problem." Tommy Joe smiled at them. "I'll bring you a fresh pot of coffee." He picked up the empty pot from the table and walked away.

"What do you think?" Styles picked up his burger and examined it.

The idea had crossed Beth's mind, but she had no idea how involved the local children were in social media in this remote area. "I can take a look and see if there are any games or chat lines that kids are accessing locally. It's difficult unless we have a device that one of the kids has been using."

"I could ask Ryder if he collected Brooklyn Daniels' computer or whatever for evidence." Styles frowned. "As it's his first murder, he may have overlooked it. It wasn't an angle I was pursuing at the time either. I had no idea kids of that age were into online games or social media. I figured all that started around the time they went to high school." He pulled out his phone and made a call. He handed an earbud to Beth. "Hey, Cash, did you by any chance take any media devices or phone from the Daniels home?"

"Yeah, no phone, but she had an iPad. They use them for school. The ME told me to ask for it and to file it just in case someone needed to go through it."

"I know it's Sunday, but can we get it today?" Styles

exchanged a triumphant look with Beth. "We're at Tommy Joe's."

"Okay, I'll go get it out of evidence and come by." Ryder disconnected.

Raising her eyebrows, Beth looked at Styles. "Well, it might be his first murder but at least he's following procedure. Everything he's given us so far has been thorough. He hasn't missed anything so far."

"Yeah, he is reliable. It's time he hired a deputy. He can't be in two places at any one time. That's when he usually calls me in to help, but now that you're here, I have a feeling we'll be handling cases far and wide." Styles smiled. "While we're waiting for Cash, I'll call the hospitals and ask if either of our suspects are working today." Styles went to work using his own brand of charm to get the information he needed.

When Ryder appeared carrying an iPad inside an evidence bag, Beth signed the paperwork to get it released to her and nodded to him. "Thanks. Why don't you join us, and we'll bring you up to date with the case?"

"Oh, Styles called me last night and gave me the rundown." Ryder indicated with his thumb to the door. "I'm in the middle of something just now and people are waiting at the office for me. Maybe next time?"

Wondering if she intimidated him, Beth gave him her brightest smile. "I'll look forward to it."

"Ah sure." Ryder backed away and hurried out of the door.

Beth watched him go and shook her head slowly. She seemed to have that effect on men. Maybe some of them were psychic?

THIRTY-FOUR

As Styles was deep in conversation with his phone pressed to his ear, Beth stood and went to the counter. She liked TJ and his bar and grill. He employed an excellent chef, and the pastries behind a glass display under a sign of a steaming coffee pot had caught her attention. Among the usual selection of pies and Danish pastries sat a delicious Black Forest cake. The thick chocolate frosting decorated with cherries made her mouth water. She sensed rather than saw TJ come toward her and lifted her gaze from the delights behind the glass. "I had no idea Wez was such a fine pastry chef."

"Well, apart from creating sumptuous mains, he likes to experiment with desserts and most times what he cooks turns out delicious." TJ grinned at her. "The Black Forest cake is new to his collection of delicacies. Can I tempt you with a slice?"

After eating a burger and fries and drinking two cups of coffee, Beth considered her calorie intake was more than enough for one day. Keeping fit and healthy was a priority and she'd become more of a salad type of person, but since she'd joined the Rattlesnake Creek field office, it seemed she'd been consuming junk food 24/7. Styles, it seemed, would eat dog food if hungry. She found it hard to believe a man in such good shape cared so little about his diet. She looked at the cake again and slowly raised her gaze to TJ. "It does look delicious, but I have just eaten one of his amazing burgers."

"Aw come on. Wez will be so disappointed if no one orders this today." TJ grinned at her. "But I'm not giving you the hard sell because what's left over I get to take home." He chuckled. "I've already eaten two slices today."

"I'll have a slice." Styles came up behind her and peered through the glass and then up at TJ. "I'm not gonna let you have all the fun." Beside him, Bear whined. "No, you're not getting chocolate cake. Didn't anyone tell you chocolate is not good for dogs?"

"I've a nice juicy bone out back if he'd like that?" TJ looked down at Bear. "On the house."

"Sure. One juicy bone and one large slice of chocolate cake." Styles looked at her. "You're not going to like me eating that in front of you, are you?" He chuckled. "Look at all that chocolate frosting and cherries. Mmm, I can taste it through the glass."

Never having friends who joked with her about anything, Beth stared at him not quite knowing what to say. She understood that something was missing in her own psyche, the part of her that didn't care about people's feelings when it was appropriate that she should. Although, without conscious effort, her lips twitched into a smile, as if it were a normal response for her. She leaned into the feeling. It was like being in front of a warm fire on a freezing day. Turning her attention away from Styles, she looked at TJ. "Okay, you forced me into it. I will have a slice, thank you."

"I have a feeling we're corrupting her." TJ winked at Styles and then went about cutting the cake and placing it onto plates. "Although Wez is getting quite creative with his takeout salads.

He loves an ego stroke and your compliments have given his creativity a boost."

Beth couldn't remember smiling so much in her life. Was this what being normal felt like? She nodded. "Yes, they're excellent. After all the takeout I've been eating on our trips, I'll be ordering one every day next week. Tell him to use his creativity and I'll be his guinea pig." She picked up her plate from the counter and carried it back to the table. At least, she didn't intimidate the chef, Wez Michaels. She smiled to herself. That was a start. She would have to work on her personality traits a little more to fit in with this friendly town. Having men run a mile from her was not a good look.

"I struck gold at the hospitals." Styles sat down and moments later Bear arrived carrying a large bone. "Go outside and eat that, boy." He pointed to the back door, and the dog wandered off, his mouth stretched wide smiling around the bone.

Beth slid the fork through the cake and lifted it to her mouth. She sighed as the delicious creamy chocolate flavor coated her taste buds. "What did you find out?"

"Luckily, everyone was very cooperative. When I asked if Ainsley Rice or Emerson Green were working today, they told me the days they'd be there. Apparently, they both have shifts at different hospitals, some at the same time. Today, we're lucky. Ainsley Rice is in town and working in the ER until eight tonight. We can catch Emerson Green tomorrow. He is working at, would you believe, Spring Grove. If you can organize a chat with the kids at the local school in the afternoon, we can catch him beforehand. He's working there all week. Ainsley Rice has shifts there as well, mornings on a few days. I have all the details."

They finished eating their cake in silence, both enjoying the rich delight. After finishing her third cup of coffee, Beth's head was buzzing with caffeine overload. She glanced at Styles to see him staring at her, a questioning expression on his face. She patted her lips with a napkin. "Do I have chocolate all over my face?"

"Nope. You look just fine." Styles pushed away his plate, drained his cup, leaned back in his chair, and sighed with obvious contentment. "I was just enjoying not arguing with you all the time."

Amused, Beth gave him a serious stare. "I blame the cake. It puts me off my game. I'll try harder for the rest of the afternoon."

"Hmm." Styles pushed on his Stetson and gathered his things from the table. "It's obvious you have quite an insight into psychopathic killers. Is it all from research or do you have any firsthand knowledge?"

Collecting the iPad and pushing her phone into her pocket, she stood. "A little of both." She indicated to Bear lying on the back porch. "You're not going to allow your dog to take that bone inside the truck, are you?"

"Nah, I'll ask TJ to wrap it to go." He smiled at her. "If you know anything about dogs, taking away food is like a punishment, and Bear has been exceptionally good during our trip."

Beth waited for Styles to speak to TJ, and when the bone was wrapped, she followed them out of the door. "How far is the hospital from here?"

"Ten minutes or so." Styles opened the back door of the truck for Bear to climb inside and then slid behind the wheel.

As they headed through town, Beth ran a few questions through her mind to ask their first suspect. Late the previous night, she'd completed a background check on Ainsley Rice and discovered he spent approximately three months in each location before moving on. This was quite common in his profession, and she'd discovered the pattern of the other travel nurse, Emerson Green, was almost identical. After correlating their movements with the murders in neighboring states, either of the two men could be the Pied Piper. This had left the courier, Lawrence Dawson, in the clear unless she dug a little deeper and discovered that he'd moved around considerably during his career, but she had only traced him to three other locations where abductions or murders had taken place.

All three men had something in common: they were single, lived alone, moved around constantly in their occupations, and had possible access to young children. All three would not be considered a threat to either parents or kids. Considering these facts, she decided that the three of them were prime suspects.

"Going back to our conversation about psychopaths, do you mind if I pick your brain?" Styles flicked her a glance as they hit the main highway.

Beth shook her head. "No. Go right ahead."

"I've worked many murder cases." Styles shrugged. "Most of them have a very plain motive. It's usually jealousy, money, cheating spouses, or gang related. When I find a woman stabbed to death, I consider the extent of the injuries to determine who was responsible. Most times men slap a woman around for a long time during spousal abuse, but a man who kills his cheating wife usually stabs them. A woman who attacks another woman for stealing her husband or boyfriend usually goes for the face. A man will often strangle his nagging girlfriend or wife, I figure to shut them up." He flicked her a glance. "I've seen opportunistic kills, where someone lets their fantasy get too much for them and strikes at the first opportunity, but afterward they show remorse. This isn't what I'm seeing in our current case. It seems to me that the Pied Piper is enjoying himself. The grooming, stalking, and murdering the girls is a game to him. What I can't get my head around is that he must be a nice guy on the outside or people would be suspicious of him."

Understanding his confusion, Beth turned in her seat to look at him. "You really should invest in reading agent Jo Wells' books on psychopathic behavior. She has spent a good deal of time visiting them in jail and conducting in-depth interviews to learn more about their behavioral variations." She pushed back her hoodie and tidied her hair, looking at her reflection in the side mirror and then tying it neatly into a ponytail at the nape of her neck.

"As I don't have time to read all of her books, give me a rundown of the basics." Styles turned onto a series of backroads. "I know you've talked about this before, but is there a ten-point plan for when we're dealing with someone like this?"

It would take a long time to run through every anomaly of a psychopath's behavioral pattern. She sucked in a deep breath and let it out slowly. Too much information at this time could point a finger at her, although her ploy to avoid suspicion by disagreeing and arguing with him should dissolve any unwanted attention. "I suppose we could work something out that could help. Let me see." She stared at the road ahead, both sides were bathed in the colors of fall, from the wheatgrass to the trees and bushes. She appreciated nature and understood that was another of her peculiarities. "There is no particular type. They can be male or female, in any walk of life, rich or poor, but one thing they have in common is that they are very smart. Not necessarily academically smart, but they seem to be able to assess situations extremely fast and act on them. If they are speaking with you and you throw them a difficult question, they can come up with an excuse in a nanosecond."

"So, they usually plan their kills?" Styles nodded as if to himself. "You mentioned an organized psychopath. Are they all organized?"

Beth shook her head. "No, some of them might see a person on the street who triggers the need to kill. This person is usually a representative of someone who triggered their violent psychopathy in the past, like a bully, an abusive parent, or someone who embarrassed them. It's not cut and dried. They're all different. An opportunistic killer would usually follow their victim until they had the chance to strike, and they usually leave the bodies where they drop. That doesn't mean to say they wouldn't return to look at them later. It's usually the opportunistic killers who have a fascination with the dead bodies of their victims. Organized psychopathic killers plan everything to the last second. These rarely make a mistake and go on to continue their killing spree for years at a time."

"You mentioned some of them going back to visit the bodies." Styles grimaced. "Wouldn't that be a dangerous thing to do?"

Beth noticed signs to the hospital and was relieved the interrogation would be over shortly. She wondered if Styles had gotten suspicious of her, although she believed she'd covered her tracks really well. She looked at him. "Another thing about serial killers is they believe they can't be caught, so if part of their fantasy is necrophilia, they'll act upon it. Going back to the scene before the cops have found the body is like a victory to them. They don't have any feelings or remorse for their victims. None of them do. They would only be visiting them again to relive the fantasy." She sighed. "The majority of them take a trophy to help them relive the thrill of the kill, but usually in their minds they're killing the same person over and over again. Once the victim is dead, they no longer have any value. They can't kill a person more than once, can they?"

"Anything else of importance, I should know?" Styles turned into the hospital parking lot and drove up and down rows of vehicles looking for a space.

Beth turned to face him. "They could be your best friend, the guy next door, the person you are working beside because you would never know. The one piece of good advice that I should give you is that, if you confront one, remember that negotiation is off the table. They will kill you at the first opportunity." She sighed. "I'm sure victims plead for their lives, but by doing this they're only feeding the psychopath's fantasy."

"Okay." Styles turned in his seat to face her. "I owe you an apology."

Beth frowned. "How so?"

"Everything you've told me is true." Styles looked abashed. "I've studied psychopathic serial killers, but not to the extent that you have, but Mac told me you had what he called an unnatural obsession with them. When he spoke to me about you coming here, he mentioned that you were too smart for your own good. He said your rash decisions and taking off alone without appropriate backup would likely make you a victim. This is another one of the reasons he sent you here to be with me. I've seen both sides of you. You have a hunger for solving crimes, but I also see a very deep-rooted desire for justice."

Shaking her head, Beth stared at him. "Apology accepted, but I'm not sure why you had to question me in such an underhand way. Over the last few days, I believe we've gotten on really well. Yeah, we've had certain procedural differences and we don't see eye to eye all of the time, but together we have made more ground on the Pied Piper killer than any other team in the entire USA." She narrowed her gaze on him. "I'm glad you came clean with me, but next time any of the directors ask questions about my sanity, come straight to the source. I'm an open book and will tell you like it is. All you have to do is ask." *Well, some of it might be true.*

THIRTY-FIVE

The redbrick building had a majestic air to it. It wasn't the usual square slab-sided construction Beth had expected. As they approached the large glass doors out front, she noticed the date, 1930, displayed on a brass plate attached to the wall. The staggered display of windows would have been an early art deco design and not one she had seen used for a hospital. The theme continued throughout and was reflected above each door and corridor. Mesmerized by the uniqueness of the building, Beth slowed her step to just soak it in. Although the contents of the hospital appeared to be brand new, the original design had been preserved throughout. When Styles turned to look at her with one eyebrow raised, she gave him an apologetic smile. "I'm sorry. I wasn't expecting such an incredible building hidden away in such a small town. Why did they build something this big?"

"Rattlesnake Creek isn't really a small town. It's just that the population is concentrated to the mining camps." He waved a hand dismissively. "This was built because in that time, accidents were frequent in the mines and we still have our share. Our town is growing year on year, and it's difficult to get staff.

We have specialists who move from one hospital to another in this part of the country. Many of the doctors on staff live here but some are like the travel nurses. They stay for three to six months and then move on to somewhere else."

Beth nodded and followed him to the front counter. "Yes, of course the mines. I keep forgetting how many of them are in this area."

After speaking to the person at the front desk they located Ainsley Rice. He was working in the children's ward on the second floor. Beth accessed a photo of him, taken from his driver's license, and showed it to Styles. Acting as casual as possible they moved through the ward until they found him, dressing the wound of a little girl. They stopped and observed him for a few moments. Rice used a soft voice as he spoke to the child and spent time with her after he'd finished. Beth had to admit his bedside manner was faultless. She lowered her voice to just above a whisper and turned to Styles. "He's smooth as silk and can obviously gain a child's trust without any problems." She shrugged. "This is probably what they all aim for when treating children. I've checked and none of the victims has been hospitalized over the last year. I don't think either of our travel nurses has been alone with them."

"We can't discount anyone until you've taken a look at Brooklyn Daniels' iPad." Styles narrowed his gaze on the man. "He's in the height range. You question him and find out if he was anywhere near the murder scenes. He might be intimidated by me and clam up."

Nodding, Beth took a notebook and pen out of her pocket. She had been told over the years that the way she looked at people intimidated them. She had been working on trying to soften her approach. Waiting until Rice moved away from the child and removed his gloves and went to a wash basin, she headed in his direction. "Could we have a word with you, Mr.

Rice?" She flipped open her cred pack and held it up to him. "Do you have a break room anywhere close by?"

"FBI? What could you possibly want to talk to me about, Agent Katz?" Rice methodically washed his hands and then dried them on a paper towel before turning to her. "Wait! Not in front of the patients. It might upset them."

Beth nodded. "You seem very good with kids. Is pediatrics part of your nursing specialty?"

"I work over a wide area." Rice straightened. "But I love kids. I've always wanted little girls of my own, but unfortunately they grow up. Marriage doesn't interest me. The thought of being tied to one woman all my life and watching her grow old isn't in my future."

"Is there somewhere we can talk?" Styles stared at him.

"The breakroom is just through there." He indicated to a passageway on the other side of a set of swinging doors.

"After you." Styles walked beside Beth.

They waited for Rice to speak to the other nurse on duty and then followed him out of the ward. The breakroom was spotlessly clean but small, with lockers down one side. A kitchenette and tables had chairs set around them.

"I can't be missing from the ward for too long." Rice indicated to the table and pulled out a chair. "What's this all about? Why do you need to speak to me? I pay my taxes."

Beth took her time sitting down and placing her notebook and pen on the table before her. She looked up at Rice. It was pointless asking him about his patients and she doubted he'd ever risk grooming his victims at the hospital. "It's not about taxes, Mr. Rice. I'm not interested in anything that happens between you and the IRS. We're speaking to people who were in Rainbow or Serenity over the last week."

"Why?" Rice smiled at her. "What could possibly happen in those two small towns that would interest the FBI? We have very capable sheriffs in our towns. So is it drug related?" He leaned back in the chair and looked from one to the other. "That's why you want to speak to me, isn't it? I work in a hospital, so you would naturally assume that I have access to drugs. The truth is the pharmacy here is very diligent. Even if I had a headache, I'd have to go down to the general store to buy some Tylenol." He pointed to himself with both thumbs. "Aw come on, Agent Katz, do I look like a drug dealer?"

Tapping the pen on the table, Beth looked at him. Trying to get inside information on a case was typical psychopathic behavior. Often, they would try and insert themselves in the investigation by being helpful. Good-looking and with an arrogant confidence, he believed he would win her over, but in fact it was the opposite. She dug in her heels and stared at him. "I'm not in a position to discuss the details of the case at this time, but if you want to remove yourself from our list, I suggest you cooperate. Let me narrow it down for you a little. We know you had a shift from nine through two Monday last at the Rainbow hospital. We're aware you worked in Serenity on the same shift Thursday last. What we'd like to know are your whereabouts between the time you left the hospital and returned to Rattlesnake Creek. I need to know if you stopped along the way and spoke to anyone. If you could give me a timeline, it would be very helpful."

"Your list for what?" Rice glanced at Styles and shrugged. "If one of my ladies is shouting rape, it's a lie."

"If you'd raped someone Mr. Rice, and been named as a possible suspect, the local sheriff would be hauling you downtown." Styles leaned on the table. He looked over at Beth and shrugged. "We're hunting down a serial killer who's possibly been seen in the towns we've mentioned. People who frequently visit or work in these towns are more likely to notice a stranger. Answer the questions, Mr. Rice."

"Ah, the kid who went missing in Rainbow? Was she

murdered?" Rice stared straight into Beth's eyes. "I figured she'd been taken by a bear, like the kid in Serenity."

How he'd obtained this information sent up a red flag for Beth. "Where did you get the information about the bear attack?"

"I was working at the hospital in Serenity yesterday and someone mentioned the local sheriff found body parts all over. So, I assumed it was a bear." He leaned on the table. "Yeah, I was in Serenity and Rainbow on the days you mentioned, and I work there all the time. Where do I spend my time after my shift? It depends. I date a lot of married women. Their husbands are often away working at the mining camps and their wives get lonely." He chuckled. "Don't look so shocked. We're not living in the Dark Ages anymore and women set their own rules."

After being held a virtual prisoner in a pedophile's brothel, nothing would ever shock Beth again. "I don't really care about your sordid lifestyle, Mr. Rice, but I would like the names of people who'll corroborate your story."

"I always go to the local diner. I go there after my shift every time I'm in town. That's where I meet my friends. You're welcome to ask the servers in the diners if I was there, but there's no way I am giving you the names of the women I see. Some of their husbands are violent and interference from someone like you would cause trouble." His eyes flashed with triumph as if he'd won. "And that wouldn't be very nice, would it?"

Beside her Styles pressed his boot against hers. He'd noticed the smug expression on the man's face as well. Beth could go two ways with this interview and she glanced down to make a few notes in her book to give herself a couple of seconds to think. She lifted her head slowly and met his gaze with a smile of her own. "Well, I don't figure it would be very good for you. I mean, gossip spreads like wildfire in these small towns, and I hear those miners can be, let's say, unpredictable, especially when they travel in gangs. Riling them wouldn't be a good idea. I can't imagine what would happen if someone let it slip about your affairs to one of them. I sure wouldn't like a group of them hunting me down." She sighed and folded her notebook and slid it back inside her pocket. "Unfortunately, if that happens, we wouldn't be able to assist you. I'm afraid you'd be on your own."

With her gut feeling screaming at her, Beth got slowly to her feet, and allowed her dark side to slide to the surface. She didn't trust Ainsley Rice and gave him the full force of her dislike. His face froze as their eyes met as if he'd stared into the face of Medusa.

THIRTY-SIX

Styles noticed a change in Beth as they walked back to the truck. She hadn't looked at him and kept her eyes front all the way back to the parking lot. "What do you think of him?"

"I think he let it slip about the girls to see our reaction." Beth pushed both hands into her pockets and headed for the passenger door. "The part about it being a bear attack was interesting. Nothing was mentioned about a bear at any time. We all know who killed the girl. So, either he's getting his information secondhand or he's the murderer. For me, the way he acted was way too smooth. All that stuff about taxes was fake. He seemed to enjoy being interviewed by us as if it made him the center of attention. Right now, he is at the top of my list. What about you? What did you get from him?"

Impressed by her astuteness, Styles stared at her over the hood of his truck. "Not quite as much as you did. For me, he seemed a bit overkeen to find out what was happening. I'd like to make my decision when we've spoken to the others."

"That's a given." Beth sighed. "You wanted my first impressions and that was it. I didn't like the fact that he liked little girls. When he said that it made my skin crawl." She climbed inside the truck.

As Styles slid behind the wheel, Bear gave them a friendly woof. The dog hadn't slept as he'd expected, and by the trails of saliva all over the window, something outside had piqued his interest. He gave him a pat on the head and then turned back and started the engine. "Bear is active. I figure he's been barking at someone."

"I hope no one has planted a bomb under the truck." Beth went to open the door.

Styles touched her arm and it froze under his touch. "He'd be going nuts if someone tampered with the truck. He went on missions and he can smell explosives. Don't worry." He started the engine. "See? It's all good."

"I'm not that confident with his abilities." Beth looked at Bear and her hand sneaked out to scratch his ears. "Although he is very intelligent. I'm sure he knows what you're saying. What do you think spooked him?"

Styles headed back to the office. "Maybe someone got too close, is all. Unless he saw a chicken."

"A chicken, huh?" Beth leaned back in her seat staring at him. "Do tell."

Driving back to the highway, Styles shrugged. "He has this thing about chickens, as in they frighten him." He looked at her astonished expression. "Maybe he was pecked as a pup. I don't know but he'll run away and hide if he sees a chicken."

"I'm sure that was a problem when he was on active duty." Beth frowned. "There were chickens running all over most of the war zones. Didn't anyone mention it before?"

Styles accelerated along the highway, enjoying the way the afternoon sun turned the tops of the pines to gold. During tough cases the scenery kept him sane. He loved living in Rattlesnake Creek. He sighed. "Nope, not a word, and I can hardly ask his handler, can I? We're dealing with it. I tried to make him feel better by holding a chicken and patting him and offering him treats, but seeing me with a chicken made him frightened of me too."

"Hmm. That's not good. Poor Bear." Beth stared out the window. "I'll start work on the laptop as soon as we get back to the office. It's going to take some time for me to check everything, so could you follow up with the local sheriff in Serenity and see if either of the victims owned a tablet or whatever? The cops might already have them in evidence, and correlating their data will help me discover if this predator is using the internet to get to the girls."

Placing Beth's instructions on a list in his mind, Styles glanced at the digital clock on his dash. "We have an order of pies coming from Aunt Betty's Café after four this afternoon. I was lucky and caught up with Dawson before he left Black Rock Falls, and then I called the diner and placed my order. Don't mention we're buying pies from another diner to TJ, will you? I don't want to hurt his feelings."

"My lips are sealed." Beth nodded slowly. "So how are you planning on getting Lawrence Dawson to talk to us? I mean you can't just say 'thanks for the delivery' and then 'are you involved in these murders?' or he'll be shouting entrapment." She gave him a critical stare. "I know you run your game close to the edge, but I figure that's pushing it a bit too far. Maybe we come in from a different angle. It would work well with a psychopath if you asked him for his assistance. You could say we're looking for strangers in these towns and noticed on his ad he travels around some. Ask if his work has taken him where they've been. If you take that line of questioning, we wouldn't make him feel like we're suspicious."

Impressed, Styles nodded. "Yeah, I'll run that through my head some. It's a good idea. When I called him, he mentioned this would be his last run for the day, so we'll bring him up here, thank him for taking on the delivery at short notice. Maybe even offer him a cup of coffee and put him at his ease before we start asking him questions? What do you say?"

"That sounds like a plan." Beth sighed as they slid into the underground parking lot below their building. "I'll sit at my desk, so it doesn't look as if we're ganging up on him."

Styles climbed out of the truck and stretched. He opened the back door and unclipped Bear's harness. "I'll be up in five. Bear needs a potty break."

"Okay." Beth headed for the elevator and turned around, walking backward. "You're a bad influence on me, Dax Styles. I'm actually looking forward to those pies." She gave him a wave and turned toward the elevator.

Grinning, Styles headed to the grassy area around the perimeter of the building. He patted Bear on the head. He'd seen a different side to Beth today. Her stiff professional, argumentative, persona had slipped a little to display someone he could grow to like.

THIRTY-SEVEN

On entering the office, Beth dropped her things on her desk and then went straight to the windows and flung them open. She often wondered why some people had an aversion to fresh air and stood for some moments allowing the cold wind to toss around her hair. The smell of death was still stuck to the inside of her nose and breathing in the fresh pine fragrance of the forest and the scent of the snow-covered mountains cleared her head. She went to the kitchenette and put on a pot of coffee before returning to her desk. Soon the aroma of the brew filled the room and she breathed in deeply. There wasn't anything better than the smell of coffee on a cold fall afternoon. She turned over the evidence bag on her desk containing Brooklyn Daniels' iPad and examined it through the plastic. With care she broke the seal, noting the dust left from collecting fingerprints. Using that method was old style and she took a tissue from her drawer and wiped it clean.

It took a few seconds for her to gain access to all of Brooklyn's social media platforms. She added in the names of the other victims and noted with interest that they were all friends. The main topic of the conversation, apart from what happened at school, was the apparent fascination with an online game. It wasn't anything special, a simple role-playing game where the girls became witches or fairies and the boys knights or warlocks, and then there was the grand warlock and the fairy queen, which she assumed must be the coordinators, but maybe not. Everything was easily corrupted. The link between the missing girls and the game was significant. Anything that linked victims together, however seemingly random, often led to arrests.

Any online platform was easily hacked. It wasn't just games that came under attack from cybercrime. It didn't seem to matter how many fail-safes were included in a game for children, hackers were able to gain access. It was a honey hole for predators, who joined the game under the identity of a child and played along for sometimes months to gain a child's trust. She shook her head in disbelief. If this was how the Pied Piper was grooming the girls, he'd managed to gain access to them through a maze of back doors. Amused by the trail he'd left behind, she smiled. The character named "The Warlock" had to be the Pied Piper. He was well hidden and very well disguised. His IP address jumped all over the world. She wondered if he'd discover her trace on his files as she scanned the lines of data. How would he feel when he realized someone like her was tracking him?

If only locating his whereabouts were as simple. Beth sighed. She couldn't trace him, not until he went online and then it would be difficult. She didn't have time before he struck again. It would be very soon, in the next day or so. She could almost see his moves like pieces on a chessboard. The next would be his last and he'd move to another area. It was something he did frequently. The MO fitted all of their suspects. The travel nurses worked through an agency and traveled all over. Dawson, the courier driver, established a service in surrounding towns and then moved on to set up another, leaving someone else to manage the business. It all seemed legitimate, but what an ingenious excuse to move around. It also left Dawson the opportunity to return to a comfort zone and kill again, maybe years down the track. *Yes, it could be him.*

The door to the office opened and Styles walked in with Sheriff Ryder behind him. Beth smiled as Bear bounded up to her, tail wagging and mouth stretched wide around his bone. She looked up as Styles came to her desk. "Is that a laptop I see in your hand?"

"It is. Sheriff Addams drove it down from Serenity. It belongs to Hailey Quinn." Styles indicated to Ryder standing beside him with his hands resting on his belt. "You can thank Cash. He chased it down after you mentioned you were looking for it."

Surprised by Ryder's sudden enthusiasm, Beth smiled at him. "Thank you so much. I'm not sure how much Styles has told you about me, but I started in cybercrime. If there's a connection between social media or any of the games the girls were playing online and the killer, I'll hunt it down. Having two devices will give me a cross-reference on websites that might be extremely valuable."

"My pleasure, ma'am." Ryder tipped his hat. "I'm sorry about before. I know none of this is your fault. Seeing the girl all cut up like that made me mad, is all."

Nodding Beth stood and went to the kitchenette. "Apology accepted. Coffee?"

"Thanks." Ryder smiled at her. "Black."

"We have Lawrence Dawson dropping by anytime now. He is a courier driver who runs all the way from Black Rock Falls through to Serenity and Rainbow, but he lives here. I've arranged for him to drop by this afternoon with a delivery of pies. It was a way of speaking to him without causing any undue suspicion." Styles' phone chimed a message and he peered at the screen. "Speak of the devil, that's a message from him saying his ETA is five minutes." He looked at Beth. "How do you want to play this?"

Beth handed them cups of coffee and poured one for herself. She leaned against the counter sipping the rich hot brew. "Why don't you and Ryder chat casually with him? If he is a suspect in this case, he'll be a typical psychopath and probably enjoy discussing the murders. You need to remember that they really enjoy reliving every aspect of the kills. If he's involved, it's likely he'll want to know everything you've discovered. Feed him some information and see if he spills his guts." She went to her desk and sat down leaning back in her chair. "I'll sit here and pretend to be working on this laptop, but I'll be listening to everything. I suggest you record the conversation with your phone. Try not to lead him into speaking about the murders, maybe say it's been a bad few days. If he starts to discuss what's been happening in town, then it's not entrapment, is it?"

"Well, I guess we're gonna find out." Styles raised both eyebrows and shrugged. "As we don't have anything at all on any of the suspects, I guess we play it by ear." The buzzer sounded on the outside intercom, and Styles went to the screen. "Yeah, that's Lawrence Dawson." He pressed the intercom button. "Come on up. Take the elevator to the third floor."

THIRTY-EIGHT

Anxious to prove her theory about Lawrence Dawson, Beth watched his progress through the security door and to the elevator on the screens. As he progressed, Styles used the controls on the security system to give him access. Moments later, Styles walked to the door and pulled it open. Dawson resembled a typical courier driver in these parts. Brown pants and a heavy matching jacket with his name in yellow on one of the pockets. When he turned around, he had the name Dawson's Couriers across his back. He stood approximately five-ten, Caucasian, light brown hair, hazel eyes. She noticed his nails and hands were spotlessly clean, not as if he'd been moving packages around all day. Turning back to the device that Ryder had given her, she listened with interest as Styles went to work.

"Mr. Dawson, am I glad to see you." Styles took the package and slid it onto his desk. "Long day? It's freezing outside and I've just brewed a fresh pot of coffee, why don't you join us?"

"You want me to sit down with the FBI?" Dawson appeared a little confused and looked from the sheriff to Styles and back and then shrugged. "This is the first time any of my customers have offered me a cup of coffee." He scratched his cheek. "This is my last delivery of the day, so yeah, thanks. It will be good to get out of the cold for a time." He took the offered chair, his attention following Styles to the kitchenette. "Black is fine."

"I know what you mean." Styles handed him a cup. "It's been a very long couple of days for us too."

Beth smiled into her coffee cup as Dawson opened up like a flower after the spring rain. She flicked a knowing glance at Styles, who kept his attention fixed on Dawson. She had underestimated Styles. His relaxed, outgoing persona would have fooled the best of them. He sure didn't look like he was on the job.

"Terrible business about them young girls. Just terrible." Dawson sipped his coffee eyeing them over the rim. "I was in Rainbow when they were searching for them. I don't recall so many people living in that town, but every man and his dog were out looking for them young'uns."

"We didn't get out there until they'd found Brooklyn Daniels in the forest." Styles indicated with his chin toward Ryder. "Cash was out hunting for days for the other girl, but we didn't find a trace of her."

"So, I hear." Dawson rubbed his chin. "What about the other two who went missing from Serenity?"

"We're still looking." Ryder stretched out his legs and crossed his ankles. "How did you hear about them?"

"People talk and ask me questions as I move around." Dawson sighed. "It just so happened I was in Serenity at the diner when the sheriff came in and asked people to join the search. I couldn't help out because I had a truckload of deliveries." He looked at Ryder. "It seems strange to me that two little girls in each town go missing around the same time and yet from what I hear no one has seen any strangers in town."

"The problem is we have miners working in this entire region from all over." Styles sipped his brew. "Many of them work here because they're living off the grid. We figure if anyone is involved in the girls' disappearance, it's probably one of them. Although we don't have any leads pointing to them at the moment."

"Maybe, maybe." Dawson pursed his lips as if thinking and then lifted his gaze to Styles. "He'd have to be near invisible to move through two towns without being noticed." He cleared his throat and looked at Ryder. "You found one girl murdered, right? So, what did he do with the other one?"

"Murder hasn't been established yet, Mr. Dawson." Ryder shrugged. "It's just scuttlebutt."

Intrigued by his willingness to talk, Beth turned in her seat to look at the trio. Dawson was relaxed and seemingly in control of the conversation. She had witnessed this type of behavior before in a guilty suspect. He was feeding tidbits to Styles to gain inside information on the case. When Styles looked at her, she gave him a nod. Hoping that he would leak the details of the second girl being found.

"Sheriff Addams has located one of the missing girls from Serenity." Styles drained his cup and placed it on the desk.

"Yeah, I heard about that one. They're saying it was a bear attack, but you don't believe that, do you?" Dawson unbuttoned his jacket in a relaxed manner. "I figure it's too much of a coincidence for little girls to go missing from two different towns and then one of each is found dead and the others are still missing."

"Maybe you should be a detective, Mr. Dawson. We haven't ruled out a bear yet." Styles smiled. "It's not safe for anyone to be in the forest alone at this time of the year, especially young kids. We've no evidence to say they were murdered or if both girls were taken by a bear. We're awaiting on the autopsy results. It wouldn't be unreasonable to imagine that the other girls were dragged off to a cave somewhere. As you say, no one has seen any strangers in the area."

"You could be right." Dawson placed his cup on the desk.

Unable to resist, asking a few questions, Beth stood and walked over to Styles' desk and leaned casually against the filing cabinet. "So, you travel all over? I've just arrived in Rattlesnake Creek and plan to visit a few of the local towns. Have you ever been to Spring Grove?"

"Yeah, that's one of my regular routes." Dawson looked her over from top to bottom and smiled. "It's a quiet little town until the miners come in on the weekend. It has three saloons and they're bursting at the seams all weekend. The music is loud and the beer is flowing."

Recognizing the look in his eyes as his way of trying to embarrass her, Beth laughed and noticed his expression change to annoyance. She lifted her chin. "That sounds like my kind of town."

"Well, I'd better be heading home. My day isn't over yet. I have to download my schedule for tomorrow." Dawson pushed to his feet. "Thanks for the coffee."

Beth had a few more questions for him. "I'm really interested in how you manage to run a courier service so efficiently between four different towns. You must have very sophisticated computer software. Styles found it so easy to book a delivery."

"Thanks." Dawson's brow furrowed. "Not so sophisticated. People call me on my cell if something is urgent. The program is just an interactive calendar. They can see what days I'm delivering where and book it in a time when I'm not busy. Payment is handled online."

Nodding as if interested, Beth gave him a confused stare. "Oh, that's so complicated. I'm terrible when it comes to technology. I have problems tracing people on the databases."

"It's not so difficult for me, but then I do most things online." Dawson smiled. "It's a sign of the times, I guess." He looked at Styles. "Good talking to you."

"Good talking to you too." Styles stood and walked him out

to the elevator. When he returned, he looked at Beth. "What did you get from him?"

"I'm not convinced he's the Pied Piper." She shrugged. "A male chauvinist maybe. Did you see the way he looked at me? One thing's for sure, I'll be checking out his webpage and finding out if he's the designer. If he is, he might be hiding something. I'm convinced the Pied Piper is gaining access to these girls via an online game."

"An online game?" Ryder scratched his cheek and stared at her. "How?"

Glad to see Ryder relax at last, she shrugged. "It's a typical hunting ground for pedophiles. They join a forum as a kid to gain a kid's trust and then lure them away from safety." She stepped away from the filing cabinet and pushed both hands through her hair. "I'm going to speak to the kids at the Spring Grove grade school about online games in the morning. I'm convinced that town is part of his comfort zone and it has to be his next target."

"So do we warn the parents to keep their kids at home?" Ryder rubbed the back of his neck. "Spring Grove is under my jurisdiction."

"No, not yet. We don't want to spook him." Styles sat down at his desk. "We have no proof he'll hit Spring Grove. It's just a hunch."

"A hunch, huh." Ryder's mouth formed a thin line as he moved his gaze from Styles to Beth and back. "If you're right and I don't do anything, this guy is going to kill again. I can't allow that to happen."

Beth took in the set of his shoulders. What part of "don't spook him" didn't he understand? One thing she had in spades was diplomacy. She guessed it came with being a psychopath. "Cash, this is why we are here. I have personally handled many cases with serial killers. You need to trust that we know what to do. It is better that you stand down until we need you. Like Dax said, if we spook him, we've lost the opportunity to catch him in the act." She shrugged. "Then he'll be out there killing more kids. We have a small window of opportunity here, and if you go in warning people, he'll know we're onto him. You do understand, don't you?"

"Yeah, I guess so, but the moment you pin him down I want to be there." Ryder grimaced. "I want to look that murdering SOB right in the eye."

THIRTY-NINE

MONDAY, WEEK TWO

Spring Grove

Unable to sleep, Beth had eaten breakfast early and headed for the office. Settled at her desk, she'd searched through aerial shots of Spring Grove, looking for clearings in the forest. She zoomed in on hunting trails leading to small clearings and similar settings to those the Pied Piper had used previously. It seemed obvious to her that he followed the same pattern in his movements when he met the girls. He gained access to the forest via a fire road, parked his vehicle, and continued on foot to the meeting place. The fire roads in Spring Grove were kept clear at all times, which made it easier for her to find them on the aerial views. None of the girls had arrived at the crime scenes on a bicycle, so she had to assume that the meeting place was in easy walking distance of their homes. When she traced back the trail the girls had taken from the scenes of the previous murders to their homes, she discovered they were less than half a mile away. After studying the maps and taking into account the distance from the local town, she came up with three possible locations. She wrote down the coordinates and stood to fill a couple of Thermos flasks with the coffee she'd just brewed. They would be driving to Spring Grove to interview Emerson Green at Spring Grove General and then head to the school, where she had arranged to speak to the children about the dangers of strangers in the area and online gaming. It had surprised her how eager the school principal had been when she suggested their visit.

An email popped into her box from Shane Wolfe. She read the contents with interest. He'd attached the autopsy report on Hailey Quinn with a note.

This is a mirror image of Brooklyn Daniels' autopsy. Time of death would have been approximately one hour after she left home. All other injuries are animal in nature and inflicted post-mortem. It's without doubt the same killer.

She filed the report and looked up as the door to the office opened and Bear bounded in and ran straight to her, his ears erect and brown eyes glossy. His thick tail wagged back and forth with excitement at seeing her. It made her feel good to be accepted by Styles' dog, even though his owner was still a little hesitant to trust her. She looked up from rubbing Bear's ears as Styles collapsed in his chair, making it groan. "Wolfe sent Hailey Quinn's autopsy report. It's the same as Brooklyn Daniels', apart from animal intervention. TOD was approximately one hour after she left home."

"I guess it's good to know we don't have two maniacs running around killing young girls." Styles flexed and unflexed his fingers in obvious pain.

Wondering what had happened to him overnight, Beth examined his pale expression. "Is everything okay?"

"Yeah, I just overdid it some in the gym." Styles rolled his shoulder. "It's an old injury that plays up from time to time. I've taken some meds to take down the swelling, but remind me next time I get mad not to spend so much time swinging a bat."

During her lifetime Beth had studied many things to assist her in her lifestyle. The herbs and various medications were only a very small part of her arsenal of knowledge. Physical therapy was another. As it was obvious that Styles didn't like her driving his truck and they would be spending a good deal of time on the road and very likely in the air, she needed him in top shape. With reluctance she pushed to her feet. "Take off your jacket. I can help with the shoulder injury."

"Ah, I'll be fine." Styles looked at her as if she'd grown two heads. "As soon as the meds kick in, I'll be as good as new."

Balling her fists on her hips Beth stared at him. "What, are you chicken?"

"You might make it worse." Styles reluctantly removed his jacket, wincing with pain.

Beth eyed him critically. "I figure it's a pinched nerve. I know meds or an injection usually work pretty fast, but some-times I can work faster. You'll need to come and sit on one of the stools." She hid her smile as he obeyed and walked round behind him. "Relax, don't fight me."

"Okay, just get on with it." Styles sat bolt upright and his jaw tightened.

With gentle care, she manipulated his shoulder and then stood back. "There, feel better now?"

"Ah..." Styles moved cautiously. "Yeah, that feels much better." He raised one dark eyebrow and looked at her suspiciously. "You're obviously a woman of many talents. Is there anything else I should know?"

Beth laughed and reached for her coat. "Probably. Not everything about me is in the files. I did once actually have a life outside of the FBI." She collected the Thermos flasks and tossed a bag of energy bars to him. "Let's go or we'll be late. I don't want to rush through Emerson Green's interview."

After a picturesque drive through alpine countryside, they arrived in the small town of Spring Grove and went straight to the hospital. A wave of antiseptic hit her as she pushed inside. It was busy for a small town. People sat in waiting areas looking depressed, glancing up at them as they walked by. Every now and then somebody coughed or groaned. After showing their creds at the front counter, they were directed to the ward where they located Emerson Green. Beth checked his image on her phone, and they found him easily enough. Styles hung back in the passageway, and they waited for Green to leave the ward before she approached him in a casual manner. "Emerson Green?"

"Yeah, who wants to know?" Green peeled off examination gloves and tossed them into the garbage before turning to look at her.

Holding up her cred pack, Beth smiled. "There's no need to be alarmed. We're speaking to everyone who frequently moves around between here, Rainbow, Serenity, and Rattlesnake Creek. I spoke to your agency and they mentioned you and a few other travel nurses in the area. Is there somewhere we can speak in private?"

"Yeah, out on the deck." Green stared apprehensively at Styles as he pushed away from the wall and walked toward them.

Beth moved to Green's side. "This is my partner, Agent Styles."

Outside on the deck, Beth took out her notebook and pen. "Can you tell me your whereabouts since Thursday last?"

"What's this about?" Green narrowed his eyes at Beth. "I'm happy to assist you, but first I'd like to know, do I need a lawyer?"

"Mr. Green." Styles tipped back his Stetson. "You heard about the girls going missing in Rainbow and Serenity, right? I mean everyone in both towns is talking up a storm about it."

"Yeah, so what's it to do with me?" Green swiped a fist over the end of his nose.

Beth cleared her throat. "As I mentioned, we're talking to people who were around town at the time they went missing. We need a timeline. We know you were in both towns and showed for your shift on time. You would have traveled through town around the time they left home. Did you see anyone with the girls? Did you see the girls walking toward the forest?"

"There are kids out all the time." Green shrugged. "I don't recall noticing anyone in particular on either day." He glanced over one shoulder toward the door. "I can't be too long. Is there anything else?"

Needing to know so much more about this man, Beth nodded. "I noticed on your social media pages you mention you're into gaming. I like to play online, do you?"

"Is there any other way?" Green's mood lightened. "It's a whole other world. A place you can be anyone you want. The ultimate escapism. I'm into VR as well. It's just like being there."

Watching his animated expression, Beth nodded. "Yeah, virtual reality is the new era of gaming. I have a gaming chair that bounces me all over. I prefer to stick to the chair or I walk into walls."

"Me too." Green smiled. "Gaming is all the kids talk about in here."

"Yeah, they make a ton of friends online." Styles leaned casually against the wall. "Kids from all over."

"That's true." Green rubbed the back of his neck. "I gotta go. They'll be wondering where I've gone." He looked at Beth.

She nodded. "Yeah, that's all we needed. Thanks."

Beth waited for him to leave and turned to Styles. "He's a maybe too. The gaming link is something we shouldn't dismiss."

"He was evasive and didn't you say they're usually over-cooperative?" Styles straightened. "What I saw was nervous and defensive. I'm not sure he's involved."

Shaking her head, Beth looked at him. "Serial killers are smart. They know the FBI is constantly upgrading their research on psychopathic serial killers. I mean there's enough shows on TV about them you'd have to be living off the grid not to know." She folded her notebook and thrust it inside her pocket. "So, they are more than capable of acting in a way suitable to the occasion. Most times the true character shows through… like when he became all friendly talking about gaming… almost childlike. He was turning on the charm… saying 'look at me I'm a good guy,' but he didn't fool me."

FORTY

He liked becoming the Warlock. It was one of his more ingenious ideas to gain a kid's trust and he'd use it again. He'd enjoyed his time in Rattlesnake Creek and could always return in a year or so when the heat died down. With the sheriffs of the local towns making inquiries and the FBI sniffing around, it would be time to go real soon, but not just yet. It wasn't as if he'd done anything wrong. It wasn't as if he'd kidnapped the girls. They always came to him willingly. What happened was their fault. They'd shared his fantasy right to the end. Online, their chats had been fun and they'd begged to meet him. He'd only given them what they wanted.

He'd need to make plans to leave town. He'd make it appear like he'd left before he planned to meet the girls. That would be easy enough as people believed what he told them. If he mentioned the day he planned to leave, that's the day they'd remember and that's the day they'd tell the cops. Too easy.

He'd selected the next two. One for him and the other to sell. He'd collected images of the girl intended for sale from social media and sent them to his contact on the dark web. The auction would take place tonight and he would lay down plans to move the merchandise as fast as possible. He usually managed to get the girl out of the forest or meeting place within an hour, but he always calculated on two as sometimes the girls arrived late, but they usually surprised him how punctual they were. Most of them didn't believe he'd actually arrive and figured he must be one of their friends playing a joke on them. It was always satisfying to see their faces light up when he walked into a clearing or turned up at the door of an old hunting cabin as if confused. It never ceased to amaze him how he was able to get them to do what he wanted. This way of meeting the girls was particular to this area of Montana. He'd discovered the latest craze for young girls was an interactive game of fairies and warlocks. It seemed that they became so engrossed with the game that they lived it in their heads, so the chance to meet a character was believable to them.

The different elements of the game had enabled him to separate the girls. He'd arrived with a special magic potion, which in fact was an herbal sleeping draft he'd discovered on his travels and grew in his backyard. It worked particularly fast on children and enabled him to leave the second girl in a safe place so he could return to his blonde fantasy. It was strange how no matter what the blonde actually looked like, the moment he stroked her long blonde hair she became Susie Parkinson. He spoke her name and the memories came tumbling back. He'd been twelve when Susie moved in next door. He'd watch her through a hole in the wooden fence, speaking to her dolls and dressing them like fairies. She was very young, but playing inside her secret garden, she mesmerized him. He wanted to talk to her and touch her long blonde hair.

Things changed when his father caught him and beat him within an inch of his life. It wasn't for looking at Susie through the hole in the fence; it was for getting caught. He'd wanted to speak to his pa, needing an explanation, but that same day his mom vanished in the night. His father insisted she'd run away with another man and that women like her were all the same. What happened next changed his life. On a lazy Sunday afternoon, he'd seen Susie wander into the woods near his home, and when she didn't return, he'd gone to look for her. On the edge of a clearing, he'd found his pa with Susie. Watching him was exciting but when his pa turned, looked at him, and smiled, something inside his head prevented him from running away. His feet glued to the forest floor and then his pa had beckoned him.

"She made me do it, son." His pa had stared at him. "You seen how she smiled at me. The young'uns are the worst." He'd pulled latex gloves from his pocket. "Put on these gloves. Now come here and do as I say or we're both going to jail."

As if an automaton, he'd walked over to him and followed instructions, collecting Susie's clothes, folding them up, and then placing her shoes neatly on top of the pile. When his father stabbed Susie, he watched in morbid fascination, unable to drag his eyes away, but when he handed him the knife with the words "no one can ever know, finish her," killing Susie had been the right thing to do. A tremble went through him as he remembered the thrill that sparked his addiction. From that day on, he'd killed them all.

His pa had insisted he find him more girls, and at first it had been difficult, but soon he'd learned how to convince them. Young girls were never afraid of him. He'd chat with them and offer to walk them home, and soon became their boyfriend. Ten-to twelve-year-olds fell for it every time and after a few days they'd do anything he asked. His pa moved them from town to town and he helped him until the cops came to the door asking questions. He'd given his pa an alibi and the cops had believed him, but his pa had made up his mind to leave town. However, his pa wanted another girl before they left. He'd followed the usual plan and packed the truck and told everyone they'd be leaving that day, but that afternoon things started playing on his mind. He'd taken all the risks and his pa was getting all the fun. He needed more and the thrill of killing was no longer satisfying his hunger. With the cops sniffing around his pa for the murders, it would only be a matter of time before they turned their attention his way. After all, he wasn't a kid any longer. It was time to do something.

As usual, he'd done his part and led the girl into the forest, but this time when his pa handed him the knife, he'd stabbed the girl and then turned the knife on him. He'd laughed when his pa grabbed his throat and looked at him bug-eyed. Then he'd turned to his Susie—she was always Susie to him, his blonde-haired fairy princess—and placed the knife in her small hand, and walked away. He'd followed the plan, taken the truck, and driven to another state.

He rarely thought of his pa and had managed alone just fine. He'd gotten a job that allowed him to move around and make his own plans. His pa had told him men like them were different to others—another lie. He'd been surprised just how many people were like him. Hundreds wanted to communicate with him and share their fantasies, but then his pa hadn't been as smart as him. He'd learned from his pa's mistakes and would never risk sharing his Susie with anyone, and by changing up his game plan frequently, he confused the cops. His idea of taking her friend had been pure genius and paid out in silver dollars. This way, he could have his Susie anytime he wanted and never worry about being short of cash. He smiled at his reflection in the rearview mirror. One thing was for sure: there was never a shortage of men willing to pay for little girls.

FORTY-ONE

The smell of the classroom brought back pleasant memories for Styles. He wondered why a kids' classroom always had the same odor. He thought on it for a time as Beth prepared to speak to the kids. Being human, people probably didn't register the familiar smell in a classroom, but they'd understand exactly what he meant if he mentioned the smell of puppies. He pushed the silly notions to the back of his mind and tried to appear nonthreatening. The mention of FBI agents in the room had silenced the noise in seconds. After being introduced to the wide-eyed kids, he went to stand beside the teacher at the back of the classroom and watched Beth cast her magic over the group of children. He hadn't expected her to have such a magnetic personality. The way she spoke was engaging and all of the children were mesmerized by her. She had kept her language easy to understand. As she was coming to the end she very carefully introduced some valid points.

"When I was a little girl, my mom always told me to be careful of strangers." Beth smiled. "Moms always say that don't they?" She shrugged. "The problem is the dangerous people who want to harm kids are usually very nice. They want to be your friend. So, if someone who has been a stranger suddenly wants to be your friend, you need to tell your parents or your teacher. If you're playing a game online and someone wants to know where you live or wants to meet you, they may not be another kid, but a stranger trying to harm you. If this happens, you must tell your parents. If this has happened to you recently, you should tell me. I'll find out if that person is who they say they are." She smiled. "You'll never get into trouble, and the person will never know what you say to me." She waved to a desk the teacher had set up for her in the corner. It was surrounded by bookshelves and offered a modicum of privacy. "If you have any questions or want to talk to me about anything at all, including being an FBI agent, I'll be sitting over there for a while."

"We'll be taking a break now." The teacher smiled at the kids. "We have fruit on the counter if you'd like a snack, and I'm happy for you to discuss everything we've been talking about this afternoon."

Styles waited for Beth to walk to his side and smiled. "You handled that like a professional. Do you think you'll get anything out of it?"

"We'll see." Beth scanned the classroom. "I noticed two of the girls blushed when I spoke about someone online. I'll go and sit at the desk and see if anyone comes for a chat." She gave him a sideways look. "To them you're a stranger, so I would suggest you stay put."

Running a hand through his hair, Styles stared at her. "Kids are smart. They know I'm an FBI agent. I'm wearing a vest and I've allowed them to look at my creds as you suggested. I don't believe they consider me a threat." He sighed. "If anyone comes over to speak to you, turn on your earbud. I need to hear what's being said."

"I'll record everything with my phone as well." Beth moved to the secluded corner and sat down with her back to the room.

It was a ploy, she'd explained, to avoid kids being apprehensive about approaching her.

It didn't take long before a young girl chewing on her fingers looked all around before heading toward Beth. Styles touched his earpiece. "Showtime."

"Don't look this way." Beth's voice came through his earpiece. "We don't want to frighten her."

He turned his back and went to read a notice attached to the wall. The earbuds they'd been supplied with were remarkable and not the old ones attached by wire to a battery pack. They fit inside the ear and were almost invisible. Everything was wireless and the sound came through crystal clear. He could hear the young girl's nervous cough as she sidled up to Beth.

"Hi there." Beth cleared her throat. "I thought for a moment that nobody wanted to talk to me. My name is Beth. What's yours?"

"Angela Brown."

Styles turned to one side. The girl couldn't see him and she was coming in loud and clear. Beth had his back to her, but he noticed as she slid her phone into the middle of the table.

"Well, Angela, how can I help you? Is there someone you're concerned about?" Beth leaned back in her chair taking a nonthreatening casual pose.

"Well, my friend Lucy Parker. We play online. There's a bunch of us from school and there is a boy who calls himself the Warlock. He said he knows where the Fairy Queen is hiding in the forest. He asked me and Lucy to meet him there this afternoon at four and he'd show us, but Lucy didn't come to school today. I think her mom's truck broke down or something."

"Where does Lucy live?" Beth sucked in a breath. "We'll go and see if she is okay, and where exactly does the Warlock want you to meet him?"

Angela gave surprisingly clear details.

Beth pulled out her phone and accessed maps of the area. She zoomed into street view and offered her the phone. "Can you show me?"

"I live three houses away from Lucy, but I take the school bus. Lucy's mom gives her a ride to school on her way to work." She moved her fingers over the screen. "This is my house and Lucy lives here. This is where we're meeting the Warlock." She smiled. "We said we'd go meet the Warlock together, but now I'm too scared to go, just in case he is really a stranger. Can you find out?"

"No, don't go. Not ever." Beth leaned forward in her chair. "Never meet anyone in the forest or anywhere else without your parents. This is what bad people do to hurt kids. Stay home and I'll go and meet him and see who he is."

"So, do you want me to pretend we'll meet him?" Angela pushed her hair over one shoulder. "I'm supposed to chat with him in the game room after school."

"Yes, but don't let him know I'll be there." Beth moved around in her chair. "I have a secret mission for you, Angela. Listen carefully. Don't tell Lucy about me either. Call her and tell her you can't go tonight but you'll go with her to meet him another day. After tonight, you can tell Lucy all about me and what we talked about in class today. Can you do that for me, Angela? It will be a special FBI mission. Just you and me."

"Yes." She giggled. "I'll be an FBI agent like you."

"Good." Beth pushed to her feet. "Remember to stay home this afternoon and never ever go into the forest to meet strangers. Leave the Warlock to me."

"Okay." Angela bounced out of the corner grinning. She walked up to her teacher. "I'm going to be an FBI agent."

Styles moved swiftly to her side. "This one will be tricky, but we have no choice."

Uncomprehending, Beth stared at him. "Tricky how?"

"Legally." Styles frowned. "We have so little on any of our suspects. People have rights and we can't ignore them."

"Says the man who beat up four guys in an alleyway." Snorting, Beth shook her head. "We'll catch him first and then worry about the legality of stopping a kid killer. Ryder can take him in for questioning for suspicion of murder. That's perfectly legal and if he's not on our suspect list I'll add him." She lifted her chin. "Don't sweat the small stuff. It's all good."

Styles checked his watch. "I'm not convinced, but whatever, we'll head out to the forest and see if he shows. We'll need to get geared up and there's no time to go back to the office." He thought for a beat. "We'll be able to get camos at the local store. There are two rifles in my truck. I'll call Ryder for the arrest and backup. It's all we've got right now."

"Okay." Beth's eyes flashed with excitement. "He calls himself the Warlock and I bet he asks them to drink a magic potion. It's straight out of the new game all the kids are playing. Now we know how he's grooming them." She took a deep breath. "Which one of our suspects do you believe it is?"

Styles headed for the door. "I have no idea, but I figure we're going to find out soon enough."

FORTY-TWO

Always thinking ahead, Beth never hunted down a serial killer without researching every move ahead of time. Unlike most FBI agents, her mantra was to stop them at all costs—stop as in removing them from this earth, not allowing them to be released on bail to kill again. Leaving them dead in an inconspicuous place with a tarot card somewhere on their person would deflect the crime away from her. For this to work, she would need Styles to believe her location was far away from the Pied Piper at the time of death. It would take all her skills to make this happen.

She climbed into Styles' truck and turned in the seat to look at him and then indicated to the pile of camouflage gear they'd just purchased. "We can't be seen getting changed in the local diner's restroom and then heading out to the forest. We don't know who's watching us. Is there a local motel close by we could use to change and plan out our strategy?"

"There's a motel attached to the back of one of the local saloons." Styles smiled at her. "I'll go get a room. Maybe it's best if you stay in the truck. The fewer people who know about us the better."

She checked her watch. "That's fine by me. I figure we need to get into the forest at least one hour before the meeting time and we'll need to take an alternative route to the Pied Piper. We already know that he'll park his vehicle on the fire road and walk into the forest. We'll come in from the opposite side. I found a hiking track we can use."

As they drove down Main, Beth crossed her arms and drummed her fingers on one forearm, anxious to be in the forest. Forcing herself to relax, she absorbed the scenery. Picturesque was an understatement. This part of the world had a unique beauty. The rivers ran fast and the term *whitewater* was evident as the rushing frothy river cascaded over and around huge chunks of rock. Alongside, boulders smoothed over the years littered the sand-covered riverbanks, offering visitors a place to sit. Across the river, the forest spread out green and lush. Miles and miles of tall fragrant pines marched up the mountainsides to surround the snowcapped peaks.

"Nervous?" Styles flicked her a glance. "I'll be right beside you."

Trying not to laugh, Beth shook her head. "Apprehensive maybe, because Ryder is an unknown. He doesn't have our training. If he barrels into the forest all guns blazing, he'll be risking our lives. We don't know if the suspect is armed. He could be holding the girls at gunpoint for all we know. I don't want him to slip through our net. This is why we should split up. I'll hide in the forest and keep watch. You meet Ryder and circle around the suspect and move in slowly."

"I've worked with Ryder for a time and he's solid." Styles blew out a long breath. "If you don't have confidence in him, by all means hide and keep watch. We are more than capable of taking the suspect down." He pulled up outside the motel and looked at her. "I'm still concerned about the legality of this bust. My worry is we only have a man walking in the forest. There's no law against doing that is there? A judge will throw it out of court, saying what the kid said is hearsay. We don't have any proof to suggest this man is one of our suspects, do we?"

Insights into human nature were something Beth had in spades. She gave Styles a direct stare. "Do you honestly believe Lucy will listen to what Angela says? Well, no she won't. She'll figure that Angela wants the Warlock all to herself. Just remember, these kids live in character. Lucy might be a warrior queen or whatever. She honestly believes she can take care of herself. She wouldn't be worried about being in the forest alone." She looked into his astonished expression and smiled. "Trust me, Lucy will be there. Angela will follow orders. She believes she's on a mission... that's another thing I discovered about the game." She sucked in a deep breath. "The tricky part is stopping the suspect before he harms the girl."

"There's no way we're using a young girl as bait." Styles rubbed the back of his neck. "No way, Beth. He'll kill her before we can get to him."

Shaking her head, Beth glared at him. "What and spoil his fantasy? Killing to him is a process, like role playing, and he'll want to follow the script in his head. For him it's the same girl every time, so it must be perfect." She sighed. "If she shows, we'll watch her every step of the way. If he as much as moves in her direction, we'll take him down. Do you honestly believe I'd risk the life of a child?"

"How do you know she'll show?" Styles' fists whitened on the steering wheel and behind her Bear growled. "I don't like this, Beth."

Astonished by his anger, Beth lowered her voice to just above a whisper. "I know because I studied the murders. He follows a pattern. Today won't be any different. All we need to make the case is to have him meet Lucy in the forest. I have Angela on tape giving the place and time they were told to meet him. Who else would know? He shows up and takes one step toward the girl and we take him down." She met his gaze. "You're a tough guy and you trust Ryder. Just pull out that six-shooter of yours and aim. The suspect won't be expecting you. He'll most likely run away."

"You're batshit crazy." Styles climbed out of the truck and stomped into the office of the motel.

Shaking her head, Beth turned to Bear. "We won't allow anything to happen to Lucy, will we, boy?" She scratched the dog's head and he licked her arm. "At least *we* understand each other."

A few minutes later, Styles emerged from the office and climbed back behind the wheel. Saying nothing, he drove to the end of a line of rooms, slid out, and opened a door before returning to get Bear. Trees surrounded the courtyard, offering privacy, and only one other vehicle was in the parking lot. Beth climbed out, grabbed the bags from the back seat, and carried them inside. The motel room was old and decrepit. Cigarette-tainted air from years gone by was the added bonus to the old musty smell, like a pair of slippers left at the back of a closet for years. The worn carpet had stains all over and some suspiciously resembled blood. Cigarette burns marked the tops of the bedside tables. It wasn't a place she'd like to sleep, that was for darn sure. Juggling the bags in one arm, she pulled back the stained comforter to expose the sheets. At least they appeared to be clean, and she dumped the bags.

"You planning on sleeping?" Styles stood hands on hips staring at her, eyebrows raised.

Beth peered into the bags and selected her things before looking at him. "Me? No, but I'm not sitting on that filthy rag on the bed either. At least the linen looks like it's been laundered this year."

"Here." Ryder handed her two sticks of chalk. "You should always carry chalk. The forests are dense and it's easy to get turned around. Marking the trees as you go means you'll always know the way back."

Wondering if she'd stepped back in time, Beth stared at the chalk. "I usually use the GPS on my satellite phone, but thanks anyway." She headed for the bathroom. "I'm getting changed. Call out when you're done. I don't want to walk in on you in your underwear."

"Not a chance." Styles rolled his eyes skyward. "Take your time. Ryder won't be here for another fifteen minutes or so. He's bringing helmets."

Beth turned at the bathroom door. "Copy that."

Dressed with her hair tied back, a shiver of excitement surged through her. Her fingers slid over the folded cutthroat razor in her pocket. It killed with efficiency and silence, but not today. She sighed and stared at herself in the mirror, allowing the dark side to recede. She prided herself on her skill and the mythical reputation of leaving no clues behind. That couldn't happen surrounded by law enforcement, but she'd find an opportunity at some time to remove this predator from existence. For now, she'd allow the law to take its course, but the moment the Pied Piper was released on bail, it would be game on. She walked to the door and knocked. "You decent?"

"Yeah." Styles looked up from the bed. He'd stripped it completely and shrugged. "I figured we'd need a clean place to sit and wait for Ryder."

Beth stared at the door. "Oh, don't tell me he's coming in his cruiser?"

"Nah, he has his own ride. We're not that stupid, Beth." He narrowed his eyes at her. "You know I've done this before, many times. You seem to believe I'm a rookie in need of guidance. Trust me, I'm not even close."

Sitting on the opposite corner of the bed Beth glared at him. "Good for you."

"I'm going for coffee." Styles stood and headed for the door.

"Watch out for Ryder and have those aerial images ready so we can brief him."

Beth took out her phone. "Yes, sir."

The look he gave her could have melted glass.

FORTY-THREE

They arrived in the forest a little after three. It was fortunate that Ryder knew the area, having lived there for a spell as a child. They hiked through the forest, splitting up well before the clearing where the Warlock had set up the meeting. Beth had listened to both men discuss the plan of attack. Styles and Ryder would be on each side of the clearing, hidden well back in the trees. They assumed that the Warlock was coming from due east as the clearing was situated a short walking distance from the fire road. In their camouflage gear, they would be hidden, and unless he passed close by, they should go unnoticed. Beth shouldered her rifle and took her position behind a boulder. After getting the confirmation that the Warlock had gone past Styles' position, she would head into the forest.

Beth's gut feeling told her that the Warlock was basically a coward and once confronted by two armed men he would hightail it back to his vehicle. Inhaling the rich fresh scents of the forest, she slid through the tall pines like a ghost, stopping frequently in the shadows to peer ahead. It was cold and dark in the dense mass of trees. Underfoot the soil squelched, pressing scattered fall leaves into the mud. Small puddles of dark rancid water abounded, left behind from last night's rain. Freezing like a statue, Beth heard him before he came into sight. Dressed in a long purple gown and wearing a pointed hat, he looked ridiculous as he crunched carelessly through the pine needles scattered over the narrow trail. It was obvious from his slow easy gait that he had no reason to be suspicious.

Heart pounding in her chest, she waited for him to pass out of view and then followed the trail to the fire road. His vehicle was just where she expected, and she walked around it a few times. She couldn't risk walking away without disabling it. Pulling a knife from a sheath on her belt, she thrust it deep into one of the tires, grinning as air exploded in a hiss, tossing the leaves on the road in all directions. She turned slowly and headed back toward the clearing, to see what was happening. Before she got halfway there, Styles' voice came in her earpiece.

"We have the suspect in sight." Styles sounded tense. *"He entered the clearing and is doing some type of ritual, walking around and muttering under his breath. He's dressed in a purple cloak and a pointed hat. This guy is really going all out to convince the kids he's a character in the game."* He sucked in a breath. *"You were right about the girl. I can see her on the trail about one hundred yards away from the clearing and heading this way."*

Anticipation gripped Beth, and her stomach clenched as if she were being dropped from a great height. "Wait until he hands her a drink. We'll have the drink and him as absolute proof he intended to do her harm. Don't mess this up, Styles. We have one chance of catching this monster. I'll have my rifle trained on him the entire time. One false move and I'll take him down. I won't let him touch Lucy. You have my word."

"Copy. I guess I have to trust you sometime."

Snorting, Beth shook her head. *"That would be nice."*

"If you two will stop arguing for a few minutes, maybe we

will be able to take this guy down." Ryder's voice boomed in her ear. *"Get your heads back in the game."*

"Moving in now." Styles' voice was just a hiss in her ear. *"Stay back until we need you, Beth."*

Shaking her head, Beth slipped through the trees until she had an almost uninterrupted view of the clearing. She took out her binoculars and searched the face of the Warlock, but zebra shadows falling across him from the trees disguised his identity. The Warlock had spotted the little girl, and slid into the forest, crouching down out of sight. A few moments later Lucy came down the trail, eagerly looking in all directions. She walked into the middle of the clearing and turned around slowly.

"I'm here." Lucy stared into the dark trees. "Warlock, Warlock, I summon you to come to me."

Excitement at seeing her prediction play out before her trembled Beth's hands. If Styles and Ryder kept their nerve, they would have enough evidence to prove that this suspect was the Pied Piper. If the killer fled the moment the others appeared, he would run straight to her, seeking escape in his truck, and she'd take him down and cuff him.

Mesmerized by the scene unfolding in front of her, she watched as the Pied Piper slipped out of the trees, looking all around as if confused. It was obvious he had played this part many times before. She tapped her com. "Open your com, Styles, so I can hear what he's saying."

The two taps on his speaker told her he'd heard her communication. She listened carefully, and the Pied Piper's voice came through the earpiece as if from down a well.

"How did I get here and who are you?" The Warlock looked all around. *"Was it you, my lady?"*

"Yes, it was me. Take me to meet the Fairy Queen at once." Lucy made some unusual hand gestures.

"First, you must drink the magic potion." The Warlock

pulled a small silver bottle from the folds of his cloak and handed it to her. *"Where is your friend?"*

"She isn't coming. I want you all to myself." Lucy grinned.

"Your wish is my command." The Warlock smiled. *"But first, you must drink the potion."*

"Go, go, go." Styles' voice blasted Beth's eardrums. *"FBI. On the ground. Hands on your head."*

Tree branches cracked, as Styles and Ryder came crashing through the forest, weapons drawn. As predicted, the Pied Piper took off through the trees, zigzagging in the direction of the fire road. He moved faster than she'd predicted. He'd obviously planned his escape and was heading straight for her, tossing his hat and cloak along the way. Assuming he'd veer back onto the fire road and make a break for his truck, Beth headed in that direction. Once she reached the fire road, she propped her rifle against a tree and waited. As he broke through the perimeter of the forest at a run, Beth stepped out from behind a tree, stuck out her boot, and tripped him. He crashed to the floor and his breath came out in a whooping sound. He lay stunned, gasping for breath, but wasn't finished yet. To her surprise, he rolled over and jumped to his feet, pulling out a knife.

Beth took a step back and, moving slowly around him, watched his eyes, waiting for him to strike. She rested one hand on her pistol. It would be so easy to take him down and it would be a righteous shoot, but she needed to know what had happened to the other girls.

"I'm going to cut you up good." The Pied Piper waved the knife back and forth. It glinted in the dappled sunshine, lethally sharp.

Heart pounding, Beth waited for the right moment and then spun and kicked the knife from his hand. As he yelped in pain, she landed a second kick to the side of his knee, taking him to the ground. In that second, she was on him, pinning him to the forest floor with her knees. "How do you like playing with the big girls?"

"It's her fault, she made me come here." The Pied Piper moved his head, his chin digging into the damp forest floor. "They're all the same. They want to play the game. You figure they're nice but they're evil. Can't you see that?"

Beth pressed hard into his spine, enjoying his whimper. They were all the same when they came up against her, like worms caught on the blade of a shovel. "You're never going to kill again. She slid from the Pied Piper's back, dragged his arms behind him, and cuffed him.

"I didn't hurt Susie." Rice tried to push onto his knees.

"Lie still, you sack of shit." She looked over one shoulder as Styles thumped down the path toward her and smiled. "Oh, there you are."

FORTY-FOUR

Unable to believe his eyes, Styles gaped at Beth. His attention snapped to the man wriggling under her knees. "It's Ainsley Rice. Who would have believed that a travel nurse who specializes in pediatrics would go around killing young girls." He offered Beth his hand and hauled her to her feet and then bent down and grabbed Rice's arm. "Get up. I figure you've got a lot of explaining to do, Mr. Rice."

"Just keep her away from me. She's got crazy eyes." Rice took two steps away from her, his eyes wide and staring. "She looks like a wolf just before it goes for your throat."

Taking a firmer grip on the deranged man, Styles gave him a little shake. "There's only one human predator in this forest today and that's you."

"I'm not a predator. I was just out for a walk, is all." Rice indicated with his chin toward Beth. "Then she came flying at me out of the forest. I figured a bear had gotten hold of me."

"What, can't you handle a grown woman?" Beth's glare was deadly. "Heck, you couldn't even handle a child without drugging her first, could you? You're a sorry excuse for a man."

Turning Rice away from Beth's glare, Styles urged him

along the track toward the clearing. He slid his attention back to Beth. "Ryder is with the girl. We'll head back. He'll take her home and explain what's happened to her parents. We'll keep Rice in custody inside my truck and then take him to the Rattlesnake Creek Sheriff's Office."

"If Ryder arrests him, I'll call the DA and have him transported to county." Beth rubbed her hands together. "It's not safe to keep him in that tiny cell in Ryder's office. Plus, he doesn't have the manpower to watch him twenty-four/seven."

Noticing the tremor that went through Beth when she stared at Rice, Styles nodded. "Call him now. We need Rice moved ASAP." He tapped his earpiece. "Ryder, the suspect is in custody. You'll need to arrest and Mirandize him before we transport him to Rattlesnake Creek. Beth is on the phone speaking to the DA to arrange transport to county, but that will take time."

"Copy that. My jail will have to do for now." Ryder let out a long breath. *"We'll escort the girl back to her parents, and you'd better follow close behind, but park some ways away from the house. I don't figure he'll be getting a good reception in town once the word gets out."*

That was the last thing that Styles needed. "Then let's hope the word doesn't get out."

"I didn't do anything." Rice looked at Styles with a tragic look in his eyes. "I'm being accused of something I didn't do. I'm innocent."

"I'm sure when we test the contents of the flask you were offering the young girl, we'll discover it's the same concoction that you gave the other two you murdered." Beth turned to Styles. "It's all set. The wheels are in motion. There will be an arrest warrant waiting for us when we get back to Rattlesnake Creek."

As Beth's gaze slid over him, Styles swallowed hard. Her eyes had changed and he suddenly understood why Rice, a brutal serial killer, had been afraid of her. Anger simmered deep in her eyes, dark and dangerous. His expression must have registered his thoughts because the next second Beth shook her head like a wet dog. "You okay there, Agent Katz?"

"Yeah." Beth shrugged nonchalantly and fell in step beside him as the trail widened. "My dad always told me I had the best death stare, bar none."

Styles tugged the reluctant Rice onward. "Your father?" Was she speaking about the serial killer? He raised one eyebrow in question.

"I only had one dad, Styles." Beth suddenly grinned at him. "Lucky for Rice here, I'm not like him." She sucked in a breath. "I see the clearing. Can you handle him and hang back some so I can take Lucy out of the forest before you arrive? She doesn't need to see this jerk again anytime soon."

Under Styles' grip, Rice tensed as if he honestly believed he could escape. "Yeah go. If he figures he'll try and make a break for it, I'll shoot him in the knee and then drag him back to the truck by his hair. After seeing what he did to those girls, my duty of care is running a little thin. In fact, I hope he does try to escape. All I need is an excuse."

"Then let him go." Beth turned around in front of him walking backward and a slow smile creased her lips. "But let me shoot out his knee. Your gun will split him in half and I want him to suffer for his crimes."

"I'm not planning on running." Rice looked from one to the other wild-eyed. "You two are nuts. I'm reporting you to the sheriff. Innocent until proven guilty, and I didn't do anything."

Styles chuckled. "You mean my good friend Sheriff Cash Ryder? Go right ahead."

FORTY-FIVE

After delivering Lucy to her parents, and Ryder had explained matters to them, Beth and the team had driven in convoy to Rattlesnake Creek. She had driven Ryder's truck and the two men escorted the prisoner. Normally she would have protested, but she'd been glad to be away from them for a time to settle the rushes of anger against Ainsley Rice. He turned out just like she expected, he'd be very dangerous if cornered, but when faced by heavily armed FBI agents, he disintegrated into Jell-O. The problem was that his addiction to raping and killing young girls would never change. If by some chance he slipped through the judicial system and was left to run the streets again, he'd kill and keep killing until somebody took him down.

Locked up in the sheriff's holding cell, Rice was safe for a time and Beth had insisted they let him sweat awhile before questioning him. She'd walked out of the office and headed to Tommy Joe's Bar and Grill to collect an order of takeout. After all, they had to feed the prisoner. Arriving back sometime later, she noticed an elderly gray-haired man sitting on a chair outside the holding cell bars. She nodded to the man, who stood at her arrival. "Agent Katz and you are...?"

"Jerry Blackwood, attorney at law." He held out his hand. "It's nice to meet you, Agent Katz. I just need a few more minutes alone with my client before you question him."

Pulling sandwiches and a can of soda from the bag she was carrying, she thrust them into Blackwood's hands. "County is sending a chopper to collect your client. It's going to be a long day. I suggest he eats something before we leave. We'll be out to speak to him shortly."

She headed for Ryder's office and walked inside. The smell of freshly brewed coffee filled the room and after dropping the bag on the table she went to the counter to pour a cup. Over-hearing the plans for Rice's transfer to county, she shook her head and looked at Styles. "Did I hear that right? County is sending two men to escort Rice and one of them is the pilot? Do they have some strange notion he won't be able to escape? Trust me, that guy is as slippery as an eel."

"Nope, I was planning on going with them with Ryder." Styles peered into the bag and pulled out sandwiches. "Oh, and while you were out Wolfe dropped by for the flask Rice handed the girl. He flew here and will analyze it the moment he gets back to the lab. He said it smells the same as the residue he discovered in Haley Quinn's stomach contents."

Annoyed, Beth held up both hands as if stopping traffic. "Whoa, take a few steps back to the part where you said Ryder was going with you to escort the prisoner."

"Is there a problem with that?" Styles took a bite out of the sandwich and chewed slowly.

Beth glared at him. "Has it slipped your mind that the Pied Piper killings are an FBI case? I'm coming with you to escort the prisoner."

"If he is, as you say, as slippery as an eel, then Ryder would be the better choice." Styles shrugged. "I have seniority over you and that's my decision."

Annoyance shivered through her and she lifted her chin in defiance. "Which one of us took down Rice?"

"Oh, give me a break." Ryder stood and glared at them. "If you two don't start getting along, all hell is going to break out around here." He turned his attention to Styles. "I agree with Beth and I told you she wouldn't like me stepping over her. I'll stay here and do the paperwork."

"The chopper from county will be here soon. It will be landing on the roof of the FBI building." Styles stuffed the last bite of his sandwich into his mouth and washed it down with coffee. "I'll go and see if our prisoner is ready to talk." He grabbed a statement book from the table and headed out the door.

Beth ignored the inquisitive look from Ryder and ate her egg salad sandwich slowly. When she had finished her coffee, Shawn, Ryder's receptionist, poked her head around the door and informed her that Styles was waiting for her to begin the interview. She dropped her garbage in the bin and rinsed her cup before walking slowly back to the holding cell. It was a very unusual setup. As there was only one cell surrounded by bars and nowhere to interview a dangerous criminal, they all had to sit around outside. She wanted desperately to speak to Rice, but Styles took the lead.

"The fact that we found you in the forest with a young girl and a flask of drugged soda isn't in dispute. Your intention was clear." Styles stared at Rice through the bars. "Right now, you're holding all the cards and it depends how you play them. Information you give us at this point might make the judge go easy on you when it comes to sentencing."

"Like what?" Rice sipped at his can of soda, apparently oblivious to the extent of trouble he was in.

Beth needed information and ignored Styles' flash of annoyance when she cleared her throat. "Mr. Rice, how did you communicate with the girls? None of them met you at the hospital. Was it in a game room?"

"You don't have to answer that question." Blackwood peered at her over half-moon glasses perched on the end of his nose. "Or any questions referring to what the agents refer to as the Pied Piper murders. Anything you say would be an admittance of guilt."

Rice remained silent.

"We know you involved two girls. We always find the body of a blonde girl, but the other one is always missing. Where are the other girls, Mr. Rice?" Styles leaned back in his chair. "If we can find them, things will go much easier for you."

Rice remained silent.

Recalling the takedown, Beth smiled to herself. She stood and walked to the bars and leaned casually against the wall. Suddenly everything about Rice fell neatly into place. "Who is Susie? Is she your little blonde-haired fantasy?" She stared at Rice. "They're all Susie to you, aren't they? How long do you figure it will take me to find out who she was and when she died? She is dead, isn't she, Mr. Rice?" She looked at Styles. "Susie was his first. When we find her, we'll know just how long this monster has been killing." She turned back to Rice. "My specialty is cybercrime and we'll get your computer. Just how long do you think it will take me to find out every sordid detail about you?"

"You're not that good." Rice grinned at her. "This time you lose."

It was a little after seven by the time they climbed into the chopper. The single guard sat beside Rice. Beth and Styles sat in the back. The chopper rose high into the air and Beth peered out the window as they headed along the mountain range and then turned east toward Black Rock Falls County. The recently built jail would rival any state pen for size. The need arrived with the increasing number of serial killer murders in the county. As they flew above an incredible pine forest a commotion broke out in the cockpit. Taking advantage of everyone admiring the scenery, Rice had leapt from his seat and had the zip tie securing his cuffed hands around the pilot's neck.

"Do as I say or I'll break his neck and we'll all die." Rice leaned back making the zip tie between the cuffs cut deep into the pilot's soft flesh.

The next second, the chopper went into a dive. The guard let out a terrified scream and clung to the seat. Beside her, Styles pushed to his feet and slid across the floor toward the cockpit, grasping the backs of chairs along the way. To her horror the pilot's arms dropped from the controls as he lost consciousness and the chopper spun out of control. Terrified, Beth gaped in horror as Styles was tossed from side to side in a desperate attempt to reach the controls. Rice must have been screaming, but all Beth could see was his mouth wide open and a horrified expression on his face as he slid to the floor. A moment later, the chopper's engine stalled and they fell from the sky.

FORTY-SIX

As if the world had been turned on, sound came back in a rush of terror. Dropping like a stone, the ground rushed up toward them. Thrown about as they smashed into the top of the trees, Rice ended up between the seats and remained there unmoving. Unable to breathe, Beth gripped the armrests white-knuckled. The spinning was sickening and with every turn Styles was tossed around. How could he possibly survive? The chopper bounced from one tree to another and then tipped to one side. The spinning rotor blades struck the boughs like a giant weed whacker, sending branches flying in all directions. and then in a screech of tearing metal, the blades spiraled away into the dense forest.

They dropped fast and impact was seconds away. Years of training sent Beth into survival mode and she ducked down, covering her head with her arms. Beside her a tree branch shattered the window, broke off with a loud crack, and filled the cabin, the sharp tip stabbing the seat in front of her. Panic surrounded her. Someone was yelling, their voice unrecognizable over the noise. In a scream of tearing metal, they stopped with a bone-shattering jolt. She lifted her head, seeing the top of the forest against the twilight sky through an open gash. Wedged between two giant trunks, the crumpled chopper whined and creaked and in the next breath it fell at a terrifying speed, tipped nose first, and speared into the ground. A shockwave hit Beth in a jolt of pain and then everything went black.

With no idea how long she'd been out, Beth ran both hands over her aching head looking for injuries. She had a small cut over one eye, but nothing was broken. Blinking as her vision came back online, she stared at the empty seats around her. Rice was gone. Where was Styles? Unclipping her harness, she stared at the broken pieces of zip tie beside the pilot's seat. Rice had used the broken window to saw through them. Gripping the back of her seat to steady a wave of giddiness, she stared into the dimly lit cabin. Both the pilot and guard hung in their seats smothered in blood. Wrapped around the back of the seats, on what was left of the floor, lay Styles. Beth slid toward the cockpit, carefully avoiding the wreckage, to get to him. Kicking away debris, she dropped to her knees, and felt for a pulse. His flesh was warm and his color good. Under her fingers, his heartbeat was strong and steady. She ran her hands down his arms and legs but found no major injuries. He had a bruise on his forehead and a few superficial cuts on his face. She gave him a little shake. "Styles, wake up." She tried a few times.

When he didn't move, she stood to check the others. Both had died in the wreck. She scanned the cabin. It was set on a steep angle and everything had slid toward the cockpit in a pile of debris. The second rule of survival was to check supplies. Her backpack had moved from under her feet and rested beside an open tear in one side of the chopper. She found Styles' backpack and dragged it back to him, rolled him on his side in the recovery position, and pushed it under his head. She released the first aid kit from its position on the wall, opened it, and removed a survival blanket. She tucked it around Styles. He was out cold, but she didn't have time to wait for him to recover.

She needed to find Rice. He might have been thrown on impact. She had to know if he was dead or alive. If he'd made it, he wasn't getting away. Night was coming and it would be freezing soon. She didn't have much time.

She zipped up her jacket and pulled on her gloves. After grabbing her flashlight, she shrugged into her backpack and stared at the darkening forest. She needed to get help and reached for her satellite phone, relieved when it lit up in her hand. After taking the coordinates, she sent a detailed message to Wolfe. She checked her weapon, and her pockets. Finding the chalk Styles had given her in one hand, she smiled. She had a small window of opportunity to search for Rice. If he was still on his feet, she needed to move fast before he vanished into the forest. She had a flashlight, and if Bear had been with them, she'd have the advantage, but it didn't matter. She'd always been a good tracker.

Taking out her lipstick, she wrote a message on the cabin wall.

Hunting down Rice. Follow the chalk marks. Time is eight-fifteen. I've contacted Wolfe with our coordinates.

Beth dropped down from the chopper, hitting the ground and rolling. The damp ground softened her fall and, standing, she searched all around, but it was easy to see where Rice had stumbled into the forest. Apart from a few indistinct footprints, there was a trail of blood. She stood listening for a few moments, but only the sounds of the forest making ready for nightfall surrounded her. She marked the first tree with a giant arrow and using her flashlight headed into the forest. The headache vanished as the predator in her rose to the surface and she broke into a run. Rice was out there, and this time he wasn't getting away.

FORTY-SEVEN

Cold brushed his cheeks and, head spinning, Styles opened his eyes. The dropping chopper in the front of his mind, he blinked into the darkness and waited for his eyes to get accustomed to the light. From the tree branches all around him, the chopper had fallen, but somehow the trees had cushioned the fall. He wrinkled his nose at the smell of blood. *That can't be good.*

A shaft of moonlight pierced a gaping jagged hole and he looked around to gain his bearings. When caught in a situation like this one, the Army had trained him to remain calm and still. Movement could be perilous and the floor below him was at a steep angle. Something crackled on his shoulder, and he carefully moved one arm and realized someone had covered him in a silver emergency blanket. Under his cheek was rough and he recognized his backpack. "Hello? Beth, are you here? Anyone?"

Only the sound of torn metal creaking in the wind and the hums of the forest answered him. He recalled dropping fast and wrapping his arms and legs around the pilot's seat and holding on as the chopper slid down between two trees. If someone had covered him, it must be safe to move around. He eased up, slowly gripping the seat, and caught a glimpse of the pilot and guard. They were tangled in the wreckage and obviously dead. The prisoner was nowhere in sight, and for him to be covered, Beth was alive and mobile. The sinking feeling that she had gone after him alone hit him in the pit of his stomach. "Beth, where the heck are you?"

He grabbed up his backpack, pulled out a flashlight, and checked his supplies. Apart from ammunition and the usual supplies, he always packed extra water, energy bars, and a change of clothes. He folded the blanket and stuffed it inside and then, pushing to his feet, moved the flashlight over what was left of the cabin. The chopper had landed nose down and the only way out was a steep climb and then a drop to the forest floor. He took a drink of water and leaned back deciding what to do. His flashlight beam hit the cabin wall, and what he had first assumed was blood was a message. He stared at it for a few seconds, and then checked his watch. He'd been out cold for fifteen minutes since she'd left, which meant she could be a mile away in any direction. Needing to contact her, he checked his phone and cursed. The attached satellite sleeve was cracked and he had no bars. "I guess I follow the chalk marks."

He pulled on his backpack and dropped from the chopper. Using his flashlight, he soon found the arrow and a trail of black spots he assumed was blood on the forest floor. Which one of them was injured? There hadn't been any first aid wrappers about the cabin, so he assumed it was Rice. He moved into the forest and scanned ahead. Beth's chalk lines lit up under the light remarkably clear, and he shook off the headache and took off at a run. The way ahead soon turned into a narrow animal trail that wound its way along the foot of the mountain ranges. Although he concentrated on following Beth, Styles' mind kept the forest in his peripheral vision. Among the usual sounds of night, the howl of a wolf could be heard close by. The scent of blood coming from the chopper would attract a wide variety of wildlife. It would be the same for Ainsley Rice. Running into the forest at night covered in blood was an advertisement for trouble. Concerned for Beth's safety, Styles picked up his pace. As a city girl, she would be completely unaware of the dangers and he couldn't in his wildest dreams figure why on earth she went after Rice alone. She'd taken the time to make sure he was comfortable, so why not wait until he'd regained consciousness so they could go after the prisoner together? Reckless was one thing, but this took it to a whole new level.

He recalled the crazy things that had happened since he met her and wondered what made her tick. He'd been reading up about warrior genes after attending a seminar on behavioral traits. Without doubt, she was an alpha female, and the list of traits filled his mind as he bounded through the forest. One sure sign of alpha-female behavior is that they're not afraid to take risks, they like to be alone, and they are used to getting their own way. They are persistent and work for the things they want and are usually very dependable. The one important thing that came to mind was that people rarely understood them. He smiled to himself. "Well, that just about sums up Beth Katz."

He'd never be able to change a genetic trait, so he'd just have to find a way to work around it. Ahead in the distance, he heard shouts. He'd found them.

FORTY-EIGHT

Darkness surrounded Beth and, heart pounding, she scanned the forest, aware of the nocturnal creatures watching her. Rice had made slow going. The drips of blood had increased substantially and now bloody handprints smeared the trunks of the tall pines. The groundcover was splattered with red droplets. At this rate he would be dead before she got there. Ahead, his cries of pain came through the night. Something inside her was glad he was suffering after the torture he'd inflicted on his victims. There was no need to rush now and she slowed to a walk. The howls she had heard earlier appeared to be getting closer. The scent of Rice's blood must be on the air, and his cries would be attracting a pack of wolves. She swung her flashlight from side to side, the beam occasionally picking up the reflections of small critters' eyes. They stared for a few seconds and then turned and ran away. A shiver ran down her spine as she recalled Styles' warning about the wildlife in this area.

The bushes close by moved and cracked. Alarmed, Beth froze midstride, switched off the flashlight, and ducked behind a tree. The crashing noise increased. She drew her weapon. If it was a grizzly, her Glock wouldn't kill it. It would just make it angry. What had Styles said to her about not using it to scare them away or was that black bears? Did he say shoot into the sky or whatever? She couldn't recall. She had no bear spray and she was sure he said to walk away and not scream. Terror cramped her stomach. How could anyone not scream if a grizzly was after them? She'd only ever seen one in a zoo and it was huge. What else did he say? Ah yeah, lie down and play dead with a grizzly but not with a black bear? So, noise made one of them attack? Which one? Confused, she slid the gun back into her shoulder holster and glued herself to the tree.

The crashing noise came close and then something loomed onto the trail. It was big with antlers and she shivered in relief as an elk lumbered past her and out of sight. Panting with relief, Beth took a few moments to grab a drink from her backpack. Ahead Rice let out another moan. He must be less than one hundred yards from her position. The sound of running water was close by, and she recalled seeing a wide fast-flowing river from the chopper, just before it crashed. Perhaps Rice was heading in that direction. He must be thirsty, especially with the blood loss, and as far as she could make out, he hadn't taken anything with him. She shook her head. Considering the Pied Piper had eluded the police for so many years, he wasn't as smart as she'd believed. If she'd been in the same position, the first thing she'd have taken would have been the weapons. The second would have been any supplies she found in close proximity. She could only imagine his need to get away was so great he'd become reckless.

An icy breeze cooled her hot cheeks. Running had kept her warm, but stopping for those few moments allowed a chill to seep through her clothes. She must keep moving. She rounded the bend. She killed her flashlight at the sight of Rice kneeling beside the river, scooping water up with his hands. Moonlight illuminated the edge of the clearing and highlighted a dark patch running down one side of him. Blood soaked his clothes.

He'd been injured in the wreck. Feeling no sympathy for the vicious child killer, Beth glanced around. The setting was perfect. Badly hurt, he wouldn't offer any resistance if she snuck up behind him and broke his neck.

Logic slid into place and Beth shook her head. *I'm acting like a crazy woman. I can't kill him. Wolfe will analyze the footprints. He'd know there'd been a struggle and I'd have Rice's blood all over me. Dammit, I'll have to take him in.* Taking a few deep breaths, she forced down her dark side. She'd always been so careful. What had gotten into her? Maybe being this close to a despicable child killer was getting to her. Shaking with the adrenaline rush, she stared at him. He'd get what was coming to him but not tonight. At that moment Rice turned slowly and looked at her. He was moving his head, not sure if there was someone in the shadows. She switched on the flashlight, holding the beam on his face. "Did you figure you'd get away from me? Not a chance."

"Stay away from me." Rice blinked and staggered to his feet, one hand wrapped around a branch he'd been using as a walking stick. "One step closer and I'll beat you to death."

Unconcerned, Beth shook her head. A man who savagely took young girls' lives was nothing but a simpering coward. She laughed. "Yeah, why not come here and give it a try? Or do you want me to come over there? I should warn you I'm armed and I don't have a problem defending myself. You got lucky in the forest before. I must have been in a good mood."

"Stay where you are." Rice looked all around. "I'll take my chances in the river if you come any closer."

Beth shook her head. "Go right ahead. We're close to the falls. It would save me the time of hauling your sorry ass back to jail." She stepped out so he could see her. "You look bad, Rice. I could just shoot you. Maybe put you out of your misery?" She stared at him as he shuffled closer to the water. "You'd die in seconds in the river. Can't you see it's cold? The rocks are covered with ice, but that would be no fun for me to watch, would it? You know how to have fun killing someone, don't you? The fantasy, the anticipation of the kill, and the rush as the blood spills, it's addictive, isn't it?" She moved closer. "Are you afraid of me, Ainsley? The girls you killed were afraid too, just like you are now. You love to cut little girls, don't you?" She pushed the flashlight into her pocket and took a step toward him. "You're a monster."

"Stay away from me." Rice turned and backed away from the river, trying to hide in the trees. "You're crazy."

A noise came from behind Beth. It was Styles calling her name, followed by the distant *thud, thud, thud* as he ran toward her. She pulled out her flashlight. Not taking her eyes off Rice, she raised her voice. "I'm here, Styles."

Beth turned and called out again. A light bobbed in the distance and she turned and waved her flashlight. "I'm here with Rice. He's injured."

The sound of something moving through the trees came close by, and sure that Rice had bolted, Beth shone the flashlight along the riverbank. It illuminated Rice staring transfixed, his attention on two bear cubs playing along the riverbank. Swallowing a rush of terror, Beth took a few steps backward and kept her voice low. "Rice, listen to me. Move away slowly. I hear their mother coming and you'll be a threat to her cubs. Don't make a sound."

As she backed into the trees, behind her Styles' footfalls became closer, and she waved her flashlight again to warn him. "Slow down. Bear cubs!"

She turned back when Rice let out a piercing scream. An angry roar made her blood run cold and she gaped in horror as a grizzly emerged from the forest. Rice was between the grizzly and its cubs. The ground appeared to shake as the bear roared in anger, its attention fixed on Rice. Beth killed the flashlight and froze on the spot as the massive creature rose up on its back legs and huffed. Bathed in moonlight, the six-hundred-pound grizzly lumbered into the clearing, its mouth wide open and saliva dripping from deadly teeth. Making strange huffing and puffing noises, it stalked Rice. With nowhere to run, Rice screamed and turned in circles.

"Shoot the bear." Rice ducked a massive swipe. "Help me!"

Frozen with terror, Beth could only stare as the bear swiped at Rice with one huge clawed paw tearing at clothes and flesh. The memory of Styles explaining why he carried a .357 Magnum flashed through her mind. Her weapon wouldn't stop a grizzly and firing it would only make it angry. She needed a powerful rifle to take it down. There was nothing she could do. Her pulse pounded in her ears and every hair on her body stood to attention as the bear moved in again and tore at Rice. The forest echoed with his screams. Unable to move, Beth gasped in horror as the bear scooped Rice into the air and tossed him to the ground like a rag doll. With one massive clawed paw, it rolled him over onto his back and played with him, like a cat with a mouse, allowing him to crawl a foot away before dragging him back. When Rice kicked out, the bear tore into him with its mouth wide open. Roars and screams filled the night, and glued to the spot, Beth could only watch in horror.

The next second, something slammed into her, taking her to the ground and rolling her into the trees. The air rushed from her lungs as a great weight pinned her to the forest floor. Terrified, she opened her mouth to scream when a gloved hand pressed over her mouth, and warm breath brushed her ear.

"Don't move a muscle." Styles covered her with his suffocating weight.

Beth wiggled beneath him and he removed his hand. "I can't breathe."

"Hush or we'll be next." Styles tucked his head next to hers with his voice so low she could hardly make out his words. "It's already too late for Rice."

Gasping for air, Beth couldn't block out Rice's terrified screams or the grizzly's growls. The ripping of flesh and snapping of jaws seemed to go on forever but only seconds had passed before everything went quiet. Trembling all over, Beth lay very still listening.

"Don't make a sound." Styles mouth was close to her ear.

Beth's nose was crushed against Styles chest. He smelled of cologne and mountain air. The rough material of his FBI jacket grazed against her skin. She pushed against him, but it was like trying to move a mountain. When he eased up again, she stared at him but kept her voice to a whisper. "Why didn't you shoot the bear?"

"It was too late to save him and, anyway, only a crazy man walks between a bear and its cubs. Rice is a local. He should have known better." Styles grimaced. "If I'd killed the mom, the cubs would have starved to death. It wasn't the bear's fault. Rice was stupid." He lifted his head to stare into the clearing.

Nodding, Beth understood his reasoning. "What's happening now?"

"It's over. The bear is leaving and the cubs are following close behind her." Styles rolled away but kept one hand on her shoulder. "There's not much left of Rice. We'll wait until we're sure the bear's gone, then we'll keep to the trees and walk away slowly. No looking back, right? That bear could return at any second. She probably knows we're here. She'd be able to smell us." He helped her to her feet. "Wolfe will send a crew to collect what's left of Rice. I'll remind him to bring a ton of bear spray."

Traumatized, Beth stared at him and wondered if her legs would ever stop shaking. Nature had risen up to remove a predator from the forest. Justice had been served. "A fitting ending for a monster."

"And I figured we'd be protecting him from the Tarot Killer until his trial." Styles shook his head. "Ain't life strange?"

EPILOGUE

ONE WEEK LATER

Winding up the case after so many incidents was a nightmare of paperwork. Beth and Styles were required to make reports on the chopper accident, as well as do a detailed background and timeline for Ainsley Rice to prove that he was indeed the Pied Piper. This not only involved the local murders but the investigation spread around the entire country. Although working as a travel nurse was a bonus, as Rice moved from one agency to another every place he lived was well documented. All his shifts at local hospitals coincided with the times and dates that the girls went missing. The fact that his MO hadn't changed for the last three years made it easy to establish his guilt. What had been difficult was trying to discover his motive. As he'd mentioned the name Susie when Beth had confronted him in the forest, she dug deeper into his background.

Convinced that Susie held the key to his fantasy, Beth researched old cases occurring in the places Rice lived as a child. As they seemed to move around frequently and, it seemed, after a particularly heinous child murder, she could only theorize that he was involved earlier than she'd imagined. At least having the name of the victim gave Beth something to use in the search engine. She came up with a handful of hits. Although the young girls had been raped and murdered, Rice had been too young to commit the crimes. On closer inspection of the murder scenes, she found one that would have put Rice at the age of twelve where the clothes had been neatly folded with the shoes placed on top.

The victim, a blonde-haired child by the name of Susan Parkinson, followed the Pied Piper's MO to the letter. The problem was that the crime had been attributed to somebody else and the perpetrator was deceased. The note mentioned another case after this one where the victim fought back and killed Stanley Rice. Beth read the name twice, unable to believe her eyes. The next moment she pulled Ainsley Rice's birth record and discovered Stanley was his father. After reading through the case file, she discovered a note that mentioned his mother went missing around the time of Susie's death. Beth turned in her seat to tell Styles, but he was on the phone and making notes. She waited for him to disconnect and laid out the information she'd discovered. "His mother vanished, and I figure he witnessed his father rape and murder Susie. I have him out of town the night his father died. All the witnesses the local cops interviewed said that they were sure he'd left town the day before. His father was a psychopathic serial killer, the original Pied Piper. He was the trigger but unlocked Ainsley's psychosis. This is why he murdered only blonde-haired girls. It doesn't tell us why he decided to kill one and take one or what he did with them. We know they were passed on or sold into the sex slave market but tracing them is near impossible."

"But you are on that, right?" Styles leaned back in his chair, twirling his pen in his fingers. "You have his laptop and those belonging to the girls. What have you found out so far?"

The time spent chasing down rabbit holes looking for leads on the dark web had given Beth a headache. She let out a long sigh. "I was able to trace the fact that he used a games room to contact the girls and used the Warlock as his name. He was very careful and moved around. I assume he used free Wi-Fi because that's what most people do who are trying to bounce their signal around the world to hide their existence. He was exceptionally good at disguising his trail. I've asked the cybercrime department to assist, as this is far too big for me to handle alone. Even with Spike's laptop, I found zip. Whoever is the kingpin changes his site address regularly." She pushed both hands through her hair. "The last time I spoke to Dominic Lowe from the San Francisco office, he said he had made headway arresting all the pedophiles who frequented Spike's brothel, but Spike was in the wind." She smiled. "He never mentioned the drug dealers. I guess they made it okay."

"Talking about Spike." Styles gave her a long considering stare and raised one eyebrow. "The local PD located his vehicle in the bay. Guess what? The judge and Spike were in the trunk." He leaned back in his chair saying nothing and just looking at her as if waiting for a reaction.

Trying to look confused, Beth stared at him. "In the trunk? How did he get into the trunk with the dead guy?"

"They're not sure, but his throat was cut and they found a tarot card in his jacket pocket." Styles cleared his throat. "You mentioned seeing someone holding open the door when he carried out the body. Can you give a description? Where exactly were you, when you saw this person?"

"Locked in a room." Beth met his gaze. "There was a small window, a slit really, in the door, so I couldn't see much, only the legs. There wasn't anyone there when I left, the place was empty." She leaned back in her chair, acting nonchalant. "I wish I'd seen him but he must have been in good shape if he was capable of lifting Spike into the trunk of a vehicle. He was a big man." She stared into space pretending to think. "I'm sorry, I wish I had more for you, but I don't. I didn't see his vehicle in the alleyway when I left." She tapped her bottom lip. "Did they give you a time of death? We're only assuming Spike died the same day. He could have driven around with the judge in his trunk for days. No one would suspect Spike, would they? I'd say not many people knew the judge was a pedophile, and with the cops all over his brothel, Spike was probably holed up somewhere."

"You could be right about Spike. The TOD isn't conclusive as they'd been in the water for a time." Styles blew out a long breath. "The PD moved in fast after they picked up the girls. They had undercover cops in position and just waited for clients to arrive."

Relieved, Beth nodded. "Well then, Spike would notice the door was open. He kept it locked. I figure it was an appointment-only setup and his calendar was full. He was careful and I figure he didn't trust anyone else to manage the girls. He didn't care for them that's for sure. He used his fists. They were terrified of him."

"The girls aren't saying anything about anyone else involved, but the San Francisco cops discovered he didn't touch his girls. He had a few favorites among the local sex workers, but none of them are talking. For all we know, the Tarot Killer could have pretended to be one of his clients and was just waiting for the chance to kill him. Maybe he followed him when he left the brothel. I guess we'll never know." Styles smiled at her. "I'm just glad we got those girls out. I still can't believe you risked your life for them. You're the most unusual agent I've ever met. Reckless, fearless, and you don't follow the rules."

Amused, Beth snorted and headed for the door. "Just like you, huh?'

"Yeah, just like me." Styles stood and went to the coffee pot and poured a cup. "With your final report, the case is wrapped up. The Pied Piper is dead." He waved to his desk. "The cases are piling up and we can take our pick. The director is convinced we are the dream team. The good news is that you're staying in Rattlesnake Creek. We're getting a budget increase, a receptionist if we want one, and a new truck." He smiled. "Take a look at the cases we've been offered. You choose what you want to investigate and I'll download all the info and set up the whiteboard." He walked back to his desk and scanned the screen. "This one is interesting. Someone is stalking and killing teenagers. The crime scenes are gruesome. Oh, and the director wants you to hand over the pedophile ring investigation to cybercrime and concentrate on a new case. They have an entire team working on finding the kingpin. Once they get a solid lead, they'll bring us back into the loop." He grinned. "You'll be there to take him down, Beth. We have the director's word."

Discussing kid killers always triggered the rise of her dark side. It came on so fast, and needing to hide it from Styles at all cost, she averted her gaze. "Fine, but I still have some loose ends to tie up in my files. You choose the next case."

"Okay." Styles barked a laugh. "But not today. I'm beat. Do you ever stop working?"

Maybe he was right and she needed to step away from hunting down the pedophile ring and leave it to cybercrime. The deep research and frustration from not getting answers was driving her nuts. So many terrible things happened to kids who became a commercial commodity. They lost their humanity and being murdered was the least of their problems. Eventually, she would take down the kingpin. It had become a personal vendetta. With the Pied Piper dead, it wouldn't be long before another uncatchable killer came to her attention. She'd already made plans to slip away unnoticed when necessary and only needed a good enough excuse to convince Styles. "Yeah, but it's the investigator side of me. It takes the upper hand sometimes. After big cases like this one, I usually request some downtime. Is that usual for you?"

"Oh, yeah." Styles leaned back in his chair, folded his arms, and sighed. "A couple of days fishing for me. Have you made plans? You're welcome to come with me."

Smiling, Beth shook her head. "Not yet but I'm looking ahead. In fact, I'm thinking of buying a cabin near the creek so I can paint in my downtime. It's been a long time since I've seen such amazing scenery. I'm by no means an artist but it's something I've wanted to try for a time now. I'd also like to spend time traveling around the local towns. I love visiting those little stores that sell handcrafted goods. I like vintage furniture as well. Fixing up a cabin would be fun and relaxing."

"You relax?" Styles chuckled. "You've had your head stuck in that computer twenty-four/seven since we solved the case. You really want to bring down that pedophile ring, don't you? I can see it eating at you, Beth. You've gotta let it go."

Stomach knotting, the faces of the missing girls flashed into her mind in a continuous stream as if demanding she bring them justice. They'd become a permanent reminder that her work wasn't finished. Not today, but one day she'd discover the big fat spider controlling the pedophile web and squash it, but for now, she'd be the perfect special agent and bide her time. "Okay, I'll let it go."

Being a special agent with access to case files across the entire country, she had a smorgasbord of serial killers to choose from and really nothing had changed. Just like all the times before, when she morphed into the Tarot Killer to bring down a monster, all she needed was an excuse to be away from the office alone. She'd leave her phone and vehicle in a safe place and use other means to get to a neighboring county or city. She could travel anywhere within reason and return unnoticed by moving around in disguise. Having Styles as a partner could put a spanner in the works if he planned on checking her every move. So she'd need to keep one step ahead of him.

Staring at him, she chuckled. "That's why I want a retreat away from the office and town. I need somewhere I can be alone and undisturbed so I can de-stress. No technology, just me and nature. Don't worry, I'll find a place on the edge of town where it's relatively safe."

"That sounds like a plan. We all need downtime and I'm glad to see you're planning ahead. There are a ton of places to choose from. I have a fishing cabin too." Styles smiled. "It's rough but all I need is a bed and somewhere to fry my fish and make coffee."

I sure hope mine is in the opposite direction. A headache threatened and she rubbed her temples. Stifled by sitting in the heated office, Beth stood and, avoiding Styles' gaze, headed for the door. "Keep that thought. I need to take a break. I'll be back soon."

Inside the gym, Beth removed her jacket and shoulder holster and picked up a bat. She switched on the batting machine and started swinging. She connected with a few balls but suddenly realized why Styles used this method to control his anger. Sweat trickled down her back, and muscles clenching with overexertion, she continued to swing the bat. Her dark side slid away but would always be there, waiting. As she batted up, Styles walked into the gym.

"I hope that's not my head you're hitting with that bat." Styles hung on the wire grinning at her.

Beth glanced at him. "Nope. Just letting off steam."

"That's good." He waited as she connected with another ball. "You know, you get this look in your eyes like you're going to tear me a new one, and then you don't. I kinda like that about you. We have our own way of doing things but it works out just fine. I figure we're going to make a great team. No, let me rephrase that. After solving the most difficult case on record, we *are* a darn great team."

Turning off the machine, Beth placed the bat in the rack

and then looked at him. She'd gained one small victory over her dark side. She'd never considered controlling it with strenuous exercise before seeing Styles' working off his anger. It wasn't a cure. Sadly, her need for vengeance could never be satisfied, but taming it would give her more time to meticulously plan her next move. Relieved, she nodded, agreeing with him, and allowed a smile to curl her lips. He was a good man. He'd always have her back and she'd come to respect him. In fact, she liked him just fine. She'd never had a soul to look up to, not ever, and then a maverick FBI agent had walked into her twisted life. Styles had proved to be a little off-kilter like her, but in him she recognized a true sense of justice. Go figure. *I needed a hero and maybe I'm looking at him.* Astonished by the realization, she laughed. "Yeah, we are and I wonder how much trouble we'll get into solving the next case."

"I guess time will tell." Styles grinned and shook his head. "You sure are one of a kind, Beth."

Amused, Beth smiled. *If only you knew.*

A LETTER FROM D.K. HOOD

Dear Readers,

Thank you so much for choosing *Dark Angel* and coming with me on the start of a brand-new series. I've been waiting to write the first Beth Katz crime thriller for some time.

If you'd like to keep up-to-date with all my latest releases, just sign up at the website link below. We will never share your details and you can unsubscribe at any time.

www.bookouture.com/dk-hood

It's wonderful to start a new series and have you along. I really appreciate all the encouraging comments and messages you have sent me during the writing of this novel.

Beth Katz is certainly a different type of special agent and it's been a pleasure to eventually see her and the unpredictable Dax Styles finally on the page. These characters have been inside my head for a few years and it's wonderful to set them free. The crimes for this pair of oddballs to solve is endless, and it will be great fun to share their stories with you.

If you enjoyed my book, I would be very grateful if you could leave a review and recommend my book to your friends and family. I really enjoy hearing from readers so feel free to ask me questions at any time.

You can get in touch on my Facebook page, Twitter, or through my websites.

Thank you so much for your support.

D.K. Hood

www.dkhood.com
dkhood-author.blogspot.com.au

 facebook.com/dkhoodauthor
twitter.com/DKHood_Author

ACKNOWLEDGMENTS

I'm always truly thankful for my wonderful editor, Helen, and the super team at Bookouture for their endless support and understanding.

My husband, Gary, endures a ton of alone time when I'm working long hours to finish a novel and is always there for me with support and encouragement.

I would also like to thank Chelle Brown, Tara McPherson, Marj Ward, Wez Brown, Wendy Steenblok, Linda Hocutt, and Christopher Wills for their wonderful comments and support during the writing of this novel.

Made in the USA
Columbia, SC
07 September 2023

THROUGH
DEATH'S
GATE

A Guide to Selfless Dying

by Joel

Center for Sacred Sciences
Eugene, OR

Library of Congress Cataloging-in-Publication Data

Joel, 1942-
Through death's gate: a guide to selfless dying / by Joel
    p. cm.
  Includes bibliographical references.
  ISBN 0-9620387-1-7 (alk. paper)
  1. Death--Religious aspects. 2. Meditation. I. Title.
BL504.J64 1995
291.2'3--dc20   95-46744
                                                      CIP

For Bonnie Linn
(1943 - 1994)
whose selfless death
set a shining example for us all.

Acknowledgements:

Special thanks are due to layout designers John Richardson and Mike Taylor; as well as to Therese Engelmann, Beverly Forster, and Merry Song Caston for both their professional advice and careful proofreading; and to Tom McFarlane for his generous financial support.

This book was written primarily for practitioners of the Way of Selflessness who are, themselves, facing imminent death. We hope, however, that it will also benefit their friends, relatives, and fellow practitioners, as well as anyone else wishing to take full advantage of the precious opportunity for Spiritual Awakening which death presents to those who are properly prepared.

IMPORTANT NOTICE:

If you are close to death and cannot read this book in its entirety, TURN IMMEDIATELY TO CHAPTERS TWO, THREE, AND FOUR. These chapters describe specific meditations (to be used during the hour of your actual death) which you should START PRACTICING NOW. Then, if you have time, go back and read the rest of the chapters in the order presented.

CONTENTS

Prologue: Facing Death

In reality, there is no death.

In reality, there is no death because there is no individual 'self' or 'I' who could die. In reality, there is only that Primordial Consciousness or God which, though appearing in myriad forms, is Itself empty of all forms and therefore without birth or death. This Consciousness is who I am. This Consciousness is also who you are. Thus, whether you Realize it or not, your sense of being a separate self is a delusion, and ultimately, so is the death of that 'self'.

Until this Realization is attained, however, the delusion of self, and therefore of death, will persist. Indeed, within the world of delusion, nothing is more certain than death. Everyone who is born is, by virtue of that very fact, doomed to die.

Although we all know this to be true, rarely do we know the actual date on which our death is to take place. This ignorance allows most of us to live out our lives under a comforting but dangerous secondary delusion—namely, that death will not come to us any time soon; that it is something which will happen only in some distant future; and that, consequently, there is nothing we need do to prepare for it now. Thus, when the legendary Hindu king, Yudhishthira, was asked, "What is the greatest wonder in the world?" he replied: "All around us people die everyday and yet no one believes it will happen to them."

For you, however, this belief has come to an end. Whether because you have been diagnosed with a terminal illness, or have reached an advanced old age (or for whatever other reason), you now know that you are definitely going to die— not on some unforeseeable date in a seemingly infinite future, but within a finite span of time. And although you may not yet know the exact hour, or the week, or even the month in which death will finally take you, such considerations are only of secondary importance. What is of primary importance is that you have been stripped of the delusion that death is a distant event which does not concern you.

To be suddenly deprived of the comfort this delusion once offered no doubt seems like a devastating thing. But for those who are willing to learn from it, having to face one's own death can also be a blessing in disguise. This, as you may recall, was just what happened to Prince Siddhartha, the future Buddha. As a young man growing up in his father's palace, surrounded by worldly delights, Siddhartha was utterly oblivious to the existence of such things as disease, old age, and death. Then, one day while venturing beyond the palace walls he encountered a sick person, an elderly person, and a corpse. Realizing that this was the fate of all sentient beings, and that he, too, would someday die, the anguished Prince exclaimed:

> O worldly men! How fatal is your delusion! Inevitably your body will crumble to dust, yet carelessly, unheedingly, you live on.[1]

Now, the Buddha was a human being no different from you. Like you, he was born into delusion, and like you he suffered from the same anxieties and fears which delusion generates. If anything, as an over-protected child, his suffering was even greater than most people's. The only difference between the Buddha and everyone else was his willingness to accept the reality of his own impermanence. It was this simple but profound insight that transformed him from being a person concerned only with worldly happiness into a fully committed spiritual seeker intent on finding that Happiness which is beyond time and change, the only Real Happiness there is. Thus for the Buddha, coming to grips with his own mortality, although emotionally devastating, turned out to be a great blessing indeed.

And it can be for you, as well.

The important thing is not to look away from death but, like the Buddha, face it squarely and take courage. Remember that death is not something that is going to happen to you alone. Think of the vast ocean of beings who have been washed up on this life's shore before you, like so many bubbles of foam, only to be dissolved back again into the deep by death's inexorable tide. Whether insect or reptile, fish or fowl, animal or human— whether strong or weak, rich or poor, ruler or servant, sinner or saint, wise one or fool—not one of us in the whole chain of being, stretching back to the beginning of time, has escaped this sea's relentless rhythm. Birth and death, creation and destruction, form and formlessness are all equally indispensable to that Ecstatic Cosmic Dance in which Consciousness constantly Realizes Itself in all Its Infinite possibilities.

But, although none of us can choose *not* to die, we can choose *how* to die. The real question, then, is: When the Angel of Death knocks at your door, how will you greet him? Are you going to receive him as a venerable teacher, or resist him as you would a thief in the night? Are you going to force Death to drag you off to the gallows like a condemned criminal? Or are you going to take Death's hand willingly, as you would that of a Divine Lover who beckons you to one last dance before your present life is over and a new one dawns?

Those who choose the latter course will, in fact, find that death has a second great blessing to confer. Not only does it awaken us to the futility of all worldly pursuits, but, as the Christian mystic, Simone Weil, wrote:

> Death will ultimately open for us an instant when, for an infinitesimal fraction of time, pure truth, naked, certain, and eternal enters the soul. I may say that I have never desired any other good for myself.[2]

Indeed, if you think about it you will see that, as a spiritual practitioner, you have actually been trying to 'die' all along. For it is only by *dying* to your separate self that you can discover the Truth which, as Jesus said, makes us free from all suffering and death forever. And while this *spiritual death* is not the same as physical death, nevertheless, the passage through Death's Gate will bring you to the very threshold of that other Gate—the Gate of Gnosis—which leads from form to Formlessness, from the finite to the Infinite. Here, stripped naked and standing between two worlds, as it were, you will find that literally *nothing* bars the way. At this point (as we shall see) it is simply a matter of recognizing this 'nothing' for what it truly is—Pure Consciousness, Itself. This is why all spiritual traditions have considered physical death to offer a supreme opportunity for attaining the ultimate "death of deaths"....provided, of course, you are properly prepared.

This book is designed to help you do just that—prepare for death. It summarizes the basic teachings found in all of the Great Traditions on how to pass through the Gate of Death as selflessly and effortlessly as possible. In particular, it contains three fundamental practices to help you transform your own death from a terrifying ordeal into what the Sufi poet, Rumi, called our "wedding with eternity." In the following chapters we will discuss these teachings and practices in more detail. First, however, it is important to get a better idea of what to expect when the hour of your death actually arrives.

*   *   *   *   *

When a man knows God, he is free: his sorrows have an end, and birth and death are no more. When in inner union he is beyond the world of the body, then the third world, the world of the spirit is found, where the power of the All is, and man has all: for he is one with the ONE.
—Upanishads (Hindu)

Chapter One: The Stages of Death

What happens during and after death?

It is commonly said that we have no idea what happens after death because no one has ever returned to tell us about it. But this is not altogether true. Since the dawn of humanity there have been those who have undergone a "clinical death" (the cessation of all vital life signs) and afterwards have been revived. According to recent studies, nearly fifty percent of such people remain lucid during these episodes, and later report having had what today are called "near-death experiences" (NDE's).[3] While the details of these experiences may vary according to an individual's temperament and beliefs, certain basic patterns and motifs recur with striking frequency. These include out-of-body-experiences, traveling through mist-filled tunnels, seeing visions, having encounters with dead relatives or other disembodied beings, and perceiving an intense white or golden light.

Another source of information about what happens after death comes to us from the world's great religious traditions. Virtually all of these traditions have attested to the continuity of consciousness beyond physical death and offered some description (usually in mythic terms) of what takes place in the afterlife. As is the case with near-death-experiencers (NDErs), the specifics of these mythologies vary considerably from culture to culture. But also (as with NDErs) cross cultural comparisons reveal underlying images and themes that are largely invariant from one tradition to another.

Finally, we now have available in the West a growing body of literature from those spiritual traditions which have made a specialty of cultivating meditative techniques that actually mimic the dying process. Perhaps the most sophisticated of these is the Tantric Buddhist tradition of Tibet. For more than a thousand years Tibetan Buddhists have been making increasingly refined observations of the mental states which occur during such simulated death experiences.

This is not the time or place to present a complete analysis of all the evidence concerning after-death states, which can be gleaned from these various sources. Indeed, a truly comprehensive study of the subject has (to our knowledge) yet to be undertaken.[4] However, enough is known to make one thing quite clear: *The mystics of all traditions unanimously agree that death will offer you a "golden opportunity" for attaining that Gnostic Awakening which has been the supreme goal of your spiritual quest.*

In the Tibetan tradition, for example, death is seen to unfold in a series of stages during which the various physical and mental constituents are absorbed into each other until, finally, there is nothing left in consciousness but an apparent void. This is the critical moment. If you can Recognize that this 'void' is actually the "fundamental clear light," (or, in our terms, *Pure Consciousness*), then you will achieve full Enlightenment, for, as Bokar Rinpoche explains:

> Recognizing this fundamental clear light means "Becoming Buddha in the absolute body at the moment of death."[5]

The Hindu tradition gives a similar account of what happens during the death process, also culminating in a moment in which the Ultimate Nature of Reality can be Realized. Thus, in the *Chandogya Upanishad*, we find this description:

> When, dear one, a person dies, his voice is absorbed into his mind; his mind into his breath; his breath into heat; and heat into formless Spirit. That is the Real. That is the essence of this whole world. That thou art.[6]

In the Jewish Kabbalist tradition, the anonymous author of the *Sefer ha-Zeruf* declares that at the moment of death accomplished Kabbalists attained:

> the essence of all apprehensions... because the interruptions and all the obstacles which are in the world left them, and the intellect returned to cleave to that light which is the [Divine] Intellect.[7]

According to both the Christian and Islamic cosmologies, if you have led a virtuous life, you will enter into paradise following the world's destruction at the end of time. Now on the face of it this sounds quite different from the Tibetan, Hindu, and Kabbalist conceptions which insist that the opportunity for Gnosis comes immediately after physical death has occured. But if we read the "world's destruction" as a mythological description of what an individual experiences during the death process, these accounts are quite compatible. From the point of view of the dying person, the progressive eradication of all phenomena from consciousness will, indeed, seem like the "end of the world." In fact, this is precisely how Tibetan master, Kalu Rinpoche, describes it:

> The internal experience for the dying person is of a great wind sweeping away the whole world...an incredible maelstrom of wind, consuming the entire universe.[8]

Moreover, according to the early Christian paradigm, although faith may earn you entry into paradise, faith by itself is not sufficient for realizing the "eternal life" promised by Jesus. Eternal life actually comes through spiritual knowledge (Gnosis), for, as Augustine pointed out, Jesus did not say, this is eternal life that ye *believe* in God, but rather, "This is eternal life that they might *know* thee the only true God, and Jesus Christ, whom thou has sent."[9] Consequently, believers who failed to attain such a "Vision of God" in this life, would, according to Augustine, be granted it in the hereafter and in this way attain salvation.

An almost identical view was held by the mystics of Islam. The great Sufi philosopher, Al-Ghazzali, for example, insisted that upon entering paradise the true lover of God would receive a "Vision of the Divine Countenance," which, he affirmed, is "none other than the gnosis (*ma'rifa*) already given in an inferior and more fleeting fashion to the saints in this world."[10]

Indeed, the link between Enlightenment and death goes back to shamanic times, for as the renowned religious historian, Mircea Eliade, writes, "all the ecstatic experiences that determine the future shaman's vocation involve the traditional schema of an initiation ceremony: suffering, death, resurrection."[11]

But in order to understand exactly *why* death should be so universally associated with an opportunity to attain Spiritual Realization, we must try to get a more precise idea of what actually happens during the death process. Because the Tibetans have developed the greatest expertise in simulating death experiences, let us combine what they have to say about the various mental states that are likely to arise with contemporary medical descriptions of what will happen to your physical body as you enter Death's Gate.

The Eight Stages of Death

Stage one: As the hour of death approaches, your body will start to shut down. Usually this begins with a loss of appetite and an inability to take in fluids. It will also become increasingly difficult for you to move your arms and legs. Mentally, you will begin to lose contact with your physical environment and become increasingly drowsy. In this stage you may also begin having confusing visions or other dream-like experiences.

Stage two: Your mouth will become dry and you will urinate less frequently. You may have out-of-body experiences, feel like you are entering a tunnel, and feel that you are surrounded by "mist" or "smoke" (similar to what many NDErs describe.)

Stage three: As your blood circulation slows, you may feel alternately hot, then cold. As time passes, however, your arms and legs will grow cooler and may turn a bluish-gray color. Your vision and hearing will become impaired, and, as less oxygen gets to your brain, you may grow confused and restless. It will also become increasingly difficult for you to recognize family members or friends who are present. Internally, you may see sparks, flashing colors, or what looks like patterns of pure "energy," which can be either fascinating or frightening, depending on your mental attitude.

Stage four: Your breathing will become irregular, with long periods of stillness between breaths. After a while, your breath may resume a more regular pattern, but this will be shallow and mechanical in nature. Eventually, your breath will cease altogether and your heart will stop beating. Inwardly, you may see something like the last sparks of a fire that is about to be extinguished. This, of course, is the moment of actual *physical* *death*, but according to the Tibetans it is *not* the end of the dying process. There are *four more stages* which take from five to twenty minutes longer to unfold.

Stage five: In stage five, your capacity to think conceptually will break down. As conceptions disappear, your mind will become pervaded by a white luminosity or light, which the Tibetans describe as being like "a clear autumn sky filled with moon-light." They call this *the mind of white appearance.*

Stage six: In the sixth stage, all traces of aggression and aversion will disappear. As this happens, the white light pervading your mind will be replaced by a red or golden luminosity which the Tibetans compare to an autumn sky "filled with intense sun-light." They call this *the mind of red increase.*

Stage seven: In the seventh stage, attachments and desires will vanish. Now your mind will be empty of all phenomena of any kind, and so appear to be a dark void or nothingness, like "an autumn sky without any light whatsoever." This, the Tibetans call *the mind of black-near-attainment*, which, in our terms, is literally *Consciousness-without-an-object.* It is here at this stage that the "golden opportunity" for Gnostic Awakening will present itself because (as we have already seen) if you can Recognize that Consciousness-without-an-object is actually the "fundamental clear light" of your own mind, then you will have discovered what you *really* are—Consciousness, Itself. (Since there is nothing else in this state besides Consciousness, Itself, what else could you be?) It is this discovery of your True Identity that Awakens you to the eighth stage which constitutes full Enlightenment.

Stage eight: This stage is called variously by the Tibetans *the attainment-clear light, the clear light of bliss,* or *the fundamental clear light of the nature of the mind.* Actually, it is not properly speaking a 'stage' at all, but simply a continuation of the mind of black-near-attainment, only now Recognized to be Consciousness, Itself. And while this Consciousness remains momentarily empty of all phenomena, It is *not* a mere *"nothingness"* (in the sense of a vacuity). Rather, It is Realized to be simultaneously the Actual Fullness (or Ultimate Reality) which contains within Itself every possible manifestation, and that Primordial Awareness (like a "clear light") which both projects and perceives these manifestations as apparent 'worlds' and 'beings'.

This is the Realization or Gnosis which "sets you free" from suffering and death forever because It makes absolutely clear that all your experiences of being a limited, transitory entity, 'I', or 'self' (which could be subject to birth, suffering, and death) have been, from the very beginning, a delusion. Put differently, you will see that every 'thing' is simply a form of your True Self, or that Consciousness which is, Itself, is intrinsically free of all things.

Why Gnosis is easier to attain at the moment of death

Of course, it is not necessary to wait for physical death to attain Gnosis. Actually, one may have a Gnostic Awakening at any time. This potential exists not only because Consciousness is always and everywhere the fundamental ground of all our experience, but also (and more precisely) because the whole cycle of birth and death (including a momentary glimpse of pure Consciousness) is repeated with the arising and passing of any phenomenon whatsoever. Thus, according to Bokar Rinpoche:

> This process of absorption...does not occur only at [physical] death, it also happens in an extremely subtle manner when we fall asleep or when a thought is removed from our mind.[12]

Other traditions attest to this fact as well. Listen, for example, to the modern Hindu mystic, Ramana Maharshi:

> The ego in its purity [i.e., the *Atman* or Divine Self] is experienced in the intervals between two states or between two thoughts...Its true nature is known when it is out of contact with objects or thoughts. You should realize *this interval* as the abiding, unchangeable Reality, your true Being...[13]

Likewise, the fourteenth century Kabbalist, Rabbi Joseph ben Shalom of Barcelona, taught that:

> in every transformation of reality, in every change of form, or every time the stature of a thing is altered, the *abyss of nothingness* is crossed and for a fleeting mystical moment becomes visible.[14]

The reason it is difficult to notice this *abyss of nothingness* is that, first of all, its appearance is exceedingly brief. Secondly, our attention is conditioned to focus only on *things*, but the *abyss of nothingness* is not a 'thing'. Consequently, our attention habitually ignores this *no*-thing as it compulsively searches out the next phenomenon to arise. If, however, we can train our attention (via meditation) to remain stable and clear, then all that is required to "point to" this *abyss of nothingness* is an ordinary gesture of the most mundane kind. This is why Zen students, for example, who have been ripened through practice, can attain Enlightenment simply by seeing a candle being blown out or hearing a bird cry. In the "intervals" just before and after the arising and passing of these phenomena, Consciousness-without-an-object stands for a split second unveiled in all Its nakedness.

But there are other moments in the course of our lives in which Consciousness-without-an-object reveals itself in a more dramatic fashion and for longer periods of time. One of these (as Bokar Rinpoche already mentioned) occurs every twenty-four hours during the transition from the waking state to sleep. Here it is not merely a single sound or sight that "dies" but the entire waking world! Accordingly, an ancient Hindu text has Shiva advising his consort, Devi, to observe carefully that moment:

> when sleep has not yet come and external wakefulness vanishes, [for] at this point BEING is REVEALED.[15]

But, again, these instructions are hard to follow because as most of us fall asleep our minds are completely absorbed in reviewing past events, making future plans, or spinning fantasies, and these mental activities so preoccupy our attention that we fail to recognize Consciousness-without-an-object when it appears. Instead, we experience it as a kind of "black out"—a state of total *un*consciousness, when, in fact, it is *Pure* Consciousness!

Finally, Consciousness-without-an-object can be experienced by practicing certain meditative techniques which lead to states of *samadhi* (as they are called in the East) or *suspension* (as they are called in the West.) Dionysius the Areopagite, one of the most influential of Christian mystics, gives this version of the practice:

> ...in the diligent exercise of mystical contemplation, leave behind the senses and the operations of the intellect, and all things sensible and intellectual, and all things in the world of being and non-being, that thou mayest arise by unknowing toward the union...with Him who transcends all being and all knowledge. For by the unceasing and absolute renunciation of thyself and all things thou mayest be borne on high, through pure and entire self-abnegation, into the superessential Radiance of the Divine Darkness.[16]

There are, however, two problems with this approach. First, attaining states of samadhi usually requires a concerted effort made over a long period of time. Consequently, this technique is usually too difficult to perfect for seekers living a householder's life. The second problem is that states of samadhi almost always generate an overwhelming sense of bliss. As a result, seekers who attain these states without having thoroughly practiced selflessness are in great danger of mistaking this bliss for a genuine Gnostic Awakening. When this happens, not only do they miss the point of the practice (which is not to bask in bliss but to attain Gnosis), but they fall into one of the worst delusions of all: they imagine they have been liberated, when they have not.

The point is that, although opportunities for Realization arise in many different situations, attaining it "in this life" (as you no doubt know) is not so easy. The primary obstacle is that we are constantly distracted by innumerable self-centered thoughts, feelings, sensations, desires, aversions, attachments, etc.—all of which seem rooted in Nature, herself. And this is precisely why death presents such a "golden opportunity" for attaining what was so hard to attain in life. As the death process unfolds, everything will be reversed. Nature (as the Tibetans say) will actually be *cooperating* with your practice by progressively removing each and every distraction from your mind, until finally there will be nothing left but Consciousness, Itself. All you really have to do is wait for this Pure Consciousness to appear, and then Recognize it for what it is. Death will take care of the rest!

Here, however, a word of warning is in order. The fact that Nature will remove all your distractions at the time of death in no way negates the necessity for practicing in this life. On the contrary, if you do not start preparing for it now, when the hour of your death actually arrives you will almost certainly be overwhelmed with pain and fear. Under such circumstances rather than being able to surrender whole-heartedly to death, your impulse will be to resist its operations with all your might. Consequently, when Consciousness-without-an-object finally does dawn, instead of recognizing what is actually happening, you will experience nothing but the onset of oblivion. Nor, unfortunately, is oblivion the end of the story as the materialists like to believe.

What lies beyond the Gate of Death?

Sooner or later, Consciousness will resume Its Divine Play. This is not a problem for one who has attained Gnosis, because when phenomena do arise again, they will be automatically Recognized simply as forms of Consciousness, Itself, possessing not the slightest reality apart from It. However, for those who remain deluded, the forms Consciousness takes following physical death will manifest as those worlds and beings which constitute the "heavens" and "hells" described by traditional mythologies.

According to the Tibetan paradigm, for example, if you fail to Recognize that the mind of black-near-attainment is actually the fundamental clear light, you will fall into a deep sleep which lasts for three days and then awaken in what is called the *Intermediate State*. In this state, Consciousness begins to manifest as various peaceful and wrathful deities. Not recognizing these deities to be projections of your own mind, you will be terrified and try to flee from them. The more you run, however, the more "hellish" your experiences will become, until at last you take rebirth in one of the six realms which make up Cyclic Existence or the world of delusion. Then, the whole process of birth and death will repeat itself

In Christianity and Islam, of course, there is no concept of "rebirth." Exoterically, it is believed that you end up either in Heaven or in Hell for all eternity. There have been mystics in both traditions, however, who have dissented from this orthodox doctrine. The early Christian theologian, Origen, for example, taught that in the end, all things (including even the devil) will be restored to God, while the Sufi "Shaykh of shaykhs," Ibn 'Arabi, wrote that, because the *Qur'an* tells us that God's mercy precedes his wrath, "all creatures must eventually find happiness."

In any case, it is axiomatic among mystics the world over that so long as you fail to attain Gnosis (whether in this life or the next) you will continue to experience states that will seem pleasant (heavenly) or unpleasant (hellish) according to the spiritual qualities you have cultivated in this life. Thus, Bokar Rinpoche, says:

> Even if we do not believe that hell exists, if we have committed negative deeds, that will cause hell to manifest; our mind will produce the false appearances causing immense suffering when the time is right. That is what hell is about. [17]

And, Al-Ghazzali writes about those who doubt that unbelievers will be tormented by snakes in the afterlife (as Islamic tradition describes):

> They do not understand that these snakes have their abode within the unbeliever's spirit, and that they existed in him even before he died, for they were his own evil qualities symbolized, such as jealousy, hatred, hypocrisy, pride, deceit, etc. [18]

In other words, in death as in life, it is we ourselves who create our own happiness or suffering. Therefore, in order to avoid suffering and be able to seize the "golden opportunity" death will present, it is imperative that you start preparing for it now. In the next three chapters we shall discuss three practices (versions of which are found in most of the Great Traditions), specifically designed to help you make a smooth passage through Death's Gate.

*   *   *   *   *

Take no pride in the body
It will soon mingle with dust.
This life is like the sporting of sparrows.
It will end with the onset of night.
I have chosen the Indestructible for my
refuge,
Him whom the snake of death
Can not devour.

— Mira Bai (Hindu)

Chapter Two: The Death Prayer

Next to the appearance of Consciousness-without-an-object, the most important moment in the dying process comes at the end of the fourth stage with physical death. At this time your mind will be particularly vulnerable so that whatever last thoughts you have before conceptions cease will make a deep impression. Thus, if you die thinking only about yourself, your sense of 'self' will be much stronger in the after-death states. This, in turn, will tend to make everything you see seem "alien" and "fearful." If, on the other hand, you die with your thoughts focused not on yourself but on the Divine, then everything you see in the after-death states will tend to appear as a manifestation of the Divine and your experiences will be imbued with beauty, joy, and bliss.

The easiest way to take your attention off yourself and focus it on the Divine is to engage in a practice of devotion. This is why virtually all traditions have encouraged those who are passing through Death's Gate to do so with a prayer on their lips and reverence in their hearts. In Islam, for example, it is recommended that a person who is dying repeat the two testimonies of Islamic Faith: "There is no god but God, and Muhammad is His messenger." A favorite death-prayer for Medieval Christians was addressed to the Virgin Mary: "Holy Mary, Mother of God, pray for us sinners now and in the hour of our death." In Judaism, to die saying the *Shema*— "Hear, O Israel, the Lord is our God, the Lord is One"—is considered to be of great benefit. Mahayana Buddhists often die praying to the Buddha of Compassion, while many American Indians have personal "death songs" to be used specifically when the time comes to leave this world.

As a practitioner of the Way of Selflessness, you should already have a *death prayer* which you have practiced in preparation for your departure from this life. If not, here are some instructions for composing one. You should do this right away so that you can practice it as much as possible in the time you have left.

Instructions for Composing a Death Prayer

Step 1: Chose an object of worship

Consciousness, Itself, has no form of its own. Rather it is that Field of Primordial Awareness in which all forms themselves continually appear and disappear. Consequently, Pure Consciousness can never appear as an object *in* consciousness. And yet, because Consciousness is the ever present ground of all forms, any form has the potential to act as a kind of "window" onto Pure Consciousness. When this potential is realized in any particular object (either by an individual or a whole community), that object becomes sacred. Historically, this process of sacralization has given rise to a great array of Divine Symbols, Images, Archetypes, and Holy Names, which can serve as focal points for devotion.

The first thing to do, then, is to choose such a Sacred Object to be the focal point of your own death prayer. This can be a simple name, like "God," or "Truth," or "The Mystery." It can also be an archetypal figure representing some particular quality of Consciousness—for example, *compassion* manifesting as Krishna, Christ, or Quan-Yin; or *wisdom* in the form of Sophia, Athena, or Khadir. If you are good at visual-ization, you may want to choose the image of one of humanity's great spiritual teachers like Buddha or Lao Tzu, Teresa of

Avila or Mira Bai. Or, you can take as your object that sense of the Divine *Presence* permeating the whole field of awareness. (This latter choice, however, is not recommended unless you have already practiced meditations which allow you to experience this *Presence* more or less at will.)

Step 2: Compose a prayer

Next choose or compose a short PRAYER of no more than a few phrases with which to address your Sacred Object. It might, for instance, be something as simple as, "O God of my heart, I surrender all to you." Make sure your prayer contains the word "surrender" or some equivalent. There are two reasons for this. First, "surrender" expresses the essence of the state of selflessness which you are trying to achieve. Second, as you approach the hour of your death, you may find that it becomes too difficult to say even a one-sentence prayer in its entirety. If this happens, you'll want to compress the intention of the whole prayer into a single word. "Surrender" says it all.

Step 3: Concentration

Close your eyes and focus your attention on the area of your heart. Feel your Sacred Object taking shape there. Fix your attention single-pointedly on your Object, while patiently ignoring all other objects, images, memories, or thoughts that may arise. Slowly, begin to address the Object with the words of your prayer. Try to feel the power and significance of each word as you say it.

Step 4: Stabilization

After a while, gently relax your attention (without letting it get carried off by distractions) until your heart grows warm and peaceful. Be careful not to let your prayer become mechanical but continue saying it with as much devotion as you can genuinely muster. There may be times when you feel your heart spontaneously "catching fire" and burning with love. If this happens, fine, but don't try to force any extraordinary feelings. The sincerity of your intention is far more important than whatever emotional fireworks you may experience.

Step 5: Inner surrender

As you continue praying, start to turn your whole life over to the Divine in whatever Form you have conceived It. Abandon all worries, anxieties, and fears—whether they concern the things of this world or the next. Think of yourself as a passenger on an airplane who has no choice but to place his or her life in the hands of the pilot. In your situation you are actually much safer because, while human pilots are fallible, the guidance of Consciousness, Itself is truly infallible...*if* you are open to receiving it unconditionally. Remember the testimony of the Mystics of all traditions: *Ultimately, the world is Good. Ultimately nothing can harm you.*

Step 6: Praying without words

Imagine that it has become too difficult for you to say the words of your prayer. Drop everything but the one word, "surrender." Merge this one word with your Sacred Object. Then, drop even this word and simply remain with your intention to surrender yourself totally to the Divine, just like a child relaxing in the arms of its mother.

Every day you should set aside some time for formally practicing your death prayer. This can be done either sitting up or lying down. It is especially important to practice your prayer while you are falling asleep, whether at night or when taking naps. This is because (as we have already seen) the states you pass through as you enter sleep are quite similar to those you will encounter at the time of death.

You can also pray informally whenever you have a few moments alone. Be careful, however, not to strain yourself with too much effort. Ideally, your heart, as the Sufis say, "should steal the prayer from your tongue." If this happens, the prayer will start to generate itself spontaneously, and there will be nothing for you to do except pay attention to it. In general what is required for success in this practice is gentle persistence and deep faith.

The Fruit of Practicing a Death Prayer

As already mentioned, saying a death prayer while passing through Death's Gate will insure that your thoughts are focused on the Divine. This, in turn, will help transform frightening experiences into blissful ones. But there is another, more significant benefit to be gained from this practice. Even though you may not recognize Consciousness-without-an-object in the seventh stage, if you are truly open to the Divine, then you will continue to receive Guidance in the after-death state which can ultimately lead to a Gnostic Awakening.

In the previous chapter we saw how this is expressed mythologically in both the Christian and Islamic traditions as a promise that those with strong faith will be granted a saving "Vision of God" once they have reached paradise. But the same motif is found in other traditions as well. For instance, the H indu *Katha Upanishad* recounts the story of a youth named Nachiketas who, after being killed by his father as a sacrifice, enters the nether world and is there taught the secret of final Liberation by Yama, the King of Death himself. Likewise, in the Buddhist traditions of Tibet and China, it is said that those who die while praying to Amitabha or Quan-Yin (male and female forms of the Buddha of Compassion) will be reborn in a "Land of Bliss" where they will have an opportunity to hear dharma teachings profound enough to make Enlightenment virtually inevitable.

If such tales arouse your skepticism, remember that the "paradisaical realms" do not, from the Mystics' point of view, represent physical places, but rather altered states of consciousness, produced by one's own psycho-spiritual conditioning. What these mythologies point to, then, is actually a fact of spiritual life well attested to in all cultures—namely, that devotional practices can generate visionary states in which Consciousness appears to devotees in Archetypal forms to provide guidance that can lead to Full Awakening.[19]

Conclusion

The death prayer is relatively easy to learn and to practice. This makes it especially suited for beginners, or for those who have been negligent in maintaining their meditative disciplines. But even if you are an experienced practitioner and intend to engage in a more advanced type of practice at the time of your death, it is still a good idea to have memorized and rehearsed a death prayer beforehand. For some people the passage through Death's Gate goes quite smoothly; for others, it can be very traumatic. Therefore, you would be foolish to rely solely on some advanced practice which may become too difficult to maintain when death finally carries you away. If that happens, you should abandon whatever practice you are doing and take up the death prayer in its stead.

*   *   *   *   *

To overcome the attitude of seeking the bliss of peace for yourself, you should train for a long time in love, compassion and the altruistic mind of enlightenment—which has love and compassion as its root.

— Tsong-ka-pa (Buddhist)

Chapter Three: The Practice of Perfect Sacrifice

A more difficult but more powerful practice than the death prayer is the practice of *perfect sacrifice*, which is the giving up of one's own life for the sake of others. This practice is universally venerated because it epitomizes a virtue fundamental to all spiritual paths—*compassionate action.*

Perhaps the best known example of perfect sacrifice in the West is the crucifixion of Jesus, who said of his own death: "No man has greater love than this, that he lay down his life for another." But the practice of perfect sacrifice is by no means confined to the Christian tradition. In virtually all sacred societies, dying for the sake of others is considered to be of great spiritual benefit. This is reflected, for instance, in the death prayer of the warriors of the Lakota Indian Fox Society who pledged themselves to surrender their own lives in defense of the tribe's women and children. Thus, when they went into battle they sang:

> I am a Fox.
> I am supposed to die.
> If there is anything difficult,
> If there is anything dangerous,
> That is mine to do.[20]

Most of us, of course, are not granted the opportunity to die in such a noble fashion, and you may wonder how your own death can possibly benefit anyone at all. But consider that when your body decays, eventually its molecules will return to the food chain providing nourishment for a host of other living creatures. What's more, in the greater scheme of things your death is absolutely essential in order to make room for future generations. Imagine a world where people were born but no one ever died. It would be like a symphony in which every note had a beginning but no end, resembling more an endless scream than a beautiful piece of music.

From a spiritual point of view, however, the real power of any practice derives not from whatever physical results it may or may not produce, but from the degree of loving compassion which motivates it. As the Christian mystic, Meister Eckhart, said:

> God has no regard for what your works are, but for what your love and devotion and intention in the works are.[21]

In other words, it is not necessary that your death actually benefit anyone else for it to be an expression of perfect sacrifice. It is enough that you die with such an intention fully enthroned in your mind and heart.

To help cultivate such an intention, Buddhists have developed a meditative practice they call "sending and taking." Although this meditation can be done at any time, it is considered especially effective when performed at the hour of one's death. As Bokar Rinpoche explains, it begins with the dying person establishing a compassionate intention by thinking:

> At the time of death all beings experience suffering and anguish...Today it is my turn to experience this suffering and anguish. Well! I hope there is enough to experience as I do not want others to suffer! I agree to take on the suffering of all beings who are dying within my suffering.[22]

This resolve is followed by a visualization practice which is coordinated with the breath. What follows are some instructions (based on this Buddhist technique) for converting your own death into a precious opportunity for practicing perfect sacrifice. However, because the degree of compassion required for fully entering into this practice usually takes a long time to cultivate, and because the moment of death is so critical, you should not make perfect sacrifice your *primary* death practice unless you already have experienced firsthand the deep joy that comes from selflessly serving others. If this is not the case with you (and be honest!), then choose a death prayer for your main practice (as described in Chapter Two), and use perfect sacrifice as an auxiliary practice.

Instructions for Practicing Perfect Sacrifice

Step One: Ponder death's universality

Allow yourself to feel deeply your own pain and suffering. Realize that, although this pain and suffering is happening to you at this particular time, it is in no way *personal*. Everyone must die just as you are dying. Everyone must suffer just as you are suffering. And everyone fears it, just as you fear it. This is what connects you to all beings at the most profound level of embodied existence. Only by undergoing death yourself can you truly understand the suffering of others.

Step Two: Pay attention to others

Pay close attention to friends and relatives who come to visit you. How do they act? Are they nervous? Embarrassed? Frightened? Shocked? Do they seem at a loss for words; or do they talk too much? Do they often burst into tears just looking at you? Observe how their own fears of death are reflected in how they react to you. Open your heart to them, and think how wonderful it would be if you could relieve them of all their fears and suffering.

Step Three: Resolve to free all beings from death forever

The only way to become "free of death forever" is through a Gnostic Awakening. Obviously one who is already Awake is in the best position to help others attain this goal. For the sake of all suffering beings, then, resolve to cooperate with your own death in order to Wake Up. (Truly, it is the simplest thing in the world. All you have to do is let go of your 'self'!) When you are Awake there will be no limit to the help you can give others—even after death.

In the meantime, be generous in communicating your current experiences to your family and friends. Tell them about whatever feelings you may be having, whether of dread or joy, sadness or delight. Share with them your confusion as well as your wisdom, your questions as well as your insights. This will not only help to alleviate their own fears, but will also provide them with a living example of how to face death in an honest and open manner.

Step Four: Visualize taking on the suffering of other beings

Start practicing perfect sacrifice by visualizing that, in addition to whatever suffering you are currently experiencing, you take on the suffering of other beings as well. Then, visualize them as relieved of their suffering and glowing with happiness.

At first, choose specific people to use in your visualizations—for instance, a family member who is particularly upset over your dying. Imagine that you feel his or her agony and grief. Then imagine that, by taking this agony and grief into yourself, the person is relieved of it. Later, extend your visualization to include other people, even ones you have never met.

In the after-death state you may well encounter apparitional beings. Some may appear as beneficent angels, gods, or goddesses. Others may appear as frightening demons, ghosts, or wrathful deities. Try to conjure up images of what they might look like, and then embrace them all with a heart overflowing with love and compassion.

Step Five: Coordinate your visualizations with your breath

Note: This is only necessary for those who intend to make perfect sacrifice their primary death practice.

Visualize taking on the suffering of other beings as you inhale. Visualize spreading relief and happiness to other beings as you exhale. At first, just practice sending out relief and happiness while you are exhaling (without worrying about taking on suffering as you inhale). Then, practice taking on the suffering of others while you inhale (without worrying about spreading happiness as you exhale). After you get used to this, start alternating the two phases of the practice more rapidly until your visualizations are coordinated with each inhalation and each exhalation.

The purpose of coordinating your visualizations with your breath is that, when the hour of death arrives, your mind may become too weak to engage in actual visualizations. However, if you have practiced coordinating the visualizations with your inhalations and exhalations beforehand, then the act of breathing itself will carry your intention to sacrifice yourself for the sake of others, and you will die with this resolve in mind.

The Fruit of Practicing Perfect Sacrifice

To speak of the "fruit" of the practice of perfect sacrifice is somewhat contradictory, because the essence of the practice is not to desire any benefit for oneself. Even Gnosis should only be desired for the sake of helping others, nor should you prefer to have blissful experiences over frightening ones. Instead, you should abandon all concern with "fruits" and, in fact, be willing to enter hell itself if it will relieve others of their suffering. This ultimate gesture of selflessness was beautifully expressed by a Sufi named Abo'l-Hasan Nuri who used to pray:

> "O Lord...if you must fill hell with people, You are certainly able to fill it and all its levels with me alone and send everyone else to heaven."[23]

Paradoxically, however, such a total disinterest in one's own welfare inevitably produces a condition close to absolute selflessness. If you enter Death's Gate in this state, then when you reach the seventh stage, and encounter Consciousness-without-an-object, it will be relatively easy to Realize that *This* is what you truly are, and thus attain Gnosis.

But even if you do not attain Gnosis at this stage, if you carry your selfless intention into the intermediate state, it will automatically transform all environments and all beings into a Play of Divine Forms. Here, again you will be able to attain Gnosis simply by Recognizing that this Play is itself nothing but a manifestation of your own mind or Consciousness, Itself.

Conclusion

It is important to reiterate that only advanced seekers should choose perfect sacrifice as their primary death practice. But never forget that the Way of Selflessness depends as much on cultivating compassion as it does on recognizing the true nature of phenomena. Both are necessary to the attainment of Full Enlightenment. This is because, without the selflessness that comes from cultivating compassion, your own sense of being a separate 'self' will circumscribe whatever insights you do manage to have. Thus, whether or not you choose perfect sacrifice as your primary death practice, the more selfless compassion you can generate for others between now and the hour of your death, the greater your chances of Awakening forever as you pass through its Gate.

*   *   *   *   *

...it is like rain falling from the heavens into a river or spring; there is nothing but water there and it is impossible to divide or separate the water belonging to the river from that which fell from the heavens. Or it is as if a tiny streamlet enters the sea, from which it will find no way of separating itself, or as if in a room there were two large windows through which the light streamed in: it enters in different places but it all becomes one.

— Teresa of Avila (Christian)

Chapter Four: Effortless Contemplation

The most difficult practice to undertake at the time of death is effortless contemplation. Essentially, effortless contemplation is a practice of inquiry. Actually, one could say that it is the *ultimate* practice of inquiry. As the name suggests, however, it does not involve any form of intellectual probing, philosophical analysis, or even mental concentration. Quite the opposite—which is why effortless contemplation is not only difficult to practice but also to describe. In fact, most explanations end up sounding quite paradoxical. For example, the great Taoist sage, Lao Tzu, writes about it this way:

> Seeking knowledge one does more every day;
> Seeking the Way one does less every day.
> One does less and less until at last one does nothing.
> When one does nothing, there is nothing that is left undone.[24]

Some people think effortless contemplation is peculiar to Taoism, but, of course, it is found in other mystical traditions as well. Thus, Ramana Maharshi advises the advanced seeker to: "Make no effort either to work or to renounce; your effort is the bondage."[25] Likewise, Meister Eckhart says of the Godhead:

> The more one seeks You, the less one finds You. You should so seek Him that you find Him nowhere. If you do not seek Him, then you will find Him.[26]

Perhaps the Dzogchen texts of Tibetan Buddhism give the most elaborate expositions of effortless contemplation. Here is one example from Longchenpa's, *The Jewel Ship:*

The way things appear are one in their pure fact of being.
Do not make any corrections here.
This king, uncontrived sameness,
Is the conceptless deep experience of the fundamental
    dimension of reality.
Simply stay with that...
When meditating on pure, unborn reality
What appears is neither concretized nor latched onto.
Just relax in the reality of this blissful
    self-generating pristine awareness.[27]

In the Tibetan tradition to die in such a state is called "dying while remaining in the nature of mind" and is considered the most desirable practice for passing through Death's Gate. Thus Bokar Rinpoche writes:

By far the best way to die is to remain without distraction within the essence of mind, which is the nature of the mind beyond illusion.[28]

It must be emphasized, however, that "remaining in the nature of the mind beyond illusion" does not mean just lying around lost in a stupor of fantasies and daydreams. Although it is, indeed, effortless, the kind of *total* abandonment of striving which characterizes this practice is actually very hard to achieve, for as Simone Weil observes: "There is an easiness in salvation which is more difficult than all our efforts."[29] The key is that you must (as Bokar Rinpoche said) be able to engage in effortless contemplation "without distraction." Consequently, *effortless contemplation should only be undertaken by advanced practitioners*—i.e., those who have attained meditative stabilization and have extensive training in this type of practice.

The following set of instructions, then, is not meant to introduce newcomers to effortless contemplation but only to act as a series of reminders for those who have had prior experience with this practice.

Instructions for Practicing Effortless Contemplation

Step One: Preliminaries

1. If you are able to, sit in your normal meditation posture. If your illness prevents this, or makes it too difficult, assume the most comfortable position you can.

2. Focus on your breath or some other meditation object to stabilize your attention.

3. After a few minutes, cease to focus on any particular object and practice "choiceless awareness," simply observing whatever objects arise and pass in Consciousness. Notice the following about each object:

   a) It is impermanent.

   b) It has no existence apart from Consciousness, Itself.

   c) Being a form of Consciousness, it is transparent to It.

Step Two: Being reminded

Note: You can either read the following reminders your-self, or have someone read them to you. In either case, they should be read slowly, giving you a chance to contemplate each one before going on to the next.

1. Without fixing your attention on anything, just consider:

Is there consciousness of sights?
Is there consciousness of sounds?
Is there consciousness of sensations?
Is there consciousness of feelings?
Is there consciousness of thoughts?

This very Consciousness, which is here right
now, is that eternal, self-luminous Reality
you have been striving to Realize all along.

Since this Consciousness is already here, your
striving is unnecessary.

2. Abandon all concepts *about* your experience and
simply observe:

See how appearances arise in Consciousness.
Since, whatever appears is already present,
how can it be avoided?

See how appearances pass in Consciousness.
Since whatever has passed is no longer
present, how can it be grasped?

See how everything appears without the
least obstruction.
Since nothing obstructs appearances, there
are no obstacles to be removed.
See how everything passes without the least
hindrance.
Since everything is self-liberating,
there is nothing to be set free.

Relax into this effortless contemplation of
how things actually are.

3. Without making any adjustments, continue to
   observe:

> Although you say,
> "forms arise in Consciousness,"
> can you really separate
> Consciousness from its forms?
> Is not Consciousness like an ocean,
> and forms its waves?

> Because Consciousness and forms are ulti-
> mately inseparable, duality never existed:
> How then can it be transcended?

> Although you say
> "I am aware of such-and-such an object,"
> can you truly distinguish
> between your self and the object?
> Where does 'self' end
> and the 'object' begin?

> Because subject and object are, in Reality,
> indistinguishable,
> delusion never originated.
> How then can it be dispelled?

4. Look! Reality is staring you right in the face:

> You say, you cannot eliminate your "self"
> but there is no "self" to eliminate.

> You say, you have not attained
> "Enlightenment,"
> but there is not the slightest thing to attain.

> You say, "I am ignorant of my true identity,"
> but how can this be?

What else is there, besides this infinite,
eternal, non-dual field of Consciousness-and-form
which is already present, right here and now...
and now... and now...

Therefore, surrender all desire for attainment
and just be what you are: Consciousness,
Itself!

Step Three: Practicing without formal reminders

Once you have gotten used to contemplating in this way,
it is sufficient to remember these three basic rules:

> *Do not grasp anything;*
> *Do not reject anything;*
> *Be whatever is.*

This applies particularly to situations where you experience states of exceptional clarity, or have feelings of great bliss, or profound insights. Such experiences will generate thoughts like: "Ah, this is Gnosis! Now, I am definitely Enlightened!" But as clarity gives way to confusion, bliss to frustration, and profound insights to mental chatter, you will think: "Now, I have lost my Enlightenment and become deluded once again. How depressing!" When this happens you must remember that Enlightenment is not a 'place' in which to settle, nor is Gnosis a 'state' that needs to be maintained. All experiences, all feelings, all states—whether sacred or mundane—are by their very nature transient and ephemeral. Without making any attempt either to hold on to them or push them away, simply remain identified with Consciousness, Itself and continue to practice effortlessly.

Step Four: Practicing informally

If you intend to make effortless contemplation your primary death practice, you should practice it not only formally (during set times of the day), but you should also try to integrate it with all your other activities—eating, drinking, laughing, crying, talking, reading, going to the bathroom, etc. Even when you are dozing or sound asleep, identify with the Boundless Space of Consciousness, Itself, and allow all things, images, and feelings to arise and pass effortlessly within It.

The Fruit of Practicing Effortless Contemplation

By practicing effortless contemplation you will develop a Realization that the self is (as the Buddhists say) "empty of any inherent existence." Thus, while objects continue to appear in Consciousness, the delusion that they are being experienced by some 'one' will temporarily subside. This state of profound selflessness, or *Consciousness-without-a-subject*, is often a prelude to Full Awakening. What is missing is the complementary Realization that not only does the 'self' lack any inherent existence, but so do objects. Consequently, as long as objects still seem to exist in their own right, there is no Gnosis. However, if you can remain in a state of Consciousness-without-a-subject as you pass through Death's Gate, then, when *Consciousness-without-an-object* finally dawns in the seventh stage, you will Realize that the now vanished objects were, themselves, only imaginary projections of this objectless Consciousness. Furthermore, you will Realize that your own Consciousness-without-a-subject is, in fact, indistinguishable from (and thus identical to) Consciousness-without-an-object. In other words, you will directly and simultaneously apprehend not only the True Nature of your 'self', but also the True Nature of all 'objects' and all 'worlds'—which is to say, *Consciousness-without-an-object-and-without-a-subject*. This is Enlightenment, the end of the path.

Conclusion

As was already said, effortless contemplation is the most difficult of all death practices and therefore should only be relied upon at the time of actual death by advanced practitioners. However, even if you are only an intermediate or beginning practitioner, it is a good idea to have some familiarity with it. The reason is that the crisis of death may, itself, spontaneously generate effortless contemplation. If this happens there is a danger that you will not recognize what is occurring because effortless contemplation does not *feel* like a practice at all. Consequently, you may think "this is too easy to be right" and try to resume your death prayer or practice of self-sacrifice. However, if the state of effortless contemplation you find yourself in is genuine, this would be a serious mistake.

But how can you tell if it *is* genuine? Ask yourself if you are thoroughly detached from, yet at the same time, totally identified with everything that is happening? In spite of pain, fear, and any other difficulties, do you nevertheless feel an unshakable peace permeating the entire field of Consciousness? Most importantly, are you Perfectly Happy? If so, stop worrying about whether or not you are practicing correctly. Drop any images you may have about what Gnosis is supposed to be and just allow the Grace of this Happiness to carry you where it will; for truly you are now beyond all striving and non-striving, and there is literally nothing more for 'you' to do.

*   *   *   *   *

People often make the mistake of being frivolous about death and think, "Oh well, death happens to everybody. It's not a big deal, it's natural. I'll be fine." That's a nice theory until one is dying.

— Chagdud Tulku Rinpoche
(Tibetan Buddhist)

Chapter Five: Other Preparations for Death

Choosing a Spiritual Guide

Just as a midwife can help a woman in the process of giving birth, so a spiritual guide can help you navigate through the difficult process of dying. If your spiritual teacher is able to be with you in person at the hour of your death, then he or she is the obvious choice for the role. If not, ask a family member or friend to serve you in this capacity.

The person you choose to be your guide should be someone whose spiritual wisdom you respect, who can assist you with your practices, and in whom you can confide when fears and doubts arise. Most importantly, he or she should know something about the stages of death outlined in this booklet and be available to act as your "bedside coach" during your actual passage through Death's Gate. This is important because if you become lost in altered states, or frightened by visions, your guide can remind you of where you are and reassure you as to the illusory nature of these experiences. He or she can also answer questions about what's happening to you, read from appropriate spiritual texts, and prompt you to maintain your death practice as you enter the final stages. After physical death has occurred, your spiritual guide should remain with your body for at least twenty minutes, gently instructing you to be attentive to the various mental appearances which will manifest, and to identify with Consciousness-without-an-object when it appears.

Once you have chosen a spiritual guide, be sure to introduce him or her to your family and friends. Let them know that
you intend to die in a spiritual manner and inform them of the
role your guide will play at the hour of your death. If they are
not thoroughly apprised of the situation, some members of
your family may become disturbed by your guide's presence.
This can cause unnecessary tensions and quarreling at a time
when an atmosphere of harmony and tranquility will be all
important.

Choosing a Practical Affairs Coordinator

It is vital that you, as a spiritual seeker, set aside time to
engage in spiritual practices or simply to be alone with God.
For most people this will not be too much of a problem.
However, if you have a lot of unfinished business to take care
of, or a large family and many friends who want to visit you,
setting aside time for yourself may become quite difficult. If
you find yourself in this situation, then, in addition to a spiritual
guide, you may also want to ask a trusted family member or
friend to act as a kind of practical affairs coordinator—
someone who can help you pay bills, buy groceries, make
doctor appointments, have prescriptions filled, arrange to get
you legal documents, tell friends when you are and are not
available for visits, and play host to them when they do stop
by. In short, a practical affairs coordinator should be a
combination business manager and social secretary.

Some people—particularly those who have prided themselves on being "independent" most of their lives—may feel
guilty about asking someone else to shoulder such responsibilities. If this is true of you, then, whether or not you have an
"official" practical affairs coordinator, allowing others to tend
to your needs will give you a good opportunity to practice the

virtue of humility. A large part of self-surrender involves giving up our attachment to the illusion that we are, or ever have been, truly autonomous beings.

From the beginning, our bodily existence has depended utterly on the sacrifice of others—whether these others were our parents who raised and supported us as children, the plants and animals that have sacrificed themselves so that we could live, or even the oxygen in the atmosphere, which has given itself freely for us to breathe. Indeed, no one stands alone, for the very boundaries that we imagine separate us from each other and the world are also what bind us together into that single vast tapestry of Consciousness-in-form. Consequently, the more you can acknowledge how much your bodily existence depends on others now, the easier it will be for you to relinquish this existence when the moment of death comes.

Moreover, in allowing others to serve you, you will also be serving them in at least two ways. First, you will be providing them with a "precious opportunity" to practice charity and compassion. This is a highly personal gift which those who care for you will remember and cherish for the rest of their lives. Second, as someone who is dying, you will be acting as a mirror in which they can contemplate their own mortality and the necessity for deepening their own spiritual practice while there is still time. To inspire someone to spiritual practice is perhaps the greatest service one human being can perform for another.

Reconciliation and Restitution

It is important to die with a clear conscience. Start by making a list of those people you have harmed or mistreated, or who have harmed or mistreated you. Do not try to remember every little incident. (Make a single but heartfelt prayer asking forgiveness for all minor offenses you have committed and forgiving those who have committed minor offenses against you.) Confine your list to those people whom you have harmed or injured in a major way and vice versa.

If some of these people are still alive, you should try to contact them personally or write a letter expressing sorrow for any grief you have caused them, and forgiving them for whatever grief they have caused you. If you have actually stolen from someone, or cheated them out of what was rightfully theirs and can make restitution, it will be of great spiritual benefit to do so. Provisions for such restitution, for instance, can be incorporated into your will. If you cannot afford to make restitution, you should still confess your offense and ask their forgiveness.

If you have lost touch with any of the people on your list, or they have already died, you can still ask for and confer forgiveness by means of meditative prayer. Recall to mind each offense as vividly as possible, along with whatever painful feelings of remorse or resentment it arouses. Notice that both remorse and resentment feel painful because the energy of these feelings is directed toward yourself. By re-directing this energy outward, you can transform remorse into repentance or resentment into forgiveness as the situation requires. Once you have done this, release the memory of what happened and do not dwell on it again. Self-pity and obsessive guilt are never signs of true selflessness. If you find yourself wallowing in these kinds of emotions, again notice that they all revolve around an image of your 'self'. Let go of this image and allow the feelings associated with it to dissolve. Then turn your attention to the present and whatever tasks are at hand.

Last Will and Testament

From a spiritual perspective, no one actually "owns" anything. Although the concept of *ownership* is socially and legally necessary, in reality, it is a fiction. As a spiritual practitioner, in order not to be deluded in this regard, you have tried to view all your material possessions as being "on loan" to you from the Divine—which, in turn, means that you have also had a responsibility to use them wisely and compassionately. This includes taking responsibility for their disposal at the time of your death.

The traditional way to dispose of possessions at the time of death is to leave a *last will and testament*. If you have not already done so, you should have one drawn up as soon as possible. It is important, however, to remember that the laws which govern such documents vary from state to state and country to country. For example, they may have to be written in a certain format, be signed by a certain number of witnesses, or be notarized by a notary public in order to be legally binding. Thus, a simple handwritten note is not likely to suffice in a court of law. To be sure that your *last will and testament* is legal, consult a lawyer. If you cannot afford one, at least find out what the laws are pertaining to these documents in your jurisdiction. You should also be aware that in some situations it may be advisable to make other arrangements, such as establishing survivorship title to your property, or setting up trusts. In order to determine which is best for you, consult a professional financial advisor or lawyer.

In addition to fulfilling your responsibilities regarding possessions, taking an active interest in their disposal will also give you an opportunity to practice detachment from them. Thus, even if you have already drawn up a *last will and testament* (or made other arrangements), you should take the time to mentally review all the things you own, say a prayer expressing your gratitude for the way in which each has served you during this life, and then make a conscious decision to relinquish it forever. By so doing, you will prepare yourself to leave this world in the same condition in which you entered it— naked and free of all things.

Documents Pertaining to Your Health Care

If your ability to make decisions about your own medical treatment becomes impaired (as, for instance, if you fall into a coma), it is usually the policy of doctors and other health care professionals (in the United States, at least) to make every effort to keep you alive for as long as possible, even if there is virtually no chance of your condition ever improving. If you do not wish such aggressive and often costly measures to be taken on your behalf, it is not enough to simply communicate this verbally to family members or friends. Because doctors and other health care professionals can be held liable for failing to keep you alive, they may have no choice but to disregard whatever your family and friends say unless it is backed up by written documentation. For this reason, it is important to draw up a *living will* and/or *power of attorney for health care,* as well as to ask your doctor to issue a *Do Not Resuscitate* order (DNR) to be given to all your health-care providers.

A *living will* gives specific instructions about what kinds of treatment you wish withheld when death becomes imminent. By signing a *power of attorney for health care* you legally empower a relative or friend to make these decisions for you should you become incapacitated. A DNR must be signed by your doctor. It informs nurses, ambulance paramedics, and other physicians that you do not wish to be resuscitated when your life signs begin to fail.

Because not all states recognize such documents as legally binding, you must again find out what the laws are in your area. Moreover, as with *last wills and testaments,* documents relating to your health care usually have to be drawn up in a specified manner to carry legal weight. In states which do recognize the legality of such documents, standardized forms can often be obtained from your doctor's office, an area hospital, a Hospice organization, or your local library. Filling them out is a relatively simple matter and well worth the effort, both for your own sake and the sake of your relatives and friends who will be trying to see that your wishes are honored.

Dying at Home

Until the turn of the twentieth century the vast majority of human beings died at home, in their own beds, surrounded by family and friends. In many places in the world they still do, but not in the United States. In the United States today, most people die in hospitals or nursing homes. This has come about partly because it is assumed that such institutions can provide better care for the dying person. With the advent of the Hospice movement in recent years, however, the advantages of dying at home versus dying in an institution have been undergoing a radical re-evaluation. Aside from questions about "death with dignity," and the quality of emotional support that family and friends can provide in a home environment (as opposed to the more technologically advanced but less personal care available in a hospital), there are good spiritual reasons for choosing to die at home:

1) There is little doubt that, all else being equal, dying at home will provide a better environment for engaging in your spiritual practices. Instead of having to follow a hospital's routine, for example, you will have more freedom to set up your own daily schedule, thus allowing for more periods of uninterrupted meditation, reading, reflection, and prayer.

2) Most people find it easier to relax at home with their own families than in a hospital run by a professional staff, no matter how sensitive the staff tries to be. This is usually true not only for the dying person, but also for friends and loved ones who come to visit. Thus, the surroundings in a home are usually more tranquil than in an institution, and as a spiritual practitioner you will certainly want to die in as tranquil an environment as

possible. This is because the more tranquil your environment, the more peaceful will be your own frame of mind and the easier it will be to concentrate on your spiritual practices when the hour of your death arrives.

3) By dying at home you will also give your family and friends a greater opportunity to experience the reality of death and to understand that it is the inevitable end of all embodied life. This will not only help them come to terms with their own mortality, but seeing you die in a spiritual manner may inspire them to strive to do the same.

The decision to die at home, however, should not be made lightly. Although it is not usually the case, the nature of your illness may be such that adequate management of pain and other symptoms is not feasible outside of a hospital setting. This is something you should discuss with your doctor. You must also take into consideration how your family and friends feel. Caring for you will require a heavy expenditure of time and energy which they may not be able to afford. Equally important they must have a genuine desire to be participants in your death. If they consent to your wishes merely out of a sense of duty, you could well find the situation at home becoming far more stressful than it would have been in a hospital. Thus, you must not only try to get them to be honest with you, you must be both honest and compassionate in your assessment of them. Some people in our society have been so sheltered from death that they simply aren't emotionally prepared to cope with the sight of someone they love dying before their very eyes.

If, on the other hand, it is medically feasible and you have the support of your family and friends, then dying at home may be easier than you might at first think. This is especially true if there is a Hospice in your area. Most Hospice organizations are staffed by trained personnel who are emotionally and spiritually committed to making dying at home a viable option in our society once again. Often, they can provide a wide range of medical and social home-care services for both you and your family, including help with such things as the administration of medication, psychological counseling, arranging for a death certificate, planning funeral services, etc. Moreover, Hospice costs are covered by Medicare, most health insurance plans, and private donations, so that lack of money is never an obstacle to receiving their assistance. Therefore, if dying at home seems the right choice for you, seeking help from a Hospice organization should be one of your top priorities.

Pain and Pain-Management

Depending on the type of illness you have, death may be accompanied by a considerable amount of physical pain. This pain can usually be controlled by a variety of pain-killing drugs. However, many of these drugs also produce states of drowsiness, confusion, and sleep—all of which may interfere with your ability to engage in spiritual practice. Because, as a spiritual practitioner you want to die in as lucid a mental state as possible, you might be tempted to abstain from all pain medication. But if the pain itself becomes so excruciating that you can no longer focus on your practice, then there will be little to gain by such abstinence. In addition (again depending on your illness), chemical changes naturally occurring in your body may produce drowsiness, confusion, and sleep even if no medication is taken. Thus, mere abstention from drugs will not necessarily guarantee the lucidity you desire.

There are two things you can do to ameliorate this problem. The first is to use pain medication with discretion, trying to establish a happy medium between physical comfort and mental clarity. The second is to rehearse your death practice whenever you take a nap or go to sleep at night. With sufficient practice, you can actually learn to meditate or pray in any state of consciousness, even while dreaming. The more you can develop this ability now, the easier it will be to maintain lucidity in the hour of your death, no matter what chemical alterations take place in your body, or how much pain medication you have to take.

Planning for the Hour of Your Death

There are many occasions in life for which we plan in great detail—births, initiations, graduations, weddings, even dinner parties. But rarely, in our modern culture, do we make the same kind of preparations for our deaths, and yet there is no more important or sacramental event. One reason that we give so little thought to our deaths is that we are not always granted the opportunity to anticipate it. You, however, have such an opportunity, and you should make the most of it.

Here are a few of the things to consider about the kind of environment you may want to establish as you make your final passage through Death's Gate—especially if you intend to die at home:

1) Would you like to have an "open house" with as many of your friends and relatives present as can make it? Or would you rather just invite members of your immediate family? Perhaps, again, you would prefer to be alone with only your spiritual guide in attendance.

2) Do you want any spiritual texts read as death approaches? If so, which ones and in what order?

3) Would you like music played? If so, what pieces?

4) Do you want any representations of your favorite spiritual teachers placed where you can see them—say, a picture or statue of Quan-Yin or the Buddha, Mira Bai, or Christ?

Even if you are not sure how you will feel about such "accessories" when death comes, you should still ask your spiritual guide in advance to have them available. That way you can avoid any last minute confusion or frantic searching about for the desired items. The more you plan now, the more the outward course of your death will proceed smoothly, and the less there will be to distract you from your inner practice.

Disposing of Your Body

From a spiritual point of view, your body (like your material possessions) does not ultimately "belong" to you, but is only held "on loan," to be used as wisely and compassionately as possible during this life. Thus, just as it is important to make arrangements for the disposal of your material possessions, so it is important to make known your wishes for the disposal of your body after your death. In this regard, there are two major things to consider: *viewing of your corpse* and its *final disposal*.

1. *Viewing of your corpse.* It will be of great spiritual benefit for others to have a chance to view your corpse after you are dead, not only in order to say a last farewell, but more importantly to be able to contemplate the impermanence of all bodily existence. To this end you should request that your body be placed on display somewhere accessible to your family, friends, and fellow practitioners, from one to three days. (In some states there are legal restraints on how long a cadaver can be left unburied without embalming or refrigeration, so check the laws in your area.) Your corpse should not be dressed up beyond the requirements of modesty, nor should any cosmetic attempts be made to disguise the fact that you are quite dead and even beginning to decay. Otherwise, the spiritual purpose of the viewing will be undermined.

2. *Final disposal.* The two most common methods for disposing of corpses are burial and cremation. As to which is best, there is no consensus in the Great Traditions. Indeed, from an Absolute perspective, it makes little difference, since your body has no reality in its own right, but is merely a

transient manifestation of Consciousness, Itself. The one thing you should specifically avoid, however, is any method of burial designed to preserve your body indefinitely (as, for instance, interment in a stainless-steel casket). Remember that you, yourself, have been able to live only through the sacrifice of other life-forms. Since you have feasted on their bodies all these years, it would be both uncharitable and unjust to now deprive them of the opportunity to feast on your body—whether this be directly, through offering your flesh as a banquet for worms and bacteria, or indirectly, by recycling it as bones and ashes that will fertilize the soil.

The Funeral Service

The funeral service fulfills many functions, most of which are social in nature. Thus, it is at once a rite that publicly confirms your death, an occasion for communal grieving, and a ceremony of closure for loved ones who must carry on without you. But it also provides an opportunity for others to assess the way you lived and to learn what they can from it. If you wish to participate in this assessment by communicating whatever insights you have gained from life, you can do so in a variety of ways. You might, for example, ask that a favorite passage from a spiritual text, an essay, or a poem be read at the service; or you might write one yourself. You might also request that a certain piece of music be played, a song sung, or that your spiritual teacher say a few words on your behalf. Keep in mind, however, that the funeral service will not be held primarily for your benefit but for the benefit of your family and friends. In talking it over with them, be attentive to their needs and considerate of their wishes.

*   *   *   *   *

"I am the murderer of joy,"
said the Angel of Death,
"The widower of wives,
the orphaner of children—"
"Why always run yourself down?"
said Rabi'a —
"Why not say instead:
'I am he who brings friend
and Friend together?"

—Rabi'a (Sufi)

Chapter Six: *Dealing with Fear and Doubt*

Two of the greatest obstacles you are likely to encounter as a spiritual practitioner facing death are fear and doubt. But these are only 'obstacles' to those who view them as such. If, instead of trying to run away from fear and doubt, you take them as "precious opportunities for spiritual practice," fear can be transformed into love, and doubt into certainty. To see how this is possible, let us take a closer look at each.

Fear

Perhaps you have seen a painting or a statue portraying the Buddha in the hour of his death. Calm and serene, he is usually shown reclining in the Lion Posture (lying on his right side with his right hand placed under his chin and his left arm lying along his left leg). His eyes are gently closed and there is the hint of a sublime smile playing across his lips which bears witness to his attainment of that "peace that passes all understanding." Indeed, this archetype of spiritual death is one of the most powerful to be found in all the Great Traditions. Above all it speaks to us of our own inherent potential for transcending the whole realm of delusion and its suffering.

Having seen such a representation, however, you may think that, as a spiritual practitioner, you too should be able to die in a similar fashion—that a truly "spiritual" person would not experience any fear, anxiety, or despair, but, like the Buddha, be able to face death with unwavering tranquility, while radiating love and compassion to all who come within range. Perhaps you are even making an effort (consciously or unconsciously) to live up to this image only to find that you cannot, that fear and other 'negative' emotions arise again and again to destroy your dreamed-of equanimity. The problem, however, lies not in the emotions themselves, but in your refusal to accept them.

This is well illustrated by another, equally powerful archetype of spiritual death: that of Christ on the cross— especially when he is depicted in that moment of supreme agony, crying out, "My God, my God, why hast Thou forsaken me?" Now, these two images—the peacefully reclining Buddha and the crucified Christ—appear completely contradictory. How can they be reconciled? In fact, they are two sides of the same coin. The archetype of the Buddha expresses that aspect of Consciousness which transcends all things, while the Christ archetype expresses that aspect which is immanent in all things—including suffering itself. When taken together, then, these complementary images of death contain one of the most profound teachings of the entire spiritual path: *we attain to the Peace of the Buddha not by avoiding the Crucifixion of Christ but by embracing it.*

But how can this be accomplished in practice?

First, be scrupulous about keeping the precept of *honesty*: "Not to deceive yourself or others by word or deed." In particular, you must not deceive yourself by pretending that you do not feel fear when, in fact, you do. Instead of denying fear, fix your attention on it and notice that the fear is not 'you', but simply an object arising in Consciousness. Feel yourself to be the "space of awareness" in which this object arises, the "womb" that gives it, and all things, birth.

Second, practice *compassion*. Embrace your fear as you would a frightened child, and ask what it is afraid of. It will answer that it is afraid of death. Why? Because death, being totally without form, is an inconceivable Mystery. But notice that the "Mystery of Death" is identical to the Mystery of God:

both are Formless. Thus, the fear of death and the fear of God are really one and the same fear! By tracing the fear of death to its source in the fear of the Unknown, you have actually touched the Unknown that is God. Realize this!

Finally, allow your fear to spontaneously *transform* itself into love. This does not require any effort. While continuing to embrace fear, simply focus your attention on the Mystery of God-in-Death and let go of all images of your 'self'. Notice, that when all your self-images are stripped away, what is left of your 'fear' is nothing but a current of pure energy. The reason you experience this energy as 'suffering' has nothing to do with the energy itself, but with the fact that it is trapped inside the boundaries of your imagined 'self'. By allowing these boundaries to dissolve, you will discover that the energy of 'fear' actually carries within it an extraordinary strength and clarity. And if you now surrender to this current of pure energy, you will experience for yourself what the great Hasidic Master, Eleazar of Worms, meant when he wrote:

> When the soul thinks deeply about the fear of God, then the flame of heartfelt love bursts in it and the exultation of innermost joy fills the heart.[30]

Doubt

Like fear, doubt is only an 'obstacle' for those who do not know what to do with it. In fact, the courage to doubt is an indispensable prerequisite for the spiritual quest. This is because, if you do not dare question those fundamental concepts about the nature of reality that you have inherited from your culture, these concepts will forever stand as a barrier between you and a *trans*-conceptual Gnosis of Reality as it truly is. Thus, it is only through doubting that you can ever arrive at the Truth. But when doubt calls into question the validity of the quest itself—that is, when you doubt whether it is worth asking such questions as, "Who am I?" and "What is this world?" and so stop engaging in those practices that will help you discover the answers—then it can, indeed, present a formidable obstacle.

This tends to happen whenever we are faced with the prospect of having to abandon the "known" in favor of venturing deeper into the Unknown. Finding that its conventional stock of knowledge can no longer be relied upon as it enters new, uncharted regions, the ego rebels and tries to flee back to the security of that familiar world it internalized as a child. This reaction often becomes particularly acute during periods of crisis because successfully navigating through most crises usually demands that we make a greater leap into the Unknown than we ever imagined would be necessary.

Needless to say, your own impending death represents this kind of crisis in the extreme. Consequently, you may find yourself from time to time being plagued by such doubts as: "Perhaps all this mysticism is nonsense after all. Perhaps death is the end of everything. Why bother with all these spiritual practices?"

The occurrence of such doubts is common and, in most cases, no great cause for concern. If they appear in your mind, do not try to suppress them, for they will only return in stronger form later. The first thing to do is notice that these doubts are just *thoughts* and, as such, have no substance and thus no power to bind you. Then, simply allow them to pass away (as you would any other distraction) and return to whatever you were doing.

If your doubts persist, the next thing to do is to take the doubts themselves as objects of meditation and follow Lao Tzu's instructions:

> The myriad phenomena all rise together
> And, by watching them, I see where they return.
> They arise in great numbers

And each returns to its root.
Returning to one's root is called stillness.
Being still, you return to your true destiny.
In returning to one's true destiny,
one knows the Constant,
And knowing the Constant, one becomes Wise.[31]

In other words, you should ignore the *content* of your thoughts and view them simply as "phenomena" arising in Consciousness. Then, by watching to see where these thought-phenomena come from and where they go, you will discover that they come from and return to that "space of awareness" which is beyond all thought whatsoever. If you now simply remain in this space, you will see that there is no need to "get rid" of thoughts of any kind: they arise and vanish all by themselves.

If you are a beginning practitioner, however, you may not yet be able to achieve this degree of detachment from your own thought processes. Then you must confront your doubts more directly and at a deeper level.

The easiest way to transform doubt into certainty is through *faith*. It must be remembered, however, that from the mystics' point of view, "faith" does not mean static belief in any codified dogma. Rather it means temporarily placing your trust in the guidance of a teacher (or teachings) who will eventually lead you *beyond* faith to your own insights and, ultimately, to your own Gnosis. This is similar to the kind of faith one places in any instructor—say, a mathematician or music teacher—in order to learn a particular subject or skill. Then, as one's education progresses, one begins to acquire one's own understanding or proficiency, so that gradually faith is replaced by knowledge and expertise.

Of course, the only way to be rid of all spiritual doubts is to finally "taste for yourself," for, as the great Hindu mystic, Anandamayi Ma declared: "Truth, THAT which IS, has to be made one's own."[32] But this, in turn, can only be accomplished through conducting your own search. By making inquiry and engaging in the appropriate practices, you too can eventually find that absolute and unshakable Certainty which comes with Enlightenment.

Thus, if you allow doubts to become a rationalization for lethargy and inaction, then they will certainly stop you dead in your tracks. On the other hand, if your doubts inspire you to find out the truth for yourself, then they will actually become a powerful motivation for pursuing the path. Here, for example, is how another great mystic, Lalleshwari, described the kinds of doubts she grappled with at the beginning of her own journey:

> Where have I come from?
> What road have I traveled?
> Which way am I going?
> I don't know the way,
> yet here I stand
> with courage and determination,
> hoping to grasp the knowledge of the Truth.[33]

And here is how she described her journey's end:

> As my faith and love grew,
> the darkness of the world diminished.
> Within and without,
> light began to shine.
> Lalli lost herself in that light...
> When the sun of knowledge rose,
> the dew of ignorance disappeared.
> When I realized my oneness
> with the name of God,
> my "I"-ness was obliterated
> and Lalli found peace.[34]

And here is what she has to say to you:

> Are you awake?
> Then stride forth.
> Walk fast and complete your journey.[35]

To summarize, then, the real difference between a spiritual and a worldly person facing death has nothing to do with whether or not they experience fear and doubt, but rather with how they *react to* these experiences. While the worldly person is normally overwhelmed by so-called "negative" thoughts and emotions (and thus becomes further lost in delusion), the spiritual practitioner learns how to transform *all* thoughts and feelings (positive or negative) into precious opportunities for spiritual practice.

* * * * *

Let me respectfully remind you
Life and Death
are of supreme importance.
Time swiftly passes by
and opportunity is lost.
Let us strive to Awaken, Awaken.
Take heed, do not squander your life.

— An evening prayer (Zen Buddhism)

Chapter Seven: Guidance for the Guide

To be asked by someone who is dying to serve as their spiritual guide is both an honor and a privilege. It is an honor because it means that that person has such a high regard for your spiritual counsel that they are willing to entrust themselves to you during the most critical time of their life—the passage through Death's Gate. It is a privilege because guiding someone through this passage can be a profound spiritual experience for you, the guide, as well. Always remember, however, that the honor and privilege which attach to this office call, in turn, for deep humility and an acute sense of gratitude. Indeed, you should take humility and gratitude to be your guiding virtues in the performance of this work. Guard against becoming puffed-up with your own self-importance, and do not neglect to give continuing thanks for being summoned to such a sacred service.

The Period Preceding the Actual Hour of Death

Depending on the dying person's illness, this period may last for days, weeks, or months. You should arrange to visit the dying person on a regular basis, perhaps once or twice a week—more if need be. During this time you should begin to familiarize yourself with the mystical literature concerning death, so that you will be in a better position to answer questions, give advice, or recommend some text he or she might want to read. You should also take up your own death practice while you serve as a spiritual guide. If you and the dying person are both engaged in the same practice, this will help forge a bond of true spiritual empathy between you.

Your primary job during this period, however, is to be a good listener.

Let the dying person set the agenda for your conversations. If you suspect the person is reluctant to talk freely about his or her feelings, you can try to initiate a discussion by openly and honestly expressing your own. If the person still doesn't respond, don't press the issue. Let it go until your next meeting. Sometimes powerful emotions take awhile to percolate to the surface. If, on the other hand, the dying person is eager to talk, you must listen with great compassion and be willing to enter fully into whatever experiences he or she wishes to communicate. Keep in mind Paul's admonition to the Romans:

> Rejoice with those who rejoice, and weep with those who weep. Be of the same mind, one with another.[36]

You must also be prepared for surprises. The period just prior to death represents a last opportunity for someone to confess misdeeds, make restitution, and otherwise clear their conscience. Consequently, you may be shocked by some secret the dying person chooses to reveal. If this happens, abandon all judgements and offer reassurances that whatever is said will be held in the strictest confidence. The trust that a dying person places in you as a spiritual guide is *sacred* and *must never be betrayed under any circumstances.*

Finally, do not forget your sense of humor. There will be many occasions when sharing a good joke will express greater compassion and provide more spiritual benefit than quoting a thousand scriptures. It was not without reason that Christendom's most celebrated poet, Dante, called the journey to God a "Divine *Comedy.*"

The Hour before Death

As a spiritual guide you must be ready, day or night, to go immediately to the dying person when the hour of death draws near. At that time your main task will be to coach the person through the eight stages of death, periodically reminding them to maintain their spiritual practice throughout the process. It is important to remember, however, that no one will have exactly the same experiences in exactly the same order, nor will the "stages" always be as clearly distinguishable as the outline given in Chapter Two of this booklet might suggest. Therefore, you must pay close attention to the person who is dying and take your cues as to what is happening directly from him or her.

For example, the dying person might suddenly sit up and wave away some frightening apparition that is invisible to you. If this happens, don't get alarmed. Simply remind the person that whatever they are seeing is only imaginary and has no power to cause harm. At other times, the person may drift off into a kind of twilight sleep, filled with troubling dreams. Again, remind him or her that such dreams have no reality in themselves and there is nothing ultimately to be afraid of. On the other hand, if the person seems to be sleeping peacefully, do not disturb them with verbal instructions, but continue to communicate silently in the form of heart-felt prayers.

Sometimes, a dying person will make what may seem to be unintelligible comments about the position of objects or people in the room. Listen carefully. He or she may be having an out-of-body experience and be viewing the whole scene from an entirely different perspective. Ask if this is, indeed, the case. If it is, reassure the dying person that such experiences are perfectly normal and encourage them to enjoy it. Whatever happens be flexible, fitting your response to the way the person's death actually unfolds, rather than to any preconceptions you have about how it *should* unfold. Above all, periodically remind the dying person to continue their death practice throughout all the stages, even after physical death has occurred. *Never assume the dying person can no longer hear you. Hearing is the last of the senses to be lost.*

Although your primary responsibility is to the person who is dying, you must also be sensitive to the feelings of any relatives and friends who may be present. Encourage them to come sit by the bed and hold the dying person's hand, while quietly saying good-bye, expressing their love, or that "it's okay to let go." Violent displays of emotion, however, should be discouraged as they can upset the dying person and be a distraction to his or her spiritual practice. You must also be prepared to counsel and console friends and relatives who may turn to you in their grief even if they, themselves, are not practitioners of the Way of Selflessness.

The Moment of Death

The most prominent outward signs of physical death are the cessation of breathing, heartbeat, and pulse. They may also include the release of bowels and bladder; enlargement of the pupils of the eyes, fixed staring, and a slackness of the jaw. When these signs appear, stay calm. Remember, a death that has been planned for is *not an emergency.* (Do *not* call 911, as the paramedics who respond will try to revive the deceased, despite his or her wishes to the contrary.) If there is a physician, nurse, or Hospice worker present, ask them to confirm that death has occurred. If not, don't worry. Nothing needs to be done immediately and, in fact, it is best if the dead person is left resting peacefully where they are for at least fifteen to twenty minutes after physical death. During this period, you should ask family members and friends to pray or meditate quietly while you sit by the deceased's side, softly reminding him or her of what happens in the final stages of the passage through Death's Gate. For instance, you might say something like this:

Dear (deceased's name):

❖ You are now dead but your journey is not yet over, so do not become distracted. Pay close attention, for soon the last obstacles to Gnosis will be removed.

❖ Now all thoughts are vanishing, and no new thoughts arise to take their place. Do not be afraid. You have no need of thought now. In place of thought, a White Light dawns. Relax and allow it to fill your entire mind.

❖ Now all resentment, anger, and animosity are fading away. Again, do not be afraid. Feel how wonderful it is to be free of these forms of suffering. As resentment, anger, and animosity disappear, a Golden Light dawns. Relax and let this Golden Light penetrate into every corner of your mind.

❖ Now, all desires, graspings, and attachments are starting to dissolve. Let them go; there is nothing to fear. Feel how peaceful it is to be free of these causes of suffering.

❖ As desires, graspings, and attachments evaporate, so does the Golden Light. Now your mind is emptied of all objects, whatsoever, and seems to be a complete Void. But look, this Void is no mere 'nothing'. In fact, it is Consciousness, Itself. Recognize this Consciousness-without-an-object as Pure Being, the Ultimate Reality, Womb of all Worlds, Radiant with Grace and Bliss.

❖ Now, Realize that this Pure Consciousness is not an object appearing in your mind. Rather, it is the True Nature of your mind itself. Recognize that your own mind and this Consciousness are indistinguishable.

❖ By Realizing that this Consciousness *is* who you *truly are*, you are instantaneously freed from all delusions of 'I' and 'other', 'self' and 'world' forever. This is Enlightenment, the end of the path![37]

Say these instructions slowly, pausing after each point so that the deceased can fully absorb it. Repeat the entire set of instructions several times during the fifteen to twenty minute period following physical death. Of course, it is not necessary to say them verbatim. You may use your own words as long as the central points are covered.

After you have given these final instructions, invite the deceased's family members and friends to approach the bed and say their last farewells. If there is no doctor, nurse, or Hospice worker present, remind whoever is responsible to inform the mortuary and/or physician that death has occurred so that a death certificate can be issued and a time arranged for removing the body after the viewing period is over.

If the deceased has had a relatively easy time passing through Death's Gate, your task as a spiritual guide is essentially complete (although again you may be called upon to counsel friends and relatives, or to say a few words at the funeral service). If, however, the person had an especially difficult time dying, you should continue giving guidance once a day in the form of a prayer, reminding the dead person that whatever he or she is experiencing is simply a manifestation of Consciousness, Itself and should be Recognized as such and be embraced with love and compassion. Different traditions have different conceptions as to how long such prayers will continue to be effective, though there seems to be strong inter-cultural agreement that the "dead" remain in contact with the "living" for a minimum of three days. (In the Tibetan tradition, passage through the three *"bardos"* of death is believed to take a full forty-nine days.) One reason it is difficult to fix a time frame for the possibility of postmortem communication is that time itself varies with different states of consciousness. Thus, what constitutes a "day" for the living does not necessarily correlate with a "day" for the dead. The most prudent thing to do is continue your prayers of guidance for as long as you feel that a spiritual connection between you and the deceased still exists.

Finally, as time passes, you may discover that having served as a spiritual guide was a good deal more traumatic than you realized at the time. In the days ahead, you may experience vivid and recurrent memories of the dying person, accompanied by intense emotions of grief, sadness, or fear. If this happens to you, the first thing to do is practice detachment. This means neither wallowing in these emotions, nor trying to push them away. Allow yourself to fully experience whatever thoughts and feelings arise, but do not dwell on them when they naturally start to pass. The second thing to do is to notice that, while these memories of death may cause you considerable suffering, they also constitute a direct experiential teaching about the transitory nature of all things. Take to heart what Black Elk, the great Lakota shaman, said:

> It is good to have a reminder of death before us, for it helps us to understand the impermanence of life on this earth, and this understanding may aid us in preparing for our own death. He who is well prepared is he who knows that he is nothing compared to *Wakan-Tanka*, who is everything; then he knows that world which is real.[38]

*   *   *   *   *

Seek water constantly, oh man of dry lips!
For your dry lips give witness that in the end
you will find a fountain. The lips' dryness is a
message from the water: "If you keep on
moving, without doubt you will find me."

— Rumi (Sufi)

Epilogue: Knowing Beyond Words

Before visiting a museum, it is always helpful to know something about the paintings you are going to see. Many guidebooks are written for this purpose and it is certainly worthwhile reading them. But have you ever noticed how some museum visitors spend more time thumbing through their guidebooks than actually looking at the paintings themselves? It's almost as though they deliberately want to fill their minds with facts and figures because they are afraid to simply stand before a work of art and allow the beauty it reflects to penetrate directly into their souls. And yet if a work of art is ever to be truly understood, such utter nakedness is precisely what is called for. All the rest is merely a preparation for this moment.

Like a museum guide, this book is also filled with a lot of facts and figures and there is a danger it can be misused in exactly the same way, for what is true of art is even more so of spiritual practice. This is why Bishop Ignatii wrote of the Christian seeker in the last stages of the path:

> Finally he becomes a child, as he is commanded in the Gospel, and is made a fool for Christ's sake, that is, he loses the false reason of the world, and receives from God a spiritual understanding.[39]

Likewise, Lalleshwari advised her disciples:

> Even though you have knowledge
> become like a fool.
> Even though you have eyes,
> become blind.

> Even though you have ears,
> become deaf...
> [For] in that state there is no knowledge,
> no meditation, no Shiva or Shakti.
> All that remains is That.[40]

And Lao Tzu declared:

> Unlike others, I am silent
> and give no sign,
> like a baby
> before it has begun to smile...
> My mind is that of a fool:
> utterly empty![41]

The purpose of this book has been to help prepare you to receive this "spiritual understanding" and attain "That" which becomes supremely available in death, precisely because, in passing through its Gate, our minds are finally made "empty," so that we can once again be filled with that wonder and awe known only to fools and children. Therefore, use the teachings contained in this book to orient yourself to death's landscape, to read the signs along the way, and to focus your attention on the Divine Mystery that lies beyond, but do not cling to these teachings like a nervous museum goer, for:

> where there be prophecies, they shall fail; where there be tongues, they shall cease; where there be knowledge, it shall vanish away. For we know in part and we prophesy in part, but when That which is Perfect is come, then that which is in part shall be done away.[42]

Death reveals "That which is Perfect." In order for this revelation to take place, however, "that which is in part" must, as the Apostle Paul said, be done away with. When this happens to you, do not be alarmed. As you enter Death's terrain it may seem at times like you are journeying through a totally foreign country. But in your heart of hearts you know this is not so. Why? Because you have already been there. Death is that Eternal Land from which you came before you were born into this world of metaphors and dreams, pleasure and pain, suffering and woe. You have only become confused and forgotten it—that's all. But now it doesn't matter—now none of it matters—because now you are going Home....

...And yet, truly speaking, you aren't going anywhere, because, in *reality*, what you are, you have always been and always will be, Consciousness without end...

Peace.

NOTES

1. Paul Carus, trans. *The Gospel of Buddha* (Chicago: The Open Court Publishing Co., 1894), 13.

2. Simone Weil, *Waiting For God,* trans. Emma Craufurd (1951; reprint, New York: Harper and Row, Publishers, 1973), 63.

3. For example, Kenneth Ring reports that 48% of the subjects in his study of people who almost died had vivid near-death experiences. Kenneth Ring, *Life At Death,* (1980; reprint, New York: Quill, 1982), 34.

4. For a fuller discussion of the trans-cultural evidence concerning after-death states, listen to my three-part audio tape, *Death: A Golden Opportunity,* available for sale or loan from the Center For Sacred Sciences' Library.

5. Bokar Rinpoche, *Death and the Art of Dying in Tibetan Buddhism,* French trans. Francois Jacquemart, English trans. Christiane Buchet, ed. Jennifer Pessereau (San Francisco: ClearPoint Press, 1993), 19.

6. *The Chandogya Upanishad,* 6:8:6-7—my rendering.

7. Moshe Idel, *The Mystical Experience in Abraham Abulafia,* (Albany, NY: State University of New York Press, 1988), 183-184—my brackets.

8. Cited in Sogyal Rinpoche, *The Tibetan Book of Living and Dying,* (San Francisco: Harper San Francisco, a division of Harper Collins Publishers, 1992), 253.

9. "On Free Choice" in *The Essential Augustine,* 2nd ed., ed. Vernon J. Bouake (Indianapolis: Hackett Publishing Co., 1974), 25.

10. Al-Ghazali, *The Remembrance of Death and the Afterlife: Book 40 of the Revival of the Religious Sciences,* trans. T.J. Winter (Cambridge: Islamic Texts Society, 1989), 250n.

11. Mircea Eliade, *Shamanism: Archaic Techniques of Ecstasy,* trans. Willard R. Trask (Princeton University Press, Bollingen series LXXVI, 1974), 33.

12. Bokar Rinpoche, *Death and the Art of Dying,* 20.

13. Ramana Maharshi, *The Spiritual Teachings of Ramana Maharshi* (Boulder, CO: Shambhala Publications, 1972), 69—my italics and brackets.

14. Gershom G. Scholem, *Major Trends in Jewish Mysticism,* (1941; reprint, New York: Schocken Books, 1961), 217—my italics.

15. "Centering" in Paul Reps, *Zen Flesh, Zen Bones,* (Rutland, VT: Charles E. Tuttle Company, Inc., 1957), 201—my brackets. (See also my spiritual autobiography, *Naked Through the Gate,* for an account of my own Enlightenment which occurred precisely at this moment.)

16. Dionysius the Areopagite, *Mystical Theology and the Celestial Hierarchies,* 2nd ed., trans. eds. of The Shrine of Wisdom (Nr. Godalming, Surrey: The Shrine of Wisdom, 1965), 9. Notice how the phrase "Radiance

of the Divine Darkness" exactly parallels the Tibetan description of the mind of black-near-attainment actually being the fundamental clear light.

17. Bokar Rinpoche, *Death and the Art of Dying*, 35.
18. Al-Ghazzali, *The Alchemy of Happiness,* trans. Claud Field (1964; reprint, Lahore: Sh. Muhammad Ashraf, October, 1983), 63.
19. In fact, my own Gnostic Awakening was prompted by just this kind of guidance: a critical teaching happened to pop into my head during the state between waking and sleep — See *Naked Through the Gate*, 239.
20. James R. Walker, *Lakota Belief and Ritual*, ed. Raymond J. DeMaillie and Elaine A. Jahner (Lincoln, NE: University of Nebraska Press, 1991), 270.
21. *Meister Eckhart: The Essential Sermons, Commentaries, Treatises, and Defense,* trans. Edmund Colledge and Bernard McGinn (New York: Paulist Press, 1981), 265.
22. Bokar Rinpoche, *Death and the Art of Dying*, 73-74.
23. Dr. Javad Nurbakhsh, *Sufism V* (New York: Khaniqahi-Nimatullahi Publications, 1991), 135.
24. Lao Tzu, *Tao Teh Ching*, 48—my rendering.
25. Ramana Maharshi,*The Spiritual Teachings of Ramana Maharshi,* 49.
26. *Meister Eckhart: The Essential Semons, Commentaries, Treatises, and Defense*, 192.
27. Longchenpa, *You Are the Eyes of the World*, trans. Kennard Lipman and Merrill Peterson (Novato, CA: Lotsawa, 1987), 36.
28. Bokar Rinpoche, *Death and the Art of Dying*, 74.
29. Simone Weil, *Waiting For God* , 195.
30. Gershom G. Scholem, *Major Trends in Jewish Mysticism,* 95.
31. Lao Tzu, *Tao Teh Ching*, 16.
32. Anandamayi Ma, *Matri Vani: Vol 1*, 5th ed. (Calcutta: Shree Shree Anandamayee Charitable Society, 1982), 33.
33. *Lalleshwari: Spiritual Poems by a Great Siddha Yogini*, rendered by Swami Muktananda (South Fallsburg, NY: SYDA Foundation, 1981), 3.
34. Ibid., 46-47.
35. Ibid., 5.
36. *Rom.* 12:15-16.
37. These instructions are loosely adapted from those given to the dead in *The Tibetan Book of the Dead*, 3rd ed., trans. Lama Case Dada-Samdup, ed. W.Y. Evans-Wentz (1976 reprint; London: Oxford University Press, 1957), 95-96.
38. Black Elk, *The Sacred Pipe*, ed. Joseph Epes Brown (1953; reprint, Baltimore: Penguin Books, 1973), 8.
39. Igumen Chariton of Valamo, *The Art of Prayer: An Orthodox Anthology*, trans., El Kadloubovsky and E.M. Palmer, ed. Timothy Ware

(1985; reprint, London, Faber and Faber, 1966), 84.

40. *Lalleshwari: Spiritual Poems by a Great Siddha Yogini*, 73 and 84 combined.

41. Lao Tzu, *Tao Teh Ching*, 20.

42. *I Cor.* 13:8-10.

Joel is the Spiritual Director of the Center for Sacred Sciences, a non-profit organization dedicated to the creation and dissemination of a new Worldview based on the wisdom of humanity's great spiritual teachers but presented in forms appropriate to our present scientific culture. Our programs draw on the teachings of the mystics of all traditions as well as the evidence of modern physics. Among the Center's current offerings are Sunday Programs with meditation and talk by Joel, meditation classes and retreats, workshops and study groups. Joel also leads a weekly Practitioners' Group for committed spiritual seekers, as well as being available for individual spiritual consultation. The Center maintains an extensive lending library of books and tapes covering a broad spectrum of spiritual, psychological and scientific subjects. For more information write:

Center For Sacred Sciences
1430 Willamette #164
Eugene, Oregon 97401-4049
(541) 345-0102